The Eagle and the Fawn

Laurie Sanford

RIVER LEAF PRESS

To Anita, my faithful friend since the age of six. I'm so glad we meant it when we said "friends forever" way back then.

One

WHATEVER THY HAND FINDETH to do, do it with thy might. The words echoed in Ellis McCraw's mind, a remnant of the father he'd left behind in Tennessee. In childhood, the verse had often been cited to rouse him when a particular job needed finishing—the barn whitewashed, the cows fed, the stables mucked out before dinner. Now they tolled again in his mind as he gazed out over the town of Gold Strike. *Is this the work you would have me do—to bring lawfulness to this wretched piece of land hardly a soul cares about beyond the western states?*

The town appeared peaceful enough, cradled between mountainous forests, its main street coming alive beneath the climbing morning sun. A well-traversed dirt thoroughfare ran through its center, flanked by business establishments of every kind—a mercantile, a leather works, a doctor's office, a tobacco shop, a hotel, and at the very end, the jail where he would work, complete with elevated gallows and ominous ropes swaying in the breeze.

His gaze snagged on the building nearest him, a homely, worn-down structure with the telltale marks of a brothel. Ellis inhaled a breath of pine-infused air. To blazes with Montana and its primitive laws. He'd been reared in God's country, a place where morality still stood for something, and God's word reigned superior to men's desires. The first place he'd see torn to the ground was that den of debauchery.

After checking his fob watch, he returned it to his waistcoat pocket and peered down the trail toward town. He'd snuck in this morning on horseback to get his own view of the town before anyone could poison him with their agendas or opinions. He rather enjoyed the view from up here, an honest look at the place he'd been hired to protect, with all her faults and raw beauty.

He still had forty-five minutes before he must report to the jail and meet with his deputies. Ellis considered grabbing a bite to eat at a corner cafe, but his stomach turned at the very thought. Who was he fooling? He could never eat before an important day, and somehow he sensed this day marked a new beginning in his life.

His gaze flicked down a path leading to his right—a trail appearing to coil through the weeds and follow the ridgeline through a thicket of spruces. From the tree where he'd tied her, his horse whinnied and stomped her foot. "Now, you stay there, Honeydew. Have a little patience." He rubbed his hands together. "I need a few more minutes to collect myself."

Sunlight sliced through the trees and warmed Ellis's back as he trekked along the narrow trail. His boots trampled stray pieces of grass and kicked at pebbles in his way. He stopped to smell the wild lupins growing verdant across the meadows and plucked a dandelion from alongside them. The filaments rolled between his fingers and dispersed on the wind as he walked.

Ellis looked over the rugged purple mountains disappearing into the fog. The air here had a crisp, invigorating quality, like a single breath of it might reenergize him for the entire day. He'd heard Montana called "Land of the Shining Mountains" before.

He understood it now, with the vast canvas of rolling clouds and sparkling sunshine stretched before him, all of nature bowing humbly beneath the ragged mountainscapes. He would miss the mysterious woodlands with their changing colors and hidden streams of home, but he couldn't deny both God and fate had delivered him into something truly magnificent.

Autumn had come to life in this awesome place. Fresh wind rustled the pines, and the faint smell of woodsmoke curled in the air. Aspens dotted the foothills, a stunning blanket of yellows splashed with orange and red standing bright against the billowing clouds.

Ellis spotted an overlook ahead where he might take a moment to think and reflect on the speech he would deliver this morning. Eyes on his dusty boots, he rounded a corner and stopped short. Two feet in front of him, a woman sat on a large boulder with her back to him, facing the vast expanse of wilds beyond.

What was a woman doing out here all by herself? After everything he'd learned of this town thus far, he instinctively wanted to order her back home to her husband or father. But something in the way she sat gave him pause.

She had on a simple gown of checkered calico hemmed in lace. She wore no outer adornments, though her shimmering strawberry blonde hair would catch the eye of any casual passerby. Pinned elegantly to the back of her head, it escaped in thin wisps on the breeze flying behind her. If he hadn't set his sights on this spot, he might never have seen her. She moved not a muscle, only stared with quiet fixation on the mountainous woodlands.

Resisting the urge to speak with her, he stepped back. He couldn't disturb the peace or prayers of whoever this mysterious woman was. He shuffled quietly backward, trying to slink his way through the trees before she noticed him. Her head snapped around at the sound, her eyes widening on sight of him.

Ellis held up both hands. "I'm very sorry, ma'am. I didn't mean to disturb you. I'll just be on my way." He motioned toward the trail behind him.

She stood abruptly. "No, I'll go. I've too long been tarrying anyway." Yet her feet stayed in place, not venturing to move past him. Her gaze darted cautiously between him and the trail.

"You don't need to fear me, ma'am—I promise." Should he tell her he was the new sheriff of Gold Strike? He'd wanted to keep that information in his back pocket a little longer. "I didn't know you were here."

She nodded slowly, though her green eyes still shone with skepticism. "I've never seen you in town before. Are you passing through?"

"No, ma'am. Just moved here." Ellis removed his hat and held it to his chest. "I arrived on the train from Tennessee yesterday. I set out early this morning to get here."

"I see." Her shoulders visibly relaxed. "Well, I suppose I should give you a proper greeting, then, if I'm the first resident of Gold Strike you're meeting."

He dipped his head at the question in her voice. "You are indeed. My name is Ellis McCraw."

Her skin blushed a beautiful shade of pink as she stepped forward to shake his hand. "Cora Blackwood."

"Mrs. Blackwood, it's a pleasure to meet you."

"Miss." She blushed a shade darker. "Miss Blackwood."

"Miss Blackwood." He allowed his eyes to linger on hers a moment before he looked at the hat in his hand. "I do hope my move here will be quite prosperous for me."

Her brow hooked. "Are you a miner?"

One shoulder lifted. "Something of the sort. I certainly like to root things out." Though criminals, rather than gold, remained his specialty.

She laughed lightly, the sound touching something deep in his core. "I'm afraid you may have come to the wrong place. The rivers and mines around here were all pillaged long ago." She gave him a gentle smile. "Don't let the name fool you."

"I believe I'll take my chances here just the same." Despite his resolve to remain indifferent to this people, her smile ignited his own. "I've come to a special place, I can already tell."

Cora lifted her skirt at the ankle and returned to her rock. "I would be remiss if I didn't give you the grand tour, then."

Ellis frowned. "The grand tour?"

"Ah, yes." She motioned to the rock beside her. "Others may bore you with endless hours of our history or take you through the town's finest establishments, but I have something better in mind."

"You do, do you?" Sauntering forward, he stopped momentarily before her, then dropped to the rock she'd indicated. "What kind of tour is that?"

"The kind that matters most, of course." An elfin sparkle lit her eyes as she turned toward the rugged terrain. "Over here we have Mount Redmon"—her hand waved toward a particularly high peak jutting from the summit—"where Gold Strike's founder climbed in the snow to plant his flag and claim it." She shielded one side of her mouth with her hand, leaning closer. "Of course, he died of hypothermia weeks later, but we don't talk about that part."

Ellis let out a hearty laugh. "And spoil all his fun? I think not."

"Down there, we have the Coldwater Timberlands." Her hand swept across the foothills, bright with autumn color. "That's where our first scouts traded with the local Indian tribes in exchange for land.

"And here"—her finger traced a distant line of trees, where gaps in the leaves revealed coursing water—"is the Beartrack River. It's a magical place. The later into fall it becomes, the deeper the leaves darken, until it's just a splash of crimson in an otherwise barren forest." She settled her chin on her hands, her awestruck gaze taking it all in. "It's rather beautiful, don't you think?" She sighed within herself.

Ellis couldn't help studying her profile, from her thick lashes to the feminine slope of her nose. "It is, indeed."

She looked at him from the corner of her eye, her lips puckering slightly, before her gaze retreated with artful coyness beneath her lashes. "You are quite the charmer, aren't you, Mr. McCraw?"

Ellis turned his hat over in his hand, holding it in his lap like a bucket. "I don't intend to be."

"But you are just the same," she said, the slightest hint of a smile edging her mouth.

Ellis scratched the back of his head through his short blond hair, unable to discern whether she enjoyed the attention or not. Women had always befuddled him, especially pretty ones. This one looked at him as if she had a bounty of secrets inside for nobody's eyes but her own.

"I suppose it's the Southerner in you," she said, resting her elbows on top of her fluttering skirts. "I've known many Southern gentlemen, and they all have a particular way about them. It drives most of the girls around here mad with excitement."

"But not you."

The color heightened in her cheeks. Her gaze slid back into his. One brow flared upward, but she said nothing, only pinned him with a look so frank yet demure in the same moment, a strange band of pressure squeezed in his middle. Yet all too soon, she dropped his gaze, leaving him stranded as she plucked a leaf off her skirt and sat up straighter.

"Where did you say you were from again? Tennessee?" Her shoulders squared, her face once again pointed toward the broad landscape before them.

"Yes, Tennessee." The word barely squeezed from his throat. How did this woman he'd only just met have such power over him? Were all the women in Montana this beguiling? He cleared his throat. "From the mountains of Appalachia. They're nothing like what you have here, though."

"No place is." She set her palms against the rock on either side of her and leaned into its beauty. "Once you've tasted it, you'll never want to go anywhere else."

The words thrummed through him, splintering over his body with magnetic electricity. Ellis inwardly shook himself—tried to shake her off. But the most he accomplished was staring straight at her, transfixed. He struggled to find his voice. "What about you, Miss Blackwood? You seem to love this place with pure, natural affection. Have you always called it home?"

She gazed so long at the landscape, he thought perhaps she hadn't heard his question. Then she turned to him, that knowing, quiet smile on her lips, before she rose up. "Forgive me, Mr. McCraw, but I think it's time I went on my way." Her head flicked toward the sun now high in the rolling sky. "I've stayed much too long."

"Now, wait just a minute." Ellis stood and took a step forward, blocking her before she could pass him. "I told you where I was from, but you won't return the favor?"

She sighed lightly. "Does it matter if I do? We're both here now anyway."

He faltered at the surety on her face. "I suppose it doesn't, but I'd like to know, if it doesn't matter to you anyway."

Cora's eyes searched his a tense moment, something vulnerable in them shining through, before she quickly put her walls back into place. "Some things are better left not spoken of, especially to strangers I've just met."

She glanced toward the town below, now bustling with activity. "You know as well as I that it's not proper for the two of us to be up here alone." Her voice caught. "For your sake, if nothing else."

His brow wrinkled. "What do you mean 'for my sake'? It's over you they'll be concerned."

Her lips flattened, but whatever remained behind them, she left unsaid. Her solemn eyes hooked with his, scarcely blinking.

"You don't fear me anymore, do you?"

Her head wagged. "You're not a man to fear, Mr. McCraw."

Ellis squeezed his teeth together, his jaw working. "And how do you know that?" He'd spent a lifetime aiming to prove himself, becoming a man who was feared and respected among his peers. But this woman, this lithe woman with the reddish blonde hair, had completely and utterly disarmed him.

"I learned long ago who to trust and who to fear." Her eyes meandered over his face. "You're a strong man, but a good man. You don't use your power to harm." The intensity in her stare lured him like a fish caught on a hook.

Ellis stepped toward her, inches past a comfortable distance, but she didn't flinch. The scent of vanilla and amber enraptured him. He let his gaze wander her smooth skin, her proud features, the plump lips softly parting. How long had it been since he'd stood this close to a woman? Not since his youth in Tennessee, when stealing a kiss was more akin to a game than actual affection.

He leaned closer, brushing a fingertip down her jawline. He hadn't meant to, and yet her glowing skin had called to him, tempting his hands to touch it. She softly inhaled, but didn't protest. As his hands found the small of her back and pressed her closer, she closed her eyes, her black lashes resting on her cheeks. Their faces came so close, her breath showered his lips. Then all reason fled him.

Ellis crashed his lips into hers, alive in the immediate warmth funneling through him. She froze for several seconds, her hands stiff in midair before she allowed herself to melt against him. Her lips responded to his with glorious, fiery heat. Her hands moved up his chest, snaked around his neck. Her fingers dove beneath his hair.

Ellis pulled her flush against him, kissing her with the ferocity of a man gasping for air. *This is a terrible idea. This is not how you wanted to introduce yourself to this town.* Yet the longer he stood wrapped in her arms, the less he could hear the nagging voice in his head. Every cell in his body had awakened with ardor for this woman whose name he barely knew.

When they both drew back for air, Cora covered her lips with her fingers and laughed. "Now, I'm sure that wasn't the respectable thing to do on your first day in town, Mr. McCraw."

He chuckled, enjoying the tickle of her hair against his cheek. "I didn't hear any protest from you."

"No." She bit her lip, her arms still snug around his neck. "I suppose I didn't."

"I won't tell if you don't." His hands squeezed her lower back. "With both of our reputations on the line and all." He could only imagine the scandal that might ensue in this town to know their new sheriff had arrived and promptly stolen a passionate kiss from one of their young maidens.

"We'll put it behind us, then." Cora slipped her arms down, letting them rest briefly on his chest, before she took a step back and extended her hand. "It was very nice to meet you, Mr. McCraw."

"And you as well." Ellis shook her hand, holding her warm fingers in his a moment too long. He grinned as she politely returned them to her side. "I hope we see much more of each other." As soon as he set up shop at the jail and inspected the town, he would call on her—do things the respectable way.

"Indeed." Casting him one last flirtatious glance, Cora swept up her skirts and brushed passed him. Ellis watched with delight as she sashayed away, throwing one last look over her shoulder before vanishing around the bend in the trail. Setting his hands on his hips, he could only shake his head and chuckle. This was *not* the reception he'd expected to find on his first morning in Gold Strike.

Two

CORA HELD THE HEM of her skirt high above the dusty street as she scampered across it. Already, the town of Gold Strike thrummed with activity. Carts transporting fresh produce to market lumbered past her, their drivers tipping their heads to her as she crossed. Cora returned the gesture, though inwardly, her stomach twisted. The sun had risen far beyond the usual spot she let it before returning to the brothel from her morning walks. Why had she let the charms of a mysterious stranger delay her?

Butterflies floated from her stomach through her entire frame as she set her sights on Madam Carey's and sprinted the rest of the way. His intense, soul-searching eyes still burned in her memory, the feel of his strong jaw flexing beneath her fingertips tingling her skin. He had kissed her with the authority of a man who commanded women for a living, yet she didn't sense a malicious side to him—not like some of the men who passed through her door.

Trying to thrust him out of her memory, she waved at a shop-keeper across the way and darted beneath the brothel's awning. A provocative whistle blasted from somewhere behind her, but she ignored it. Madam Carey often instructed her girls to encourage such advances, to feed her customers' vulgarity. *Convince them you want them as much as they want you.* Yet Cora didn't possess the strength to pretend today—not after being truly and perfectly kissed this morning by a man whose touch still raised glorious gooseflesh on her arms.

Within the safety of the brothel's foyer, Cora leaned against the front door and exhaled. She'd been tempted to tarry in town and ask questions about this newcomer, but it wouldn't serve her anyway. Not with her current occupation. Once he found out who she was, he'd either utterly scorn her, or pay for the privilege of her companionship. Neither prospect left her with any hope in regard to their future.

"Oh Cora, there you are. Finally." Madam Carey's scathing tone made her jump to attention. The aging madam glided down the sweeping staircase with practiced grace, clad in a glittering evening gown despite the time of day. *One never knows when an important guest will arrive, and one always needs to look one's best,* she often told them.

Cora pulled her shawl from around her shoulders and knotted it in her hands. "I'm sorry, Madam Carey. I went for a walk and lost track of time. There was a"—she bit her lip—"an animal up on the trail that I had to bypass." Her cheeks flushed. He had certainly behaved like an animal.

"And that is precisely why I tell you those trails are dangerous." Madam Carey came to rest before her on the Belgian rug. "That, and ruffians, of course. They may pay for you here, but if they find you by yourself in the woods, I promise you they won't be so obliging."

Cora resisted the urge to curl her lips in disgust. The madam had not a concern about her being raped. She only thought about the money she would lose if someone were to take her services for free. She nodded, swallowing back her quiet rage. "I shall try to be more careful."

"Good." Madam Carey's scrutinous gaze wandered over her, returning to her face with abhorrence. "You look absolutely dreadful, my dear. No wonder nobody tries to accost you when you are out. Why is your hair disturbed in such an unkempt fashion?"

A bubble of laughter threatened to erupt in Cora's throat, but she pressed it down. *Because I let a man push his fingers through it while he kissed me so hard I lost my head?* "It was the animal, Madam Carey. The whole ordeal disheveled me, I'm afraid."

"Ah." Yet a dubious sheen remained in her eyes. "Well, no matter now. Try to maintain your appearance better the next time you're out, will you? I can't have my best girl looking like a rat who has just climbed out of a sewer drain."

"Yes, ma'am."

Madam Carey turned abruptly, her salt-and-pepper hair catching rays of sunlight from the front window. "Follow me. I have work for you to do."

"I'll start on the laundry right away." Cora jogged to catch up with her quick pace. "And I have those tapestries finished that you asked me to mend."

"Nevermind about all that." The madam's fingers waved dismissively in the air, her jewels glinting. "The laundry can be finished later. I have a special task for you this morning."

Cora's stomach roiled. Usually, Madam Carey's "special tasks" required something uncomfortable or downright immoral of her—if she could concern herself with morality in this place. Whatever project she had conjured this morning promised to test her in more ways than one.

Trailing after Madam Carey past the lounge area with only a few stray patrons sprinkled around the bar, Cora soon found herself in the girls' private dining area. Most of the women had dispersed by now, but a handful remained, seated at long dining tables and munching on fresh-baked bread. They all straightened upon Madam Carey's blustery entrance.

She clapped her hands. "Hurry up, girls. There are already patrons at the bar. I need four of you dressed and ready to greet them, while the rest of you should commence with your daily chores." The order snapped them into motion. Nobody wanted to face Madam Carey's wrath when the only other work for miles was at the Wild Rose Saloon, where their labor was cheap, and the girls had to entertain the proprietor as often as his customers.

"Now then, come along." Madam Carey clasped Cora's wrist, leading her toward a table with a lone girl sporting a braid of tangled raven hair. "This new one is named Damaris." She leaned conspiratorially close. "Escaped from the market, or so I've been told."

Cora's gut constricted, harsh memories flooding her. How many years had to pass before they no longer haunted her? "She was a slave?"

"I can't be sure. She talks very little. I need you to take extra care with her." As if someone had ignited a lamp, the madam brightened as she reached the girl's table. "Damaris, my darling, I have someone I'd like you to meet."

The girl's vacant gaze rolled up toward the pair, dazed as if looking through them. She let the spoon in her hand clatter to her bowl with a loud ping.

"This is Cora Blackwood. She's the finest of my ladies." Madam Carey propelled Cora toward her. "She dresses all my new girls and makes sure they're comfortable in their new home. I'm sure you two will have instant rapport."

Despite the girl's dubious expression, Madam Carey turned cheerfully Cora's way. "Do make sure she has appropriate attire and *instruction* for tonight."

Cora stepped closer before she could turn away, speaking quietly. "You want to start her tonight? She doesn't appear anything close to ready."

The madam's eyes flashed indignantly. "Yes, well that is why I pulled you from laundry duty today. It is your job to *make* her ready."

"But ma'am—"

"I'll hear no excuses." With that, the madam bustled away, her skirts a flurry and small heels clicking on the dining room floor.

Cora's throat dried as she angled toward the new girl and tried to conjure a smile. "Are you finished with breakfast? I'd love to take you to my room, so I can show you my gowns." At Damaris's hesitant expression, she laid a reassuring hand on her shoulder. "I have many beautiful dresses. I'll let you keep whatever you'd like."

With a cautious glance around her, the girl scooted her chair back and rose. Cora tried to ignore the absolute wrestling match transpiring in her stomach as she led Damaris up the back stairwell and down the corridor toward her room. She couldn't be more than sixteen years old—common for new arrivals, but tragic just the same.

Damaris silently surveyed her room from the ruffled curtains to her hand-embroidered bedspread. Inhaling the scent of cornflowers she'd plucked from the trail yesterday, Cora marched to her wardrobe and threw it open. No sense in delaying the inevitable when she had only hours to prepare the poor girl.

"There now, this might do." She pulled an embellished gown of purple satin from her collection, holding it up to the girl's thin frame. "You are quite petite. I made this for just such a girl in mind."

Damaris's eyes rounded, her fingers venturing out to gently touch the slippery fabric. "You made this?"

"Indeed, I did." Cora laughed a bit self-consciously. "I make most of the gowns for the girls here. It's a passion of mine."

Dark eyes flitting up to her, Damaris pinched her lips together. "So you're a seamstress. You're not a—"

Compassion expanded Cora's chest. How bizarre of a world to step into for the very first time. "I am a prostitute. I've just learned to do many various jobs since I first walked through Madam Carey's doors." Developed skills that would lead her back out the doors eventually, she hoped.

"Oh." Damaris buffed a hand up her smooth, olive-toned skin. Her forlorn gaze dropped to her shoes.

"You can leave, you know. Madam Carey doesn't own you—not yet." As the girl's surprised gaze darted back into hers, Cora's head angled. "She won't fuss after a girl who has merely eaten a meal and left. But once you've hit her market, that's a different matter entirely. She has claws on her girls that don't release unless she tells them to."

Damaris swallowed. "Why would I consider leaving? This is a home with food and fine clothing, is it not?"

Exactly the argument that had won her over as a girl of seventeen, alone in the world. "Yes, but there are other places to find such amenities. That path may seem harder at first, but I can assure you it's not." Her chest tightened. "There is no path harder than the one you've chosen."

The girl blinked, her abundant lashes fluttering several times, before she lifted her chin. "This is the most I've eaten in months. I've never even dreamed of wearing something like that." Her eyes lingered on the gown draped over Cora's arm. "I will take my chances. I can learn how to please a man if it means having a full stomach and a comfortable place to sleep."

Cora nodded, though the ache inside her only intensified. If she could explain what this job did to a person—how it ripped the soul apart, how it left one hollow and devoid of meaning—she could successfully get every new arrival to turn away. But they wouldn't believe her until they experienced it themselves, until they looked into the eyes of yet another man in an endless line, bearing their bodies as their souls became lifeless. They never turned away until it was too late.

"Well then, let's get you a bath." Cora did her best to paint on a smile despite the tears blooming behind her eyes. She had not the time or luxury of mourning yet another soul brimming with innocence about to be crushed. "I have much to teach you before tonight."

The Gold Strike jail looked nothing like Ellis had pictured it when the offer had arrived from clear across the country for a sheriff's title of his own. As a lowly deputy riding the Appalachian hills in search of trespassers and moonshiners, he'd fallen prey to glossy visions of grandeur. He'd seen a whitewashed building with a proud sign over the door, a host of deputies eagerly awaiting his arrival, a clean jail with everything he'd need to take charge of this wayward town. Reality hit him hard in the face.

Standing at the entrance to the sheriff's office with its rickety door and rusted hinges, he surveyed the meager space. Several desks were jammed together across the front room, with papers strewn everywhere and coffee stains marring the wood. Beyond that, a dingy floor stretched to a dark hallway he assumed led to the jail. Nobody came to greet him, not even whatever drudge was assigned to work the front desk.

Sighing, Ellis trod forward and threw his hat on top of a stack of pages marked "classified"—out in the open for everyone to see, of course. Behind the desks, he spotted a closed door with a plaque reading "Sheriff Lester Jones" in bronze. "I suppose that's where I'm supposed to land." If someone ever got around to changing the name on the door.

He expected a locked office, but instead, the wobbly knob turned beneath his hand. The door squealed inward, revealing a cramped rectangular room with a single desk, a file cabinet, and two bookcases only half filled with a haphazard display of books. He ran his fingertips over the gold-embossed titles—*The Compiled Statutes of Montana, United States Revised Statutes, My Life on the Plains.* What good had all these resources done the dead sheriff when he'd decided to turn his back on his duty and resort to evil?

A door clicked somewhere down the hall, followed by the clatter of boots across the floor. A face appeared around the door seconds later—red, plump, eyes round. "Hey, you!" One chubby finger jabbed his way. "You can't be in here. This is a private office."

Ellis revolved toward the stout man with a lopsided hat and deputy's badge pinned to his stained waistcoat. "There was no one here to stop me from coming in"—he waved a hand toward the lobby—"from browsing the stacks of classified papers, from rifling through Sheriff Jones's things if I chose to."

The deputy flushed a cherry red, trying but failing miserably to appear taller. "Well, there is now, and it's time for you to go." His hand covered the hilt of his gun. "Don't"—his throat bobbed—"don't make me use force."

Spreading his legs wider, Ellis knotted his arms across his broad chest. "I wouldn't do that if I were you."

The deputy's fingers began to tremor atop his gun. "Why—why's that?"

Ellis's mouth tipped up on one side. "You don't want to shoot your new sheriff on the very first day, do you?"

Eyes expanding and mouth falling open, the deputy hopped up as if a spring had unloosed beneath him. "Sh-Sheriff McCraw? We didn't expect you until later today. I'm sorry, sir. I—"

His steady stream of self-censure halted at Ellis's upraised hand. "That's enough for now. I don't expect a soliloquy on your apologies. I only want the promise that you'll fix these deficiencies as soon as possible."

"Yes, sir." The deputy folded his arms behind his back, standing at attention like a soldier facing a drillmaster. "What else can I do for you, sir?"

"You can start by telling me your name."

"Yes, of course, sir." His chest billowed with pride. "I am Arnold Wainwright II."

"Well, Arnold Wainwright II"—Ellis rested his hands on his hips, silently scrutinizing his charge—"how many deputies work for this office—and where are the rest of them at this hour?"

"Five in total, Sheriff McCraw. A couple are around the county performing patrol duties. The others constitute our night shift."

Ellis's lips cinched in dissatisfaction. "Meaning half are in bed asleep and the other half are wasting the day away however they see fit." His fingertips skimmed the top of his desk before his knuckles pounded the wood. "I want every single one of you here at two o'clock this afternoon—sharp. Do you understand?"

Wainwright nodded with frantic zeal. Ellis could practically see the globs of sweat forming beneath his curling hairline.

"At ease, soldier." His eyes scanned the office, noting its cold presentation and lack of ornamentation. "Tell me a few things about the late Sheriff Jones, would you?"

Shifting nervously from foot to foot, Wainwright wrung his hands. "What do you want to know?"

Ellis spun in a slow circle, inspecting every piece of the office he could see from where he stood. "What kind of a man was he? I don't see any photographs in here. A man normally keeps those he loves best at the forefront of his mind."

"Jones was a bachelor. No wife, no children." Wainwright leaned in as if hoping to pluck a bit of personal information from his new boss. "Much like you, Sheriff McCraw."

Eyeing him coolly, Ellis grunted. "I'm twenty-seven years old, Wainwright. And Jones was—"

"Fifty-two, sir."

"You do recognize the difference." He'd often imagined himself as that lone wolf, the world passing him by as his hair turned from golden to white. He hadn't the time for romance, after all. Yet after the morning he'd enjoyed, he could almost imagine anything of his future.

"I do, Sheriff. I apologize." Wainwright blinked at him expectantly a few times before he folded his hands together. "To your question, I worked with Sheriff Jones every day for the past three years, but I failed to know him well. I'm not sure who did in this town. He kept to himself mostly. He was very serious about his job, and he ran a tight ship. Beyond that, I'm not sure."

Ellis released a sardonic laugh. "From the looks of things out there, he didn't run much of anything."

Coloring, Wainwright stuttered again before collecting his words. "I admit I let things run amuck since he passed. It's been several months, you know. That's one reason nobody wanted me as their new sheriff." His self-depricating laugh fell flat in the small space.

"We're going to work together to change that." He had to if he wanted anyone to take him seriously as sheriff after the hoax of a leader they had before him. "I'm not as gruff as I seem, and I would appreciate all the help I can get."

"Well, I am here to help, sir."

Ellis turned toward the cluttered bookshelves and squinted again at the titles. "You can start by collecting everything laying around on those desks out there and bringing it in here. Stack it on the floor in the corner. I'll go over everything one page at a time."

"Right away." Wainwright's boots thumped over the floor as he scurried out the door to follow orders. Within seconds, the mad rustle of papers filled the lobby area.

Setting his arms akimbo, Ellis studied the bookshelves a moment longer before swinging his gaze to the desk. It had compartments down each side just waiting to be explored. He glanced at the file cabinet, large enough to hold hundreds of files.

"I have a feeling there's more to your story, Jones," he muttered to the empty air. "I'm going to tear every inch of this place apart to find it."

Three

Even in the quiet street, the din of Madam Carey's brothel created a spectacle for anybody passing by. The homely clapboard building, quiet and plain by day, sprang to life at night. Gaslight spilled from the windows, painting the street in splashes of yellow. Bawdy laughter and chatter carried across the night. Ellis let his gaze rove the lively establishment, noting that every window in the place was lit. Even the tavern down the street didn't entice like this one, a lone shining beacon against the feathered forest.

A chill scampered over him. So far he'd wandered through each of Gold Strike's evening venues, his gun concealed beneath his jacket and his shiny new sheriff's badge deep in his pocket. Anonymity allowed him a certain degree of freedom he'd never have again in this town. At the Mountainview Inn, a concierge had greeted him with a bow and offer of champagne. His introduction to the Wild Rose Saloon had proved less grandiose. Only a well-worn stool and a bar littered with peanut shells had met him.

A burly bartender had pushed him a shot of whiskey at his request, thumping his finger on the bar for payment. From his perch atop his barstool, he'd observed how the lumbermen and mountaineers of Gold Strike passed their Friday night—sucking on cheap cigars and gulping whiskeys like water. Most of them threw their last few dollars into games of poker, inevitably bellowing in despair when luck dashed their fervent hopes.

Ellis watched the charade with dwindling interest, eyeing the women circling their games and leaning over shoulders provocatively. The prostitutes at the tavern appeared rough, worse for the wear, with stained low-cut dresses and gaudy makeup resembling stage clowns. This place was more hopeless than he'd imagined.

Poverty, gluttony, alcoholism, lusts of the flesh. Gold Strike imbibed in each wicked vice more deeply than the last. It practically thrived on them, without a hint of misgiving at their sins. From what he could see, Madam Carey's was the deepest well of debauchery in the whole town, a snake pit crawling with temptresses. His stomach turned to imagine the reception he might expect inside.

"Well, are you coming or you going, darlin'?" A feminine voice ripped him from his musings, pinning his attention on a curvaceous brunette standing in the business's open doorway. She giggled at his startled expression, the sound rattling his nerves. "I promise we don't bite."

Ellis forced down the nausea threatening to overwhelm him and climbed the porch steps. "I was only out here having a smoke."

"Uh-huh." She hooked one dubious brow. "I saw you out here staring in the windows like the whole place might be hit by a flame of fire like Sodom itself." She leaned closer, her revealing neckline accentuating her natural assets. "I promise God won't strike you down if you come inside. Heck, half the people in here you'll recognize from church."

Ellis's throat closed in on itself. How vile to blaspheme the name of God in such a fashion. Yet it would do no good to condemn her on the spot. He'd stick out like an oxen among horses if he didn't at least try to play the part. "I'm not afraid. Why don't you take me inside?"

At his invitation, she bit her lip seductively and seized his arm. The overabundance of floral perfume assaulted him as she snuggled in close and wrapped both arms around his elbow. "So you were just waiting for an invitation, were you?" Her sly gaze ascended his chest to his face. "I hope you're planning to have a good time tonight, because that's all we're good at here."

Ellis forced himself to return her forward grin. "What's your name?"

"Allison. What's yours?"

Would anybody in this town have heard of the new sheriff? Better not to take a chance and use his middle name instead. "I'm Daniel."

"Daniel?" she purred as if the very sound enlivened her. "What do you do for work, Daniel?"

"I'm a hunter." It was true, wasn't it?

"That's why you have such strong muscles." She squeezed his arm as they passed through the front door. "You must be lonely, spending all those hours by yourself in the wilderness. Why haven't I seen you here before?"

He opened his mouth to answer, but a squeal pulled his attention elsewhere. A petite blonde approached them, her hand already plastered across Ellis's other arm. "Who is this you've brought in with you?"

"This is Daniel." Allison laughed, though she tugged him against her protectively. "And he's mine. I saw him first."

"I believe the man has a choice, and a voice of his own." The newcomer's eyes raked him suggestively before she batted her lashes a few times and pouted at him. "My, you're a handsome fellow. Wouldn't you like to come have a chat in my room?"

Allison pulled him backward. "I told you he's mine."

The new girl's hand clamped harder on his arm. "You don't own him just because you brought him inside."

"Ladies." Ellis freed himself of both their grips, raising two placating hands. "That's enough squabbling. Let me have a look around first, hmm?" He tossed them a wink amid the churn of his stomach. What a disgusting charade to play night after night, pretending to desire a man's attention when their only aim was to line their own pockets.

Leaving behind his two sulking companions, Ellis wandered the crowd in an attempt to blend in while ingesting every detail. Claret drapes with golden tassels flanked the wide foyer with its curved staircase. Each set of drapes appeared to section off another room. Ellis wandered through the archway to his left, finding a barroom similar to the one at the Wild Rose, only flashier and more sophisticated.

This one, too, held tables full of men locked in heated concentration over games of cards. Yet beyond them sat couches for guests to lounge upon, a sitting area crawling with scantily clad women. He perused the room a few moments before turning aside. He couldn't tolerate another drink on an empty stomach.

A hand stopped him before he could take another step. Ellis turned, ready to defend himself against another eager prostitute, but instead an elegantly dressed older woman smiled back. "Well, hello there, sir. Pardon my interruption." Her hand flattened over her beaded chest. "I noticed you looking around, and it appears this is your first visit, correct?"

Ellis tipped his head, trying to cover his misgiving with a casual smile. "That's right, ma'am."

"How delightful." The woman laughed, her headpiece catching the lamplight in crystalline sparkles. "I am Madam Carey, the proprietor of this establishment. I'm happy to answer any and all questions you may have."

"Is that so?" Ellis raged within. *I have a million questions for you, lady.* "How many girls do you have working in this place?"

"Well, now let me think." She tapped a finger on her slightly wrinkled chin. "I believe we have fourteen now. We just had a new girl join our ranks—if virginity is of interest to you."

His stomach dropped. What a disgusting human being. "That's quite all right. I doubt I could afford her." His eyes swept the sea of jewels and too-thin gowns. "All of your women are housed here?"

"Yes, of course." Madam Carey paused, a flicker of concern marring her brow. "I consider this a haven for my girls. I feed them and house them as queens, for that is what they truly are."

Queens who are forced to be intimate with whomever you say. He plastered on a false smile. "That paints a lovely picture, madam. Forgive me. I'm always particular when I enter an establishment such as your own."

The light of understanding brimmed in her eyes. "Ah." She leaned in, speaking in a low tone. "With all the literature sprouting up about disease, you mean. I can assure you my girls are clean. I make sure of it daily."

Ellis nodded as if satisfied. What kind of ritual she put these women through, he didn't want to begin to imagine. "I trust you do. And you have a fine selection, if I may say so."

"Well, thank you, young man. I pride myself on having the cleanest, most beautiful, most *knowledgeable* girls in the whole of Montana." Her arm swept the milling crowd. "You may have who you choose tonight. I guarantee it. I don't care who has put money down before you. You will have top priority as a first-time customer."

"Much obliged, ma'am." Ellis's gaze moved from one girl to the next, to every shade of skin and color of hair, from tall ones to petite ones—a collection of women presented like cattle at market, less than human. What was wrong with these men who frequented their doors every night, to keep a brothel of fourteen women running in comfort? Why, with only one day in this town, he'd found a true woman of substance and beauty who put all the rest of these to shame.

Cora. The very remembrance of her name sparked electric tingles racing down his forearms into his hands. He'd spent a day trying to focus on work and forget her, but how could he when her green eyes and supple lips still haunted his every thought? Once he got out of this den of sin, he'd seek her out—tomorrow, at a respectable hour. Any woman worth her salt had taken to bed hours ago. He'd simply have to dream of her tonight, content with the memories of holding her in his arms.

"Do you see one that strikes your fancy?" Madam Carey's eager voice brought him back to the present.

Ellis sucked in a breath, aware he had been staring at the swarm of prostitutes when he noticed several blushing and flirting with him from behind their fans. His chest still ached for Cora, not these women of little substance, all dressed in strategically-placed ruffles and trained to allure the weakest of men. If only he could reach out and touch her this moment, could hold her rather than pretending to want one of these women who paled in disgrace to her.

Forcing a sly smirk Madam Carey's way, he steeled himself against his foolish rush of emotion. "I think I may have just the girl in mind."

"You're still sure about this?" Cora glanced at the woman beside her. "There's still time to run."

Damaris pushed her chin up, her back straight, though her fingers gripping the railing showed the slightest tremor. "I'm sure, thank you. It's either this or dying in a ditch somewhere." She wore a confident expression, though her voice sounded feeble within the lively brothel.

Cora's heart pumped for her. Standing at the top of these stairs, she couldn't help but remember the first time she descended them to a crowd of greedy men, knowing she was placing her innocence up for sale. She understood better than anyone the desperation consuming Damaris to even consider such a profession. Yet try as she might, she couldn't convince her to turn away. Neither could she move backward in time and keep herself from the crooked path she'd traveled toward destruction.

Madam Carey had wasted no expense on the arrival of her newest milch cow. The brothel sparkled like never before, gaslight hissing in all the sconces, candelabras winking with flames, her best crystal clinking together as men gorged themselves and ogled the prospective *items* for sale.

Her belly roiled, threatening to make her vomit. She'd spent all day trying to prepare Damaris—bathing her, teaching her Madam Carey's rules in regard to interactions with her guests. Like the greenhorns before her, she had assured Damaris knew what to expect in the bedroom and what she could do if she fell into danger. She'd even briefly mentioned the auction, but she wouldn't—no, she *couldn't* properly explain what it felt like to stand like a lone tree before their licentious, leering eyes and be sold like chattel to the highest bidder. Madam Carey had explained it to her in youth as if she were an exquisite piece of artwork, valued especially because no man had touched her before. She had twisted the reality to make her feel honored. She refused to foster such delusions in Damaris.

Despite the madam's orders to keep the atmosphere light and refreshing with bouquets of sweet-smelling roses and clematises, the scent of sweat, body odor, and alcohol still lifted to them. No amount of pretending could ever cover up what this place truly was—nothing but a home fit for dogs.

"You will survive tonight, and you will go on," she heard herself say, almost without her consent. Damaris turned wide, unblinking eyes to her. Cora's heart almost broke at the naivety on her face. "No matter what happens, I promise you will survive—and I will be here in the morning if you need me."

Nodding dully, Damaris swallowed as her gaze turned back to the crowd of anxious guests. The bosom beneath her lavender sequined gown began to surge as her breath came hard.

Cora caught her hand and, simultaneously, her attention. "I am here when you need direction or simply escape. I am here." Her heart screamed out to throw the girl out the nearest door and tell her to run. But like all the other times in her life it protested, she silenced it with a shake of her shoulders. "Now, it's time to go. Madam Carey will be cross if we tarry any longer."

Her own heart galloped as Cora led Damaris down the stairwell. She pressed a hand over her crystal-studded bodice and seized a handful of her sea green satin skirts. Just because she spent a day leading a young girl down the path of evil didn't mean she could be lax in her responsibilities. With practiced regality, Cora lifted her head and put on a smile. She would play her part to a tee. She always did. The perfect employee, the perfect woman, the perfect lover.

"Cora, my dear, you look ravishing tonight." One of her more genteel regulars stepped up as she reached the base of the stairs, laying a warm kiss upon her hand.

Cora feigned a grin equal parts bashful and wicked. "Why, thank you. You look rather dashing yourself, Mr. Sullivan."

"And who is this you've brought with you?" another man asked as he eyed Damaris's tightly cinched form.

"This is my good friend Damaris." Cora laid a gentle hand on her shoulder, prodding her forward with the barest of touches. "Go easy on her, gentlemen. She isn't the social butterfly that some of our girls are, and she's not yet accustomed to such lavish attention." She kept her voice light, all the while steering her companion toward the guests she knew would treat her better than others.

"A newcomer." The men's eyes rolled knowingly toward one another. "Are we to have an auction tonight?"

"Indeed, gentlemen. We are." Cora's hand pressed reassuringly on Damaris's forearm. "This one is as acquiescent as she is beautiful. She'll make a perfect companion for one lucky man tonight."

"Perhaps she'll have time for more," a bearded guest shouted, jostling his comrades with an elbow.

Keeping her chin high, Cora commandeered Damaris toward a more opulent section of men. Better to parade her before a single man who could afford to keep her all night than let her loose on the revolting dregs of society who would pool their money.

She scanned the crowd, her gaze at last landing on Madam Carey. The proprietor appeared locked in conversation with an unseen guest in the lounge area. Cora exhaled her relief. At least she'd have time to put poor Damaris in the right hands before the auction commenced. Nothing dampened a young woman's life like a wretched first experience.

"Let's have a talk with those gentlemen over there, shall we?" Indicating a plush sofa containing some of Gold Strike's most wealthy citizens, Cora weaved Damaris through the clouds of cigar smoke, laughter, and suggestive propositions.

She couldn't miss the fellow prostitutes whose narrowed gazes followed them everywhere. Indeed, Cora couldn't step foot from her room without attracting vitriol from somewhere. She had the largest and most luxurious room in the brothel—save for Madam Carey's—the fullest wardrobe, the best pick of customers. To her chagrin, Madam Carey considered her the cream atop her milk, the finest of all under her employ. Somewhere in the span of her devastating existence, Cora had learned how to charm in a way that made her stand out. She never felt the weight of it more than when girls like Allison glared at her every move.

Time wore on, chock-full of empty conversation filled with lazily masked innuendo. She gulped down a glass of champagne when offered, letting the bubbling liquor sizzle through her. The time for the auction quickly approached, and Madam Carey's foot tapped with impatience on the floor, her eyes darting to the grandfather clock in the hallway. She would expect them all to find partners by the end of the party—disenchanted bidders who'd been outmaneuvered at the auction. She had only minutes to prepare Damaris for her fate, an hour if lucky before she found herself yet again unclothed in a stranger's presence.

As if reading her thoughts, Madam Carey's gaze hooked her like the claws of an eagle. One finger motioned Cora her way, the look on her upraised brow saying she would accept no other response but quick compliance.

Cora sighed. "I need to find out what Madam Carey requires of me," she told Damaris. "Do you think you will fair all right here by yourself while I'm gone?"

The girl's eyes opened round like a doe's, but she nodded. "I'll be fine. Thank you, Cora—for everything you've done."

Cora tossed her a reassuring smile and squeezed her hand before making her way through the crowd. What could Madam Carey possibly need at a time like this? A throng of tall men still blocked her view of the woman's companion, no doubt someone rich or influential by the amount of time she spent greasing his wheels. Madam Carey would expect her to perform for him like the trained poodle she was. With a steadying breath, she bolstered herself, preparing to put on her very best show.

"Ah, my dear. There you are." The expectant madam flapped her hand harder. "Hurry up, girl. I have a very important guest who is impatient to meet you. I've told him what an absolute star you are around here."

So he will expect even more of me. Fantastic. If only she could skip over all this pretension and curl up beneath her covers—alone, for a change. To strike out on her own and never have to please another man again. *Someday.*

"Come, come." Madam Carey's hand jetted out to capture her wrist, pulling her through the last of the crowd and into the glorified space of her presence. "Cora, I'd like you to meet Mr. Daniel

Barton." Her free hand swept up a tall, broad gentleman with neatly combed, sandy blond hair.

The world tilted on its axis. Cora stepped back, refocusing her eyes. They must be deceiving her. Yet even after she blinked away the fog, his image remained. His jaw clenched, his eagle-eyed stare grinding her to the floor. She had no choice but to look into the face of the man who'd kissed her this morning and admit exactly who she was.

Four

CORA'S BODY FROZE AS if dropped into a pool of cold water. The man's scrutinous gaze raked over her, from her much-too-revealing neckline down her shimmering skirts. Cora had never wished so badly to put on a coat, a blanket, anything that would hide her skin from those eyes that seemed to look through her.

"Well, aren't you going to say hello to our guest?" Madam Carey laughed nervously. "This is his very first visit to our fine establishment." *Of course it was. He'd just arrived in town today.*

Trying to steady her breathing, Cora blinked rapidly. She hadn't taken him for the kind of desperate man to find the first brothel he could the moment his feet hit town. But how much did she really know about him? He had, after all, kissed her upon their first meeting. Kissed her with such passion she could still sense it radiating through her body.

Compelling an expression she hoped was pleasant across her face, she forced herself to look at him. "Forgive me. It's so good to meet you, Mister—Barton, was it?" Funny. She seemed to remember an Ellis McCraw.

He cleared his throat. "Yes, Daniel Barton. It's good to make your *true* acquaintance, Miss Blackwood."

The sardonic bite to his words wasn't meant to be missed, but Madam Carey did just the same. "I was just telling Mr. Barton here what an accomplished young woman you are." Her eyes glowed with false sincerity. "Why, she's the finest I've had the privilege to employ. Always helpful, always graceful, and her *talents* are beyond compare." Her brows wiggled suggestively.

Cora clamped her lips shut. Of course, the madam didn't refer to the lengths she went to make the girls feel safe, or the endless hours she spent sewing beautiful costumes. She had a fondness for lending Cora out to first-time callers, especially if they had money or any societal rank. No doubt Cora's unique charms kept them wanting more.

"Is that right?" Ellis's lip curled ever so slightly, his incredulity quickly converting to disgust.

"Madam Carey exaggerates." Cora flattened a hand over her pulsating chest.

"On the contrary, my dear." Madam Carey's hand waved her off like an obnoxious bird begging for food. "You practically keep a roof over my head with your talents. I'm proud of the woman you've become." She reached out to cup Cora's chin.

Ellis licked his lips. His brows gathered. "Forgive me, Madam Carey, but might I have a word with Miss Blackwood—*alone*?"

Cora's body heated. The last place she wanted to go was anywhere alone with this man—not with the absolute fire raging in his eyes.

"Alone?" The madam covered her rouged lips with the tips of her fingers. "Why, you may certainly have her to yourself once the auction is over."

"Auction?"

Before Cora could explain, Madam Carey tittered again. "Why, of course. Why did you think I held this grand party tonight?" She nodded toward poor Damaris, who stood like a deer caught in a hunter's trap within a swarm of eager men. "The new girl I told you about. She must be auctioned off. Claiming her virginity is no small prize, sir."

His skin whitened. How bizarre a practice it must appear to anyone looking in—indeed, anyone with a soul. Even a man who went looking for a night's comfort may not condone such a callous display.

"Anyway, all my girls will be available for purchase once the auction is concluded." She gestured to the soiled doves sprinkled about the room, her gaze finally coming to rest on Cora. "Even this one."

Ellis took a brief moment, as if shaking himself, before taking one step toward Cora. His head shook. "I have no desire to purchase her. I'd simply like to have a conversation." He reached for Cora's hand, but before their fingers could touch, Madam Carey intercepted.

Yanking Cora backward, she stepped in front of her like a shield. "My girls do not converse, Mr. Barton—at least not alone. Their time is more valuable than that."

His jaw flexed. "It won't be more than five minutes."

The pleasant look on her face turned cold. "This is not my first night on the job, sir. I know the tricks men play to keep from paying my girls what they deserve."

"You mean to keep from paying *you?*" His mouth flattened at the look of shock on Madam Carey's face. "Forgive me. I promise you I have no intentions with Miss Blackwood here. I would simply like to talk with her."

Flipping her fan in front of her face, Madam Carey fluttered it sharply. "And I told you that is impossible, sir. If you would like to speak with Miss Blackwood, you need to pay a price." Her gloved hand shot out, her fingers rubbing against each other.

"Fine." Ellis reached into the back pocket of his pants and slapped his wallet into his hand. "How much?"

Throwing a bewildered look Cora's way, Madam Carey's mouth hinged open before she closed it and stood taller. "She usually goes for thirteen dollars."

"Thirteen dollars?" His brow arched, but he dug into his wallet and produced several crisp bills. "Here. Here's your thirteen dollars." He flung the bills across Madam Carey's hand and reached for Cora's wrist.

"Wait! You can't just run off with her like that. We have rules!" Madam Carey snapped her fingers, summoning her ever-present bouncer. "Randolph! I'm in need of your immediate assistance."

Sighing irritably, Ellis turned her way. "What rules have I broken? You insisted I pay to speak with her. I gave you what you asked."

Madam Carey plopped both fists on her rounded hips, his bills crumpled safely in her fingers. "I told you she cannot go until after the auction is over. All of the girls must wait."

"And why is that?"

"We have an order to things here." She glanced around at the ever-increasing number of stunned faces pointed their way. "What if you decided you'd rather spend your time with Damaris?"

"I don't want her. I want this one." His pointed finger poked toward Cora, who'd turned red with humility over the exchange.

Madam Carey rose up on her tiptoes. "What if someone else wishes to claim her?"

Ellis laughed sarcastically, the sound rumbling from deep within his chest. "I doubt there's a person here who hasn't yet tasted this flavor." His scathing look twisted Cora's middle.

"She is very sought-after. I often get more for her."

Ellis's wary gaze rounded on the hushed group in the foyer, whose every eye pinned on him now. "Is she to be sold at auction too? Can I take liberties with her if I toss in the highest bid?"

Madam Carey huffed. "She is not, but there are conventions." Randolph had now arrived at her side, ready to follow her orders. "Please see this man out. He's overstayed his welcome."

Standing proud, Ellis shot a warning glance Randolph's way. "I am simply trying to conduct a business transaction." He looked back at the men in the foyer. "Who else here wants her? Who will pay more than thirteen dollars?"

"Mr. Barton!" The madam blushed a rosy hue, a color Cora had never seen on her before.

"I'll take her for fourteen!" one of the men shouted.

"Fifteen!"

"I paid eighteen not a month back and I'd do it again!"

"All right, it stands at eighteen dollars!" Ellis wrenched out of the grip Randolph tried to get on his arm. "Anybody else?"

"For Cora? Nothing short of twenty!"

"Excellent." Ellis's large hand spurted up, a lone symbol in the pressing crowd. "I'll bid twenty-five. Does any man want to challenge me?"

Stillness fell over the group, save for a few derisive laughs and lewd jokes. "Twenty-five dollars it is, then." Retrieving the rest of the amount from his wallet, Ellis stood before Madam Carey, crushing her with the heat of his gaze. "I will give you twenty-five dollars to take her *now*."

Madam Carey's skin tightened around the jaw, but she dared not spit back the venom on her face. She hadn't gotten such favorable prices for Cora in years. "I suppose a few rules can be bent from time to time." She glanced toward Randolph. "You may unhand him. So long as you take this display elsewhere, Mr. Barton, I'm prepared to overlook it."

"Good." Ellis snatched Cora's hand and led her through the crowd of onlookers.

"But the auction!" Cora pulled back toward the crowd.

"The auction can wait," Madam Carey hissed, a warning gaze darting Ellis's way. "She'll be fine. Take care of him."

Before she could find another way to protest, Ellis had dragged her through the milling throng to the base of the staircase. "I assume your chambers are up there?"

Throat dry, Cora nodded. The guests around them were already whistling and making suggestive comments. She couldn't address her feelings here—not with this drunken lot buzzing in her ears.

Cora allowed Ellis to lead her up the staircase only because she had to. As soon as they reached the landing and the cover of shadows, she pried her arm out of his hand and marched down the hallway in seething silence. A thousand times, she'd been objectified, made to feel less than human, to acquiesce to a man's desires. But she had never experienced this gut-wrenching fire curling through her insides. She had never felt so hurt and humiliated she couldn't look at the person standing next to her. Instead, she clenched her jaw and kept on walking, even as he studied her stoic profile. Pressure built behind her eyes, but she shoved it down. He was not the man she'd imagined this mystical morning.

The confines of her bedroom, normally fresh and comforting, layered Cora in an eerie sensation. She closed the door and locked it, then leaned against it. She wanted to hit him. She wanted to scream. Yet staring silently as he paced the floor beside her bed proved all she could muster.

Ellis raked both hands through his hair, clenching it into fists. His gaze, smoldering with ire, landed everywhere but her—her hand-sewn lace curtains, her wardrobe with skirts peeping through the open door, her rose-patterned bedspread with intricate stitching. The wrath on his face tangled with mourning, his hands clenching and unfurling at his sides.

In the wake of his outburst, Cora found her voice. "What were you possibly thinking out there?" she asked through clenched teeth. She had worked too long and hard for a stranger to walk in and treat her with such contempt.

Ellis's fiery gaze shot to her. "What do you mean—the part where I had you thrown at me, or the part where I had to pay money just to speak with you?"

Her stomach roiled. "The part where you made me a spectacle in front of everybody. You humiliated me."

"Humiliated you?" His head angled, his lips contorting. "Isn't that what you did to yourself? What every other man out there was doing to you?" His hand swung toward the door, through which the sound of revelry seeped through.

"Those men and I—we have an understanding." Her fists balled at the base of her desperate throat. "I know what to expect, and so do they. I never would have guessed that you, of all people—"

"What?" His voice held the lilt of mockery. "What about me, of all people? You hardly even know me."

Cora's hands fell limp beside her. "How right you are. I was foolish to harbor a different kind of hope." She tried to suppress her tears, but still they emerged beneath her batting lashes.

The slightest hint of remorse shone through his eyes. "Try to imagine how I feel."

Her defeat quickly erupted into fire. Cora stepped forward in challenge. "How do you feel? Tell me. What does the brave man who kisses a strange woman then visits a brothel that very night have to say? Please, share your wisdom with the rest of us fools."

He stared at her a quiet, vulnerable moment, his chest surging. "That's not the kind of man I am. I don't go kissing strange women."

"You kissed me."

His nostrils flared. "I won't deny it. Perhaps I had a momentary lapse in judgment, but I had hoped—" His words trailed off, thick with emotion.

Cora's chest ached. "You'd hoped what?"

"I'd hoped to find out who you were, to properly court you. I didn't intend to kiss you and never let it mean anything."

Her arms folded across her chest. "Yet you wound up here." How convenient for a man's logic—to claim pure motives while dancing with the devil. She'd heard this story a hundred times before.

He sighed heavily. "It isn't what it seems."

"Really? Then how, pray tell, is it?" Marching past him, she reached for the silk robe hanging on a hook. She'd craved its protection all night. Now it slid across her shoulders, hiding her heaving bosom. "From where I stand, it looks like you came looking to go the rounds tonight, and now you're angry because you found me."

She whirled on him. "That's it, isn't it? You imagined I was some chaste, sanctimonious woman who would stand there and wait for you while you sowed your wild oats. That you could kiss me and pretend you cared, all the while feeding the lusts of your flesh. It's disgusting." She spat the last word, drops of spittle spewing from her lips.

"I never pretended to care." He took a step toward her, his jaw working. "I had genuine feelings for you from our conversation this morning. I felt things when I kissed you, things I never—" He breathed, the sound rasping from his throat.

The look in his eyes held such sincerity, Cora could almost sympathize with him. Then she remembered glaring reality, and rage overwhelmed her. "You felt so strongly for me, you had to come looking for a strumpet to satisfy you."

"If you would only give me a chance to explain," he growled. He'd come close now—close enough for her to see the flecks of green in his bright eyes, to feel the heat of his breath on her skin.

Cora set her teeth, staring him down, determined to meet his every accusation and win. "I'd like to hear this elaborate explanation. Please, do tell me why such a righteous man is standing in a brothel after having paid *twenty-five dollars* to indulge himself with me as he saw fit."

The arms clenched beneath his jacket. He stood over her, eyes narrowed and nostrils fuming. Yet the words wouldn't come. He bit back whatever he wanted to say, all probably lies. What could he possibly say to dig himself out of the hole he'd fashioned?

A wild streak pulsed through her, perhaps from years of ignoring her conscience. "Maybe you did all this with the aim to get me alone." She pressed toward him, her body brushing his. "Well, here I am, Ellis McCraw. You paid for me. Do as you wish."

He blinked, his gaze dropping to her throat. Before it could fall any further, he forced it up again. A scarlet hue climbed his neck, brimming from his shirt collar.

"Don't have anything to say? I'm not a fool. I know what *all* men come here for." Her arms hooked around his back, hauling him against her.

"Cora," he ground out, more a plea than a statement. "Cora, don't."

"Why not? This is what you want, isn't it? You said it in front of everybody." Her hands slithered up his solid chest to grip the shirt covering his rapidly thudding heart. "What you refuse to say with your mouth, your body speaks for you."

He was trembling now, like wax in her hands. Just like every other man who walked through her doors, he was a fool. Cora drew her other hand up his hip, pausing when something solid met her fingertips. She frowned. "What is that?" He tried to pull away, but her hand had already dipped into his pocket, feeling for the pointed edges of whatever rested inside.

"That isn't your business. Cora, don't."

She yanked the item out of his pocket, holding it to the light. Her mouth fell open, then burst with astonished laughter. Gleaming in her curled fingers rested a silver badge with the word "sheriff" etched across it.

Awareness tingled over her one piece at a time. "No wonder you were observing everyone as if you thought someone might want to kill you. No wonder you used a fake name." Her eyes met his over the glimmering badge. "You're nothing but a spy, aren't you?"

"Give me that." Ellis snatched it from her hold and shoved it back in his pocket.

Crossing her arms over her chest, Cora looked him over. "I ought to tell Madam Carey about you. The mob downstairs wouldn't take kindly to a lawman in their midst."

He shook out his jacket lapels. "Tell her if you want. You think I'm scared of a few angry drunks?"

"Perhaps you should be." She cocked one brow. "They're very protective of me—especially that bouncer you insulted downstairs."

"I suppose he protects you in exchange for your *superior* talents I've heard so much about. Isn't that how these things work?"

Dumping her casual facade, Cora marched toward him, clutching two fistfuls of her silk robe. Randolph had been nothing but a kind, respectful friend to her since she'd come under Madam Carey's thumb. But what good would the truth do her now? "That is not your concern. What I do with myself is none of your business."

He leaned over her, much like he had this morning—only the light of admiration had fled. "Just like it was none of my business when I found you on that path."

"Yes, it was none of your business." Her face tilted toward his, matching his passion. "Am I to tell every person whose acquaintance I make about my profession so they can judge me before they even know me?"

Ellis glared down at her. "Do you kiss every person you meet the way you kissed me?"

A disbelieving huff lifted from her. "You are unbelievable. *You* kissed *me*, and you didn't bother to tell me you were the sheriff, even when I asked what you did for a living." Their faces had drawn close again, their fervent breaths mingling, their eyes shooting daggers at each other. If he didn't dwarf her in every way possible, she might have hit him. The urge speared up her forearms, bursting into her clenched hands.

"Yes, I kissed you." His gaze plummeted to her lips before finding her eyes again. "I didn't know at the time I was being lured by a professional, enticed by a practiced woman who knew exactly how to hook me."

His accusations pooled in her stomach, ice draining through her. After years of parading herself in front of men for their attention, she knew indeed exactly how to ensnare them. Yet this morning, before he'd learned what inevitably clouded his vision of her, she had spoken to him as herself—the true Cora, the one she could show hardly a soul in this town. Now he stomped on her, grinding that existence to dust.

"If that's what you think, you should have paid me." Her voice rose, raw and jaded, a reflection of the soul hiding somewhere inside her, tucked away from the world's prying eyes.

"Isn't that what the twenty-five dollars was for?" His unforgiving eyes searched her face. "For one spectacular kiss, and the chance to tell you to your face that I'll never allow that to happen again?"

Cora blinked back the hot tears flooding her eyes. She couldn't show him how his words cut her, how the disillusionment on his face made her want to hurl herself in the depths of the river. She had lived a hollow, soulless life for a very long time, but she couldn't remember when it had disappointed anyone but herself.

"Go, then. You've had your say." She flattened both hands against his chest and pushed him backward. "Go! Leave me be! Don't let my sin encroach on your perfect life again."

Ellis stared at her a painful moment, anger and sorrow warring in his eyes. Then he turned, tramped toward the door, and unlocked it. He threw one last condemning look at her before he vanished into the hallway, slamming the door in his wake.

Cora's body tremored like a leaf in the wind. Tears rushed over her face freely now, burning paths down her cheeks and dripping off her chin. She fell to her bed and tucked herself into a fetal position, crying until she had no tears left.

Ellis McCraw had been a fleeting dream. He was gone now. The empty life ahead stretched into oblivion. She would go on, exactly as she deserved—condemned, alone, and wishing for death.

Five

CRISP AUTUMN AIR SWEPT through the trees and fluttered Ellis's shirt against his chest as he rode. The pines gave off a bold, effervescent scent that reached down and grabbed a part of his soul. How it reminded him of Tennessee's backwoods, of riding the trails as a boy. Yet here, the handiwork of God was marred by thieves and murderers. Such truth burned his gullet as he climbed the foothills and trampled the fallen leaves underfoot.

After his display last night, he doubted a person in Gold Strike wouldn't recognize him. He'd trodden down the brothel hallway beneath the lamplight, righteous indignation funneling through him. His hand still trembled from her closeness, his heart slamming against his ribs. He'd wanted with every fiber of his being to pull her close and kiss her again, even as she spewed hatred his way. Even knowing every man in that brothel had touched her before him.

Ellis cursed himself. No matter how focused his mind, his body was a traitor. He wanted her with a fire that frightened even himself. He'd stopped in that hallway, pacing the floor, wringing his hands. The destructive voice inside urged him to return—not to claim what he'd paid for, as the rest of the drunks crowding this brothel would do, but to satisfy the raging desire to kiss her one more time. To feel her slender frame wilting within his arms.

You are a fool, he told himself. *She only kissed you to make you want more. It's only a job for her.* Yet oh, how his heart ached to consider his dashed hopes. He'd seen in that one glorious kiss a future filled with light and laughter, family and joy. He'd imagined an unearthly connection between them as they'd spoken on that mountain trail, but it was all a lie.

Ellis pulled at his collar to keep it from strangling him. She wanted nothing but money. There was no joy in loving her. The laughter bounding off the walls of the brothel crashed over him like a wave pounding against the seashore. He descended the stairs, appalled to find every man in the place pressed into a parlor, bidding over a woman's virginity.

"I'll give you sixty!"

"Seventy-five!"

The young woman, hardly older than a girl, shivered as she stood before them in a gown too tight, her broad eyes bright with fear.

"The two of us will pay eighty!" someone shouted, jabbing the fellow to his left with an elbow.

Something inside Ellis snapped, whether born of his anger over Cora or this sickening display, he couldn't be sure. Yanking his gun from his waistband, he held it to his side and pushed his way through the crowd.

The bidding continued, the prices rising higher, the lewd jokes and laughter breaking to a fever pitch. Ellis waited until he stood in the room's center beneath a crystal chandelier, until the poor woman being auctioned off shook with such fright he thought her liable to faint. Then, without warning, he lifted his hand and shot two bullets into the ceiling over his head.

Shouts erupted around him. The woman screamed, diving behind a settee. Others shrieked as shards of crystal rained across the crowd. People ran to and fro, men grabbing their guns, others seizing pieces of furniture to protect themselves.

Ellis set his jaw, stomping through the melee until he reached a lounge chair and stepped atop it. He faced the crowd, his chest expanding. "Listen up, everybody, and listen good!"

The shouting subsided, every eye turning his way, even as many hid themselves in quaking fear. "My name is Ellis McCraw." He reached into his pocket and held his badge high in the lamplight. "I'm the new sheriff of this town. I know the worthless debauchery you've become accustomed to in this place, and I'm here to bring you a very clear message."

His intense stare met with each of theirs. "The freedom you enjoyed to run amuck as you pleased—to steal, to destroy, to hurt innocent women—it's all over. I'm going to bring each of you into the just hands of the law, to pay recompense for your sins against her name. Not a soul in here will escape the judgment of the law. I promise to hunt each of you down, one by one, until she has been satisfied."

A fearful hush had overtaken the crowd, but now they stirred, whispering to one another.

"We haven't done anything wrong!"

"I don't know where you came from, but prostitution ain't illegal here."

Ellis swung his incensed gaze toward the man who'd said it. "Legal or not, it is immoral and an abomination in God's eyes. I will not let this town fester in its blatant immorality."

"He's just mad he had to pay so high a price for Cora!" someone shouted from the back, inciting a barrage of laughs at his expense. "Was she too much of a woman for you?"

Ellis's fingers coiled around the hilt of his pistol. "Be careful what you say. I have a single strand of patience, and it isn't very long."

Several men reached for their guns, their eyes shifting warily to their comrades.

"I wouldn't if I were you," Ellis warned. "You might get away with killing me, but you won't withstand the force of deputies I have waiting outside these walls."

Their fingers reluctantly retreated, though Ellis understood the unseen messages passing between them. They would find a way to unseat this new and inconvenient sheriff before he disassembled their hedonistic way of life.

"I want you to remember this moment, gentlemen." His eyes scanned the crowd, waiting with anxious expressions. "This is the last time your antics will be tolerated in this place. Gold Strike shall become a town of honor and dignity. I will see to it or die trying."

His pledge to them still rang in his mind as he maneuvered his horse down the meandering trail, through the dense foliage beyond Jeremiah Anderson's ranch. In the light of day, he could admit that his rant had been foolish. He was lucky to have escaped it with his life. Thankfully for him, the men at Madam Carey's had never sat down with him to a game of poker. Otherwise, they would have recognized his bluff and called him on it.

Breathing in the familiar, comforting odors of wet bark and sap, Ellis flicked his reins over Honeydew's neck and urged her across a narrow stream. Upon hearing his plan to confront the town's most notorious outlaw, his deputies had lined up with guns ready and chests puffed like strutting roosters, volunteering themselves to aid him in his mission. But Ellis didn't trust anyone yet— certainly not enough to put his life in their hands. Besides, he preferred solitude. If Anderson wanted to kill him, he'd just have to step up and do it like a man.

Through the trees, he spied a modest ranch house with shabby siding and a stone chimney with smoke wisping into the sky. Ellis clicked his tongue, directing the mare down a sloping ravine that emptied into an open field. Most of Anderson's men had crawled into Madam Carey's or the Wild Rose Saloon this afternoon, wasting the few coins they could rub together on frivolous pursuits. Through careful prying, he'd learned that Anderson had stayed home—to plot his next move, no doubt.

Ellis didn't bother to hide his approach as he galloped Honeydew across the bare field toward a corral of horses. They neighed and stomped at his arrival, a beautiful collection of Mustangs and American Paints. So he had a similar interest with Anderson after all.

The horses' whinnying attracted three men to the cabin's front door, all holding rifles at their hips. Two looked like nothing, mere grunts destined to take orders from another man. Jeremiah Anderson stood unmistakably between them, his long, straggly blond hair lifting with the breeze and his brawny shoulders twice the width of the other two. He shook his head when one of his companions murmured something to him.

The three held their guns at their sides until Ellis trotted up to them with his badge pinned to his chest in full view. "Good day, gentlemen." He spoke the greeting casually, as if passing a parishioner at church.

Anderson's suspicious gaze slid over him. "Fine day to you, Sheriff." His large hand coiled menacingly on his gun.

"Being new to town, I thought I'd drop by." Ellis tipped his hat toward each of the trio. "I hope it isn't an inconvenience."

"Inconvenience? No." Anderson squinted. "But I'd be lyin' if I said it weren't a bit strange for the new sheriff to come to me."

"That's funny." Ellis's head cocked. "From what I hear, you had quite a close relationship with the last sheriff of this town. Or am I misinformed?"

Anderson ran his tongue across his teeth. "I think we both know the answer to that question."

"Indeed." Refusing to be cowed by Anderson's commanding presence, Ellis swung off Honeydew's back and landed in the dirt with a thud. Spinning around, he strode easily across the dusty ground, and didn't stop until he stood but two feet before his foes.

"As you may know, I have a particular interest in you, Jeremiah Anderson."

"Well, don't that make me feel like a tickled little girl?" Anderson's booming laugh spread over them, prompting his associates to chortle along with him.

Ellis shook his head. "Laugh all you want, but you won't be when you see what I have in store for you."

Sniffing, Anderson looked at him sideways, like one might glance at a bothersome fly. "You sure you're up for the challenge, Sheriff? Things have been goin' the same for quite some time in Gold Strike. People don't like change."

"Like it or not, it's coming."

"Yeah, I heard you say the same last night at Madam Carey's." So he *was* there, no doubt lurking at the edges of the room, concealing himself. "You was awful mad. Couldn't have been over a woman, could it?" His mocking eyes pinned on Ellis, searching him. "Wasn't hard to notice you fallin' all over yourself for her just a minute or two before."

Tongue dry, Ellis could do nothing but stare in return. Blast his feelings for Cora. If they were so easily deciphered, they would prove nothing but a thorn in his side.

Anderson's mouth tipped. "I can't fault you for it. That one there's quite a looker—and handy when a man gets lonely, if you know what I mean." His brows waggled. "I've lost my head over her a time or two myself."

Clenching the backs of his teeth, Ellis forced his ire to stay buried in his balled fists. He released a slow breath through his nostrils. "I didn't come here to talk about a woman. This is about you and me and the future of this town."

Anderson's lip snarled. "Far as I can tell, it might not have a future with the both of us in it."

"You're probably right." Ellis took a commanding step forward. "And I won't be the one to falter, I promise you."

"You want to bet on that, McCraw?" His upper lip pulled back, revealing stained teeth. "You took an awful big risk ridin' out here on your own. What's stoppin' me from puttin' a bullet in your head and buryin' ya where the only one who will find ya is a pack of hungry wolves?"

"I believe his name is—Isaiah?" Anderson's eyes slightly widened at Ellis's words. "Yes, that's what it is. He's sitting in my jail as we speak."

"Hogwash." Anderson loomed nearer, growling. "You're bluffin', just like you was last night at the brothel."

Ellis shrugged. "Perhaps. But do you really want to take a chance? I'm holding him on a serious charge of robbery. The townspeople are calling for his hanging." His hand came to rest on the hilt of his gun. "So I can be lenient, or my deputies can officially charge him for his crime when I go missing."

The outlaw's cheek twitched. "You don't have Isaiah. He went to the Wild Rose at noon."

"Yes, and then he decided to try and steal an old woman's reticule." Ellis touched his fingertip to his jaw, trying to remember the youth's words just before he left the jail. "He had a message for you, though. He said to bring the oxen to market."

Anderson swore, spitting in the dirt. "He's got Isaiah, all right," he said to the anxious men next to him. "I told him to say that if he ever got in trouble." He looked back at Ellis, his rage only harnessed for the moment. "I won't forget this, McCraw. You're skatin' on some mighty thin ice."

"Neither will I." Back rigid, Ellis tramped through the dirt and reached for Honeydew's reins. "I meant what I said. It's either you or me, Anderson. I'm going to see to it you're out of this town come spring—and that's my solemn vow."

Seizing the horse's saddle in one hand, he stepped up and swung his leg over her back. He would forever relish the image of Jeremiah Anderson, incomparable outlaw, bursting with wrath that had nowhere to land. How easy it proved to fell a mighty tree when the one cutting it down knew its weak points.

"Come by the jail," he said, leading his mount in a circle. "We'll see about getting your brother released and maybe a new town for you to terrorize." With a tip of his hat, he kicked Honeydew into motion, knowing the trio of bandits behind him could do nothing but stare in utter weakness.

Six

THE TIDY PARLOR OF Madam Carey's, filled to the brim with men last night, now sat in destitute silence. Cora perused the intricate rug, littered with crystal shards only hours before, now cleaned to perfection. Randolph had pulled down the broken chandelier, leaving a bare ceiling marked with two bullet holes. She shivered. How utterly incensed was Ellis at her last night to take it out on Madam Carey's ceiling?

"I thought I was going to die," Damaris said. "I thought someone was shooting at me."

Cora turned back to the young woman seated next to her on the velvet settee. She reached for Damaris's hand, holding it in hers. "I don't blame you. That must have been terrifying. You were already having such a stressful night as it was."

Damaris swallowed, her cheeks flooding with color. Her gaze tumbled to her lap. "Yes, it was much more than I had imagined."

"An auction always is." Cora squeezed her fingers. "But it's over now, and it will never happen again." She laughed humorlessly.

"Unless some maniac of a sheriff barges in and decides to put you up for auction himself."

Damaris laughed with her, yet it didn't reach her eyes. "He was quite insane, wasn't he?"

"Without question."

"But he was handsome, too." Damaris's dark brows rose in subtle question.

Cora pushed a hand over her light blue crepe skirts. Did her inescapable attraction to him show so completely? "He is, I suppose. The other girls say so, anyway."

Scooting closer, Damaris leaned inward. "Is it true what you told the madam? He really didn't even touch you after that whole charade with having a bidding war?"

Cora forced a smile. "Every word I said was true. I think the only reason he purchased me at all was to berate me over the evils of prostitution. He yelled at me the entire time." No need to mention she'd screamed and pounded his chest in return.

"But why you in particular?" Damaris frowned. "Why pay such a high price to get you alone only to lecture you? He could have yelled at us all together. That seems far more effective."

"I don't know." Cora hugged her arms around her torso, fighting the chill sweeping over her. "Perhaps I reminded him of someone who once wronged him." Or I was the only girl unlucky enough to stumble across his path that morning.

"I thought he was going to bid on me the way he came trampling through the room." Damaris's eyes expanded, their coffee-hued depths full of remembered fear. "He looked at me with such intensity, I wanted to swoon on the spot."

Cora resisted the urge to roll her eyes. "I know the feeling."

Evening had nearly set over the vast expanse of forest outside, and girls plunked down the stairwell for a hasty dinner before work time began. Cora glanced out the window at the purpling colors of dusk gathering above the trees.

"Before the guests arrive, I wanted a chance to chat about what happened last night. The auction, I mean."

Damaris's body stiffened. "You mean what happened after Sheriff McCraw disrupted it."

"Yes." Her throat burned at the pained look in Damaris's eyes. "What happened after he left and all the commotion died down? Madam Carey shooed me back to my room so quickly, I didn't get a chance to find you."

The girl's lithe hand rested upon her chest. "The bidding was up to eighty dollars before he shot the ceiling and stopped everything in its tracks. The men were angered about the auction ending so abruptly, but Madam Carey chose not to cause another squabble after what had just transpired."

Cora's breath stuck in her chest. "So she didn't make you go through with it?"

Damaris's lashes fluttered. "She accepted a private bid of one hundred dollars from Mr. Fletcher."

"Mr. Fletcher?" Cora's shoulders eased. He was of the older, wealthy class of gentlemen in Gold Strike. He had never been anything but gentle and respectful toward her, a man left lonely after his wife departed the world too soon. "I trust he treated you well."

Damaris nodded, though her skin paled. "I am lucky he was my first. I don't know what I would have done had some of the men who were bidding won." A chill shook her frame.

"Well, you needn't worry." Cora patted her arm. "Everything gets easier after the first. Soon you won't be able to distinguish one man from another." Her stomach turned with the statement. What a callous and sad reality her world had become.

"Are you faring well?" Cora asked. "Do you think you'll be ready for tonight?" She'd tried to petition Madam Carey to allow the girl a night of reprieve, but her request fell on deaf ears. The men were hungry for fresh blood in this place. Cora felt that fact more with each passing day.

"I'm fine. In fact, I look forward to it." Damaris sat with practiced determination, already spouting Madam Carey's ideals. Perhaps she might have looked believable if her lips didn't tremble.

"Well, you know I'm here should you ever need me." Cora's insides tightened. Who would support *her* on days such as this, with her very existence caving in?

"Girls, what are you still doing in here?" Madam Carey's brash voice ripped her from her musings. They both turned to find the middle-aged woman clad in her typical evening gown, a feather in her salt-and-pepper hair. "Everyone else has gone to dinner. You'll miss it if you don't hurry. Our guests will arrive within the hour, and I won't have you dilly-dallying in the dining hall while they wait to be entertained."

Cora bit her tongue. "We'll be right there, Madam Carey. Damaris and I were just wrapping things up."

"Well, see that you do." The madam dramatically tossed her skirt as she whirled and vanished down the hallway, her heels clicking over the floorboards.

Dinner passed with Cora hardly aware of the fact. She ate a few bites of chicken pot pie, but the savory vegetables only sickened her. The usually pleasant blend of spices tasted bitter to her tongue. Throwing down her fork with a clank, she wiped her mouth and reached for her water. The cold glass pressed into her quaking palm as she gulped the water down.

Ignoring the curious glances around her, she pushed off her chair and started for the hallway. No use putting off the inevitable—another night of painting on an artificial smile, of bearing her feminine assets and convincing a man she could solve his every worry with a few minutes in her bed. Another night of burying the soul inside her so far down, she feared she'd never find it again.

Quickly ascending the back stairwell to her room, Cora washed the scent of dinner from her face and hands in her washbowl and reapplied rouge to her lips. Spritzing violet-scented perfume into the air, she walked through it. Following a moment in front of her full-length mirror, she felt ready to face whatever came tonight.

She adjusted her jeweled bodice so it hugged her torso perfectly, with her bosom on full display. After tucking a few stray pieces of strawberry blonde hair into her chignon, she positioned a silver and jade dragonfly comb into her hair. Despite the fact that she had seven years on some of these girls, she still looked as youthful and vibrant as ever. To blazes with Ellis McCraw and the cutting remarks he had to say about her.

The brothel sparkled with gaslight as she reached the base of the stairs and readied herself to welcome the guests. It always boasted an enchanted feel, lamps glowing in the windows and elegant tapestries draped from every corner. One could almost forget about the cold and depressing acts taking place here. One could pretend they'd entered a palace if they truly wanted to.

Cora summoned her most charming welcome to each of the men who passed through the doors. Despite the battle raging inside, she kept up her genial facade, batting her lashes and flirting with barely concealed innuendo. This was her identity, after all. Why not embrace it?

When a familiar face came into view, her hand gripped her champagne coupe tighter. Jeremiah Anderson hadn't called on her for at least a year, but now his determined stare told her she wouldn't escape him tonight. Elbowing past everyone in his path, he didn't stop until his heavy boots rested inches away from her slippers. His appreciative gaze took all of her in.

"Why, Cora Blackwood. It's been a long time."

"Indeed, it has, Mr. Anderson." She simpered. "As I recall, you've preferred the company of *younger* girls more recently." At twenty-three, she was hardly an old maid, but she knew men like Anderson. They wanted youth, a new adventure, not something they'd tried a hundred times before.

A low chuckle emanated from his throat. "You'll have to for-give me. I've been a bit busy, is all. Didn't mean to ignore you, honey." He winked, the gesture revolting her.

After all that had transpired between Anderson and Caleb, the last thing she wanted to do was stand here and pretend to have any interest in this ruthless blowhard. But Madam Carey edged her vision, her hawk-like gaze scrutinizing every move Cora made.

"Here I thought you didn't care." Her mouth tugged up in a smirk. "I'd almost given up hope." *The hope of never seeing your face again.*

"I still have a sweet spot for my Cora." He stepped toward her, shouldering the men she'd been speaking with out of the way. "Be gone, gentlemen. Find someone else."

Cora's skin heated as he sidled up to her, his licentious gaze drifting down her jeweled necklace at a painfully slow pace. Her skin crawled to imagine him touching her, to imagine submitting to him after all he'd done to Caleb and Lily. But she didn't have a choice. Denying the most influential criminal in the valley would have severe consequences.

"You sure are a sight for a poor man's eyes." He continued to peruse her openly without a modicum of decency. "Have you given any thought to what I asked you before?"

A laugh bubbled up her throat. "What? You mean leave Madam Carey's for your ranch? Madam Carey would brain you."

"She wouldn't have much say in the matter now, would she?" He leaned close, his breath hot on her neck. "You could have whatever you wanted and I wouldn't have to share you."

Her insides recoiled. At least prostitution was more appealing than being Jeremiah Anderson's personal slave. "Ah, but I would have to share *you*, wouldn't I? You would never stop coming here."

His eyes rolled toward the ceiling, a smile on his whiskered lips. "That's the way of things between a man and a woman. You understand better than anyone how it works."

She could almost believe the lie if she hadn't once seen something different. It wasn't how it had worked for her parents, for her grandparents, for everyone she'd known back home. "I like it where I am." The champagne in her glass chilled her fingertips. "I enjoy having many men who adore me."

He leaned closer, his lips skimming the sensitive skin of her ear. "Suit yourself—as long as I get to be one of them." One broad hand swept from her wrist to her elbow. "What do you say we take this upstairs? It's been too long."

Cora's breath hitched. What was wrong with her? She'd endured Jeremiah Anderson dozens of times by now. Why did the thought of it send sprinkles of ice down her spine? She swallowed. "I suppose that's up to Madam Carey."

"You know she never denies me." He smiled against her skin, his bristly jaw scraping her cheek. "Plus, I got my money back. I have enough to pay for you every night if I want to."

Her heart lurched into her throat. *Every night.* How could she not fall into a broken shell of a person if that were true? Her gaze jumped to Madam Carey, who still watched her from across the room. She nodded, the look in her deathly eyes clear. A war already waged between the sheriff and the underbelly of this town. Madam Carey needed Anderson on her side. *Appease him, or there will be hell to pay.*

Turning away, she seized a handful of his shirt and dragged him behind her. "All right, then. Let's go."

A satisfied rumble vibrated from his chest to her fingertips. A dizzy sensation took hold, tilting her world on its axis. Cora reached out to steady herself on the banister, shutting out the voices in her head screaming at her to turn back. If only she had a choice in the matter. If only she hadn't taken this path a long time ago. But the damage was already done. She captured Anderson's warm hand in hers, leading him up the stairs to the hollers and cheers of the men below.

Her bedroom had never felt so silent. Cora dragged him inside and shut the door, quickly detaching herself from him. She strode across the hardwood floor, removing her dangling earrings as she walked. Hopefully he would make this quick and leave her to the isolation of her thoughts. She stopped at the dressing table, letting the earrings clatter against the wood as she shakily unlatched her necklace.

Two hands rested on her shoulders. Cora shivered, the weight of his fingers like rocks against her skin. He moved in closer, his presence a looming threat. "Why are you in such a hurry, hmmm?" His breath skittered over her neck. "Let's enjoy ourselves, like the old days."

As if she'd ever enjoyed a moment in his presence. As if the smell of cheap liquor and cigar smoke lifting off his clothes didn't nauseate her. She finished unlatching her necklace and let it slip to the dressing table. "It doesn't matter to me how long it takes, just as long as I get paid." Just as long as he went away when it was over.

Anderson spun her around, his eyes piercing hers. The loose hair beneath his wide-brimmed hat framed his face as it always did. Cora could easily reach out and punch that face if his money didn't keep them afloat. Her stomach turned with misgiving. Had he ever looked at her like that before—with meaning and intention? What could he possibly want?

"What do you know about this new sheriff?" he asked, his voice converting from raspy to devious.

So that was it. Cora laughed at the absurdity in his question. "He announced himself in town yesterday. What am I to know of him?"

"You know something." His head angled, his gaze probing. "You know a lot more than you let on."

Cora knotted her arms defensively across her bosom. "What gives you the idea that I know anything about him? He was clear last night in his declaration, wasn't he? He hates us. He wants to destroy us."

His brows narrowed. "Yes, indeed he was." His gaze darted across every plane of her face. "But he caused quite a ruckus with you. In fact, he paid twenty-five dollars just to get you alone."

Biting her lip, Cora let her gaze drop to her shimmering slippers. What kind of a fool would make such a scene, then proclaim himself sheriff in front of everyone? Had he intentionally marked her for trouble?

"Apparently he has a special hatred of me." She managed to look into his eyes again. "His twenty-five dollars bought him a lecture. He yelled at me until he had no more breath left in him."

"So I heard"—Anderson's jaw worked—"but I still don't believe it. Why would a man like that single you out—the most expensive girl in here? Why would he make such a display?"

Her nostrils fumed. "I told you, I don't know!"

He grunted, the sound low and irritating. "I think you do. I think you know exactly why he called on you, and why he got so angry in the first place."

"Well, if you know the answer, I'd like to hear it too!" Her eyes went wild. "I only met him yesterday. I don't know him beyond what happened here. I don't know why he took a special interest in me."

Anderson slowly sucked his upper lip into his mouth, but said nothing—only judged her with those cold, calculating eyes of his. Then his breath hissed out his teeth. "You can tell him when he calls on you again that I'll be waiting for him."

Cora huffed. "Are all the men in this place immune to listening to me? I'm not part of your games. I don't want to be a part of them!"

"You were certainly a part when it came to Caleb Broderick and Wesley Pierce." At her look of bewilderment, he shook his head. "Can't tell me you didn't help them. I know you did."

Cora stepped back. "I will always help the people I love."

"Then don't get upset when you get caught up in their games."

His callous words snaked through her, squeezing until she thought the life would drain from her limbs. How true they were. She wanted no part of the evil deeds performed here in Gold Strike, yet she planted herself firmly in their midst. She grasped at a false sense of morality while inviting a different man into her bed every night. The whole charade was exhausting.

She pressed her lips together. "I'll tell you what I can if he ever speaks to me again, but I doubt from our parting he will." Her gut twisted to embrace the painful reality of her own words.

"That's a good girl." Anderson's thumb skimmed her jaw. "It will be best for all of us when he's gone. We can't have a man like that running the law in Gold Strike. We'll both be out of a job in months."

Cora sighed, her breath lingering on her lips. "I'm trying to remember the last time we agreed on something." Her brows rose in good humor. "I'm trying to remember the last time a man came in here to do something other than berate me or hound me for information."

"Oh, I came in here to do a lot more than hound you for information." He seized both arms, yanking her to him and capturing her in a passionate, fiery kiss meant to turn a woman's legs to mush.

Yet Cora felt rooted to the ground, even as she returned his advances, her hands gripping his shirt. His kiss was like all the others—empty, meaningless, meant to thrill and nothing more. Cora retreated into the person she had to be when duty called, trying to forget the feel of Ellis's lips against hers, the touch of his strong hands. Trying to erase him from her heart forever.

Seven

ELLIS'S BACK ACHED AS he bent over his desk, sorting through yet another pile of unorganized papers. Did nobody keep accurate records around here? It seemed as if Sheriff Jones had dumped every paper he'd received into a giant vat and swirled them around to confound his deputies. Perhaps he had.

Rubbing his eyes, Ellis sat back. He'd grown weary of reading names and dates, sorting the endless piles into something half resembling an orderly manner. Reaching for the cup of coffee he'd left sitting atop his desk, he shook his head. This whole business of uncovering Jones's crimes and motives proved more daunting than he'd imagined. His ceramic mug warmed his hands as he lifted it to his lips and took a swig of steaming black coffee. The answer had to lie in all this mess. It had to.

Wainwright popped his head in, his smile alarmingly cheerful as ever. "I see you've made it through the last two piles in the corner. I'd say that deserves a lunch break."

Ellis ignored the grumbling in his stomach, setting his coffee mug back on the littered desk. "I'll eat later. I feel like I'm *this* close to finding something." He held two fingers out, only an inch apart.

"I've been through all the papers you asked me to look at." Wainwright thumped his hand on the doorframe. "I still haven't found anything, but I'll keep looking."

"Good man." Ellis returned to his stack of papers, inhaling the swirling scent of his coffee. Despite his initial display of incompetence, Wainwright had thus far proven himself a loyal, hardworking employee. Ellis doubted he had anything to do with the schemes of his former boss.

"Well, I'll leave you to it," Wainwright said. "Let me know if you need anything. I'll be over at Yvette's."

Ellis grunted, not bothering to look up. He had in his grip what appeared to be dossiers for every girl who worked at Madam Carey's. He quickly flipped through the pages until he spotted her name: Cora Elizabeth Blackwood, age twenty-three, immigrant from Scotland, employed at Madam Carey's since 1884. Ellis frowned. *Strange.* He hadn't detected an accent.

So she'd held her position at the brothel for six years. His stomach soured. Six years of entertaining every man who threw her a few dollars. Six years of selling her soul to the devil.

Uncomfortable in his thoughts, Ellis tossed the dossiers down and laced his fingers together. Was it disgust or jealousy he felt? And why had Jones kept records of all the local prostitutes if he'd shown no ambitions to inhibit their business? He'd even heard it whispered among his deputies that the former sheriff himself visited Madam Carey's on occasion—*not* for business reasons.

Drumming his fingertips on the desk, he shifted his eyes again from the desk drawers he'd already scoured to the filing cabinet that had yielded nothing but more useless information. Sheriff Jones had been conducting an illegal operation for years. He'd known exactly how to keep it going without being caught. No one had suspected him until he trapped people in a cave and chased one headlong off a cliff.

The memory of his interview with Caleb and Lily Broderick tickled his mind as he rose from his chair and sauntered toward the bookcase. Days ago, he'd ridden up to Miller's Crossing to find them. Residing in a posh hotel owned by her grandmother, they had welcomed him and answered every question—except one. Her father had taken leave to recover from his ordeal, and she did not know where he'd gone. Ellis had a sneaking suspicion this Jude Hammond could help him explain a lot more than anyone else in this town after working so closely with the Anderson Gang.

Ellis sighed, propping a hand against the bookshelf. Jude Hammond's daughter was safer with him living elsewhere, and he doubtlessly knew that fact. To forge a trail after him in hopes of learning something new would derail his mission. He had to focus if he hoped to save Gold Strike from the evil clutches of Jeremiah Anderson and all the other soulless outlaws holding this town hostage.

His brows dove as he skimmed a finger along the bookshelf and lifted it to find a thin layer of dust clinging to his skin. Could the county not afford maintenance in their sheriff's office? The books, too, appeared dusty and untouched—for far longer than the handful of months it had taken to appoint a new sheriff. If Jones ever actually *used* these books, his office didn't reflect it.

A peculiar sight caught his eye, and Ellis crouched down to inspect it. On the second-to-bottom shelf of the far bookcase, the dust appeared thinner than the other shelves. In fact, only a section of the wood looked darker from use, as if someone had recently dragged a book across it. His fingers meandered over the books, finding a large volume that had no dust marring its binding.

Ellis pulled it out, examining the space behind it. His hand felt around in the dark, but found nothing. Sitting back on his heels, he held the book to the sunlight streaming through the window. *History of the Pacific States of North America*. Not exactly anything incriminating. Ellis peeled back the cover and flipped a few pages, his mouth falling open.

Inside the thick volume lay a hollowed-out cavern, cut into the pages. The space contained a stack of folded paper with writing across it. Ellis closed the book and got to his feet, carting it over to the desk and setting it down. He crossed the office to close the door with a glance down the hall in either direction.

Easing into his chair, he opened the book and retrieved the first page. A correspondence from Jeremiah Anderson—no surprise there. In the letter, Anderson outlined the pay he expected in return for whatever job Jones had asked of him. A few others from Anderson lay beneath it—all what he'd expect between a duplicitous sheriff and his minion of a criminal. His staff couldn't know anything about this. Why would they leave this in his new office to find?

Ellis dug deeper, finding another letter from Anderson regarding the stagecoach robbery that had taken Colton Baxter's life. *The plans are set in motion, and there will be no stopping it now. Baxter expects me to stage a robbery, which I will. I plan only to bring a few of my most trusted men, enough to make the robbery look real, but not so many that tongues can wag.*

Ellis leaned forward, his eyes madly skimming the page. *As you know, our benefactor has grown tired of Baxter. They want him gone. So I will rob the stage as agreed upon, which shouldn't be hard considering Baxter expects it. He'll have that Broderick boy with him to pin any blame on if things go awry. But once the gold is secured, I'm moving in. Give us enough time to kill Colton Baxter, and our plans will go forward.*

Kill Colton Baxter. Leaning back in his chair, Ellis blew a breath out his lips. He'd learned from Caleb and Lily Broderick that Colton Baxter was not the paragon of virtue everyone in this town expected, along with the true reason he was shot dead by Wesley Pierce. Yet all of this—a plot to murder Baxter involving Anderson himself—had never crossed their lips. As far as he understood, Anderson had been working *with* Baxter, not against him.

If you agree to his terms, our benefactor is prepared to pay you handsomely in return. He only asks that you stay out of the way long enough for the job to be done, and that let you release any of our men if caught—discreetly, of course. I'll do the execution myself. If need be, I'll kill the Broderick boy too. Baxter thinks he's an insurance policy, that he will only be a witness if everything goes properly. My bet is that he'll run off into the woods before any of the real fighting starts.

Rifling through the next few folded pages, Ellis found one with distinctly different handwriting—a bold, commanding font that didn't welcome arguments. Several more lay beneath it, all signed with a cryptic "X" at the bottom. Ellis shook out the first, his pulse pounding. What else could this duplicitous sheriff have been hiding in his chest of secrets?

The trial of Caleb Broderick was botched from the very beginning, and I blame you for its outcome. Ellis laughed, the sound reverberating back in the little office. That trial had ended with a conviction and a surprise confession. If it weren't for the incompetent deputies now under his charge, Wesley Pierce would have hanged for the crime.

While you were running around Gold Strike doing God-knows-what, a confessed killer walked free. Then, if the rumors are to be believed, you allowed Caleb Broderick to waltz back into town without a care. I need stricter order from you, Sheriff. I need to know I have a firm hand in Gold Strike, minding its comings and goings. I need to know you will not allow this next mission to fail.

The reverend in Gold Strike—Reverend Sommers, I'm told—is causing a great amount of mischief for me. Ellis bolted to his feet, pacing the floor as he read. *Most of the town is now sold on the developments I have planned for the region, but he remains stubborn and steadfast in his ways. He will not budge when it comes to his ideals, and any amount of bribery I've tried to send his way proved useless.*

He encourages his congregation from the pulpit to fight against my every vision. I cannot have this.

Ellis's heart beat in his ears, sweat emerging on his hands as he ambled from one end of the office to the other. A murder plot on the reverend had already transpired this summer. Was he witnessing its beginnings? The man who'd penned this letter certainly appeared at the heart of it.

I've commissioned the Anderson Gang to carry out what must be done. You need not take part in it or know any further than that. It's better if you don't. My plan will present no harm to the public. Just know that when it takes place, and the reverend succumbs to his terrible fate, I need you to step in. I have ideas for the person who should succeed him. I need you, with your revered and influential sway in this town, to step up and guide Gold Strike into a mutually beneficial place, where we may both thrive. Work with me, Sheriff Jones. I won't let you down. X.

Ellis's stomach ached, burning from his throat down. What kind of a disgusting man had occupied this chair before him? How many innocent lives had they destroyed in the name of greed? The potential answers swirled about his brain, too great and disheartening to think about. Whatever had taken place before his arrival, he would claw through the dark web tangled over this town until it covered him if need be. He wouldn't stop until he found this mysterious benefactor and buried him.

Reverend Sommers—the one man who had dared to stand against them and lived to tell the story. Ellis pushed everything back into the book and slammed it shut, then shoved it into place on the bookshelf. If nothing else, he had to keep this a secret. It could end a man's life—or save it.

Cora folded the last of her mending into her basket and placed it on the bed. *There.* Now, at least there would be coats and sweaters for the church to hand out as the cooler months crept across the valley and turned to ice. Some of these poor mountain families couldn't afford coats for their children, let alone winter clothing for themselves. Over the years, she'd turned her passion into charity work—at least a contribution, with so few hours of freedom allowed her by Madam Carey.

Turning to the hook on her wall, she retrieved her cashmere shawl and pulled it across the shoulders of her gown. Cora stopped at the mirror to fluff her hair and replace a few strays before grabbing her basket and heading for her bedroom door.

The brothel was quiet this time of day—so quiet, it launched shivers up her arms. At night, the walls swelled with the expected ruckus—drunken men squabbling with one another, getting drunker, shoving their attentions on any woman who stood within arm's reach. During the day, the atmosphere proved less predictable. Cora never knew when to expect a storm to brew among the girls, or when another would fall ill. Madam Carey's was far more depressing in the light of day without the glitz and glamor to make it shine.

Cora descended the stairs to the scrub of brushes on the foyer's floorboards. Several of the newer girls had the distinct pleasure of cleaning them after their guests trounced them with mud, sloshed liquor, and globs of spat tobacco. She greeted them as she crossed the foyer and reached for the brothel's front door, but before her hand could fall on the knob, the swish of skirts flurried up the hallway behind her.

"Cora, where are you going this time of day? I need you here tending the chores."

Exhaling through her nose, Cora took a moment to calm herself before turning on her heel. "I only have a short errand to run. It won't take but twenty minutes." She held up the basket in her grip. "I just finished these for the reverend's clothing drive."

Madam Carey rolled her eyes, bustling across the foyer until she stood only inches away. "If the people of this town had a mite of ingenuity, they wouldn't need others to give them their cast-offs."

Cora studied her in the sunlight—the strands of white striping her hair, the sagging skin beneath her eyes. Even her elegant clothing, normally so groomed, appeared rumpled and barely holding in her figure. Stress marred every line of her aging face.

"What kind of ingenuity is that?" Cora's head cocked. "The kind it takes to run a brothel?" The second the words fled her lips, she wished she could reel them back in.

Madam Carey's brows creased, showing her age all the more. "I do not need such insolent talk from you, young lady. I saved you from a life of squalor, remember?"

She nodded. "I do, Madam Carey. I'm sorry." For allowing herself to be saved, more than anything.

"Good." The madam ironed her dress with her hands. "Now, this is the last time I will allow these shenanigans to proceed."

"What do you mean?" Cora frowned. "You've never interfered with my works of charity before, as long as they didn't hinder my job here."

"Yes, well, times are changing. I simply can't rely on the system we used to have in place."

A disbelieving breath rushed up Cora's lungs. "So I'm to have no free time? Is that what I am to understand? That you'll keep me under lock and key until I'm too old to be of any use to you?"

Eyes snapping, Madam Carey stepped closer. "That is exactly what I am saying, and you would do well to maintain a bit of gratitude, young lady. I'm liable to throw you out on your backside for speaking to me in such a fashion."

"Me? The top-selling woman in this brothel?" Cora tried to bite back her next words, but after the week's events, they refused to stay inside. "You wouldn't dare risk throwing me out and tossing away so much money."

Something cold and evil slithered through Madam Carey's eyes—a darkness she usually concealed. With a quick glance toward the girls scrubbing the floors, she snatched Cora's hand and yanked her toward an empty sitting room, slamming the door behind them.

"You will do as I say." She advanced toward Cora with her finger wagging, her eyes wide as two full moons. "Ever since that sheriff walked into town, he's been nothing but trouble for us. Because of him, I will most likely need to cut my staff. That means only the best girls will have a place here. The beautiful girls. The skilled girls. The *young* girls." Her eyes descended Cora as she said it, assessing her with a distaste reserved for the rotten meat of the pile. "You may be my top earner now, but don't expect that condition to last as your skin wrinkles and your body begins to sag."

Despite her raging heartbeat, Cora lifted her chin. "I have years before that will begin."

Madam Carey's scathing laughter tunneled deep inside her bones. "The years pass quickly, my dear. You have less time than you think, and you'll soon be nothing but a dried up old hag who will be lucky if she can even sew anymore, with her arthritic fingers and failing eyesight."

Cora's teeth gritted. "Like you?"

Without warning, Madam Carey took two swift steps forward and struck her across the face. Cora held her throbbing cheek, her mouth hinging open. Tears of pain stung in her eyes as she stared in shock at the madam.

"I have allowed you girls free rein around this place—especially you." Madam Carey's eyes darkened. "That ends today. If you want a place here, you will obey my orders."

"Or what? You'll hit me again? You'll threaten me with Randolph?" They both knew he would take down Madam Carey herself long before he would touch a hair on Cora's head.

"Randolph is gone."

Cora's hand plummeted from her face at Madam Carey's callous assertion. "What?"

"Don't look so shocked." The madam's brow arched. "For a large man, he was as useless as a kitten. He never could have handled the job ahead of us." She brightened, her hand sweeping toward the sitting room window. "Ah, here he comes now. My new bouncer."

Cora turned to watch a man in shabby attire climbing the porch steps. If she couldn't make out his face from here, his arrogant swagger gave him away. "You hired one of the Anderson Gang to watch over us?" Cora spun back to Madam Carey. "Have you taken leave of your senses? Not one of them can be trusted."

A clever smirk passed over Madam Carey's wrinkled lips. "He's perfect. He's exactly the type of man who will get the results I need. You girls need a strong hand."

Cora's chest tightened. "You hired him to protect us from outsiders, correct?"

Her brows waggled. "Protect you. Discipline you. Two sides of the same coin."

Discipline. The word tasted bitter. "Why would he need to discipline us?"

"For behavior exactly as you've displayed today!" Madam Carey's arms crossed, as if shutting out her conscience. "From now on, you will remember who you work for and the consequences of disobeying me."

"Madam Carey, I've worked for you loyally for years. I've done everything you've asked of me. I've never refused you, never refused a client. I've shown you my loyalty in spades." Her soul *bled* from the effort.

Madam Carey looked off to a far corner, refusing to meet her gaze. "Yet you spend hours mending clothes for people you don't even know. You fritter away your days in that dress shop across the way." Her jaw hardened. "You refuse to tell me anything about your association with this new sheriff."

Cora's lips parted as if she'd punched the breath from her. "I told you everything I know. I'd never met the man before the day he walked into this place." And she hoped never to see him again.

The madam's gaze swung back, cold and accusing. "I know what you said, but I don't believe you. That man was rabid to get you alone."

"After which he did nothing but argue with me." Her hands shook. "He didn't even touch me." How many times did she have to tell the truth before somebody believed her?

Not a shred of humanity remained in Madam Carey's eyes as they anchored on Cora. "Well, if you have nothing to hide, you have nothing to fear, do you?" She waved one bejeweled hand toward the door she'd just slammed. "Now be gone with you. Deliver your pathetic scraps to the poor, but be back before the hour. Jorgen will begin interrogations, and yours must conclude before dinner."

With a flurry of her skirts, she stomped away, leaving Cora with nothing but a sour taste in her mouth and a deep sense of foreboding.

Eight

"I APPRECIATE YOU MEETING with me, Reverend." Ellis stood at the front of the Gold Strike Methodist Church, taking in the neat rows of carved pews and finely-hewn wooden beams across the ceiling.

"It's my pleasure, Sheriff McCraw." Reverend Sommers paced the floor behind the pulpit. "Though perhaps you'd be more comfortable in my office?"

"No." Ellis wagged his head. "I'd like to stay here, if you don't mind. I want to see where the action of Caleb Broderick's trial took place."

"Ah, yes." The reverend's hand spread wide. "Our sacred space was turned into a circus that week, I'm afraid. We had so many people crowded into this room at one point, I only prayed to God a fire didn't break out." His eyes sparkled with humor. "If only I could attract that many on Sunday mornings."

Ellis laughed. "I hope I can help with that problem."

"So I hear. The town is buzzing with your calls for change."
Reverend Sommers stood behind the pulpit and gripped it as
if delivering a sermon. "I appreciate your support. There aren't
many who stand against the lawlessness in this place."

"It's only the beginning of what I hope is a long and success-
ful stint as your sheriff. I hope to change this place from the
ground up."

"It seems you already have." Reverend Sommers leaned on
his elbows. "I've never seen those in opposition to God's laws
so frightened and fired up. It gives a man hope."

Ellis's boots tapped the wooden floor as he strode to the front
pew and sat down. The wood groaned beneath his body. "I'd
like to talk about the trial, if you don't mind—and the recent
threat to your life."

"I don't know if I would call it a threat. They managed to
destroy a perfectly good scarecrow, though."

Ellis joined in the reverend's chuckling before growing serious once more. "Still, someone did seek your life. I doubt
whatever plan they had is finished."

The reverend's shoulders lifted. "My life is in God's hands,
and he will deal with it as he sees fit. What can man do to me,
after all?"

"The Bible's authority. Can't argue with that." Ellis swung
his foot to perch on his knee. "I do hope the good Lord agrees
with my plan to keep you safe, though."

"Nobody wants that more than I." The reverend stood taller,
his thin form resolute. "But I will not be cowed by these criminals. They cannot scare me into submitting to their evil ideals.
I don't care what plans they have up their sleeves."

A slow smile spread across Ellis's lips. He needed more men
like this on his side. "I don't expect you to, Reverend. In fact,
I welcome the chance to work together."

Reverend Sommers's head angled. "What exactly did you
have in mind?"

"Well, first of all"—Ellis leaned inward—"who do you think attacked you?"

"That isn't a difficult thing to deduce. The Anderson Gang has all but owned to it."

"But they weren't acting on their own authority?"

Silence spread across the empty church for several beats as Reverend Sommers thought on his question. "What makes you say that?"

"The simple fact that Jeremiah Anderson had nothing to gain from your death. You never stood up there and spoke against him, did you?"

"The evils of his practices, yes." The reverend shook his head, thumping his knuckles on the pulpit. "But no, I never said a thing about the Andersons, or the Red Fox Gang, or any of the other ruffians running around this country. Those men already know their sins and wallow in it."

Ellis let his fingertips trail across the pew's glossy wood. "So you could say it's a fair assumption that somebody you *did* preach against had a motive to kill you?"

Reverend Sommers swallowed, his eyes like granite. "It's like you've read my mind, Sheriff."

Ellis shrugged. "Glad to know we're on a similar page. Do you have any ideas who might have summoned such an act?" A secret wealthy benefactor, perhaps?

The reverend hesitated, as if assessing Ellis, before sighing. "I've thought about that question much in the last few months. In fact, I've thought of little else." He idly thumbed through the Bible atop the pulpit. "There are a number of citizens in the area with enough sway to carry out such plans. I've spoken freely of my distaste for greed and plundering of forests. There have been ongoing efforts in this town for many years now to wipe the land clean and develop it. I suspect whoever tried to kill me wanted to see these plans to fruition."

Ellis nodded. "You are as powerful a player in this town as they are."

"In a way I am. I might not wield money or business acumen, but my social capital is substantial."

"Substantial enough for someone to put a bounty on your head."

"Exactly."

Setting both feet on the ground, Ellis pushed off the floor and walked across the sleek boards. "What if I told you I can verify your suspicions?"

The reverend frowned. "Sir?"

"I won't say how I procured them, but I have in my possession several correspondences detailing your unfortunate demise at the hands of the Andersons." He came to rest before the pulpit, inhaling the building's rich cedar. "You may read them if you'd like."

"No." Reverend Sommers shook his head, holding up one hand. "That's quite enough for me. It chills me to the bone just to think about it." His hand pressed over his heart. "What do you need from me?"

Ellis's broad hands rested atop the pulpit. "A list of suspects if you have it. Details of the trial that took place here, names of anybody who could make my investigation easier."

Bending, the reverend reached for a ledger he had lying on a table. "I do have a list of everyone who testified at Caleb Broderick's trial, if that helps." He opened the ledger to a page of scrawled names. "I tried to keep detailed notes of their testimony, but I got lost in the midst of it."

"This will be just fine." Ellis took the upraised page from him, briefly skimming the names. *Adam Graves, Edward Carter, Abeline Baxter, Leonard Higgins.* The monikers marched one after the other down the paper, all perhaps useless red herrings or his next lead. His pulse beat faster at the possibilities. "Thank you, Reverend. This is a mighty good start."

"I'm glad to be of service."

The front doors of the church squealed open, followed by the clack of footsteps across the floor. Reverend Sommers leaned in conspiratorially. "We'd better finish this discussion another time." Snapping his ledger closed, he held it to his chest and turned to greet his new caller. Too fixated on the list of potential witnesses in his hand, Ellis hardly heard the clatter of approaching shoes.

"Ah, Miss Blackwood." Reverend Sommers rushed forward with hands extended. "How good of you to come. I see you've brought us more treasures for the clothing drive."

From his spot before the pulpit, Ellis swiveled around with one brow raised. Cora Blackwood in a church? This was an amusing new development. Her stare had already latched to him, her cheeks aflame. Cora opened her mouth to answer the reverend, blinked, and closed it again.

"My apologies." Reverend Sommers genially extended a hand toward both of them. "Cora, this is our new sheriff, Ellis McCraw. Sheriff, Cora Blackwood."

He made the pronouncement so enthusiastically, Ellis dared not shatter his excitement. Did he know he had a woman of the night traipsing down the aisle of his church, waltzing around as if she didn't harbor dark secrets beneath her woolen cape? Biting back his compulsion to censure, he simply nodded. "Miss Blackwood."

Her lips flattened, her nostrils billowing. "Sheriff McCraw. So pleased to make your acquaintance."

Oblivious to their silent war, the reverend reached for the basket in her hands. "Cora makes the most beautiful clothes for the local children, and she fills our baskets with coats whenever we appeal to the congregation."

"Does she now?" Ellis's stomach turned at the way she feigned modesty. "Miss Blackwood must have a great many talents." His lips curled into a smile, yet his eyes glared back at her.

"She is a blessing, indeed—to all our community." Reverend Sommers bowed her way. "Thank you for this, Cora. I'll make sure it gets into the right hands."

"Certainly." She smiled warmly at Reverend Sommers before her gaze flicked with irritation toward Ellis. "Sheriff McCraw. Good day." With a curt nod, she spun on her heel and marched back the way she'd come.

Good riddance. Yet why did his heart swell against his chest wall at the thought of her departure? Ellis nodded toward the reverend. "Thank you, sir. I'll be in touch about these names." He waved the list in two fingers as he marched down the aisle toward the church's entrance.

Cora stood in the dirt beyond the front steps. Ellis waited a moment beneath the doorframe, watching the way her cape billowed in the wind and her hair shimmered like bronze in the soft sunlight. She wore a forest-green dress that accentuated both the brightness of her hair and the fiery eyes that still snapped in his memory. *This is foolish. I shouldn't speak with her.* Yet the need thrummed through him like ripples of water disturbed by a single stone.

As if sensing his eyes on her, she pivoted back. Her gaze held no curiosity anymore, no earnest longing. Instead, she regarded him like a stray who wouldn't stop following her home. "I knew you would come out here."

"You did, did you?" Ellis jogged down the steps and stopped short in the dirt before her. "How'd you know that?"

Her head snapped away as she knotted her arms over her bosom. "Because you can't leave anything alone. Why waste a perfectly good opportunity to attack me?"

A burning sensation speared across Ellis's chest. "You know me so well from two meetings, do you?"

"I know enough."

"And it seems I'm only beginning to understand you." He moved in front of her so she could no longer avoid his gaze. "Does the reverend know who you are?"

Her chin raised, a vulnerable look passing through her eyes before they converted to stone. "He knows exactly who I am, and

77

yet he welcomes me—which is more than I can say for most of the people in this town." She glanced around at the clusters of citizens already whispering behind fans.

Ellis laughed. "Can you blame them? You aren't exactly the kind of influence most people want around their children."

"I suppose I'm not"—she squared her shoulders—"but Reverend Sommers is a firm believer in the gospel of Christ. Christ welcomed women like me."

Chills scampered over his skin. How did this woman know how to disarm him so effortlessly? How did she know just what to say to leave him tongue-tied?

Her brows rose. "Is that all, Sheriff McCraw? Am I free to go now?"

Before she could take a step, he halted her with a hand to her forearm, which she swiftly yanked away. "Not so fast. I have a few more things to ask you."

"Ask me, or tell me?" She drew her shawl protectively around her shoulders. "I really don't have the time to stand out here all day and endure your onslaught of my moral shortcomings."

Ellis slid a glance toward the nosy townspeople watching them from in front of the businesses. "This isn't about your moral virtue. I need your help piecing together what happened before I arrived in this town." At her questioning gaze, he motioned with his head toward the church. "Come back inside? It will only take a few moments."

Deliberation battled in Cora's eyes before she finally huffed. "All right, but make it quick. Madam Carey is already calling for my head on a platter, and she warned me not to be late."

"What could she possibly hold over your head that you aren't willing to do for her already?" Ellis fell into step beside her, clattering up the stairs and holding the door open for Cora to pass through.

She visibly shivered as she strode past him and into the church foyer. "Things you could never even begin to imagine, I'm sure."

Ellis let the door clang shut, his heart stuttering. What other secrets lay in that den of hell, posing as an oasis to ease one's trouble? A piece of him didn't want to ask, the other longing to know.

"Is someone there?" Reverend Sommers's voice rang through the chapel.

"It's only us, Reverend," Ellis called back. "I needed a quiet place to ask Cora a few questions, away from prying ears."

"Take all the time you need!"

Turning back to Cora, Ellis set his hands on his waist. "Poor man has to watch his back every second of the day."

She nodded. "I'm surprised Jeremiah Anderson hasn't tried again to kill him."

Ellis's brows lifted. "What do you know about that?"

"Only what I've heard around town." Her chin rose defiantly. "I had nothing to do with it, if that's what you think."

"I didn't—" He paused, his eyes searching the wounded ones staring back. Did she care what he thought of her? Is that why she'd chosen to keep her true identity a secret? "I didn't think you were involved, but I couldn't help noticing your presence among all the happenings in town."

She tapped her foot impatiently. "Such as?"

"Your association with Caleb Broderick, namely. He's been at the center of every crime and scandal this town has seen in the past few years."

Her gaze cast into the shadows. "It's a small town. Many people know Caleb."

"Not like you do." He released an exhausted breath. "You were at his wedding, for goodness' sake."

Her startled gaze fluttered up to his. "How did you know that?"

"He told me himself when I traveled up to Miller's Crossing to interview him and his new bride."

Cora shook her head. "I told him not to involve me in any of this. I've seen enough trouble."

His forehead wrinkled. "He was only telling me the truth, as any law-abiding citizen would." He examined her expression a moment longer, gleaning unsaid words from her wide eyes and cinched lips. "Would you have him lie? Why is it so important to you to avoid the truth?"

Fire lit her face, her skin flushing despite the coolness of the darkened room in which they stood. "You want the truth? Fine. Caleb is my best friend. I hid money for him, not knowing he was working for a criminal. Of course, he didn't know he was working for a criminal either at the time.

"I watched his trial. I helped Wesley Pierce rescue Caleb's sister when Jeremiah Anderson kidnapped her. I gave Caleb and Lily clothes and blankets when they were on the run from Anderson's men."

Her toes lifted her with every sentence until she stood nearly eye-level with him, their faces mere inches apart. "So, as you can see, I've done nothing but fight against Anderson and the sway he's had over this town. Isn't that your goal too?"

Ellis held his breath, staring into the emerald eyes blazing back at him. His thoughts whirled like a raging storm, blasting in circles and having nowhere to land. She smelled of pressed lavender, the scent clouding the thoughts he desperately tried to rein in.

"Anderson kidnapped Julia Broderick?" he finally asked. The dossiers from Sheriff Jones's office flashed through his mind.

"That's what you got from everything I said?" Cora landed back on her heels. "Yes, Anderson kidnapped her. She knew too much, and he wanted to keep her quiet."

He stared off into the shadows, his mind racing. "Has he kidnapped anyone else that you know of?"

"What?" Her brows gathered. "No, I mean—well yes, he kidnapped Jim Sawyer, the stagecoach driver, for the very same reason. But I don't see how this—"

"I don't know." Ellis gnawed on his bottom lip. "I only know he was doing much at Jones's bidding that the town knows nothing about."

Cora drew back. "I don't see what any of this has to do with me."

"Anderson frequents your brothel, doesn't he?"

Her lip curled. "That doesn't mean he confides in me."

"He has to confide in someone." Ellis drummed his fingers over his jaw. With Anderson spending so much time within Madam Carey's walls, perhaps he had informants there. His gut twisted. Perhaps he spoke with one such informant this very moment.

She covered herself in her shawl, her look incredulous. "Sheriff, I want nothing to do with this investigation, and nothing to do with you." In her angered state, with rosy skin and shimmering eyes, she somehow managed to look more beautiful. "The madam is already pressing me about our association."

His mind focused back on her. "Our association?"

"You can't expect to waltz in and cause a scene like you did and not have it raise questions." Her nose flared. "You put me in a terrible position with what you did. Now everybody in that brothel suspects I'm working with you to destroy them."

Curiosity subsiding, Ellis's familiar ire rekindled in his belly. How convenient to place all the blame on his shoulders. "Forgive me for having a human emotion. I was in shock."

Her hands fisted on her hips. "Shock or no, you could have handled yourself better. My life isn't a game."

"And neither is mine." Ellis stepped closer, his breath coming harder. "Pardon me for seeing you for the first time dressed up in fancy clothes, displaying your every God-given asset for the world. Pardon me for reacting to finding out you were a prostitute when I thought one day I might—" He stopped short, his chest pumping.

Cora's lips parted. "Thought you might what?"

He shook his head. He refused to humiliate himself at her feet—to admit that kiss had brought on visions of courting her, of dances beneath the stars at community barn raisings, the hope of marrying her one day. She couldn't have that much of him. He wouldn't give her the satisfaction.

"You thought that kiss meant you owned me, didn't you?"

He shook his head again, but she'd already made up her mind.

"I've had enough of men thinking they own me." Her jaw clenched, holding back whatever emotion played behind her eyes. "You may think I have nothing, *am* nothing, because of my profession, but I have the decency to look at other human beings as fellow men and not property."

His chest ached. "Cora, that isn't—"

"I know what you meant to say, Sheriff McCraw. I can see it written all over your face. I've seen it a hundred times before."

Clutching her shawl tight, she brushed past him toward the front doors. As she swept one back, sunlight spilled into the foyer, blinding his eyes. Only the flash of metal registered before gunfire blasted through the air. Ellis lurched toward Cora, but she'd already stepped outside, into the line of fire.

Nine

CORA'S BLOOD POUNDED THROUGH her veins as she stepped out of the quiet church and into the afternoon sunlight. That insolent sheriff. How dare he presume to know anything about her, let alone delve into her relationship with Caleb? If only she could go back and erase their clandestine kiss, shove him away upon their first meeting. Ensure he never spoke with her again. Now they were bizarrely tied together, like two twisted pieces of string that had no business uniting. What could she possibly do to make him leave her be for good?

The thought had barely breached her mind when commotion ahead made her pause on the porch steps of the church. Jeremiah Anderson's younger brother Isaiah, always caught in some sort of trouble or another, stood in the middle of the street. Scattered men surrounded him, pressing closer, each reaching for their holstered guns.

Isaiah threw both hands in the air, signaling his surrender. Yet the group of men laughed in response, mocking him with cheers and lewd insults.

"What's the matter, boy? Not so tough on your own?"

"Why don't you show us all that fancy footwork your brother taught you?"

Drawing his weapon, Isaiah took a defensive stance. "I ain't scared of you cowards. Give me your best shot!"

A single gunshot boomed, whether from Isaiah's gun or his opponents', Cora couldn't be sure. She stumbled backward as bullets whizzed through the air, one tearing at a chunk of wood in the porch post to her right. Her heart battered against her ribs. Just as she turned toward the open church door, a bullet sliced the air over her head and embedded in the wall.

Ellis. But his strong hands had already found her, shoving her down the porch steps and away from the ruckus. Ellis's face flashed before her eyes as his arm hooked her waist and yanked her around the side of the church. Her perception became a blur of aftershave and muscles. Ellis flattened his form against her, pressing them both to the church's wall.

"Are you all right?" His breath wheezed, a warm dew on her neck and face. "They didn't hit you, did they?"

"No." She examined her body to be sure. "I'm fine."

"Good." His chest pumped against hers, his heartbeat pounding through his shirt. He looked into her eyes for the briefest of moments, scouring their depths, before his gaze fell and he reached for the gun on his hip.

Bullets still zinged past each other, their strident thunks echoing against the walls. Men shouted from every direction. Women screamed, horse hooves pounding, doors slamming. Ellis peeled himself off Cora's quivering frame, adjusting his hold on his gun.

She shook her head. "You can't go out there. They'll murder you."

"What kind of a sheriff would I be if I stood down when trouble ensued?"

"A live one." Cora huffed in annoyance when he ignored her and crept to the edge of the church. "You're going to get yourself killed!" *Stubborn, pig-headed man.*

As if oblivious to her, Ellis peeked around the corner at the active brawl. He shook his head, straightening to stand beside her along the wall. "It looks like Isaiah Anderson is dead. He's lying in a pool of blood in the street."

Her pulse picked up speed. "Then who is still shooting?"

"Townspeople," he said between gasps for air. "My guess is shopkeepers who don't appreciate their windows being blown out." A low growl emanated from his throat. "This place is a hopeless disaster. No wonder they were so eager to employ a man of so little experience."

Cora blinked through the acrid haze. He'd appeared so confident when he stood before a crowd of people and declared their way of life an abomination to the image of God. Where was that brazen, arrogant man now?

Pushing off the side of the church, he held his gun near his throat as he inched toward the melee.

Cora launched forward, stopping short of seizing his arm. "You're bound to catch a stray bullet wandering out there."

"I can't sit by and do nothing." He kept his back to her, creeping into the open until he disappeared altogether from her sight.

Cora bunched her fists against her eyes. The fighting had died down now, but the blast of bullets hadn't ceased to nothing. Her heart dropped to her stomach. Why did she care so much if he lived or died? He'd proven nothing but an absolute menace to her since he'd stepped into town. Yet her entire body convulsed with shivers as she imagined harm befalling him.

Cora's eyes slammed shut as she felt her way along the wall. Flipping to her stomach, she peeked around the church's side and squinted through the dust and smoke. Isaiah Anderson indeed lay in a pool of crimson in front of the tannery. Only a few men shot now, the others racing toward their mounts and scattering off like wild turkeys being hunted.

Her gaze darted frantically from man to man until it clamped on Ellis, still sneaking across the churchyard to a man stationed near the steps. Ellis had his pistol holstered now, both hands spread like a vulture's claws toward his target's back. In one swift movement, he wrestled the gun from the man's hand and yanked him backward, not stopping until he dragged him to their hiding spot.

His captive hollered and swore as Ellis dumped him into the dirt beside Cora and trained his pistol on the man's head. "Quit talking or I'll shoot you dead on the spot." His thumb pulled back, a bullet clicking into the chamber of the man's own gun.

The outlaw swallowed, pushing back into the church's siding. "I don't want no trouble, mister."

"Sheriff." Ellis pulled back his jacket to reveal the silver star on his chest. "Sheriff McCraw."

"Sh—Sheriff McCraw," he stammered. His eyes shifted to Cora, narrowing with vague recollection. She'd seen him in the brothel a time or two, but he was barely old enough to toss down a stiff drink, let alone bed a woman.

"What's your name, son?" Ellis stared down the barrel of his pistol.

"Adrian." The man licked his lips, raking a hand through his dark hair. "Adrian Fox."

"Fox, is it?" Ellis's lips drew down in thought.

"He's Red Fox's son," Cora said. "I knew I recognized him."

Adrian's brow wrinkled. "Aren't you that pretty girl from Madam Carey's? The one who costs the most money?"

Cora rolled her eyes. "You Foxes are all the same—cheap as the dirt you're sitting on."

The youth laughed, presumably forgetting the gun fixed on him. "It's my pa who's the miser. I told him I wanted to pay you a visit for my sixteenth birthday, but he said it was a waste to spend so much on one night."

Ellis cleared his throat, prompting both sets of eyes to snap toward him. "This is a lovely chat, but may we get back to business, please?" He had that look on his face again. His features assumed an expression of disgust whenever anyone mentioned her profession. She would never be anything but a disease to him.

"What was all that back there?" Ellis flicked his head toward the unseen street behind them. "Why did you all start a fight with Isaiah Anderson?"

"We didn't start the fight." Adrian sat up, chest puffing. "Anderson started it a long time ago. He deserves everything he gets."

"Yes, and now his brother is dead." Ellis leaned over him, his shadow falling across the boy's face. "You killed his closest family member. Who do you think Jeremiah Anderson is going to come for first?"

Swallowing, the boy let his head fall against the wall. He said nothing, only pulled his knees against his chest and hugged them like a child who'd just been scolded and sent to the corner. Cora couldn't help but reach out and touch his shoulder.

Ellis's hard stare landed briefly on her hand before revolving away. "Tell me about this feud between the Andersons and the Foxes. How long has it been raging?"

When Adrian refused to speak, Cora sighed. "Their feud has existed for generations. It's older than this town itself." She squeezed Adrian's shoulder. "I believe this most recent flare-up is a result of the stagecoach robbery and Colton Baxter's murder. Isn't that right?" Dipping her head, she met Adrian's dark, forlorn eyes.

Reluctantly, he nodded. "The Andersons killed two good men that day. We owe them two lives for our fallen comrades." He held his index and middle finger in front of his face.

Ellis lowered the gun to his side. "Your men died in commission of a robbery, did they not?"

Adrian's cheeks billowed. "We weren't planning on killin' no one. We was just tryin' to take the gold and leave. Anderson's men attacked us unawares."

"I see." Ellis's square jaw worked as he mulled the information over. He had to have known this already if he'd interviewed Caleb in any detail. "So you think your killing of Isaiah Anderson is justified, do you? That you can surround a man, outnumber him, and shoot him dead in the street like a dog because he attacked you first?"

"The Andersons ain't nothing but trash." Adrian sniffed, his feet stomping out clouds of dust. "They've done a whole lot more to us over the years than just killing two of our men."

Ellis's brow hooked. "Such as?"

"Stealing my ma—that's what."

Ellis' startled gaze latched with Cora's. She lowered her hand from Adrian's shoulder, her palms beginning to perspire. Hadn't Ellis hounded her earlier about kidnapping?

He grunted. "What do you mean, boy? Don't speak in riddles. How long ago did this happen?"

"I ain't talking in riddles. It was just this summer. My ma knew she was in danger. She tried to run, and Anderson took her."

Cora found herself inching toward him. "How do you know he took her?"

Adrian hung his head. "She told me she was leaving. Said she was in a lot of trouble. Told me she was going back to my pa's family in Billings."

Cora frowned. "So she left of her own volition?"

"Nah, she never made it to Billings." He held his head in his hands. "Pa wrote letters back and forth to our family out there. They said she never showed up. Never even heard from her."

"What is your mother's name?" Ellis asked. "Maybe I can find out what happened to her."

Adrian's head wagged sadly. "You won't. Anderson has probably killed her by now."

Ellis stepped forward impatiently. "Still, it's my job to try. If kidnappings are happening in my town, I *must* know about them."

Adrian's eyes lifted Ellis's way. He had never looked so young and defenseless. "Her name is Sylvia Hammond."

A harsh breath sucked through Cora's lips. She covered them with her hands. "Sylvia Hammond?" The woman who ran Diamonds and Rubies, who she'd spent countless hours with, learning her intricate trade?

Ellis's careful gaze flicked her way. "You know this woman?"

Cora nodded, her hands lowering from her face. "She had a seamstress's shop across from the brothel. I've spent much time over the years there."

Adrian brightened. "So you're the woman she was teaching embroidery to."

"Yes, I was." Memories paraded across her mind's eye—of sitting next to her shop window, laughing and chatting over stitching lessons. "I wondered where she had gone when her shop was suddenly vacant. It"—she gave him a sad smile—"it broke my heart a little."

"She knew everyone's business in town. The ladies would come into her shop and chatter away. She would never tell me much, but I got an earful whenever I came to visit her."

"Is that why you think they took her?" Cora asked. "Because she knew too much about the Andersons?"

He shrugged. "It's the only answer I've come up with."

Above them, Ellis pursed his lips, his brows drawn in deliberation. He wore that look whenever he'd lost himself in the forest of his own ideas.

Cora stood, her skirt releasing loose dirt. "What are you thinking?"

He gazed back at her silently for several beats before his eyes shifted to Adrian, still seated on the ground. "I've done a lot of research on both the Andersons and your family. I don't recall hearing anything about your father having a wife."

"That's because he doesn't," Adrian said. "My parents were together a long time ago. They had my brother and me and then they split. Haven't even talked to each other much in years."

"Yet your father felt obligated to let her hide out with his family and follow up with them regarding her safety."

"I know it don't make much sense." Adrian's shoulders lifted. "Pa won't admit it if you ask him, but I know he still cares about her. The way he tells it, she couldn't handle the pressure of staying with an outlaw. She didn't want to raise children always looking over her shoulder."

Cora nodded. "I can't imagine how hard that would be."

"She bought that little shop with what she had. Raised the two of us. She let us see him from time to time, but she didn't want us living in a criminal's home. Didn't think it was safe."

"And you stayed on the virtuous and narrow path, I see," Ellis said with a derisive chuckle.

Adrian glared at him. "I got loyalty to my pa. My brother ran off to some fancy school in Chicago, but I wasn't meant for that life. I was meant to be a part of the Red Fox Gang."

Ellis swung around, pointing his pistol at the now deserted street behind the church. "Soon you're going to be just like him—lying dead in the street, barely old enough to be called an adult, with no future ahead."

"At least I'll have honored my pa." His jaw set, his eyes fixed ahead. There would be no convincing a boy wanting desperately to please his father.

"Come on, then." Ellis motioned him up. "You're coming with me."

Slowly climbing to his feet, Adrian frowned. "Where are we going?"

"We, young lad, are going to the Gold Strike jail." Advancing on him in two quick strides, he whirled the boy around and clamped handcuffs on his wrists behind his back.

"Hey, this isn't fair." Adrian wrestled within his hold. "I didn't shoot him. I didn't even fire my gun. You can check the chamber."

"That will be valuable information at the trial." Ellis finished securing his handcuffs and yanked him forward. "There was a shootout in my town today, right in the street, with women and children walking around. I'd be remiss in my duty if I didn't arrest someone involved."

"You can't take me to the jail." He dug in his feet, his head swiftly shaking. "I've seen what they do to men like me in the jail. I'll be hanged!"

Ellis laughed through his nose. "Relax. You're not even a man yet. I'm not going to let anyone hang you."

Cora jogged to catch up. "You'll be safer in the jail. Anderson won't be able to touch you in there." Yet still, the boy looked back at her as if longing for the mother who'd vanished like a desert wind.

"She's right. Jeremiah Anderson has no sway in my jail, and I'll make sure you're guarded by my best men." Ellis glanced at Cora. "Are you safe to get home?"

As they walked, her gaze darted around the wreckage in the street. Glass had shattered everywhere, sprinkling the dirt in glinting light. People were just emerging from storefronts, aghast at the body lying dead before them. Cora's stomach ached, and tingles prickled her spine as she beheld Isaiah Anderson sprawled in the dirt, caked in blood, his head twisted at an unnatural angle.

"Don't look at him, Cora." Ellis's commanding voice snapped her back to attention. She found him amidst the fog, his steady gaze anchoring him to her. "Are you safe to get home, or should I send my deputy to escort you?"

"I'm fine." She shook off the heaviness clinging to her, willing her gaze not to wander back to Isaiah Anderson's dead body. "There's going to be chaos in this town tonight. People are bound to storm the jail."

"I have it under control." Ellis set his jaw with a determined air. "I'll make sure he doesn't get hurt."

She stepped sideways, off balance. How did he know she already cared so much about this young man she'd only just met? His ability to see beneath the layers she presented to people left her feeling exposed. Her arms flattened across her chest, her hands clamping around them.

"His mother means a great deal to me. She's my mentor." She stepped toward him. "I'll do anything I can to find out where she's gone."

Ellis gave her a long, concentrated look before he nodded. "I'll let you know if you can help. For now, you should go. It won't be a friendly place out here much longer."

Already, the street had begun to fill with moving bodies, pointing fingers, skirts swishing through the muck. Everyone wanted a look at the Anderson boy, gunned down before his twentieth birthday. They hid behind shocked expressions and eyes closing in disgust, but Cora knew the truth. They couldn't wait to glean as much gossip as they could from the situation. They couldn't wait to run off and tell others what they'd seen.

As she walked backward, the growing crowd swallowed her up. Voices raised at Ellis, demanding answers, calling for Adrian's head on a spike. Yet Ellis kept walking without a glance in their direction, marching the Fox boy up the street toward the Gold Strike jail. Something warm bloomed inside her. At least he meant to keep his word, even if he couldn't in the long run.

Cora glanced at the sun, cursing beneath her breath. It already dipped below the roofline, indicating late afternoon. Madam Carey would kill her if she stood in the street any longer. Aiming herself toward the brothel, Cora shoved through the crowd and ran, determined to put the ghastly scene she'd just witnessed behind her.

Ten

A GHOSTLY SILENCE HAD descended over Madam Carey's as Cora clambered up the front steps and pushed the door in. She glanced around, noting the usual chatter from the barroom didn't drift into the foyer. Wandering forward, she glanced past the tasseled curtains into the common spaces, finding only a handful of men sprinkled around the bar, with not a woman in sight. *Strange.* Madam Carey always had someone attending to their needs at all times of day—usually the older women who didn't fetch a high price in the afternoons.

Her stomach squeezed as she ascended the staircase one creaky step at a time. The freshly polished banister slid beneath her fingertips, guiding her upward until she reached the landing. Something wasn't right. She sensed it in every tense muscle of her body.

Choosing a door at the top of the stairs, Cora quietly rapped on it and waited. Footsteps tapped on the floor inside. At least she knew someone was here. The door swung open just enough to reveal the face of Charlotte, one of her more amiable companions at the brothel.

"Oh, it's you." She let out a breath. "I thought you were Madam Carey."

"What's going on?" Cora glanced past Charlotte to another woman huddled behind her with an equally frightened expression. "Where is everybody? It's like a tomb in here."

"I don't know." Charlotte's head shook. "Madam Carey ordered everybody to stay in their rooms until dinner. She threatened to have us beaten if we didn't."

"I saw her pulling Laurel into the stairway to the cellar," the cowering girl behind her said. "She didn't look like she wanted to go."

Sweat rose on Cora's skin. Laurel was a favorite of Red Fox's. It couldn't be a coincidence.

Charlotte gripped the door in white knuckles. "We have to get back inside before she sees us. We can't be seen with you."

At her apologetic expression, Cora dipped her head. "Of course."

The door shook as it closed, rattling the doorframe. Cora trod the hallway with uneven steps, each one weighted and laden with trepidation. When she reached her door, she eased it open, half expecting a surprise attack. Yet no one waited on the other side.

She slipped inside, gently clicking it shut and turning the lock. Despite the brothel's eerie flavor tonight, her bedroom felt normal, just like every evening as she prepared for dinner and the theatrics that ensued afterward.

Her fingers trembled as she removed her shawl and hung it on a hook by her vanity mirror. The window was shut against the chilling autumn winds, yet she shivered as if hit with a gust of it. *You're imagining things. Madam Carey won't let him hurt you.* Yet an ominous sensation still tortured her middle. Did she even want to ponder the depths Madam Carey would go to protect her glistening kingdom?

The clop of shoes climbing the stairwell grabbed her attention. She stared at the closed door as the footsteps approached, the familiar gait both relieving and teasing her with the threat of the menacing unknown.

Madam Carey, demure as ever, tapped on the door. Cora sidestepped toward the window, contemplating how long it would take her to climb out and shimmy down the drain pipe. But where would she go? She'd walked back into this trap of her own accord. She would face whatever plans Madam Carey had conjured and survive with her head held high, like always.

"Cora, my dear, are you home?" Her airy voice divulged not a hint of the tense conversation they'd shared earlier that day. To deny her would only anger her.

With a breath of courage, Cora stepped across her bare floor and unlocked the door. She summoned her most believable smile—the one she reserved for the vilest of Madam Carey's clients. When she pulled the door open, the madam showed no sign of anything amiss—only a coy smile that drove Cora's fears even deeper.

"Yes, Madam Carey? What may I do for you? Am I late for dinner?"

"No, dear. That's not for another hour or so." She glanced at the hallway clock. "Though you are rather tardy if that was you I heard slinking through the doors just minutes ago."

Cora pressed her palm to the cold doorknob. "Forgive me, Madam Carey. There was an incident in town."

"An incident?" Her eyes lit with fire more than interest. "What kind of incident?"

"It was a shootout." Cora's voice trembled against her will. "Isaiah Anderson was killed."

"*Killed?*" Madam Carey recoiled, whether from genuine concern or not, Cora couldn't be sure. "My, that is unfortunate. The Andersons have always been loyal customers."

Customers? Was that all she could think of at a time like this?

Belatedly, Madam Carey's face wrinkled with worry. "Are you all right? That must have been a terrible shock."

Cora tried not to flinch beneath the hand that brushed her arm. Madam Carey had never worried for her in all her years of service—not even after she'd been with a man for the first time.

"I'm shaken, but I'm fine." She gently pulled away. "I'll be ready for work tonight."

"Good. I can always count on you, can't I?" She patted Cora's cheek, her fingers icy and lifeless. When Cora stood silently in the threshold of her room, Madam Carey hooked one finger in a "come-hither" motion. "I do have a task I need you to complete before dinner. It is of the utmost importance."

Her stomach tightened. "Must I leave my room? I'm quite tired, and I'd like to prepare myself for tonight."

"My darling, don't you remember?" Madam Carey's soulless laugh pricked at her skin like needles. "I told you there would be an inquiry tonight, and you are the star of the show. It can't go on without you."

Everything within her screamed to jump out the nearest window, yet Cora steeled herself. "How could I have forgotten?" Better yet, how could Madam Carey expect her to waltz willingly into something she called an inquiry? "What, may I ask, am I to expect from this *inquiry* you speak of?"

Madam Carey giggled again, tossing her head back. "Don't look so worried. It's only an interview. You have nothing to hide, remember?" Her fingers closed around Cora's wrist. "Hurry up, now. Jorgen is waiting."

Every step Cora took behind Madam Carey felt like the swing of an anvil, forging her road to destruction. They swept past the barroom, ignoring the curious stares of patrons, following the hallway until it ended at the kitchen. Only the cook stood beside the washbasin, a disturbed look on her rotund face. She tried to toss Cora a smile, but it fell flat before it even reached her.

Muddy footprints besmirched the kitchen floor, stretching into a smear as if someone had been dragged. Madam Carey stepped over them with her nose in the air, as if she didn't even notice anything beneath her imagined self-importance.

The cellar door groaned inward, the blackened stairwell below lurching up at them. Without bothering to light a lamp, the madam daintily lifted her skirts and descended them with only a handrail to support her. Cora trailed on increasingly tremulous legs, imagining herself descending into hell. She'd always likened the upstairs of this place to that devilish inferno, so what crept in its underbelly?

An orange flickering light cast shadows over the floor as they reached the ground and stepped into the cellar. Cora had come here once or twice to retrieve canned vegetables or goods for the cook, but the atmosphere had shifted since those careless days. Now, instead of mere shelves filled with preserved foods, a single chair sat in the room's center. Beside it on the floor, a cast-iron lamp spread twitching shadows across the room.

The man she'd watched climb the brothel's front porch only hours before stood with his hands braced on the chair back, a malicious smile stretching his lips into a thin, curved line. "Welcome, Cora. So good to see you again."

She stiffened at the smooth Norwegian accent. He'd called on her once before. She'd never forget it. A man like that wanted more from a woman than simply her body.

Breath stuck in her throat, she squared her shoulders and feigned a sense of bravery so very far from her true emotions. The shuffle of her feet echoed against the stone walls as she approached the chair. Cora averted her eyes from the evil ones grinning back at her and noticed splashes of blood on the floor. She gasped, doing an about-face. "Madam Carey, is this—"

"Hush, girl." Hatred pierced Madam Carey's wrinkled eyes. "I've had enough of your sass. You will answer Jorgen's questions, or I'll put an end to your days here." She cleverly masked her true meaning beneath innocent enough words, but Cora suspected she meant more than simply leaving her without a job.

She gulped back her raging fear and forced herself to sit in the empty chair. Every time she'd cowed to Madam Carey's wishes, she had written this day into the history of her life. Now, after a million bad choices, she had to face the consequences of her decisions.

With one final sneer in her direction, Madam Carey whipped around and stomped her way up the stairwell. All of her casual charm had fled. Her desperation seethed through every inch of this dark space.

Two hands squeezed Cora's shoulder blades like spider legs crawling over her body. She clenched her teeth, determined not to react. *I have nothing to hide. I've done nothing wrong.*

"You're so very tense." His fingers kneaded her muscles, digging until barbs of pain shot through her.

Cora breathed through her nose. He would not make her cry out. He could not. He tried harder, squeezing until tears emerged beneath her eyelids, but she refused to make a sound.

"Ah, this is the girl I remember." Seizing a handful of her hair, he tilted her head back to look into his beady eyes, a fearsome sight in the shifting lamplight. "You never let yourself have a human reaction, no matter what I did to try and hurt you."

Cora shut her eyes, blocking out the memory. No wonder he'd never sought her out again. She didn't give him the reaction he desired. She failed to let him shock her.

Jorgen shoved her head forward, bouncing it off her chest. The patter of his boots across the stone floor sent her pulse racing. He stood in front of her now, his eyes scouring every inch of her, searching for ways to invade.

"Tell me what you know about the sheriff." His voice was hollow, devoid of emotion.

Cora lifted her face and leveled her gaze with his. "I know nothing about him—just as I've told Madam Carey. I met him the day he came to the brothel."

He smirked, tossing back his sandy blond hair. "Madam Carey doesn't seem to believe you. She says he was quite forceful in trying to get you alone."

"A lot of men are forceful in trying to get me alone."

His tongue clicked, his head wagging. "Yet you claim he never touched you." He reached out, letting his clammy fingers brush her jawline. "Why would a man pay so much money simply to talk?"

Cora's teeth clenched at his unwelcome touch. "The man is a lunatic, clearly. Or did you not see the two holes he blew in our ceiling?"

"Ah, yes." His fingertips snaked down her skin until they reached her throat. "But even a lunatic is no match for your peculiar charms, no?"

Her pulse quickened as his thumb moved down her airway. His fingers constricted, pulsing against her neck. She had to get his hand away. "You tell me. Were *you* able to resist my charms?"

Fire erupted in his eyes. His hand lifted from her throat and thwacked across her cheek. Searing pain inflamed her face, but she made not a move to cover her throbbing skin. Better to endure a smack or two than tempt him to choke the life out of her.

"This interview isn't about me." He leaned over her, his bourbon-tinged breath showering her skin. "You will answer my questions truthfully, or you will pay the consequences."

Cora met his wild eyes, determined to display sheer defiance in hers. "Ask me, then, so I can be done with you. I have work to do, and I'll need a shower after enduring your presence."

Gritting his teeth like a snarling wolf, he set his face inches from hers. "What do you know of the sheriff? What did he tell you?"

Her nostrils fumed. "He told me nothing, as I've said. He told me I was sinful and worthless for being a prostitute. Is that what you wanted to know?"

He studied her closely, the lamplight making the whites of his eyes glow. He reeked of body odor and desperation—the kind that could make a man do anything. "Madam Carey said he recognized you on your first meeting—that he tried to hide it, but she saw the truth."

Sharp breaths wisped from Cora's open mouth. To tell the truth could give the madam a deadly upper hand, but to lie meant certain torture. "I saw him in town earlier that day. I didn't know who he was."

Jorgen leaned over her, the chair creaking as it absorbed his weight. "Tell me more."

"There isn't much else to tell you." Cora's mind swam, grasping at something, *anything* she could reveal that wouldn't put her in further danger. "We spoke mostly of the terrain here, of the mountains and the forests." Her shoulders rose. "He told me he came from Tennessee."

"And you didn't think to tell any of this to Madam Carey?"

Her skin blazed at his nearness, as if he could burn her simply by looking at her. "Why would I tell Madam Carey about a casual conversation I had with a man I didn't even know?"

"You chose to keep your conversation a secret, even after he revealed his true identity. Isn't that right?"

Her throat closed, barely allowing breath to get through. "I didn't think it would matter."

"You're lying, girl!" He slapped her again, triggering pain from her cheekbone to her ear. "Tell me the truth."

"I *am* telling you the truth." Cora fought the hot tears stinging her eyes. "I only met him that day. He told me briefly of his home in Tennessee, and that's all. That's all I remember."

His hand crashed against her again, colliding with her temple. Her entire skull exploded in agony, stars dancing across her vision.

"I know nothing, I swear it. He told me nothing of his plans or what he wanted here in Gold Strike."

His fist came again, bashing the sensitive skin above her ear. Cora understood with gut-wrenching clarity that he wouldn't hit her with such force in the face—not when it would cost Madam Carey a sizable sum to distort her good looks.

She sucked through her teeth as she lifted her head. "I know nothing else. I know nothing. There is nothing more I can tell you."

Her words cut short as his fingers found her throat again, this time not teasing her, but squeezing like a cobra wound tight beneath her chin. Cora's heart battered her ribcage, her throat aching, her head pounding. Her vision swam, liquefying, as she tried for another breath but couldn't. No matter how hard her chest pumped, no air came.

She would die here in this chair, in the darkness of a brothel cellar, in the company of a madman. *She won't let me die. She won't let me die.* Yet her sureness of that fact waned with every second his hands commanded her throat.

"What else happened?" His palms released just long enough for her to gasp in one breath before clamping again at the base of her throat. He shook her, jarring her aching head until she thought she'd never see straight again. "What else happened?" His hands lifted again, still sweaty against her skin.

She gulped in several breaths. "He kissed me!"

Jorgen paused, his hands hanging at her collarbone. "What do you mean he kissed you? When he went to your room, you mean?"

"No." She shook her head, strands of hair falling out of her combs and flinging against her face. "The first time he met me, he kissed me."

His lips peeled back, revealing teeth stained with brown. "Did you tell him you were a prostitute?"

"I didn't tell him anything about myself. I swear it." She panted, drinking in every breath of the stale cellar she possibly could. "He didn't know I worked at Madam Carey's."

"Why would he kiss you, then?"

"I don't know." Her brows climbed her forehead, imploring him. "We got along. We talked. We liked each other. He kissed me and I let him. I think maybe he thought—" Her words hung in the dense air.

"He thought he would court you," Jorgen finished for her, his nose snarling in distaste. "That a woman who would allow him to kiss her at first meeting was something more than a useless trollop."

Cora nodded frantically. "He told me he had feelings for me."

Jorgen stared back at her in disbelief before his lips spread into a wicked grin. Laughter bubbled up his throat, echoing in the small space. "Well, that's delicious, isn't it? Our new sheriff, pining after a little harlot." His eyes narrowed. "Why didn't you tell this to the madam?"

Cora bit her bottom lip. "I didn't want to get in trouble. We aren't supposed to kiss men without making them pay. It's against her rules."

"I see." Jorgen stepped backward, peering down at her like a hawk circling lower, sure of the kill. "Is there anything else you want to tell me, love? Or can I report to Madam Carey that you gave up everything?"

She shook her head, diverting her gaze to the darkened corner. "No, that's it. There's no more." She had nothing left to give.

"I would suggest you tell Madam Carey everything from now on if you want to avoid a future meeting like this." His fingers reached out again, coiling beneath her chin. "Though another meeting between the two of us is inevitable."

Cora held back the vomit threatening to spew from her throat, cursing herself for giving him higher ground. He only wanted her when he could elicit a reaction. How appealing her fear must have looked to him tonight.

Icicles pricked her arms as she rose and fled up the stairwell. Even the safety of her room couldn't pacify her. A gloom followed her everywhere, a shuddering fear that had taken root so deeply she could no longer try to escape it. With terrifying awareness, Cora sensed the end was coming, and with it, the destruction of everything she'd built her life upon.

Eleven

THE NIGHT WAS STILL—so still, it shrouded Ellis in unease. He leaned against the doorframe at the jail's front, looking out over the empty street. Nothing met his gaze but dense blackness and the glittering lights of town. Yet still he scanned the emptiness, waiting for the first stirrings of trouble.

"Anything yet, boss?" Wainwright asked, appearing at his side.

Ellis glanced over his shoulder and shook his head. "Nothing yet, but that doesn't mean much." Whatever Jeremiah Anderson was doing out there beyond the borders of town could only bring strife. "How's the kid eating?"

Wainwright half-grunted, half-laughed. "He's sure got an appetite. Hope we don't have to feed him for too long."

A smile spread across Ellis's lips. "He's only sixteen years old. He's still growing."

"Sixteen years old and destined for a life of crime." Wainwright sighed, his rounded belly heaving. "His pa didn't even give him a chance."

"He'll find out soon enough—if he lives that long." At the dismal thought, he pushed off the doorframe and closed the door to the sheriff's office. "I've had enough watching for now. If they come, they come. We can't do anything about it by waiting."

The front office, lit with only a single lamp, was bathed in an eerie quiet as Ellis tramped through it with Wainwright at his side. He'd asked the other deputies to stay tonight in anticipation of a riot, and they had scattered themselves around the perimeter. Ellis's shoes squeaked across the floor, punctuated only by a dripping faucet somewhere in the building.

The hallway to the jailhouse, no longer burdened with a layer of dirt as he'd found it, closed in tight as they passed through the doors and along the narrow corridor. It smelled cleaner now—like fresh lemons instead of grime. The other jail cells stood empty, just waiting for the underside of Gold Strike's community. Only the cell at the end was occupied with the form of a boy, not quite a man, slumped over on the cot.

"How are you fairing, Adrian?" Ellis slipped his key into the lock and turned it, pushing until the cell door grumbled inward.

Adrian rubbed his eyes, peering dismally through the scant light. "I've had better nights, Sheriff."

"Well, this isn't the worst place you can be. At least there's food and a warm place to sleep." Ellis passed through the bars, turning toward Wainwright. "I'll be fine in here, deputy. Thank you."

As Wainwright locked the door behind him and his footsteps receded, Ellis pulled the cell's lone chair near to the pathetic mattress they called a bed and sat down. The two of them wallowed in silence a few minutes, as if the world didn't keep going, hatching its plans and devising mayhem. As if certain trouble didn't await them both.

"Wainwright said you ate a good dinner."

Nodding, Adrian drew his legs in and settled his arms over his knees. "The food here ain't half bad. Of course, I'm used to my pa's cooking now."

Ellis chuckled. "Not as good as your ma's?"

"No, sir." The first spark of light he'd seen in hours lit the boy's eyes. "He tries, but he don't do nothing as good as Ma." His words floated about the air, a vulnerability to them Ellis didn't quite know how to handle. He'd never raised a child, and though he liked to think of himself as an honorable role model, he fell short of the mark so often.

He rubbed his hands together to expel the chill. "Is there anything else I can get you?"

Adrian's mouth dimpled. "Do you have Cora hidden away somewhere in here?"

"We don't provide that kind of entertainment."

He hugged his legs tighter. "That's not what I meant."

The truth of his statement shone out through his fearful eyes. He needed her like he needed a mother. He craved the gentle care that vanished when Sylvia took off on that train.

"She knows just what to say, doesn't she?"

Adrian smiled shyly. "Yeah, she made me feel better about getting arrested. Not quite so—" He stopped short of admitting his fear.

Leaning back, Ellis knotted his arms over his chest. Cora had a way with people. In his short time here, he'd already noticed the easy communication she shared with Reverend Sommers, the way she ignored a boy objectifying her and comforted him anyway. His gut constricted, remembering the stolen moments they'd spent above the town. Strangers yet already friends. Did this talent of hers derive from the practiced art of charming male companions, or did people just resonate with her?

"I don't know what Cora would say right now, but I can tell you the truth." Ellis set a solemn look on the boy. "The things to come will be hard, scary. But you will come out of this on the other side if I have anything to do with it. I always keep my word."

Adrian eyed him warily from the corner of his dark eyes. "I don't put much stock in the words of a lawman. Pa always told me not to trust you."

"And your pa knows all of us lawmen, does he? He knows we're all corrupt."

"The ones he's known are." Adrian motioned down the hall with his head. "Just look at Sheriff Jones. Look who he turned out to be."

Uncrossing his arms, Ellis set his elbows on his knees and leaned forward. "I am not Sheriff Jones, Mr. Fox. I promise you that."

He scowled. "More empty promises."

Ellis's head shook. "Not empty promises. My solemn vow." His hands folded together as if in prayer. "I promise to uphold my duty, to protect you while you're under my care. To see justice served."

Silence pervaded the cell as Adrian studied him in the muddled light, his brows working. What must have passed through his mind in these moments, with an outlaw for a father and a mother who had left him behind? Something buried deep within cried out through his eyes before he hung his head again.

"You seem to see the world in only one color, Sheriff."

Brow creasing, Ellis angled his head. "What does that mean?"

Adrian sighed and slumped back against the wall. "The world has all sorts of colors. It's full of them. You see only black and white."

"If you're referring to right and wrong, then yes. We all have a sense of morality, and we've been given clear instructions. It isn't hard to understand unless one chooses not to."

Letting his long legs stretch out over the crumpled bed, Adrian looked back at him almost in pity. "With all due respect, people ain't black and white, Sheriff. We're made of color and substance. There's a lot more to a person's soul than lists of right and wrong."

Ellis stared back, his lips parting. He didn't want to admit this juvenile's words had stirred something within him, yet they echoed again and again across his mind. *People are made of color, not black and white.*

Ellis pushed off his chair and began to pace the small room. He pictured his father standing over him, reading the words of the Good Book, fashioning the paths that would become Ellis's lifelong trails. Had he ever stopped to question them? Had he ever paused long enough to consider another person's point of view? He raked a hand through his hair, confounded by the dizzy sensation washing over him. He didn't need this. What room had he for pondering life's philosophical questions when an entire town stood against him, both good and evil? What room did he have to reorganize his perception of them?

"You're wrong, boy." His voice slightly tremored. "I stand on the side of good. What your father has taught you is evil."

"My father is a rotten man. I'll allow you that much." Adrian paused, his voice strained. "But my pa ain't never been evil. His life is a fight, just like everyone else's. Only he embraces it. He doesn't push it away."

Before Ellis could consider the idea, boots clomped down the hallway. A moment later, Wainwright appeared at the bars, his face pale. "They're here, Sheriff."

Adrian rose up from the bed, his rounded gaze ricocheting between both lawmen.

"I'll deal with whoever is out there." Ellis clapped the boy on the shoulder as he passed him by and waited for Wainwright to unlatch the cell door. "Try not to worry yourself."

Yet his heart drummed as Ellis traversed the corridor toward the waiting mob. Would it be angry townspeople, gathered to demand swift justice—or perhaps Red Fox, impatient for his son's return? How could he hope to conduct proper business in a town so used to running wild without consequences?

Torchlight shivered beyond the open door as Ellis moved through the front office. The vague outline of men on horseback began to form, blocked from view only by the chain of deputies who'd materialized around the jail's exterior. At least he had loyal employees on his side.

When his boots reached the creaking boards of the porch, Ellis found himself face-to-face with a familiar foe. Leering eyes and twisted lips, whiskers so thick they almost made a beard, long hair flapping in the nocturnal breeze. Only an outlaw as brazen as Jeremiah Anderson would walk around town so freely, unconcerned with being apprehended.

"My deputy says you requested a word." Ellis kept his voice flat. Already, a growing crowd had pooled around Anderson's men. No use giving them a show.

Anderson glared down from atop his broad, snorting stallion. The flickering torchlight revealed uncharacteristic shadows beneath his eyes. "I hear you caught one of the rats who shot my brother this afternoon. I came to fetch him."

Ellis crossed his arms over his chest and set his legs wide. "I did arrest an involved party in the unfortunate incident today, but there will be no fetching. He is my prisoner, and as such, he is not free to go."

Anderson's large hands adjusted on his horse's reins, his fingers curling. "Free or not, you will bring him out. Let us deal with him proper."

"That is not the way justice works, Mr. Anderson."

"It's the way it works around here." Anderson's jaw clenched, rage and mourning warring in his torchlit eyes. "This ain't Tennessee, Sheriff. This is the West. Here, when one man murders another, he answers to those who are left behind."

Ellis steadied himself, refusing to falter. How did Anderson know he'd come from Tennessee? He'd only told Cora on that first morning. A cold, nauseating sensation filled his gut. Of course she had told him. How had she nearly tricked him again into believing her to be anything but a deceiver?

"That's the way you've done things for a long time, but it's not anymore." Ellis stared through the wavering torchlight, his voice firm. "This is no longer the vigilante West of your fathers and grandfathers. Whether you like it or not, you are a part of the United States now, under her protection and authority. It is my job to uphold her laws the way they were written."

Anderson shared a laugh with his comrades before sneering down at Ellis. "The laws of the people were in effect long before the government moved in. They tried to have their say, tried to take our money." The heads around him bobbed. "It's our right to govern ourselves as we see fit."

Ellis scanned the burgeoning crowd beyond the Anderson gang, huddling together to hear the exchange with rounded eyes. "What about *them*, huh?" He nodded toward the onlookers. "What about all the people you've stolen from, whose cattle you've taken, whose land you've encroached on? What about all those you've murdered because you couldn't be bothered to make an honest living of your own?" His words sparked murmurs across the throng, heads nodding, a few calling their support.

Anderson's fists clenched around his horse's reins, the muscles in his jaw shifting beneath the glimmering light. In seconds, he'd swung his long leg over his horse's rear end and tramped across the dirty street toward the jail's front porch. Ellis's deputies tightened the space between them, hands ready on their guns.

"Let him come, boys. I'm not interested in controlling this town by force."

The side of Anderson's mouth perked up. He climbed the porch steps, the boards groaning beneath his weight, every step juddering the entire structure. He came toe-to-toe with Ellis, only an inch or two taller, but still seeming to dwarf him with his brawny form. "You're awful foolhardy for a man who doesn't have any friends in town yet." He growled every word, as if he could command an army by sheer intimidation.

Ellis stood steady, refusing to flinch at his close proximity. "Foolhardy or brave, depending on which way you look at it."

Anderson's tongue clicked. "Bravery never saved a man's life, Sheriff."

"Are you saying my life's in danger?" Perhaps the last sheriff had bowed down to such blatant threats, but he would not prove so cowardly.

"Look around you." Anderson's arm swept toward his posse of waiting henchmen. "All of them do as I say when I tell them to do it."

Ellis's eyes narrowed into slits. "Are you going to tell them to hurt me, Anderson?" His muscles clenched, his stare refusing to waver. He'd met a hundred men like this back home, but in Tennessee he'd known the hills and valleys and rivers like old friends. Here, he was more akin to a river fish floundering in an ocean.

"That all depends on you." Anderson neared, his cigar-laced breath puffing clouds of vapor between them. "Do you want to play the game by the house rules, or will you stick to your sanctimonious law? It don't go both ways here."

Ellis set his hands on his hips, allowing his expanded chest to nearly collide with Anderson's. His school days frolicked before his eyes—days when, no matter how much effort he put into his work, some schoolyard bully could still come along and trounce his spirit. Ellis had learned a long time ago how to fight back. The quivering child within him had vanished, the years forming him into a strong man with an even stronger will. For all the times he'd shivered beneath a bully's threats, he shored himself up and looked Anderson square in the eye. Gold Strike was no playground, and he did not give in to bullies.

"It rests on me, does it?" He surveyed the cluster of disheveled outlaws on horseback, each holding a weapon. "I say you'd all better go home before I arrest you for obstruction." His gaze settled again on Anderson. "The boy stays here until he can get a proper trial. As the sheriff of this town, I owe him nothing less."

Humor lit Anderson's eyes, even as something darker passed through them. "If that's the call you want to make, Sheriff." His head wagged, disturbing the hair sitting on his shoulders. "I tried to warn you."

"And I'm warning you." Ellis's fingers coiled on his belt. "You will leave this property at once, or my deputies will arrest you." The men in question shifted from foot to foot, glancing nervously his way. Did the idea of arresting criminals frighten them so much?

Air blasted from Anderson's nostrils in twin bursts. "Cora said you were a stubborn man."

The remark emptied Ellis's lungs, knocking him off balance. "Cora?"

"Yes, Cora." Anderson hissed her name like a venomous snake. "She told me all about you, about your"—he licked his teeth—"*meeting* on Dusty Fork Ridge. Gave us both a good laugh."

Swallowing back the burning acid surging up his throat, Ellis could do nothing but stare back in silence. She had told Anderson, of all people, about their clandestine kiss? Even after finding out who she truly was, he still cherished the memory as special, unlike any moment he'd ever shared with a woman before. Now that she'd cheapened it, the moment made him sick. Clearly it did not mean to her what it had meant to him at the time.

"What? Shocked that you're not the only man in town she's laid her charms on?" Anderson released a jarring laugh. "Don't trouble yourself. She's bewitching. I've spent many a night learning just how bewitching."

The suggestive arch of his brow launched fury through Ellis's tense body. Of course he had slept with Cora. Likely more than half the town had slept with Cora. Why did the thought of it rankle him so? Why did he care what company a prostitute kept? Yet even as he tried to harden himself against his spiraling thoughts, her luminous eyes flashed in his mind—the way she smiled, the way her hair glittered beneath the sunlight. She was a siren, designed to tempt and beguile, to leave a man empty-handed and broken-hearted.

As if coming out of a fog, Ellis refocused on Anderson's face, the slight shift of his eyes, the movement of his neck muscles. His talk of Cora was a distraction. Adrenaline shot through Ellis. *He's reaching for his gun.* Without thought, Ellis expertly snatched his pistol from its holster and shoved it beneath Anderson's whiskered chin. Anderson froze in mid-motion, both hands flattening in surrender.

Several of Anderson's men readied their weapons, but Ellis yanked him up by the collar and positioned him to face them. "One move and I'll blow his head off. I mean it. Holster your weapons."

Anderson nodded, his skittish gaze wandering down Ellis's pistol. "Do it." His men complied at a hesitant pace.

Gritting his teeth, Ellis shoved the gun harder against Anderson's throat, eliciting a grunt. "I'm going to say this one more time, Anderson. You stay away from this jail and out of my way." Reaching around him, he pulled the pistol from Anderson's holster and held it skyward in his left hand. "The law will be upheld in this town. I don't care about your house rules."

The hatred blazing back at him burned in Ellis's mind even after he shoved Anderson back and allowed him to remount his horse. Those eyes promised so much more to come—the battle Ellis had vowed to wage the moment he accepted the badge of sheriff. Anderson would not go down quietly, and he had a mob at his back.

In dismal understanding, Ellis returned to the jail. He was alone in this fight, but he would fight until his very last breath.

Twelve

ONLY THE NEED FOR proper sustenance incited Madam Carey to release Cora into the wild. She'd tried for several days to send others to the market, but their inexperience had brought them back with the wrong items or not enough to fulfill the needs of over a dozen hungry girls.

Finally, after three breakfasts without her favorite raspberry jam, Madam Carey at last relented. Cora could make the market run as long as she went nowhere else and saw no one else. She had even commissioned that brute of a man, Jorgen, to accompany Cora.

With the sunlight warm on her skin and the crisp autumn air filling her lungs, Cora left the brothel for the first time in days. Never mind the lapdog trailing her every move. She could finally breathe right again—air not tinged with perfume and cigar smoke, but alive in nature's bounty. She could finally feel the wind in her hair. As dismal as the brothel had seemed to her before, it had never sucked the very life out of her as it had these last few days.

Clutching her shawl high around her shoulders, she hurried across the street and down the dusty thoroughfare. Madam Carey had warned her she only had half an hour before she needed to be within the brothel's confines again. Half an hour to walk and to breathe, to savor a freedom she'd so long taken for granted.

Madam Carey had provided her little explanation for the interrogation and subsequent beatings she'd received. When Cora had gone to her, incensed over her treatment after so many years of service, the madam had stuck up her nose and reminded her of her place. "I can replace you at any time."

The words still echoed through her, a harbinger of her future. Cora had expected this years down the road, when age stole her appeal to Madam Carey's customers. Yet she'd never imagined the madam would resort to such cruel measures with her top-earning girl.

Laurel had fared no better, she guessed. Nobody had seen her since the incident, and her closet had been cleared. Cora hoped with a shiver that Madam Carey had thrown her out. After witnessing the splotches of blood across the cellar floor, she refused to consider the alternative.

Positioned against the large glass windows of the mercantile, the farmers' market burst with vibrant color and voices as Cora wandered up the boardwalk. She had grown accustomed to visiting the stands of fresh fruits and vegetables nearly every morning after her walk, picking up items the girls would enjoy with their meals and taking them to the cook. After days spent trapped inside her bedroom, perusing the dewy greens and polished apples felt like heaven.

"How are you today, Cora?" Fred, the local shopkeeper, greeted her with a dip of his hat. "I haven't seen you much around here this week."

She sighed, determined to keep her cheerful demeanor despite the emotions weighing on her. "I'm afraid I've been far too busy to shop this week. I'm so happy to have the chance today, though."

"As am I." Fred leaned in, hanging his thumbs on his waist-coat pockets. "Between you and me, those other girls Madam Carey has been sending don't know the difference between a beet and a turnip. I shudder to imagine what you girls have been eating."

Cora laughed. "It has been rather a burden on our cook. Thankfully she has an imagination." Glancing over her shoulder, she eyed Jorgen, who stood on the tips of his toes and watched her over the milling throng. At least he had the decency to let her shop on her own.

After selecting a bushel of carrots, several heads of cabbage, and an entire sack of onions, Cora turned toward the fruit. In the midst of harvest season, the colorful selection of apples thrilled her. She purchased a pound of Baldwin apples, followed by an equal amount of Grimes Golden. Perhaps she could help the cook make pies during her confinement.

"Are you planning to haul all that back by yourself?" a friendly voice at her ear made Cora jerk to attention. The full smile staring back injected life into her.

"Oh, Faith." She flattened a hand over her chest. "I didn't see you there."

"Well, no wonder. You were so enraptured with your shopping." Faith tossed her blonde braid over one shoulder. "You're picking up quite a lot there." She eyed the large burlap sacks collecting at Cora's feet.

"Normally I shop for produce from day to day." Cora shrugged as nonchalantly as she could. "I don't know when I'll have occasion to get out again."

If Faith suspected anything to be amiss, she didn't show it. Instead, she stalked to the posts lining the boardwalk and leaned out toward the street. "Well, you must come to the pony show this Sunday. Do you see my new sorrel out there? She'll be the talk of the show." Her fingers splayed toward an auburn horse tied up among others at the water trough.

"She's beautiful." Daughter of a local businessman, Faith always had the loveliest mounts, trained to trot and perform tricks at her command. Her natural talent and love for the powerful beasts pervaded her entire life. "I'll try to make it." Cora's stomach twisted at the look of confusion on Faith's young face. "Madam Carey has me working on many special projects right now."

"Special projects?" Faith swung back to stand beside her, looking so much more mature in her white blouse and beige riding skirts than she had only months before. "How does she have you working on Sundays? Who comes to a brothel on Sundays?"

Clearing her throat, Cora glanced around. "Some people do."

"Well, they ought to be in church." Faith stood to her tall, slim height, looking every bit her seventeen years. "You're coming to church, aren't you, Cora? Didn't you promise the reverend you'd help with his bake sale?"

Cora winced. "That's right, I did." How could she have forgotten? She had pledged herself to bring a hundred cookies to church on Sunday. What would Madam Carey think of that? "I'll see if I can come."

Faith expressed her dissatisfaction in a pout. "I'll be terribly disheartened if you don't come. I've practiced for months for this show. Papa says this is my best trained horse yet."

"I'm sure your father would be grateful to know I'm not coming. Didn't he warn you about me?" *The devil's temptress,* he'd called her on their last meeting. Cora couldn't blame him for wanting to deter his daughter's friendship with a harlot.

"He doesn't need to know you're there"— Faith hooked a roguish brow—"nor that you snuck me into the brothel once."

Gaze darting quickly around, Cora pressed a finger over her lips. "You aren't supposed to tell. I should never have brought you in. I just wanted—"

The glow of Faith's smile reached her soul. "You wanted to see how I'd look in one of your magnificent creations, and I'll never forget it." She reached out, squeezing Cora's arm. "You're going to make an excellent seamstress one day, Cora. I know you are."

Cora's throat wedged back her words, emotion swathing her. If only everyone believed in her like this young girl did, she might actually accomplish something from her worthless life. If only she could return to her age and start again. But Faith would never have to contemplate the choices that had plagued Cora in her younger years.

She stood before her, fresh as a summer daisy, her blonde hair tethered with cashmere ribbons, her simple dress made of the finest silks available in the West. She had equestrian training, knowledge of languages, musical skills. Her family had reared her to make the perfect wife for a gentleman as rich as her father. Cora had learned nothing from her home life but the devastating weight of poverty.

Flattening her thoughts beneath her aching bosom, she forced her lips to curl upward. "Thank you for your kind words, Faith." She needed them more than her friend could comprehend.

Faith's smile faded as her eyes wandered Cora's face and anchored at her hairline. "What is that?" She stepped forward with fingers extended, but Cora quickly jerked away.

"It's nothing." Cora stepped back, rearranging her hair to cover the purple skin along her temples.

"It isn't nothing." Following her, Faith reached out again, her fingertips gently prodding Cora's skin. A breath sucked through her lips. "You have bruises all along your hairline. On this side, too. Cora, who did this to you?"

Cora shook her head. "It was an accident. I fell, and—"

"You don't get bruises on both sides of your head from falling." Faith stepped closer, speaking in a lower tone. "Did Madam Carey have you beaten?"

Memories of that night rushed in like an unstoppable flood. Cora tried to close her eyes against it, but the images flashed brighter each second—Jorgen's hand as it sailed toward her head, the lancing pain, the stench of his sweat in the musty cellar. If she told anyone about it, she'd have to relive it, and possibly worse. She couldn't let Faith get involved.

Yet already, the girl's hand had found her arm, hauling her off the boardwalk and into the street. "We'll be back to collect these items in a moment, Fred," Faith told the friendly shopkeeper.

The morning sun bathed the bustling street in warmth and yellow streams of light. Cora felt exposed beneath it, as if the world could see her pain, could sense she teetered on the brink of insanity. The people of Gold Strike tolerated her because of her acts of charity, but without them she would fade into the rest of the girls at Madam Carey's, forgotten except to condemn and whisper about behind closed doors.

Once they reached the edge of the street bordering the forest, Faith dropped her arm and stood near. "Tell me about who hurt you, Cora. I want to help."

"You can't help. There's nothing you can do."

Faith knotted her arms defiantly across her chest. "That can't be true. My father is an important man in this region. I know he doesn't like you, but he won't ignore something like this."

Glancing over Faith's shoulder, Cora spotted Jorgen, already at attention and stomping through the dust their way. "Please don't get your father involved in this, Faith. This is my problem to handle—not yours."

"But you're my friend." Faith seized her hands, holding them between hers. "I can't let you suffer when I know you're hurting."

Dear, sweet Faith. She had such an innocent view of life. Her only dilemmas thus far revolved around which gown to wear in the morning and how to please her expectant father. She had never tasted reality—not really, and Cora wished to keep it that way.

"Please, Faith." Cora darted a look at Jorgen, only steps away from them now. "I am fine, I promise you. I'll find my way out of this."

Before Faith could open her mouth, Jorgen jammed himself between them and clamped a hand on her arm. "It's time to go now. The madam is waiting."

Yanking free of his grasp, Cora let her gaze climb to his. She swiveled to the side to keep Faith from hearing. "Do you know how suspicious you look right now?" she hissed. "Her father owns half the valley. If she senses something is amiss, she will tell him and bring attention to all of us."

Jorgen sneered, his beady eyes ricocheting off them both before he took a step back. "Five more minutes. I won't get in trouble for you."

Once he had retreated up the street, Faith sidled near. "Who was that?"

"Madam Carey's new bouncer. He has a heavier touch than Randolph did." Her skin still crawled where he'd lain his hand.

"He looks fearsome." Faith's brows pinched together. "Cora, he isn't the one who—"

"No, Faith." Cora stopped her with a hand to her arm. "Please don't worry yourself about it anymore. It isn't worth your concern."

"But you *are* worth my concern." Her head angled. "Is there nothing I can do for you?"

Heart picking up speed, Cora reached into the pocket of her dress. "There is one thing, actually." Her fingers closed around the letter she'd penned earlier that day. She'd snuck into Madam Carey's quarters to do it—the only place she could find fresh paper and ink. Her pulse thumped in her throat as she pulled it out and handed it to Faith while Jorgen's attention was diverted elsewhere.

Without bothering to read the outside, Faith tucked it into her reticule. "What do you need me to do?"

"Mail it for me, please. It's very important. Madam Carey has Jorgen following me everywhere, and I can't risk him seeing."

Faith swallowed, then nodded briskly. "Of course. I'll send it out today."

"Thank you." A sigh of relief pressed from Cora's stifled lungs. That letter could mean her freedom. She had thought out exactly what she wanted to say as she lay in the safety of her bed, then snuck off to Madam Carey's quarters when she went down for breakfast. The madam had allowed her a trip to Miller's Crossing for Caleb's wedding once, but she'd never make the mistake again. Cora needed Caleb's help this time, the funds to escape, the power to get her free of Madam Carey for good. With his wife's grandmother behind him, surely he could help.

The scent of fresh-cut cedar drew Cora's attention to the sawmill. They stood only yards away from it, where men hauled logs onto rollers and fed them into water-powered saws, slicing rough boards for building homes. The machines' loud grinding conveyed memories of Caleb working there in the early days, staining his fine city clothes in oil and sawdust. The foreman, Adam Graves, stood a head above the other men, giving orders and overseeing production. He could be Jeremiah Anderson from the back, they looked so much alike with their long, scraggly hair and powerful build.

Another form caught her eye, wandering around the perimeter, asking questions of the foreman. Her stomach clenched. Could she never get away from him?

"Who is that?" Faith asked from her side, studying him with curiosity.

"He's the new sheriff. Haven't you heard? His name is Ellis McCraw."

"Oh, that's Sheriff McCraw." Faith tapped her fingertips on her chin. "My, he certainly is a handsome fellow, isn't he? How many women do you think will commit crimes just to land in a jail cell near him?"

Cora laughed at the girl's spunk. "I'm sure I don't know. He is handsome, but he's also a heel."

Faith's brows rose in question.

"He's already sworn to tear down the brothel and put us all out of work." Cora sighed, trying not to look at the way the sunlight glinted off the muscles of his exposed forearms. "He's been nothing but rude and presumptuous every time we've met."

"You've met him more than once, have you?" Mischief sparked in Faith's eyes. "Look at the color in your cheeks. I've never seen you so perturbed by a man before."

Cora tossed back an escaped strand of hair. "I'm not perturbed. The man means nothing to me."

Faith's lips pinched into a smirk. "So you don't mind if I have a friendly chat with him? My father is supposed to meet with him on Sunday."

Edward Carter, meeting with the new sheriff? What could they possibly have to speak about?

Ignoring her curiosity, Cora shrugged. "Speak with him all you like. Just please wait until I'm gone."

"I don't think that's possible," Faith said, so much glee brimming from her face, Cora wondered if her smile might crack in half.

"Why do you say that?"

"Because he's coming right this way."

Cora diverted her gaze just far enough to watch him march up the dusty street toward them. Jorgen stood only yards away, still looking elsewhere. Her palms slickened. If the two of them clashed, there could be trouble.

"Good day, ladies." Ellis glanced briefly at Cora, his eyes lingering a moment too long, before he looked Faith's way. "I don't believe I've had the pleasure."

"I'm Faith Carter." She genially shot out a hand. "I believe you've spoken with my father, Edward Carter?"

"Ah, yes. Of course." Ellis shook her offered hand. "You must know I'm Ellis McCraw, then." He shot a bashful yet knowing look Cora's way.

121

Faith chuckled. "How could I not? The whole town is abuzz with your plans for revitalizing it. My father could not be more delighted to have a new man at the helm of the sheriff's office."

Ellis nodded cordially. "It is my honor indeed, miss. I look forward to discussing my plans with your father."

"And to see my horse show, I hope." At his wrinkled brow, she laughed again. "Forgive the shameful advertisement. I'm just so excited about my new sorrel. She's bound to win the blue ribbon."

Following her pointed finger toward the horse glistening in the sunlight, Ellis clasped his hands behind his back. "It sounds like a festive occasion. I wouldn't miss it."

"Cora here might." Faith simpered at the look of annoyance on Cora's face. "She's too important for my little horse shows."

Cora released a breath. "Not too important, just busy." *And please leave it at that.* Ellis McCraw was the last person she needed to involve in her troubles at the brothel.

"Yes, Miss Blackwood has a demanding schedule, between her charitable ventures and"—he cleared his throat—"*other* endeavors."

Heat spread up Cora's neck. Did he have to identify her with her occupation every time he stood within a foot of her? Did he always have to remind her? "You seem disturbed by my endeavors, Sheriff McCraw. Do they occupy your mind?"

He stiffened at the suggestion. "Certainly not. I was simply making an observation."

Her fingers squeezed around the handle of the basket in her grip until the wicker indented her palm. "An observation you seem keen to comment on each time we meet. What else am I to think but that you have nothing better to do than to ponder my daily goings-on?"

Fire lit his gaze. "I can assure you, my mind is far too occupied with actual problems to consider your daily routines, though you are clearly the empress of all in your own mind."

Empress of all. What a self-important blowhard. "I suppose I should bow to your moral superiority, throw myself at the feet of your mercy." She slapped a hand on her chest, feigning a dramatic pose.

"No, but you would do well to find a little moral ground in your own life." His jaw hardened, his neck muscles clenching. "I suppose you've so long practiced the art of using men for your petty games that you've forgotten what morality actually is."

Her stomach turned at the notion. He had no idea what she had crawled out of. "At least I don't put on an air of self-right-eousness. At least I know who I am."

He stepped forward, gaze burning into hers. "Are you saying my lawfulness is only a front? That I'm no better than the devious sheriff who last served this town?"

"Funny you found those words by yourself." She crossed her arms, shielding herself from the tall approaching frame. "I don't need to tell you who you are, Sheriff."

"No, Miss Blackwood, you do not." He stood so close now, mere inches away, his light eyes scouring her face. This close, she could see the sheen of sweat on his skin, make out every piece of stubble dotting his jawline. How had she swept her hand across those whiskers and into his hair? How had she al-lowed him to kiss her? Now, nothing but self-righteous venom shone from his hard face.

"Just as you have no room to judge *me.*" The words barely sounded on her trembling lips, drawing his gaze to them. Cora held her breath, remembering the moment he'd swept her into his arms and pressed them against his. The feel of his magnetic kiss still tingled on her lips when he looked at them. But he'd promised her before—it would never happen again.

"No, but your actions speak for themselves." Pain crept into his eyes, no longer masked by sheer anger. "Anderson has already told me all about the way you laugh at my expense behind closed doors, about our conversation that first morning. You just couldn't keep it to yourself, now could you?"

Cora searched his eyes, his passion unsettling. How did Anderson know about their first meeting? Then, cold realization emptied into her stomach. *Jorgen. Madam Carey.* Of course they'd used every piece of information they could lay their hands on against her.

As if remembering with a jolt that Faith still stood by watching them, Ellis blinked. "Forgive me, Miss Carter." Stepping back from Cora, he ran a hand through his hair. "How terribly rude of me."

Toying with the strings of her reticule, Faith watched them with delight crimping her lips. "Think nothing of it, Sheriff."

Cora rolled her eyes. If God had blessed her with a sister, she imagined she'd get under her skin in much the same way as Faith. "Well, I, for one, must be going." She clasped Faith's hands in hers. "It was so good to see you again, Faith." Rounding a disapproving look on Ellis, she voiced her feelings without words.

Traipsing down the street and up the steps to the boardwalk, Cora shook out her arms, still tense and bursting with energy. The smell of him lingered in her nostrils, all pine and aftershave—as if he belonged perfectly in two worlds. If only he hadn't stepped into hers.

She gave a friendly nod to the shopkeeper before paying for her purchases and hoisting them into her arms. Before Jorgen could protest, she dumped the heavier bags into his grasp and whirled toward Madam Carey's. "It's time you make good use of yourself, Jorgen." Tilting her chin up, she marched past Faith and Ellis, determined never to look his way again.

Thirteen

THE TIDY YARD OF Colton Baxter's farmhouse bespoke friendliness and serenity. Ellis stood in the shade of an elm tree, his eyes roaming the tall dormer windows and steepled roofs, the gingerbread trim painted white against cheerful yellow siding. In front of the porch sat neatly trimmed hedgerows bordered by hydrangeas in blues and pinks. Despite her age, Abeline Baxter kept a lovely home.

Ellis walked the cobbled pathway, climbing the front steps to the wraparound porch. A few raps on the door brought the elderly woman to the threshold, her buoyant smile welcoming him in before she stood back to admit him. Finally, a gracious hostess. After nearly a week of interviewing anybody he could who had participated in Caleb Broderick's trial, the old woman with the warm smile eased his frazzled nerves.

He'd interviewed boys more concerned with his guns than answering his questions, women of the night, an elderly gentleman who could hardly remember testifying, let alone what he'd said. His most recent visits to the Gold Strike lumber mill had yielded little. Adam Graves, its formidable owner, had graciously answered his every question, but clearly knew nothing beyond Caleb's strange behavior before Baxter's death. He needed someone close to the man, someone who could unravel the contradictory ideas channeling his way.

"Sheriff McCraw, how delightful to see you." Mrs. Baxter swept a hand over her comfortable sitting room. "Please, do come in."

Stepping inside, Ellis removed his hat and held it to his chest. "I do hope this is an acceptable time."

"Yes, yes, of course." She waved him further in, shutting the door behind him. "I just made fresh muffins."

"So that explains the lovely smell." Wisps of blueberry wafted from her kitchen, tempting Ellis's middle.

"That is exactly what you smell." She smiled, holding up one wrinkled finger. "Why don't you have a seat while I fetch us some refreshments? How does sweet tea sound to you?"

"Sweet tea sounds delightful."

"Very well, then. I'll be right back."

Relaxing against the corduroy stuffed armchair, Ellis took in the room. White lace curtains framed the windows, letting sunlight spill across the wooden floors. Matching doilies adorned every piece of furniture, all a rustic shade of green with mahogany finishings. Everything about her home signaled simplicity and elegance. This was not a woman who'd spent her widowhood mired by grief. No, this woman had a strength of character absent from many he had met in this town.

Ice clinked in the glasses on her tray as Abeline Baxter shuffled back into the room. Age had slowed her movements, yet not dampened her spirits. She beamed back at Ellis as she set the tray on the tea table before him. "I was wondering when you would make your way to my humble abode."

Ellis reached for a tall glass of tea. "You were expecting me?"

"With my unique position in this town, I assumed the new sheriff would have some questions for me." She eased onto the settee nearest him and arranged her bright silk skirts over her knees. "It's not every woman in town who has suffered the loss of a husband in quite the same way I did."

Ellis gripped the cold glass. "I'm very sorry to have heard your story. I can't imagine the difficulty of losing a spouse to murder."

She sighed, settling back against the settee. "It has not been easy, especially at my age. Colton was still spry and active. I thought we'd have more time together."

"Would you tell me about him?" Taking a sip of tea, he watched her over the edge of his glass. She gazed down at the hands in her lap for several moments before lifting her head.

"Forgive me. It's not always easy speaking of him, knowing his life is in the past now." Her face brightened. "We shared over forty happy years together. He was such an industrious man, such a hard worker. I want for nothing, even in my old age."

Ellis savored the blend of honey and lemon sliding down his gullet. Baxter's widow was clearly unaware of his nefarious deeds, like the rest of this blinded town. Ellis had learned the truth from Caleb Broderick that Colton had been secretly working with both Jeremiah Anderson and Sheriff Jones to steal the stagecoach gold for himself. Letters from Baxter's office had confirmed this, but the information had never come to trial and seemingly failed to reach Abeline Baxter's ears. He smiled at her fond memories. Why taint a woman's picture of her husband with him already buried in the ground?

"He was always kind to me," she said. "Never had a harsh word or raised his voice, even when he was angry. If we could all be so patient with the ones we love in our lives."

"Indeed." Ellis set his glass on the tray next to the basket of freshly baked muffins she'd left there. "If you don't mind my asking, how do you feel about the outcome of the trial? About what happened afterward?"

Her wrinkles deepened with her forlorn expression. "I am relieved that a man did not hang for something he didn't do; that much is positive." Her head shook, her tightly wound white hair glinting in the sunlight. "Though I must admit I was shocked to learn that Wesley Pierce had committed the act."

"Do you know Mr. Pierce?"

"Not personally, no." She reached for a glass and held it in her hands. "He spoke with me once at the trial after I testified. We went to a cafe and had a conversation. He seemed so troubled and riddled with guilt. Now I see why."

Ellis nodded slowly, fixing the pieces together in his mind. As he understood it, Wesley Pierce had indeed shot Mr. Baxter. But as Caleb told the story, he was only defending Caleb's life. "Interesting that a man guilty of a crime no one suspected him of at the time would risk speaking with you so intimately."

"That's what I thought when I learned the truth." Abeline sighed. "Strange of him to confess and take the blame on his own shoulders too."

"Not quite the man you pictured killing your husband in cold blood?"

Her gaze swung back, a troubled light kindling behind them. "There must be more to the story, but I don't know what. I can't ask my husband, nor can I inquire after Wesley Pierce, now that he's absconded from the hand of the law."

Ellis tented his fingers, carefully selecting his next words. If Wesley Pierce ever returned to Gold Strike, Ellis would have to see his execution completed by order of the court. The thought twisted his gut with nausea. He'd entered into this business to protect the innocent, not to punish them. "I believe there is more to the story, and that's why I've come today."

Her head angled curiously. "A reason my husband was killed? Mr. Pierce claimed self-defense in court. I can't imagine anybody needing to defend themselves against my husband unless he were in fear for his own life."

"He had just encountered a skirmish between two different sets of outlaws." Though he had summoned the Andersons himself.

Her frail frame shivered. "I can't imagine what he experienced that day. I hope he didn't suffer." Her last word faded into a whimper, grabbing hold of Ellis's heart and squeezing tight.

"Let's speak of something happier, shall we? I didn't come here to make you relive your horrifying experience." Ellis plastered on a false smile and reached for one of her warm muffins. "You said you and your husband were married for over forty years?"

Pulling her shoulders back, she nodded. "Forty-six last April. We had a good life. We only had one child who left long ago, but we were enough for each other."

"You must have settled here in the town's very beginnings." He glanced around at the farmhouse's cheerfully decorated walls.

"We did. We came here from North Dakota when we were newly married." Pride overwhelmed her gaze as it washed over her well-maintained home. "Colton built this home with his own hands— with the help of men from town, of course. It was barely an outpost when we decided to settle here, and it quickly grew into something beautiful. I'll never forget those early days."

Ellis enjoyed a few bites of blueberry muffin before speaking. "So you were among the town's founders, I take it. How many of you are left?"

The sly smile of an adolescent girl graced her lips. "That, Mr. McCraw, is better answered with your eyes." Rising from the settee, she ambled across the room and retrieved a framed photograph affixed to the wall. With loving care, she carried it across the room and deposited it into Ellis's hands. "We took this photograph the day we broke ground on the church."

Ellis sat up, awed by the weathered tintype, among the first of its kind. A group of people stood in an open space before a backdrop of forest, a shovel proudly positioned before them.

"Many of these people are gone now, but a few remain." Abeline lightly touched his shoulder. "Can you find me?"

Scanning the slightly blurred faces, Ellis searched until his eyes pinned on a pretty young woman in a floral dress. His finger tapped her face through the glass. "Is that you?"

"Very good, Sheriff. I wondered if I could be recognized after all these years. You honor me." She touched the glass beside her image, indicating a young man in a smartly fitting suit. "There's Colton. My, I'd almost forgotten how handsome he was in those days."

"Who else in this picture is still alive?"

"Well, there's Jake Schulman, who still runs the local distillery." She indicated a portly man smiling from ear to ear. "And the Bakers, who now have seventeen grandchildren. And, oh—do you recognize this one?" Her finger moved to a rail-thin boy, not much older than a child.

Ellis squinted. "Can't say as I do."

"That's Edward Carter," she said with a laugh. "Of course, he resides in Missoula now, but he's up here all the time. He was an orphan child who wandered into town and made such a name for himself. We are all so very proud of him."

Ellis smiled at the sentiment. "I have yet to meet him, but I plan to on Sunday after church."

"Oh, will he be here on Sunday?" She clasped her hand to her heart. "That is very good news. I'll have to bring him some of my baked goods."

Ellis's gaze wandered the brown-tinged photograph, landing on a young, sharply-dressed couple. The woman's face looked so familiar. "Is that—" He tapped the glass, the name eluding him.

"Why, that's Clarice Foster. I haven't seen her in years." Abeline turned a questioning gaze on him. "Do you know her?"

"Only casually." Ellis stared into the proud face smiling back in the picture. "I traveled up to Miller's Crossing to interview her granddaughter and her husband. She has a beautiful establishment."

"Isn't it lovely?" Abeline stared out the window, a far-off look clouding her eyes. "We were best friends once. We did everything together. The day they picked up and left for Miller's Crossing left a hole in my heart. I've never ceased to miss her."

"Well, perhaps you should have a visit. It's not too far."

"In my old age, traveling is a bit of a hassle." She took the frame from him and held it to her bosom. "Though perhaps I shall. It has been far too long since I've seen my old friend."

Her words marched across Ellis's mind. Why hadn't Clarice mentioned their connection when he'd asked her about her history in Gold Strike? Perhaps he shouldn't voice his next concern, but the words escaped him anyway. "Did Clarice ever have anything against you or your husband?"

Abeline's graying brows narrowed. "Anything against us? Why would she?"

His shoulders lifted. "Just thought I might ask. I'm trying to understand the dynamics of this town." After all, Clarice Foster was among the few rich enough in these parts to coordinate the kind of attack he'd read about in Sheriff Jones's letters.

"We never had even the slightest quarrel. Our children grew up together, could have married—" She stopped short, as if her mention of the past belonged there.

"You were nearly in-laws?" Ellis leaned in, polishing off the last bite of muffin in his hand.

"No, not nearly." Abeline stared listlessly at the photograph. "My son had quite the admiration for their daughter, Angelica. But it wasn't to be. She loved another."

"Lily Broderick's father."

"Yes. Jude Hammond." She laughed lightly. "He was quite the looker in his day."

"It sounds like a beautiful friendship." One he probably had no business prying into.

"It was." Abeline crossed the room and hung the picture in its place beside the mantle. "I really should go and visit her. We're both widows now." Her voice faded on the last word, and she buffed a hand up her arm.

131

Ellis thought. "There's nobody else you can think of who might have harbored a vendetta against your husband? Not Edward Carter? Any of the other local businessmen, nobody from the bank?"

She frowned, suspicion peering out from her troubled gaze. "We know who killed my husband, Sheriff McCraw. He admitted it from his very own lips."

"Yet you said yourself you thought there was more to the story."

She nodded, her face thoughtful. "There could be more, but what evidence of that do I have? Colton was loved in this town. Nobody wished to hurt him." Her fingers spread on either side. "What reason would they have to kill a hard-working banker, an institution in this town for years?"

"That, I don't know." Ellis rubbed his palms together, warming them. "But I plan to do everything in my power to find out." Setting his palms on his knees, he pushed to a stand. "I shouldn't take up any more of your time, Mrs. Baxter. You've given me everything I need."

"Yet you've managed to disturb me." At his questioning look, she rested her hands on her thin hips. "I was perfectly happy living out here alone, enjoying my elder years in the home of our dreams." She implored him with a steady look. "Should I be worried about my safety? Do you think someone had something to gain from Colton's death?"

A quiet breath passed through his lips. His mind screamed in emphatic *yes* after everything he'd learned of her husband's sordid past, but he could not risk his investigation and divulge any of it to her. He doubted she would believe him anyway. "Forgive me, ma'am. That wasn't my intention. I'm just trying to do my duty." He shook his head. "Leave no stone unturned. That's what my pa used to tell me."

"He was a lawman too?"

"Yes, ma'am. One of the best." He traversed the hardwood floor, coming to stand near the front door. "If I believed you to be in any danger, I would tell you. Right now I'm only grasping at straws, but grasp I must."

Abeline met him at the door, pulling it open and standing aside. "I hope you find your answer, Sheriff McCraw—for both our sakes."

Stepping onto the porch, Ellis donned his hat and tipped the brim to her. "Good day, ma'am. Thank you for the tea and muffins." His hand made a circle on his belly. "I don't believe I've had finer, even back home in Tennessee."

The trepidation hadn't fled her eyes as she watched him go with a wave.

Ellis jogged down the porch steps, noting the way they creaked beneath his feet. The wind rushed through the trees, carrying the distant caw of a bird unlike any Ellis could remember hearing in these parts. A thumping sound brought his attention to the side of the house, where a set of cellar doors flapped against the ground in the baying wind. Her home certainly appeared in fine condition, but an old woman alone could only do so much.

"Your root cellar doors appear in need of tightening up," he said over his shoulder. "Would you like me to arrange for someone to come fix them? Perhaps mend the porch steps?"

Abeline smiled back, a bit of pride pinching her lips together. "My home is aging along with me. Let me retain a little dignity and make the arrangements myself."

"I understand." With a tip of his head, he sauntered down the walkway toward the trail leading to Gold Strike. He could appreciate an independent woman, especially when he had another plaguing his every waking thought.

Fourteen

"COME, THOU FOUNT OF every blessing, tune my heart to sing Thy grace." Cora sang the words of the old hymn, her words contrite, but her soul floundering. She gripped the hymnal in both hands, attempting to steady it despite her quaking fingers.

The words, so elegant and beautiful, rolled off her tongue to the organ's jubilant voice, but they found no root inside her. The church's walls, normally a haven against the outside world, bore down upon her. The voices raised in poetic harmony around her blended together until a strident hum buzzed in her ears. She had no business singing these words of praise when she thwarted the principles of God day after miserable day. Could he even hear her beneath her heap of transgressions?

Refocusing her eyes, she started in on the next verse. *It won't matter soon anyway. This will be my last Sunday in church.* She'd only managed this foray into the world because of her prior commitment to the church bake sale.

Her pleas had been met with an emphatic no—until Cora reminded Madam Carey of the last time Reverend Sommers had visited the brothel. With his father-like presence and encouraging words, he'd managed to convert three of the girls and convince them to abandon their posts on the spot.

"I always keep my commitments," she'd told the wary madam. "If I'm not there to attend church and deliver the cookies, he'll be here before nightfall spreading the good news among your girls."

The threat had proven enough to convince Madam Carey to let Cora out—alone this time. Jorgen had paled at the idea of stepping foot in a church. She had until noon before Madam Carey set him loose after her.

The feel of eyes prompted Cora to glance to her left. Ellis held her gaze a moment, then returned his to the hymnal in his hand. No doubt he resented her attendance in this place, as did several others who periodically clamped a condemning gaze on her. She never sat anywhere but the back row, the safest place to flee if necessary.

Despite her best efforts to resist, she found her eyes pinned to Ellis several more times. Normally he wore a cotton or wool shirt tucked in his trousers, a thick jacket over the top. Today he had on a crisp black suit and necktie, his hair combed and his face shaven. He could almost pass for a dignified gentleman if it weren't for his rugged bearing. His commanding stance gave him away. He was meant for nothing but seizing the world on horseback and battling the lions of injustice.

A sermon commenced on the everlasting love of Christ. Cora concentrated on the uplifting words, all the while battling their veracity. God loved the sinner, yes, but did he love the person with no more conscience? The one who'd pushed him away so long he appeared more as a vague shadow than a true father?

As the final notes of the closing hymn drifted from the pipe organ, Cora shot to her feet and made for the door. Madam Carey would expect her soon, and she'd do best to escape the judgmental looks of her fellow parishioners. They needed her here no longer than necessary.

"Cora!" She froze at the masculine voice who summoned her from the church doors. "Cora, wait!"

She kept walking, ignoring the boots pummeling the dirt behind her. If he wanted to make a spectacle of himself, let him. She had no intention of letting him reel her into another trap.

"Slow down, would you?" Ellis jogged to catch up with her, his long strides reaching her in seconds.

Cora tossed a flippant look his way. "I have to be getting back. I don't have much time."

"Don't you have a few seconds to spare?"

"No, I don't." She kept her gaze to the street ahead and the line of businesses leading back to the brothel. "You would do best not to be seen with me here, anyway. The gossips are in full force on Sundays."

"Hold on just a minute." Ellis caught her by the arm, luring her back like a fish caught on a wire.

Cora's nostrils widened, her gaze flinging to where he held her captive. "Kindly let me go, Sheriff McCraw. I have committed no crime here worthy of your detainment."

His fingers instantly released her. "I do not wish to detain you, I just—" His chest pumped, his breath still hurried from the short jog.

"You want to ridicule me again."

Before she could whirl away and run, he blocked her path. "I want to apologize."

Cora scowled, her eyes questioning his. Only the light of sincerity shone back.

"I should never have argued with you the way I did the other day in front of your friend." He clutched his hat in front of him, turning it over in his hand. "That was very poor form of me."

Drawing back, she angled her chin up. "And auctioning me off at the brothel? How was your form then?"

His head shook. "Terrible. The lowest point of my life."

"And kissing me first, then scorning me because I wasn't who you imagined I would be?"

"Blast, woman. Can't you accept a simple apology?" His jaw flexed, the muscles of his forearms rippling.

"I see how genuine your apology is." Picking up her skirts, Cora elbowed past him. A crowd had already gathered outside the church, hanging on their every word.

"Wait. You're right. I'm sorry." Ellis seized her arm again, gentler this time. Heat crept up Cora's neck, but she didn't pull away again. "Please listen to what I have to say."

She blew out an impatient breath. "Say it quickly, please. I'm late as it is." She could just imagine Jorgen dragging her back by her hair, extending the beating he'd given her already.

Ellis glanced furtively around before he stepped closer, much too close for propriety's sake. The action sparked whispers and surprised looks from those watching in the churchyard. "I need your help."

Cora protectively crossed her arms over her bosom. "I can't imagine the kind of help I could bring to you."

"Oh, but you can." The fingers still clutching her arm restricted. The scent of his aftershave touched her nose, stirring a bizarre sense of excitement within. "You're the only one I know at Madam Carey's."

She laughed. "That's not true. I'm sure a dozen girls would step into whatever role you need them to."

His head wagged solemnly. "I don't trust any of them."

The implication of his words made her gulp back her growing trepidation. She searched his face, letting her gaze trail across his smooth jaw before landing on his gray-rimmed eyes. "What is it?"

"I need to know—" He licked his lips, shifting from one foot to the other. "Well, have you noticed anything strange at Madam Carey's? Have any girls gone missing?"

"Missing?" Her brow wrinkled. Madam Carey's was a terrifying place, but women didn't vanish into thin air. They were too valuable to the operation. "No one has gone missing. Women leave from time to time—when they age or decide to move on, but—"

"Nobody has left without explanation in the recent past?"

Cora's mind shifted immediately to Laurel, whose blood blotched the cellar floor and clothes had vanished along with her. Her breath hardened. If she mentioned any of that, he would want to know more, and her life would hang in a precarious place.

At last, she shook her head. "Nobody." Until she had the means to escape this town, she couldn't risk Madam Carey's wrath.

Ellis gnawed his lip. "I thought surely there would be."

"Do you suspect someone is kidnapping girls in this town? Have there been other occurrences?" Suddenly the madam didn't pose the only threat to her safety.

Eyes troubled, Ellis stared at her a breathless second before he broke her gaze. "No. I don't know. What Adrian Fox said about his mother, it got me thinking, and"—he drew back his suit jacket, resting his hands on his trim waist—"I suppose my imaginings went too far." Yet that turbulent look hadn't left him.

"I'll look out for anything suspicious."

Her words brought his head up, his gaze turning hopeful. "Thank you, Cora—and I am sorry. I'll try not to behave that way again."

Before she could answer, a man's voice sailed through the air. "Sheriff McCraw?"

Cora turned to see Faith and her father headed their way. "I must go." *Before I cause you even more trouble.* Mr. Carter had never hidden how he felt about prostitution. Doubting she had the fortitude to endure his verbal assaults, she slipped away before Ellis could say another word.

It was better this way—better for them both. As soon as Caleb could send her the funds, she'd be on her way to Miller's Crossing and a new life. And Ellis McCraw would be nothing but an unpleasant memory.

Ellis couldn't help watching Cora flurry across the street, re-treating into the cloud of dust that clogged his vision. She had an urgency to her step, a need to run away as quickly as she possibly could—for fear of a scolding from Madam Carey, or because she couldn't stand another second in his presence? He shook his head, reminding himself of the truth. He'd apologized for his wanton actions. He could bear her self-righteous indignation no further.

"Sheriff McCraw!"

At the sound of Edward Carter's second call, Ellis turned on his heel. A broad man with a bald head, trim mustache, and tailored suit approached from the direction of the church. Beside him happily walked the young lady he'd met only days before, dressed to perfection in a lavender lace gown and crisp white parasol.

"Edward Carter, I presume?" Ellis forced a smile, his hand shooting out in greeting. "A pleasure."

"Likewise." Carter pumped his hand with a strong, solid shake. "I hear you've already made my daughter's acquaintance."

"Only briefly, but yes." Ellis dipped his head toward the friendly blonde. "Good day to you, Miss Carter."

"And to you, Sheriff McCraw." A smidgeon of adolescent playfulness skittered over her lips as she peered past him toward Cora's fleeing image. "Is that Cora Blackwood I see in such a rush? I hope you didn't scare her off, Sheriff."

Mr. Carter wagged his head, fixing her with a disapproving scowl. "That is precisely what he should do. A prostitute openly flaunting her sin in the church? It's a disgrace."

Faith pursed her lips. "I beg to disagree. She looks perfectly presentable, and it isn't like she's attempting to drum up business by her attendance on Sundays."

"And how do you know she isn't?" Mr. Carter clicked his tongue, pivoting his attention to Ellis. "You will have to forgive my daughter. She's a good girl, but she enjoys testing the bounds of propriety at times. I can assure you, she does *not* associate with the likes of that harlot."

Ellis pushed back the grin that edged his lips. From the looks of their conversation only days before, the two were good friends—a fact that seemed to elude the sharp business man. Or perhaps he chose simply to ignore it for the sake of appearances. Faith showed no fear of discovery in her unbothered expression.

"No need to apologize," Ellis said. "Who your daughter chooses to befriend is no business of mine."

Mr. Carter's hearty chuckle filled the air. "You'll soon learn anything that happens around here is everybody's business." He nodded toward the group of gawkers now only beginning to scatter. "Did you not notice the swarm of busy bodies watching your every move?"

Ellis shrugged. "I did. Perhaps I simply do not care what they have to say or think about me."

"I would advise against that if you want to keep your job long in this place." Mr. Carter's eyes narrowed. "What business do you have with Cora Blackwood, anyway?"

"Father!" Faith's hand shot out, gently swatting his wrist. "How obtuse of you to ask such a question."

"Nonsense." Ellis held up a hand, painting on a neutral look. "I'm perfectly happy to explain. We both happened to be at the church when the shootout transpired between the Red Fox Gang and Isaiah Anderson. I wanted to see how she was fairing after witnessing such a horrific ordeal."

"How thoughtful of you." Mr. Carter's lips lifted beneath his thick mustache, but his daughter didn't appear so convinced. She had witnessed their argument on the street, after all.

"I hear the Andersons tried to hang Adrian Fox themselves," Faith said, her eyes widening with delight.

"The rumors have been grossly exaggerated." Ellis clasped his hands in front of him to keep his restless fingers from twitching. "Mr. Fox is safe in my care."

Mr. Carter's mouth flattened into a sober line. "You've managed to get a trial underway quickly, or so I hear."

Ellis nodded. "Proceedings will start tomorrow. The town has been vocal about their wish to see him hanged, but it is my duty to ensure he has a proper trial." He paused, drawing a breath as he considered his next words. "This feud between the Foxes and the Andersons is part of the reason I wished to speak with you, Mr. Carter."

With a quick glance around, the large man hooked Ellis's arm away from the church. "Come, let's speak as we walk, shall we?" He steered them toward the side of town not dominated by businesses currently rife with people. Here in the shadows of the tannery and feed stores, the trio walked with a fragile sense of calm. "What, exactly, did you want to know?"

Mind racing with possibilities, Ellis dove ahead. Better to start with the obvious reasons for his inquiry, without bringing Jones's mysterious letters into the mix. "I heard you testified at Caleb Broderick's trial."

"I did indeed." Mr. Carter fastened his hands behind his back as he walked. "The prosecution had questions for me regarding the burglary that took place at my home not long before Baxter's murder."

"A dreadful night." Faith shuddered, clutching her parasol tight. "I heard shooting downstairs. I was afraid someone had broken in and attacked my father."

Ellis frowned. "Is that a fear you often have, Miss Carter?"

"I think she means her first thought went to my safety." Mr. Carter patted Faith's shoulder. "A man never had a more caring daughter."

She beamed back at him, the sunlight illuminating her tawny hair. "With Mama gone, we look out for each other." Her thin shoulders lifted. "Anyway, the shots I heard were from Papa's gun."

"I was forced to shoot at the man invading my home. My daughter's life was at stake."

"Understandable." Ellis thought back to the conversations he'd shared with Wainwright and his many colorful accounts of the trial. "Caleb Broderick was involved in that burglary."

"He was in the carriage, yes." Mr. Carter took a breath, his shoes disturbing the pebbled ground as they walked. "I've heard since then he had no idea why they'd come. It seems a good boy got mixed up with the wrong crowd."

The scent of hay and alfalfa drifted in from the feed store as they passed a narrow barn. "I'm curious then, Mr. Carter. Who *did* invade your home that night? Who did you shoot? I don't believe I've ever heard the answer to these questions."

"No, you wouldn't have." Mr. Carter squinted against the harsh rays of sunlight. "Caleb Broderick was on trial—nobody else. I, myself, still don't have a clue."

Ellis's gaze swung his way. "What do you mean?"

"Nobody ever turned up with a gunshot wound in town, as far as I've heard. I'll never know if any of my bullets hit flesh or not—or if the blood on my windowsill was only from scraping the broken glass."

"Perhaps the intruder came from another town."

"Perhaps." Mr. Carter shook his head. "I suppose only Caleb Broderick himself knows who broke in."

Ellis looked toward the sky ahead, a vast expanse of blue with bushy white clouds drifting across it. He'd already brought these questions to Caleb Broderick's door and received the answers he sought. Colton Baxter had indeed taken a bullet that day, though how he'd covered up the fact, Caleb couldn't be sure. Perhaps Jeremiah Anderson had a shady backroom doctor under his employ for just such circumstances.

"I know Anderson was involved in the whole thing," Mr. Carter said, as if reading his very thoughts. "I could only describe him as a large man with long hair in court because I didn't see his face. Anyone with eyes can tell who that rogue is from a mile away."

Another fact confirmed by Caleb Broderick. "Yes, I've come to a similar conclusion myself. Mr. Anderson certainly possesses the moral bankruptcy to commit such a crime."

"He's a perfect cad," Faith put in. "Nothing but a scoundrel."

Mr. Carter shot her a warning glance. "And you're to have nothing to do with him, young lady."

"Relax, Papa." Faith laughed blithely. "I only meant in passing. Of course I have no association with him, but that doesn't stop him from throwing looks and comments my way."

Mr. Carter's jaw clenched, the muscles beneath his suit coat bulging. "If he gets near you, I'll kill him."

She simpered back. "If he gets near me, you're welcome to."

As if remembering he stood in the presence of the sheriff, Mr. Carter straightened up and brushed off his coat. "I don't like threats to my daughter's safety, if you hadn't noticed yet."

"I've gotten the inkling." Ellis turned his hat over and screwed it back on his head. "I was hoping you would be able to tell me more about what happened, but I see you're just as much in the dark as I."

Mr. Carter stopped short, facing him. "I'll do anything I can to help, Sheriff. I want to make this a safe place for my daughter to reside."

They'd nearly reached a wide corral where Faith's glossy sorrel waited to be shown. "I want that too. I believe with the help of some fine upstanding citizens, we might make Gold Strike into the place it once was again, like when you wandered in here as a boy."

Mr. Carter's mouth opened. "Now, how did you come upon that piece of trivia?"

Ellis grinned. "I met with Abeline Carter at her farmhouse only days ago. She showed me the tintype of the church's first ground-breaking."

His eyes darkened—from sympathy, resentment, pain—Ellis couldn't be sure. "Abeline Baxter. How is the old bird?"

"As good as can be expected for her present circumstances."

"We all miss Colton." Mr. Carter managed a ragged breath. "We should go see her, shouldn't we, Faith? Perhaps bring her some of your fruitcake you always like experimenting with."

"That would be lovely." Faith's light eyes flashed Ellis's way. "Mrs. Baxter is like a grandmother to us all."

"I hate to think of her out there living all alone." Mr. Carter reached out an arm, hugging his daughter to his side. "This town takes care of one another. We will not leave her to her own devices."

Strengthened by his exchange with the Carter family, Ellis looked back at the lonely jail sitting beneath misty rays of sunlight. *This town takes care of each other.* He was a part of this tradition now. Inside that jail's walls sat a child with the weight of a man on his shoulders. Ellis would see him get a fair trial if it was the last thing he managed to accomplish in this town.

Fifteen

GOLD STRIKE METHODIST CHURCH, so subdued the day before, now buzzed with voices and activity. A crowd had filed in for this impromptu set of proceedings, giving Ellis a glimpse of what Caleb's trial must have looked like. Even the same local justice agreed to perform his duties in the absence of a circuit judge. His tall, thin frame filled the doorway as he gazed across the bustling structure.

Many had laughed in Ellis's face when they discovered he was demanding such lengths for a member of a known local gang, but he met every protest with unshakable earnesty. Adrian Fox deserved every bit a fair trial as a common citizen of Gold Strike, just as Isaiah Anderson deserved justice for a rival gang surrounding him and gunning him down in the street. If his responsibility only extended to keepers of the law, Ellis would consider himself a hypocrite.

He watched in silence as Justice Morgan tramped across the front of the church and once again took up his gavel. The man had a weary look on his face, as if the forty or so years he'd lived on this earth had worn on him harder than they should have. He banged his gavel on the table, disrupting the clusters of conversation around the room. "The court will come to order!"

A hush fell over the assembled crowd, the tapping of a few stray boots bounding off the walls before every eye turned toward Justice Morgan. Their expectant silence was palpable. What grand adventure awaited them at this trial, so soon after Gold Strike had flipped on its head over the murder of Colton Baxter?

"Ladies and gentlemen, we have assembled here today to hear the case of one Adrian Fox." Justice Morgan indicated the defendant with one hand. "He is accused by the state of Montana of willfully causing a disturbance in the streets of Gold Strike, of unlawfully rallying a crowd, and murdering one of its citizens. The court will now hear evidence for and against these charges. Prosecution, the floor is yours."

Ellis had spent the better part of a week procuring an attorney fit enough to represent the prosecution. His efforts displayed themselves now as Mr. Donald Culver stood and approached the hastily assembled jury members flanking one wall. He wore a wrinkled suit with patches on the waistcoat and pants that looked six inches too short. His hair, a bundle of white curls, stuck out from his head in every direction, and he peered at the jury over gold-rimmed spectacles balanced on the tip of his nose. What he lacked in stature, he accounted for in comical display.

"Gentlemen of the jury"—he cracked his knuckles, the sound popping across the quiet space—"what we have here is an open and shut case. The man you see before you, Mr. Adrian Fox"—his hand flourished toward the despondent youth—"is a known thief and offender of the law, a local deviant. He and the other members of his notorious group, the Red Fox Gang, surrounded the victim, Mr. Isaiah Anderson, taunted him, and shot at him until he fell dead in the street."

Puffing out his chest, he faced the jury head-on. "This will all be proven beyond a shadow of a doubt throughout the course of these proceedings, which I cannot imagine will last longer than a day or two." He smiled, an alarmingly cheerful display. "Then we may all be on our merry way, for we already know Adrian Fox, just like the rest of his crew, deserve nothing but the harshest penalties of the law and certain death. Thank you."

The click of his shoes across the wooden floorboards had a deafening quality in the wake of his pathetic opening state-ment. Ellis rubbed his face in hard strokes and looked over his hand at Adrian, slumped forward in his seat. His thumbs twiddled over one another, his eyes pinned to the desk. He had the bearing of a child, yet he stood trial for his very life.

Knotting his arms over his chest, Ellis leaned back and watched Adrian's lawyer take his place before the jury. A wave of nausea rolled through him. The defense attorney, barely older than Adrian himself, looked on like a scarecrow caught in the wind at the waiting faces of the jury. Who had drummed up this sad excuse for a lawyer from the dredges of Gold Strike's society? He couldn't hold a proper license to practice law. No doubt, whatever degrees he claimed had been forged, dreamed up when Red Fox couldn't afford better representation.

"Gentlemen"—his voice cracked, straining to be heard, yet falling dismally short—"you may think because Adrian Fox carries a notorious last name that you should condemn him without hearing the proper arguments." He stood taller, clear-ing his throat. "But you would be wrong, and that would be a great disservice to Mr. Fox here."

The men of the jury, seated in two uneven lines beneath a row of windows, eyed him speculatively. Their narrowed gazes followed him as he proclaimed Adrian Fox a victim, the squish of his shoes nearly drowning out his voice. At the end of his speech, Ellis felt like crying. Neither side had a hope of hearing the facts presented properly, with a disinterested old man on one side and a frightened little boy on the other.

He drew in an exasperated breath, watching as the prosecution called their first witness. Citizen after citizen traipsed across the crowd's eye—shopkeepers, customers, children who'd been playing in the streets. Each had a more fantastical tale than the last, building upon each other's fiction with impressive detail.

By the time Ellis trudged to the front of the church to take the witness stand, the town had painted Adrian Fox as a maniacal devil sent from Hades itself, who'd stalked Isaiah Anderson from the outskirts of town, waiting for his chance to pounce. Never mind that the Anderson Gang had committed as many atrocities as the Foxes had. The whites of their eyes bulged, their veins standing out against their skin as they wove a tale so outlandish, he wondered if he hadn't stepped into a storybook.

"You were near the scene of the crime when it occurred, weren't you, Sheriff McCraw?" Mr. Culver stared over the rim of his glasses like a bird looking for a leftover crumb.

"I was. I happened to be just outside the church when it happened." From his lone chair, Ellis pointed toward the back doors at the end of the aisle.

"Did you see who pulled the trigger that delivered the fatal shot, Sheriff McCraw?"

"No." Ellis softly shook his head. "Shots were being fired all around. It could have been almost any one of the group that cornered Isaiah Anderson that day."

Mr. Culver's head cocked. "Yet you only arrested Mr. Fox here. Why is that?"

Ellis's nose flared at the unspoken insinuation. "He was simply the only one of them I could safely arrest without being shot myself. I was hoping to find out more information from interrogating him. I only chose him because he was easy prey."

Against the scattered murmurs wisping across the crowd, Mr. Culver stopped his pacing to send a look of confusion Ellis's way. "Easy prey?"

"He's sixteen years old." His arm swept toward the boy. "Look at him. A strong wing could knock him over. He was cowering in the back, so I saw my opportunity and I took it." The remark tinged Adrian's cheeks a rosy hue. Let it. He'd rather the boy suffer a little embarrassment than die for his pride.

The prosecutor gave him one last dissatisfied look before announcing he'd finished his questions. Did he expect Ellis to bend the truth his way just because he'd hired him? What kind of law was practiced in this backward place?

The defense lawyer rose up, his youthful face still swathed in timidity. "No questions, Justice."

"*Yes*, you have questions." Alarm shot through Ellis, the words materializing before he'd even thought them through.

Adrian's lawyer shot a startled look Justice Morgan's way before his rounded eyes landed back on Ellis.

"I was there when that Anderson kid was shot." Ellis leaned forward, his chair squeaking with the movement. "Come over here and ask me questions, boy."

The courtroom erupted in snickers as the shamed lawyer made his way toward the makeshift witness stand. Even when he reached the front, his eyes stayed glued to his shoes rather than meet Ellis's face. He stepped from foot to foot, as if waiting outside an outhouse for his turn.

"Sheriff McCraw, you were here at the church when Isaiah Anderson was killed?"

"I was right outside." *Come on, boy. Get to the meat of the questions. Ask me something I can work with.*

"And you saw the Red Fox Gang shooting at Anderson?"

"I did."

The young lawyer swallowed. "And he shot back?"

"He had to. He was outnumbered, and they were going to kill him either way." *Come on, come on.*

His eyes shifted, as if searching for something important to ask, yet finding nothing within the recesses of his mind.

"Ask me about Adrian's gun," Ellis said in a low tone. When he was only met with a quizzical expression, he leaned forward. "Ask me about the bullets."

"Sheriff McCraw," Justice Morgan's warning thrust Ellis back in his seat. "May I remind you that just as leading a witness is prohibited, so is leading a lawyer."

"Apologies, Justice." Ellis couldn't squelch the smirk edging his lips as the audience broke into fits of laughter.

The lawyer's face brightened with understanding, his shoulders squaring despite the throng of spectators openly mocking him. "Did you take Adrian Fox's gun when you arrested him?"

Ellis dipped his chin. "I did indeed."

"Did you notice anything about the bullets?"

Thank heavens. "Every single one was still in its chamber."

The lawyer bounced on the balls of his feet now, his childlike eyes illuminated. "What would you say if I suggested that perhaps he simply reloaded?"

Yes, boy. "There was no time to reload in that fight. The bullets were flying constantly, and he could have been hit by taking the risk of looking down. Besides"—Ellis knit his fingers together in his lap—"the gun was cold. There was no powder on it whatsoever. It was not fired during that gunfight."

"Did Mr. Fox perhaps have another gun on him?"

"No, sir, he did not. I searched him thoroughly."

"Thank you, Sheriff McCraw." A relieved breath blew from the attorney's lips as he returned to the defense table and settled himself next to Adrian.

Justice Morgan shook his head, sitting in shocked silence a moment before he looked Ellis's way. "Sheriff McCraw, you're free to go. Mr. Culver, call your next witness, please."

Ellis's back cracked as he stood and ambled across the floor to the front pew he'd taken before. He barely registered Culver standing and glancing over a sheet of paper in his hand until his words sounded across the quiet church: "The prosecution calls Miss Cora Blackwood."

Butterflies danced in Cora's middle as she stood up from among the crowd and scooted to the edge of her pew. All morning, she'd waited with spiraling dread to take her place on the witness stand. How had she, of all people, been dragged into this? Why hadn't she listened to Madam Carey and been safe within the brothel's walls when Isaiah Anderson found himself swarmed by Foxes eager to end his lawless existence?

The madam, seated on the pew by the spot Cora had just vacated, warned her silently with eyes like sharpened daggers. *Don't say too much. Get this over with as fast as you possibly can.* Chills skittered up Cora's arms as she marched down the aisle with every eye in the building fixed to her.

When the lawyer had first appeared at the brothel door and summoned her to court that day, Madam Carey had refused to let her go. No girl of hers had time to waste on such trivial matters, she'd told the aging attorney. Yet after hearing the potential consequences, her mind had been changed. She couldn't lose her biggest seller to the confines of a prison. Thus she sat, probably for the first time in her life, within the walls of the Gold Strike church with her head held exceedingly high.

Murmurs swept over the audience as Cora reached the front of the church and swore to tell only the truth. She had donned her most modest dress that day, a long-sleeved cotton gingham with a neckline ringing her throat. No matter what they said about her, she'd not have them accuse her of indecency in the Lord's house, nor of dishonoring the court with her appearance. Still, she couldn't ignore the condescending looks and outright glares thrown at her, nor the licentious leers from some of the men.

"Miss Blackwood," Mr. Culver began, "you were with Sheriff McCraw here at the church when the shooting began. Is that right?"

"Yes, well"—she tried to temper the heat rising in her face—"we did not come together, but I was speaking with Sheriff McCraw when the shooting began." The remark sparked more whispers, and Cora felt as if floundering in a dark ocean at night while the stars looked on from the safety of the sky.

"Did you see Isaiah Anderson being shot?"

Her head wagged. "No, sir, I did not."

"But you were there when Sheriff McCraw apprehended Adrian Fox."

"Yes, sir." Her eyes drifted toward the defendant, who cast her a sad grin from his spot at the defense table. "I watched him arrest Mr. Fox."

Mr. Culver studied her closely. "Did the shooting of Isaiah Anderson occur before or after Sheriff McCraw apprehended our defendant here?"

Cora thought for a moment, the unpleasant memories playing across her mind's eye. "It was before. Sheriff McCraw told me he thought Isaiah Anderson was dead before he snuck up on Mr. Fox and took him into custody."

"I see." Stroking his whiskered chin with his thumb and forefinger, Mr. Culver peered over his glasses at her. "What kind of response did you witness young Mr. Fox have to his arrest?"

"He was scared."

"Scared because he knew he'd been caught?"

Cora blinked. "Scared because he was just a boy caught in the games of men. I don't believe he ever intended to kill a man. He was only trying to please his father by being a part of his group."

Mr. Culver's mouth dragged down in displeasure. "Have you ever met Adrian Fox before, Miss Blackwood—or his father?" His eyes turned to slits. "Do you have much association with Red Fox?"

Blood pumped furiously through Cora. She knew *exactly* what he was suggesting—that she'd colluded with Red Fox on a visit to the brothel to make his son look better. "We are hardly acquainted. We've said no more than 'hello' on sparse occasions."

"And yet you seem to know a lot about his son's motives." His lips pursed accusingly. "How can this be?"

Cora glanced out at the waiting crowd—the way they bent toward her, hanging on her every word, eager to glean any bit of salacious gossip they could. "Because he told me himself. When Sheriff McCraw questioned him, Adrian said he'd mainly lived with his mother, but he rode with his father now, seeking his approval."

"Very interesting." Mr. Culver tapped his fingertip on his chin. "So it very well could be the case that in order to please his father, Mr. Fox took down the brother of his sworn enemy, the unsuspecting man now lying dead in a coffin because of the actions that transpired that day."

"I don't believe so, Mr. Culver." Before he could react to her statement, Cora plunged ahead. "I watched Adrian Fox from the side of the church while some of the shooting was still going on. He stood there with his gun in the air, pointed skyward. Shaking in his boots. I never saw him fire a single shot."

The lawyer lifted his brows in condescending mockery. "Just because you didn't see it, my dear, doesn't mean it didn't happen."

"No, but Sheriff McCraw already testified to the fact that Adrian Fox never shot his gun." Her gaze landed back on Adrian, seeing instead the faces of the younger brothers she'd left behind in Scotland. How would she feel to have them paraded around, put on display for a town's entertainment? "The fact that Adrian Fox could not have fired his gun is quite damaging to your case, is it not?"

The chatter began anew. Justice Morgan rubbed his temples, but failed to get involved. Even at a distance, Madam Carey's scornful glare burned through her. Cora stole a glance at Ellis, who sat with his elbows on his knees, seemingly fascinated by the whole ordeal.

"Miss Blackwood"—Mr. Culver's saggy jowls tightened as his mouth clamped—"remind everyone in attendance what you do for a living."

Her stomach dropped as every ear in the building angled closer. "You know exactly what I do, Mr. Culver." She kept her voice steady, though every instinct tempted her to wither in her seat.

"It isn't an option to be evasive with the court, Miss Blackwood." His bushy brows rose in question, taunting her.

Cora stuck out her chin, her breath growing louder. "I work at Madam Carey's." The breath pressed from her nose. "I am a prostitute."

Triumph flared over the old man's face. He turned to share a knowing look with the crowd before pivoting back to her with unsolicited pity. "A prostitute—one who happened to be in an advantageous spot to witness the crime in question, yet no scholar of the law. Your opinion matters little here." He turned away again, as if to brush her off like unwanted dust.

"Perhaps my opinion matters little, but my experience does not." The volume of her voice surprised even her, hooking Mr. Culver back with a startled expression. "I know what I saw, and that boy was terrified. He was shaking. He was in fear for his life. That isn't a matter of opinion."

Cora looked across the crowd, each person waiting with bated breath for Mr. Culver's answer. They'd come for a show, hadn't they? Her gaze caught on Ellis, eyes transfixed upon her. How justified he must have felt in that moment to hear her name dragged through the mud, to have his hired lawyer question her existence in front of the whole town. Yet as his eyes met hers, she saw nothing but concern in them.

"You spend a lot of time around criminals, I suppose." Mr. Culver fairly spat at her now, his eyes white with venom. "Your chosen profession makes you an expert, does it? Do you take a measure of a man's soul when you bed him?"

Cora gasped along with the watching spectators. Her gaze darted to Justice Morgan, but the man's eyes practically rolled up in his head. He had washed his hands of this town long ago.

Cora's back teeth clenched as the attorney ambled toward her. "You need not get any closer, Mr. Culver. I can already see your measure from here."

The man froze in his tracks as fresh whispers ricocheted off the walls.

"You think you can hurt and humiliate me by dragging my personal life across the public eye like the act of a circus clown, but I stand for more than a job, Mr. Culver. I am a human of flesh and blood." Her chest pumped. "I breathe just like you. I weep, I laugh, I fight. I have a soul just as you do. Don't try to diminish my testimony because you think my kind is beneath yours. Our bodies will all return to dust in the end. When we stand before our maker, you will have just as much explaining to do as I."

The church bloated with awestruck silence, not a soul moving a muscle. Even Mr. Culver stood fixed in place, his jaw hinged open.

Cora pushed to her feet, her veins pulsing with rampant blood. "May I go, Justice Morgan?"

With a grim expression, he waved her on. "You may, Miss Blackwood. In fact, I think we all need a recess." He banged his gavel on the table. "We shall reconvene in ten minutes. Everyone get a breath of fresh air"—his scathing eyes raked the prosecuting attorney—"especially you, Mr. Culver."

Keeping her gaze far above the sea of curious faces aimed her way, Cora marched down the aisle. She couldn't let them see her turmoil, couldn't let them sense the tears burning beneath her unbothered eyes. They'd come for the satisfaction of watching her squirm, and she refused to give it to them.

A moment before she reached the open doors leading to the foyer, Cora whirled around with distinctive purpose. She found Mr. Culver near the witness stand, touching his fingertips together as if calculating what had gone so horribly wrong for him. "By the way, Mr. Culver." His head popped up at her mention of his name. "Esther should be free tonight. Don't you prefer her on Mondays?"

To the explosion of riotous laughter and gasps around her, Cora reeled back and made for the outer doors. Madam Carey would surely punish her for exposing one of their regulars, but at this point she didn't care. She thought only of the way he looked at her, as if peering through translucent glass. As if she mattered not enough to consider human.

The doors clattered behind her as she marched down the front steps and into the churchyard. Perhaps it was only the first step in her journey toward freedom and standing up for her true self.

Sixteen

ELLIS STARED AFTER THE church doors as they swung open and crashed in on themselves again. In the wake of Cora's riotous exit, he could look nowhere else, think of nothing but her words as she'd stolen away that loathsome lawyer's accusations and pointed his mirror of self-righteousness back at him. He'd never seen anything like it.

Adrian hooked his attention, clapping his hands and laughing despite the looming death sentence hanging over him. The church had erupted in a similar fashion, stoic faces lifting with glee, jokes replacing their furtive whispers. She'd masterfully transformed this place into the true circus it was, pulling back the curtain on the actors playing their roles.

Without even registering the movement of his feet, Ellis pushed through the crowd and trailed her. The pain in her eyes had been tangible, reaching out to him as he sat on the front pew of that church. Her courage had made his heart stop.

In spite of everything—knowing she gave herself freely to different men every night, knowing she'd shared their intimate moments with Jeremiah Anderson, he couldn't resist the pull. She'd spoken to *him* in that brave testimony, to everyone who'd pigeonholed her for her life choices. And instead of the urge to change her, he now felt compelled to *ask* her about her life experience.

His breath came in painful jabs as he reached the front doors and flung one open. Sunlight spilled over his face, warm and exposing, revealing her distant fleeing form, now halfway down Main Street. His heart squeezed as he stumbled outside. He *must* speak with her before she went on another moment thinking he reviled her.

"You'd best stay here, Sheriff McCraw." A woman's voice caught him off guard. Ellis turned, wide-eyed, to see Madam Carey circling him from behind. "You've already made enough of a spectacle running after her. The town will not forgive you if you try to chase her down."

His mouth hung open, shock spidering through his middle as if she'd hit him in the gut. "I don't care what the town thinks." He only cared about *her*. The realization stung after so much strife between them.

"You say you don't care, but you will. When they turn against you and take your job—you'll care then." Her slightly wrinkled eyes surveyed him, the fan in her grip slapping against her palm. "The last sheriff learned quickly. It doesn't matter what you do. It matters only how you look to the people of this town."

Ellis's hands clenched into fists at his sides. "Am I to be compared to a rogue like Jones? To a thief and a murderer who cared only for himself?" His breath came hot as he glared down at her. "I am not so easily bought. I take my responsibilities seriously, and I will not let you intervene."

Before he could shove past her, she laid a commanding hand on his forearm. Her gaze climbed to his, polite on the surface, yet stewing with malice. Her glittering fingers tightened. "You will not let someone who can help you intervene, yet you chase after a little harlot as if you're her lapdog?" She shook her head, tongue clicking. "My, my, Sheriff McCraw, do you have your priorities scrambled. Let me help you unravel them, hmm?"

His eyes narrowed. "What are you talking about?"

Just then, he noticed a man creeping from the shadows. He stood obediently behind Madam Carey, lacing his hands together in front of his tall, wiry frame. Ellis had seen him before among Anderson's men. He comported himself as a pompous weasel, his stained grin betraying a man of no scruples, only greed.

"I've hired Jorgen here to oversee the girls." Her crystal headpiece flashed in the sunlight as she looked his way. "He protects them from men like you—those who seek time with my girls without paying the proper fee."

Ellis's jaw worked. "I've never sought out any of your girls, and I've spoken with Cora only in the commission of my job."

A laugh burst through her rouged lips. "Is it not your job to be honest, Sheriff?" She tossed him a pitying look. "Come, now. Everyone can see you desire her. It's written all over you." She assessed his tense frame with unconcealed mockery.

Ellis could do nothing but clamp his teeth together and stare back at her. He could not deny his attraction, nor the unstoppable force that had led him to kiss Cora upon their first meeting. Yet everything that had come after—the lies, the arguments, the betrayal—he'd stuffed so far inside, he didn't comprehend his true feelings. He knew only the compulsion to understand and to learn more, to find out who she truly was.

"Do you think the citizens of Gold Strike have missed your interactions with her?" Madam Carey opened her fan, fluttering it despite the autumn winds. "Do you think they don't talk about the night you came to the brothel and purchased time with her so publicly?"

His nostrils flared. "That night—"

"I'm not judging what you did, Sheriff McCraw." Madam Carey's gloved hand silenced him. "You paid for that time. You could do whatever you liked, so long as she was unharmed. But the town will never believe you didn't have your way with her. They've already deemed you a hypocrite."

Stomach roiling, Ellis stared into the blustering trees, the curtain of evergreens dotting the mountainsides. If he'd already lost the town's trust, what could he do? In just weeks, he'd managed to alienate them, Cora, likely soon the few people still working for good on his side. What change could he possibly make when they all abandoned him?

"Don't look so hopeless." Madam Carey's inauthentic laugh rang in his ears. "I may have just the solution for you."

His gaze drifted back to the madam, who fluffed her salt-and-pepper hair with one hand. "What kind of solution?"

"You clearly have affection for my girl, and I'm not willing to lose her. Besides"—her manicured brow hooked—"there's no way a man like you could marry a strumpet—not if he wants anybody to respect him ever again."

A cold, devious light slithered across her gaze. "If you want to have her, you can. But I must warn you—she brings in a hefty commission every week."

His lip curled. "What are you saying?"

"I'm saying, my dear sheriff, that you may have what you'd like and retain your public front." Her hand slid to his, grasping it as if she understood him in a way nobody else could. "You pay me the right amount, and Cora will come to you. You won't have to set foot in the brothel. She'll be discreet, and best yet, you won't have to share her." She smiled seductively. "Doesn't that sound like a lovely plan for everyone?"

Ellis yanked his hand back, his eyes hunting her presumptuous face. She wanted Ellis to pay her money so he could use Cora however he felt, so she would come to him night after night without a say in the matter, her presence in his life no better than a slave? His stomach lurched. What a despicable woman.

"I do see the moral dilemma this must cause you." Her head angled in feigned sympathy. "Think of how this could change Cora's life. It's bound to be better serving only one man than whoever pays for her each night. You wouldn't just be paying for your own pleasure."

The agonizing truth of her words splintered through him. He could pay simply to relieve her burden, to let her come to his home and rest, rather than having to imagine her in the arms of somebody else every night. Still, she would have no say. Would she even want that? And what else would Madam Carey expect with such an arrangement?

"Perhaps we could discuss the fee." She laid the charm on thick again, as if luring a fly to honey. "I'm happy to negotiate. There may well be more than just financial contributions with which you could benefit me, Sheriff McCraw."

There it was. Her true aim amid the subterfuge—to have another sheriff she could lead around like a trained pet, who would do her bidding without question. He would not play into her games.

Ellis finally spoke, his voice clear and unshakable. "If you know what's best for you, ma'am, you will desist from trying to bribe me. I have no tolerance for people like you, and I promise I will see your game ended before it even begins."

Horror flashed through Madam Carey's gaze, shattering her sugary composure. She stepped closer, challenging him despite her diminutive height. "You've made your decision clear. Now both you and the girl will face the consequences. Don't try to speak with her again unless you want her to taste the penalty of your foolish actions."

Grabbing her companion's arm, she pointed him toward the brothel. "Come along, Jorgen. We have better things to do." Wicked delight captured her lips. "You may have the girl tonight. I know how spirited you like to get. Just leave her without bruises this time." Her look of satisfaction could have melted Ellis.

He stood on the porch steps long after they flooded with people, staring off at the distant shadows of Madam Carey's brothel. He had to convince Cora to leave before it destroyed her—and perhaps him, too. He had to get her out.

The little town of Gold Strike, quiet beneath the purpling colors of dusk, had never looked so dismal. Cora leaned her forehead on her window pane, the glass cold beneath her skin. The shop where Sylvia had once shared her trade sat abandoned and desolate in the thickening shadows. Once upon a time, Cora had harbored dreams of working in that shop alongside her, perhaps starting her own. Those visions had long ago fled, giving in to painful reality. She would never realize her dream of making clothes for a living with the hands of suppression so tightly clamped around her throat.

She drew in a breath, catching a whiff of her own jasmine perfume. Chatter skittered up the stairwell, laughter already booming from the walls. Guests trickled through the front door as night set in and Madam Carey's came alive with the luring sheen of lamplight.

Cora touched her fingertips to the glass, each adhering to its translucent surface. She doubted she possessed the strength to descend those stairs and affix a smile to her face. How could she pretend gaiety and attraction when all she wanted to do was jump from this very window?

That morning she'd faced Mr. Culver's assault with bravery, an undefeated front—but inside she crumbled, remembering every word said to her. Recalling the way the townspeople looked at her like nothing more than an ant to be stepped on. She was nothing, *nothing*. The sooner she embraced that, the less her heart would have to break each time the world rose up again to remind her.

The tap of footsteps in the hall brought her head off the window. Madam Carey come to force her downstairs, no doubt. What kind of punishment would await her if she refused? With sickening morbidity, she pondered letting it happen—defying Jorgen again and again until he killed her in his fury. At least then it would be over.

Whispered voices near her door prompted her bare feet across the floor. It didn't sound like Madam Carey. Sinking to her knees, she pressed both hands against the door and squinted through the keyhole. At first, she saw nothing—only blurry figures moving in between the soft shadows. Then, as details emerged, she froze.

Several doors away, Jorgen stood against the wall, embracing a female figure. Cora squinted harder, focusing on that curvaceous frame and beaded shawl. Her laughter lit the air, leaving no question. *Allison.* What was Allison doing cavorting with Jorgen behind Madam Carey's back?

Ducking his head, he kissed her neck. The action produced moans of encouragement from Allison's throat, sounds that made Cora's hair stand on end. She wedged her ear against the door, straining at the low tones drifting through it.

"You should stop before Madam Carey catches us," Allison said breathlessly.

Jorgen growled, continuing to kiss her. "Madam Carey won't care—not after the money I'm going to make her."

Cora bit her lip. *What money?* What had Jorgen ever been good for but hurting people?

Allison laughed again, the sound reverberating against Cora's door. "Did you really beat Laurel within an inch of her life? I would have paid good money to see that. She always treated me like I was beneath her, like being Red Fox's favorite was such a claim to pride."

"Yes, well, she's nobody's favorite anymore." Jorgen joined her in a rumbling laugh that twisted Cora's middle. "She did make me a hefty commission, though. You could practically see the greed sparking in Madam Carey's eyes. She had enough of her haughty ways."

"We all had—just like Polly and Elizabeth and that snob Elena." Allison's tone scathed. "I'm glad they're gone."

Cora's palms slid down the grainy wood of her door. *Polly and Elizabeth and Elena.* Each woman had left in the recent past for various reasons, but when she thought about it, Cora couldn't remember their actual parting. Ellis's questions about abducted girls zipped through her mind. Could there be anything to his claims?

"I hope you haven't gotten too attached to your friend Damaris." Jorgen's voice pulled her from her funneling thoughts. "I hear she's not performing well."

"She's fine. It's Cora I wish would meet an untimely end." Allison's purring voice took on the edge of annoyance. "She's been Madam Carey's pet for too long. She thinks she owns this place."

"I don't think you have anything to worry about. I heard the madam trying to sell her off today."

"Sell her off?" Allison giggled. "Who did she try to sell her off to?"

"Sheriff McCraw, of course. The only man fool enough to follow her around all moon-eyed. He refused her. Couldn't be bothered to step down from his lofty heights, even for the princess of Madam Carey's."

Allison huffed. "It figures. Cora is overpraised and approaching an age where she's hardly desirable. Soon she'll be about as useful as a wooden nickel." She paused, as if expecting validation. When she received none, her voice rose, more bitter this time. "Come on, let's do what Madam Carey told us to. She'll be expecting me downstairs by now."

Cora scrambled to her feet as their steps approached her door and a knock landed hard against the wood. "Cora, are you in there?" Allison's call could be mistaken for sweet if she hadn't just wrung her out to dry.

Straightening her hair and disheveled skirts, Cora took a moment to breathe before reaching for the doorknob. Whatever lay on the other side, she doubted she wanted to face—but her hesitation could only intensify it.

"Yes? What may I do for you?" She stood back from the door, keeping her eyes pinned on Allison and off the taller frame at her side.

Allison rolled her eyes. "You do know it was time to be downstairs half an hour ago, don't you? Or are you superior to our timetable, just as everything else?"

Cora gripped the door. "I was just putting on my shoes. I lost track of the hour." She lifted one bare foot, wiggling her toes.

Allison scrunched up her nose as if Cora had stuck them in her face. "Don't bother. I came only for that sapphire blue gown you sometimes wear." She shouldered into the room, looking around with raw envy. "Madam Carey thinks Damaris will look prettier in it, that perhaps she'll fetch a higher price"—a laugh bubbled out her throat—"as if the men care what she's wearing."

"Of course." Cora made for her wardrobe and opened it, quickly selecting the mentioned tulle gown and shoving it into Allison's arms. "Here you are."

Allison glared at her. "What's wrong with you tonight? You're behaving so pleasantly."

Cora forced a smile. "Would you rather I scorn you?"

"It wouldn't make me wonder if you were up to something." Allison eyed her skeptically a moment longer before turning toward the door.

Cora jogged a few steps after her. "What do you mean by telling me not to bother coming down? Does Madam Carey have a special assignment for me?"

Ignoring her question, Allison slipped from the room, pausing only to slide a triumphant look Jorgen's way. "I'll see you later."

In the wake of her parting, Jorgen stepped into the room and closed the door. His teeth bared in a greasy smile as he perused her the way he had the first time he came to the brothel.

"I must get downstairs. Madam Carey will be wondering where I am." She tried to angle past him, but he caught her around the waist, his breath hot against her cheekbone. When Cora dared to meet his leering eyes, the truth settled deep within her.

He ran a clammy finger down her face, anchoring his hand at her throat. "You have no assignment tonight but to please me." His lips spread to reveal stained teeth. "Tonight you are mine."

Seventeen

Ellis leaned back in his office chair, his limbs weak and head pounding. Perhaps Madam Carey was right, and he wouldn't last long in this town. Already his every effort had proven futile. Pushing himself out of the chair, he rose up and stretched his back. The day's proceedings had worn on him until he pictured himself as nothing but a thread frayed down to a single string.

Despite his every effort to present the facts of the case, the jury had ingested every bit of salacious gossip presented on the witness stand. Hanging for young Adrian Fox—it was their only answer, despite clear evidence that he'd merely stood there while the rest of his gang gunned down Isaiah Anderson. The boy would die for trying to please his father.

Ellis cleared his blurred vision with a few rubs of his eyes before yawning and making his way toward the lobby where Wainwright stood guard. Most of the deputies had fallen asleep by now in various parts of the jail. He couldn't risk sending one of them home—not with the certainty of Red Fox showing up to rescue his boy.

Shuffling up behind Wainwright, who stood in the open door, Ellis clapped him on the shoulder. "You're a good man, Wainwright."

The deputy half-turned, clutching a pistol at his chest. "I'm only doing my job, Sheriff."

And a fine one at that. "Maybe you should take a rest. Let one of the others handle it for a while."

"No, sir." His head shook. "I'll stay right here if it makes no difference to you. I'm not tired."

"Suit yourself." Ellis glanced at the clock on the wall. The hands indicated 1:20 a.m. When had it grown so late? He'd been swimming alone in the sea of his worries—Adrian, Cora, the mysterious benefactor who had ordered Colton Baxter's death. The deep night had crept in without his say in the matter.

"What about you?" Wainwright's question brought his attention back to the doorway. "I thought you'd found a place to live. Why don't you use it?"

Ellis tossed him a lopsided grin, shaking his head as he walked toward one of the long desks situated across the room. "I couldn't go home on a night like this. Besides"—he eased himself onto the top of the desk and leaned against the wall—"I try to go there as little as possible. I'd rather the darker forces in this town not know where I live."

"That's not a bad idea. They will probably try to kill you in your sleep."

The two men exchanged knowing grins. Sometimes grim humor was all one had in the face of crushing defeat.

"I don't mind it here." Ellis rested his head against the wall. "I'd rather be in the company of partners than alone in the vast hollow of my thoughts."

Wainwright turned back toward the porch, scanning the darkness. The chirp of crickets carried in on the cool wind. "Are you still blaming yourself for the boy?"

Ellis winced. "How could I not? I brought him here, didn't I?"

"You were only doing what you thought was best. If he'd have been guilty, you'd be singing a different song now."

A heavy sigh lifted Ellis's chest. Knowing the truth didn't help anything. If he hadn't arrested Adrian Fox, he wouldn't now carry the burden of watching a sixteen-year-old die. "Can I tell you the truth?"

Wainwright glanced back at him with brows raised and nodded.

"If I could take it back, I would. I would let that boy run off with all the others and keep on living his life."

Wainwright's thoughtful eyes turned back to the night. "But you wouldn't know that without the knowledge you have now. You would have blamed yourself for letting him go, for not catching anybody responsible for Isaiah Anderson's murder."

"I suppose so." Ellis crossed his ankles over one another on the desk. "Though I still didn't catch anyone for the crime either way."

Wainwright leaned against the doorframe. "You didn't know what this place is like. Most people here are more excited for an execution than actually learning the truth."

"But I do know human nature. I know how men are." Closing his eyes, Ellis let memories of home drift over him. Of comfort amid uncertainty. Of long talks with his father before the fire and singing with his mother in the church choir. How distant it all felt now, with the world rising against him and his every concept of reality shaken.

Boots scraping the floorboards prompted his eyes to open again. Wainwright's body had stiffened, his ear turned toward the night. Movement from far down the hall launched Ellis to his feet.

Wainwright squinted against the inky blackness before his voice came, strained and quivering. "They're here. I can see forms moving down the street."

"Close the door. Don't stand in the direct line of fire." As Wainwright obeyed, Ellis moved toward the hallway that led to the jail. "I'm going to see what's happening in back. I'll summon the deputies your way. Don't fight anybody unless you have to."

"Yes, boss."

Drawing his pistol from its holster, Ellis held the gun at his side as he traversed the hallway. He threw his head into rooms where men slumbered. "Everyone, wake up! To the front to help Wainwright! Everyone up!" He left them, confused and disoriented, his heart thrashing against his chest wall.

More sounds rose from the cells—whispered voices, the clink of metal. They'd already breached the interior. When Ellis got within sight of the three cells lined in brick walls, his stomach dropped. The jail's back door, normally locked with a steel bar, was completely gone, presumably removed by the hinges. Next to the gaping doorway admitting the earthy smells of night, Adrian's cell stood open in a similar fashion, the door off its hinges and leaning against the bars.

Ellis glanced around. Had he remembered to leave a guard on duty to watch the boy—or had his torn ideals chosen to let him forget? His hands began to sweat, wetting the cold steel of his gun. With stealthy movements, he crept closer to the cell, where another form materialized beside Adrian. *Red Fox.* His distinctive hair gave him away, even in the low light. He had Adrian by the arm, ready to lead him into the night.

"I wouldn't do that, Mr. Fox." Ellis's voice froze them like startled opossums.

Red Fox stepped back with hands raised on sight of Ellis's pistol aimed his way. "This doesn't have to get bloody, Sheriff. I only came for my son."

"And your son is my prisoner." Ellis tramped forward, his boots echoing in the bare hallway. "He was convicted today in court of murder."

Red grunted. "You know that ain't true. I heard what you said about my boy in court. You know he didn't kill nobody."

Ellis's jaw tightened. If only the jury would have listened and not put him in this precarious spot. "Nonetheless, he was convicted in a court of law."

"Blast your courts and juries and law." Red's eyes flashed with a stirring fire. "You know my son is innocent. What kind of justice lets a youth die by the hangman's noose when the evidence says he didn't commit a crime? What kind of a man are you to allow this to happen?"

Ellis's mouth went dry, his gaze darting between Red and his frightened son. Adrian implored him with wide, vulnerable eyes, eyes that dove beneath his skin and into his soul. *What kind of a man are you, Ellis McCraw? What kind of a man did you vow to become when you assumed the badge of the law?* His hand shook ever so slightly.

How could he ignore his duty to ensure the court's decision was upheld? He'd been hired to do a job and do it well. That didn't include thwarting the will of a jury who had been lawfully appointed. Yet as he gazed into Adrian's injured expression, the alternative made his lungs beg for air. A sixteen-year-old would walk to his early end tomorrow simply for standing on the street while his father's gang gunned down a man so much guiltier than he. His father stood beside him, desperate to save him, and Ellis understood with crippling awareness that only he had the power to set things right.

"My boy didn't hurt anyone, Sheriff. You know it." Red Fox's hand slipped over Adrian's head, ruffling his dark locks. "He's a good boy. I never should have brought him into my corrupt world."

"No, you shouldn't have." Fire blazed from Ellis's core down the tense arm still aiming his gun at the outlaw. "This is your fault, Mr. Fox. You've made countless bad choices, chosen a life of greed over your own family."

"I know it," Red said, his voice strangled. "Don't you think I know it?"

Despite his every effort to remain hardened against the faces looking back to him, pity swelled in Ellis's chest. Hadn't Adrian himself said the world wasn't black and white, but a myriad of gray shades? The truth of it had never rung so palpably as it sank into him and settled down in his soul. This quandary had no good answer.

Shouted orders from the front office diverted his mind. Ellis stepped closer, training his pistol firmly on Red Fox's chest. "Do you have the power to stop your men, to signal them before any of my deputies get hurt?"

Red swallowed and nodded. "I do."

"And do you promise to keep your son out of your affairs from now on, to keep him safe, and to teach him the right way to be a man?"

Red's head bobbed again, this time more aggressively. "I will, Sheriff. I promise. I'll send him off to live with his brother if I have to, or"—his shoulders raised—"whatever I need to do. I won't let him become like me."

Against his every instinct, against the years of training that had taught him what to do in this moment, Ellis lifted his gun and held it at his side. His gaze washed over Adrian, willing his father's words to be true. He deserved so much more than a life of thievery, killing, running from the law. He deserved a future.

Ellis's head ticked toward the open back door as he holstered his pistol. "Go quickly, then. Call your men off my deputies. Speak of this to no one." He caught Red Fox in a solemn stare before he could pull Adrian out the door. "Don't cross me again, Mr. Fox. I'm doing this for your son, not for you. I'll gladly string you up the minute you put my citizens in harm's way."

Red dipped his head in understanding. "Thank you, Sheriff."

In seconds, they'd slipped out the door, a mess of stomping boots and kicked-up dust. Red's whistle blasted through the air, summoning his gang back to his side. No gunshots blistered the night's perfect silence, only the rise of befuddled voices from the front office. *Follow my orders. Don't chase after them. Don't fight.*

Legs weary, Ellis dropped to the thin mattress laid across a simple wooden frame and plunked his elbows on his knees, burying his face in his hands. He stared into the vast canvas of black enshrouding him and questioned his every decision. Would he look back on this day and regret it? Would he wish Adrian Fox had met his appointed execution when he turned into a glass image of his father and terrorized Gold Strike with his crimes?

He couldn't know the outcome. He could only embrace the truth of this night. A wayward child would go on. He would keep breathing, keep living out a new chance every day to become something new. By defying everything he held dear, Ellis had given him that chance. Now he had to live with the consequences.

Eighteen

THE NIGHT, BATHED IN an ominous fog, surrounded Ellis as he and Honeydew ambled through it. He urged her on with a click of his tongue, through the shadowed patches of forest and under a canopy of winking stars masked by slithering clouds. Every once in a while, Ellis threw a glance over his shoulder. He couldn't afford anyone following him—not with his mission tonight.

An owl hooted from somewhere in the dense trees, echoing from limb to limb. Wind rustled the pine branches against one another, lifting their spicy scent across the air. Ellis glanced at the full moon overhead, casting a brilliant light on the trail. It couldn't be far now. Just a few more minutes, and he could let Honeydew snack on some wild grasses while he scratched his way out of the hole he'd dug for himself in this town.

Since the night of Adrian's escape, he'd noticed the looks he received from the citizens of Gold Strike, their dubious expressions, their judgmental glances. Fewer trusted him by the day, with rumors swirling over his relationship with Cora, his failure to keep a condemned murderer locked up, and whatever other shreds of titillating gossip people had cooked up. He needed more than theories at this point. He needed concrete evidence to make these people see the truth, perhaps to save Cora from certain disaster.

A rocky incline led him to the top of a hill that rolled into a clearing ringed in fir trees. Ellis led Honeydew across the open space, shivering slightly against the October winds battering his jacket against his frame. The air held a chill he wasn't used to, the looming promise of snow earlier than he'd ever known in Tennessee, and a colder winter ahead than he might have predicted.

A small house materialized in the moonlight—one story, simple, a utilitarian structure of stained wood without the homey touches one might expect in a person's abode. Sheriff Jones had been a bachelor, had he not?

After slipping off Honeydew's back, Ellis left her tied to a tree with easy access to grass and a trickling stream. With a few strokes to her glossy coat, he let his eyes wander the shadowed house and yard. The forest behind him swayed in the nocturnal breeze, but he saw no signs of human life.

Ignoring the twinge of misgiving in his middle, he untethered his lantern from Honeydew's saddlebags and set to work lighting it. No use coming all this way and allowing fear to keep him from conquering what lay beyond. From what Wainwright had told him, not a soul had traversed this property since Sheriff Jones plummeted to his death.

The house sat in eerie silence, a foreboding mass against the quiet night. Ellis took one step up the porch at a time, attempting to minimize the creak beneath his feet, as if it might rouse the sleeping giants within. Jones had no family to speak of, and those listed in his will had yet to make the journey west in order to claim or sell his property. There should be nobody here, and yet he found it difficult to shake off the bizarre premonition of being watched.

Finding the front door locked, Ellis bashed his elbow through the window beside it and reached in to unlock it. "Forgive me, Sheriff Jones." He'd pay for the damages if necessary.

Inside, the house smelled of tobacco tinged with mildew. The strands of light streaming from his lantern illuminated a scant sitting room and a kitchen off to one side. Beyond a couch and set of chairs, a narrow hallway stretched, presumably to Jones's bedroom.

The floorboards groaned beneath his weight as Ellis crept across the space and stopped at a braided rug. Would he find anything here, or just a lonely graveyard of a man's wasted life?

Compelled to a stone fireplace, he stood at the mantel and lifted a cedar box sitting atop it. Inside lay a collection of cigars. Ellis lifted one from its bed and held it to his nose, inhaling tobacco and cinnamon. Beside it, a collection of expensive whiskeys graced the fireplace. For the humble home he dwelled in, Jones appeared to have savored the finer things in life.

His gaze swept the meager furnishings and undecorated walls, but nothing of interest stood out. If Sheriff Jones spent much time in this house, it didn't show. His kitchen held only the bare necessities—a few pots and pans, a stove in need of a good scrub, mismatched dishes in a cupboard about to fall off its hinges. Even his dish towels appeared as if cut from a broad cloth and hastily stitched around the hem. Some good his ill-gotten money did him. His home appeared no better than a pauper's cabin.

Weary, Ellis crossed back through the sitting area to inspect the hallway. As expected, an equally sparse bedroom lay beyond the open door. Beside a narrow bed topped in a patchwork quilt sat a small chest of drawers. In the corner lay a writing desk, complete with several scattered sheets of paper and an unorganized collection of pens. It was a start.

Ellis crossed to the chest of drawers first, upon which rested a few scattered books and trinkets. His fingertips grazed their worn covers, a comforting smell lifting off the pages as he rifled through them. The drawers held mostly clothes—vests and linen shirts, trousers meant for heavy wear. The type of wardrobe any man who'd spent a lifetime on the Western frontier would need.

Locating a few folded slips of paper beneath his woolen socks, Ellis drew them out and carried them to the writing desk. Using the light from his lantern, he spread the pages over the desk's surface and scanned the elegant writing. Their contents held private correspondences, declarations of love, a woman's heart poured across the pages. *Interesting that he never married.* Ellis flipped them over one by one, finding the name Elena at the bottom. Whoever she was, she hadn't held back her affection for the dubious lawman.

Ellis sighed, sitting back against the chair and eyeing the sloping writing desk. Perhaps he'd find nothing here. Maybe Sheriff Jones had burned any evidence that would matter. Yet something inside urged him onward. He had to know, even if knowing only created more questions.

Folding the letters into his jacket pocket, he bent down to inspect the narrow tower of drawers beneath the desk. Each one barely slid from its cramped position, but Ellis managed to look through them all. *Nothing*—only spare pens, ink, wax, and a seal.

He rose up, staring into the yawning darkness only punctuated by bands of yellow light from his lantern. "Where were you hiding, Jones? What don't you want me to see?"

After rummaging around the bed and searching the floor beneath it, he wandered back into the hallway. Whatever incriminating evidence stood against him, Jones had hidden it proficiently.

Perhaps he'd buried it beneath the ground in some secretive spot so deep in the woods, Ellis would never find it. Perhaps he'd made it so impossible to discover because he knew this moment would come, when another man would take his place and delve into the horrifying recesses of his malicious mind. Perhaps Ellis still fought a man whose final breath had ended in a scream and a cry for salvation.

A strong mountain wind beat against the sides of the house now, drowning out Honeydew's soft wickers. Outside the window, tree branches swayed and scraped. Ellis thought briefly of searching the property under the cover of night, but he knew he'd find little, especially in this weather.

Turning to the side, he rested his hands on a chair back. He'd discovered the other letters so easily in Jones's office. Yet here, without a bookshelf in sight, he found himself at a loss. His fingers scrunched the chair's rough fabric.

Ellis frowned, lifting his fingers in the lamplight and dusting them against one another. A crumbling residue remained across the ridges of his fingertips. He bent and squinted at the chair, finding more traces of chalky debris resembling pieces of chinking.

His heart picked up speed as he rounded the chair and stood before the stone fireplace once again, holding his lantern high. Beams of light shed over the rocks, and Ellis studied them in concentration until one in particular caught his eye. It appeared less uniform than the others, somewhat dislodged.

Ellis set his lantern on the mantel and stretched to his toes, seizing the stone in both hands. To his surprise and pleasure, it smoothly came loose from the others. A thin sprinkling of mortar followed after it. Ellis set the rock at his feet and stood tall again, burying his hands inside the cavern he'd exposed until they closed around a box. With a laugh, he pulled it into the lamplight and dusted it off.

"You certainly were a sneaky devil, Sheriff Jones."

The sleek cedar box swathed him in its earthy scent as Ellis lifted the lid. Inside, a thick stack of bills lay atop a pile of papers, no doubt payment for whatever nefarious deeds he performed for the underbelly of this town. Ellis dug beneath the money and pulled out the sheets of paper, a well-kept record by the look of it.

Setting the box aside, he thumbed through the papers as he sank into an armchair. They all appeared to be receipts with transactions and sums of money neatly added into columns. He held the first to the light, his eyes soaking up every word.

Blonde, five feet three inches, slim build, hard-working, attractive. His throat tightened as his gaze swung from a description of a woman to an amount of money and a record of purchase. The next page read similarly: *Chinese, black hair and eyes, five feet two inches, thin build, bilingual.*

His stomach turned as page after page listed the description of a female and recorded an amount of money exchanged. The sums appeared much higher than those passing through Madam Carey's fingers every day. He'd stumbled upon more than a simple prostitution ring.

When he reached the end of the stack, he held the papers to his aching chest. Was this where Adrian's mother had gone, exchanged for hundreds of dollars and shipped off to God knows where? The thought made his brain start spinning. How could he even begin to remedy this problem if he hadn't the first clue where to look for these women?

With his new evidence tucked in his jacket pocket, Ellis left the rock on the floor and made for the front door. It was time to get back to the jail, where he could put himself to good work and run his discoveries past Wainwright. Perhaps he could make sense of them.

The wind whistled and blew his hair around as Ellis ventured into it. The night had grown colder, near freezing, the ground wet with icy dew. Honeydew stood where he'd left her, but something had shifted. The air had scattered his path with foliage and obscured the way back.

A smell carried on the wind—not the lush scent of forest, but sweat and grime, the distinct odor of a man. Ellis lifted his lantern toward the source just as an unseen force barreled into him. The lantern slipped from his fingers, shattering on the ground and igniting the grass. A body pressed against him, all grunts and ragged breaths.

Ellis grappled with the hands attempting to seize him, fighting back as muscles strained against him. Several punches flew at his head, prompting him to duck and weave. He returned the assault with forceful hits of his own, managing one to his attacker's gut and another to his firm jaw.

"Damn you, McCraw," a voice he'd become all too familiar with lit the air. Anderson stumbled backward, holding his face.

Ellis panted, shaking out his stinging hands. "I'm not the one who launched an attack in the dead of night." He peered through the firelight accentuating the curves and hollows of Anderson's face. "What are you doing all the way out here?"

"Following you, obviously." For the first time, Ellis noticed the knife he held gleaming in the building fire.

His throat dried. "You were planning to kill me."

"I *am* planning to kill you." Anderson sneered, a few silver teeth glittering. "I told you there ain't room enough in this town for both of us, Sheriff. It's got to be you or me."

Before Ellis could react, Anderson lunged at him with teeth exposed, his ominous blade extended. Ellis jumped back and back again, as quickly as his body would allow. Anderson's blade cut through the air, whooshing past Ellis's ear as it plunged downward. A split second before it could sink into his gut, Ellis twisted around and seized the outlaw's arm, pressing it at an unnatural angle.

A string of curses lifted off Anderson's lips, moans of excruciating pain. His fingers released the knife into the dirt, and his elbow swung back, jabbing Ellis hard in the stomach. Ellis stumbled back, his blood hot and pounding in his head, barely comprehending the vision of Anderson charging him once more.

Anderson's fist came again, smashing into Ellis's cheek, whipping his head to the side. A million stars overwhelmed his vision, clouding his senses. Yet still his fists flung wildly, guarding himself, preventing another assault. As soon as he could decipher anything, he landed another solid blow across Anderson's face, forcing him momentarily back.

Chest heaving, Ellis spat what tasted like blood and swiped a hand across his mouth. Anderson stood a short distance away, bent over and bracing his hands on his knees. His long hair, haphazardly hanging in strings about his shoulders, had matted with blood and dirt. His clothes were stained with sweat, traces of crimson licking the fabric.

The fire that started when Ellis's lantern pitched from his hands had grown waist-high, throwing cinders and illuminating the quiet night. From her tethered spot by the tree, Honeydew kicked and whinnied, protesting the ensuing fight.

"Give it up, Anderson," Ellis said between rasps for air. "I was called to this town for a reason. You cannot defeat me so easily."

Anderson wheezed, his head wagging. "I can't give up. I'm dead either way. Either you kill me, or I lose everything I've built here."

A bizarre sense of pity swelled inside Ellis. What a miserable existence—to assemble one's entire life on deception. What a pathetic human being. "Take what you've built somewhere else. Go terrorize another town."

Anderson gulped in several hasty breaths before his eyes met Ellis's in the firelight, cold and shimmering. "I refuse to believe you can't be beaten. You ain't but flesh and blood." Despite his obvious signs of pain, he lurched toward Ellis in a staggered, uneven walk. "I always knew a man would come who would test me, who would make me prove my own strength. I ain't about to back down now."

With a guttural roar, he surged at Ellis, but the sheriff had prepared for him this time. Flexing his forearms, he waited with hands out and seized Anderson by the shirt. Before the outlaw could snatch him, he whirled and threw him to the ground. Ellis climbed on top of the struggling mass of muscles and teeth, the fists flying his way.

Anderson managed several hits to his face before Ellis wrestled his arms down and subdued him with a punch, and then another, his fists pounding against flesh and bone until Anderson lay weakly at his mercy. His head lulled to the side, his hair veiling his defeated eyes.

"Enough!" Ellis pinned his arms to the ground on either side of his head, his chest heavy and breath quick. "Enough of this fight. Admit your defeat."

Silence settled over them, interrupted only by the occasional moan from Anderson's tremulous lips and the fire's sizzling pops. Anderson's muscles slackened beneath Ellis's hands—a trick or a result of the fight, Ellis couldn't be sure. He leaned over to catch his breath and still his rapidly thudding heart. Power surged through his arms and fists, adrenaline urging him to fight, but the moment had passed.

"Stealing a horse is one thing; kidnapping a woman is another." He barely heard his own voice in the baying wind. "I won't let this happen in my town."

Anderson tossed him a scornful look. "I ain't never kidnapped no woman except that Broderick girl, and I never intended to keep her past the trial or hurt her. I only wanted to keep her quiet."

Ellis's hands tensed on his wrists. "I just found evidence that Jones was selling women for money. The names matched dossiers he had on file in his office. Girls from the brothel." His face heated, bile rising in his throat. "Jones took those girls from Madam Carey's. I know he did."

"So what if he did?" Anderson scoffed. "It don't mean I had anything to do with it."

"You worked with Jones. I know you did."

"Yeah, I worked with Jones." His hateful glare slid into Ellis's. "I did plenty of work for him, but I ain't never had a hand in stealin' no girls. Women ain't like horses. You can't buy 'em and trade 'em and steal 'em. You may think I don't have no conscience, but I ain't about takin' a woman's life from her. That ain't who I am."

Ellis shook him in frustration. "Jones couldn't have acted alone. I know he had help."

Anderson cringed with every shake, air hissing through his teeth. "He had help, but I didn't give it to him."

Ellis's fingers curled around his shirt, hauling him upward, ready to shove him into the ground. "Then who did?"

"Madam Carey!"

At Anderson's sputtered words, he stiffened. "What?"

"Madam Carey's the one who sold them girls. She entices them to her brothel, and if they don't perform the way she expects, she gets rid of 'em."

Ellis's head angled. "She forces them back to the street."

"No." The single word chilled him. "If they ain't makin' her enough profit, she sells 'em. You can make a lot of money turning people into slaves."

Stomach turning, Ellis sat back on his heels. "Slaves?" How deep must the depths of depravity run in a person to sell another human being—to garner money from their pain? How far had this world sunk into pure depravity?

His gaze fixed back on Anderson, his fingers tightening. "Tell me what you know. You must know more."

"I don't." Anderson's head shook vehemently. "I've only heard whisperings, nothing concrete."

Ellis leaned near, his teeth gritted. "Tell me everything you've heard. Leave out one detail and I'll kill you, I promise."

Anderson hesitated, then swallowed. "The buyers are coming to town again soon. They plan to take Damaris, and—"

"And who?" Ellis shook him again. "Who do they plan to take?"

"And Cora. Maybe Cora."

With those simple words, Ellis's world collapsed in on itself.

Nineteen

CORA'S BEDROOM FELT COLDER with the wind whipping the sky outside, tossing the trees and bashing them against the sides of the brothel. She sat atop her disheveled blankets, barely noticing the man who laced his boots at the end of her bed. Would she even recognize him if she saw him again on the street? Would she recognize any of them?

He threw a sly smile over his shoulder as he trudged toward the door. "Thanks, Cora."

She couldn't find enough strength to acknowledge him, the most recent in a string of men who paid hard-earned cash to own her for an hour. They didn't care. She fed their depraved fantasies.

Alone in the quiet of her room, her thoughts ran wild. She imagined herself one of the scattered leaves blowing on the wind, thrashed and beaten but free. How many years had passed since she'd tasted such liberty? The freedom to think and to choose? The will to decide her own destiny?

Cora. *Cora.* Her mother's voice still echoed across her mind, a mere fragment of a memory. She could still see her standing atop the verdant, windswept cliffs, her red hair floating behind her on a breeze, her bright green eyes wide and inviting. She could still taste her Scotch broth and bannocks, feel her hands as they picked her up and held her close, as they soothed her after a nightmare. The notes of a lullaby still hummed in her ears, quieter now but just as sweet.

Had her mother cried when she'd been torn from her arms? Did she miss her still? Attempting to breathe against the raw ache of remembering, Cora turned on her side and hugged her arms around her middle. Her corset and silk robe did little to temper the chill rushing over her. She'd performed this trick a thousand times. Why did it seem to matter now? Why did her demons rise up, torturing her, calling her names she'd only heard in the secret shadows of her dreams?

The wind rushed in again, rattling the shutters and howling a morose tune until she couldn't stand it anymore. Cora pushed off the bed and walked barefoot across the floor to her wardrobe. Surely she was done for the night and could change into comfortable clothing. The festive din had died down in the main parlor, masculine voices chatting and hooting with laughter as they departed into the street.

She slipped her silk robe off her shoulders just as her door swung open. *Oh, no.* Why hadn't she thought to latch it after the last caller? Memories of Jorgen flashed through her mind, bolting through her like lightning. She couldn't handle another night of his proclivities, his desire to inflict harm. Her fingers closed around the hilt of a knife she kept hidden in her wardrobe, the only weapon at her disposal. If he tried to hurt her again, she'd kill him.

"Cora," another man's voice called through the dusky lamplight.

Cora dropped the handle of her knife, reeling back to find Ellis slinking through her door.

He exhaled when he saw her, snapping the door shut and leaning against it. "Thank God I got here in time."

"What do you mean? How did you get in here?" She froze at the color flooding his cheeks. How must she look standing there in nothing but a frilly corset and thigh-high stockings, her bosom pushed forward to amplify her every curve?

Cora quickly reached into her wardrobe and yanked out her robe, draping it over her shoulders and cinching it around her waist. "If you'd have come a few minutes earlier, you would have seen a lot more of me than that."

His jaw tightened, his look stony. Then, as if recalling whatever had brought him, he shook himself to life. "I snuck up the back stairwell—the one only the women use."

She planted her fists on her hips. "And how do you know about that?"

"Caleb, of course. He told me everything he could about this place."

"I see." Had Caleb divulged information about her? Had he provided the sheriff with everything he needed to trample her heart in one go? She shook her head. "You shouldn't be here. If Madam Carey finds you, she'll—"

"Let her come for me." He lifted his strong chin. "She wouldn't be the first person I had to fight off today."

Stepping forward, she discerned open wounds on his face, marks where someone had hit him. "Ellis, are you bleeding?" Without thought, her feet carried her to him. Her hand stretched outward until it suspended in the air, mere inches from his pinkened lips.

He averted his gaze. "I'm fine. It's nothing—though I suspect Jeremiah Anderson will be laid up for days after the fight we had."

A breath sucked through her lips. "Jeremiah Anderson? That scoundrel did this to you?"

"It doesn't matter now." He seized her arm. "We must get you to safety."

A warm sensation sprouted beneath his fingertips, but Cora pulled her arm away. "You're talking like a madman."

Ellis clenched his teeth. "We wouldn't even need to talk at all if you could listen to me for once. Your life is in danger."

Taking an unsteady step back, she studied him, from his tense arms, lashed with wounds, to his restless legs, preparing to run. He meant every word he said, but how could she trust him after all that had transpired between them? Cora had learned long ago not to put faith in anybody but herself.

She backed slowly in reverse, her head wagging. "I can't just go with you if I don't know why. This is my home, my—" The words choked her. This place had ceased to be a home so very long ago. "I can't leave. Madam Carey will kill me if she catches me."

"She'll kill you if you stay." His words yanked her gaze to his. She searched his face in the lamplight. After all these years, could it really be true? Would Madam Carey allow Jorgen to finish the job he started that dreadful night in the cellar?

Her legs gave way, and Cora sank to the unmade bed. "You must tell me what you know, Ellis. I can't make a decision unless I know."

Ellis huffed and drove his fingers through his hair, but in seconds, he'd nested beside her on the pliant mattress. "I went by Sheriff Jones's house tonight to search it, and I found these." Dipping his hand into his jacket, he produced a stack of folded pages.

Cora's fingers shook as she unfurled them and examined the printed text. "What is this?" Descriptions of women, sums of money. No, her mind wouldn't comprehend it.

"They're sales, Cora. Sales of girls from this brothel." He pointed to the first sheet of paper. "Think about it. You know her, don't you?"

Blonde, five feet three inches, slim build, hard-working. It sounded just like—no, not Polly. It couldn't be her. Then the next portrayal—a Chinese girl with bilingual skills. Madam Carey had never liked Sung Lee from the moment she hired her.

Tears burgeoned in her eyes. "I know them. These are"—her hand rose to cover her mouth—"these are all women who once worked here and have left."

"Not of their own accord." Ellis unfolded another few slips of paper with fanciful writing sprawled across them. "Did you know a girl named Elena?"

"Elena? Of course. She lived two doors down." Her mind produced a picture of a Mexican girl with olive skin and the deepest, most beautiful eyes Cora had ever beheld. "Don't tell me he sold her too."

"I don't know." The papers crinkled slightly beneath his fingers. "I found love letters she wrote to Sheriff Jones, declarations of her devotion."

Warm tears slipped down her cheeks. "She thought he would take her away from here, that his visits meant he loved her." She shivered. "She never listened to me."

"What happened to her?"

"I'm not exactly sure, but her room was empty one day. I always assumed they'd fought and she'd left." She glanced at the door, memories of Allison and Jorgen's conversation trickling back. "I suspect she was one of them."

Ellis shifted beside her on the bed. "Why so?"

"I heard them talking in the hallway the other night—one of the girls and our new bouncer. They mentioned Elena, along with Polly and another girl. Jorgen said Madam Carey was making money off whatever he was doing for her."

His nostrils flared. "Money off trafficking women. What a deplorable excuse for a human."

"And she's part of this?" Cora turned imploring eyes his way. "Madam Carey is the one who sold them?" As hostile as she'd turned these last few months, Cora couldn't help remembering the woman who had taken her in and given her a chance when she lay dying in the street. In some twisted way, she'd replaced the mother Cora had left behind in Scotland.

"That's what Jeremiah Anderson told me under the threat of death. I have no reason to believe he would lie." He sighed, his expression soft. "The woman essentially tried to sell you to me during the trial like a subscription to a newspaper."

Cora's gaze tumbled to her lap. "They mentioned that too. I'm aware that Jorgen is no friend of mine. He seems to have replaced me in regards to Madam Carey's favor."

A hush had overtaken the brothel now as feminine voices faded into rooms and doors closed behind them. Cora breathed in the perfumed air and pulled her robe tighter around herself. The material felt thinner now, the protection she'd imagined a mere illusion. The weight of Ellis's eyes rested upon her. She couldn't look at him, open and exposed, her soul lying vulnerable.

At last, his voice touched her ears, volleying a shiver through her. "Has he hurt you?" At her silence, his finger hooked beneath her chin and pushed it upward. "Cora, has Jorgen hurt you?"

Her eyes filled, even as she tried to summon the strength to keep her emotion at bay. She blinked, her lashes batting away tears. How had he *not* hurt her? Her mental anguish rivaled the skin still bearing the ache of his beating, even after the bruising had eased. Her gaze shifted to his, finding rest in the honest concern shining back.

She felt herself nodding. "Yes, he beat me." She bit her lip to suppress the sobs starting to rack her body. She would leave it at that. No need to mention Jorgen's dark depravities and pile added shame upon herself.

Ellis's jaw clenched, his eyes like granite. "I'll kill him."

"You can't kill him. That will only bring more trouble for you."

His fingers slipped from her chin. "Do you think I care what trouble it brings me? I can't just sit idly by while a man like him is harming women."

"You *must*, Ellis." Cora rose from the bed and faced the far wall. "It will get worse if you do anything."

"What does that mean?"

She clenched her fists. "All of the girls are in danger here now. To provoke Jorgen or Madam Carey can only bring more problems on us." His silence drove a knife through her. Didn't he understand? She had a responsibility to the girls in this place as a sister to helpless souls like hers, who'd wandered in without hope and deserved to survive.

Ellis stood behind her. She could sense him at her back, feel the intensity of his stare. When he spoke, his voice had softened to a tone she'd never heard from his lips. "Let me take you from this place, Cora. *Please.* I can't stand by and watch you suffer."

She swiped at the tears peppering her cheekbone. "I can't leave them. I have a purpose here, girls who depend on me."

"Girls who will suffer just the same if you're dead."

His words dropped an anchor in her stomach. Cora spun to face him. He looked desperate, harrowed. What did he know that she didn't?

"Anderson told me tonight"—he paused, his hands flattening on the legs of his trousers—"he said you're next. That you are one of the next girls Madam Carey intends to sell."

A dizzy sensation showered her. Cora reached for something to balance herself, but found nothing. Madam Carey—sell her? It was impossible. She brought in more revenue than any girl here, but the more she allowed herself to think about it, the warning signs she'd chosen to ignore blared in her face. Jorgen's beating. Her captivity. Madam Carey's sudden coldness to her. If only she hadn't defied her so publicly.

"I won't let you be sold, Cora." Ellis's voice snatched her from her spiraling thoughts. "I know you feel a burden to protect the girls who live here, but you can be of better use to them from the outside."

She nodded, her tense body relenting. "All right." The word barely strained from her aching throat.

Ellis's shoulders relaxed as he looked toward the door. "How many people are around this time of night? Do you think we can sneak out unnoticed?"

She shrugged. "If you got in, I don't see why we wouldn't get out." As if in a dream, she moved toward the wardrobe and began pawing through it. "I'm going to need something decent to wear. I'll catch my death in this robe."

He nodded. "Do it quickly. I don't know how much time we have."

Cora worked through the fear churning inside. Did Madam Carey plan to abduct her tonight? Her fingers closed around a sturdy woolen gown. She'd have to put it on with Ellis in the room, but what matter did it make now with death dangled precariously between them?

"Did Anderson say how soon Madam Carey planned to sell me—or whom she planned to sell me to?" She closed the wardrobe with gown in hand.

"He didn't know, or so he said." Ellis watched her remove the dress from its hanger. "He just knew you two were slated to be sold soon."

Cora halted in mid-motion. "Us two? Me and who else?"

His hand splayed beside him. "Damaris? I think her name is Damaris."

Cora collapsed against the wardrobe door. "They're planning to sell Damaris?"

"That's what he told me. She isn't performing as Madam Carey expected."

All hope fled Cora's body. She hugged the gown to her bosom. "She's our newest girl. I trained her. I knew she was having trouble fitting in, but I thought Madam Carey would give her a chance." Damaris was only a girl, barely older than a child. The thought of her locked in the chains of slavery for the rest of her life chilled Cora to the bone.

Ellis's boots scuffed the floor toward her. "We must hurry."

Her head shook. "I won't go without her. She needs me."

"Cora, we must." Fear edged his voice. "If we have to, we'll try to get her on our way out."

"You can't. She lives in the lower quarters with the other girls. You could never get down there without being seen."

"Then we'll come back for her." He seized her hand, pulling her toward the door.

"*No.*" Cora tugged her hand back. "I told you—I won't go without her. She's only a girl, Ellis."

A frustrated grunt issued from his lungs before he dragged his hands through his hair. "Why must you be so stubborn? Why can't you listen to reason?"

"Why do you care?" Her hasty words hooked his gaze, eyes that drove into her like the rush of a waterfall. Her chest surged. "Why are you suddenly so concerned for my safety?"

"I don't wish to see anybody harmed—"

"But I'm not just anybody, Ellis." She stepped closer. "You chose to seek me out—above Damaris, above the other girls. *Why?*" The word sounded more like a cry than a question. Why did he insist on leading her through these endless games that tore her heart open?

He swallowed, looking to the floor again before he dared to gaze into her eyes. "I don't know. I mean—I've tried to deny my feelings, but I—" His lips parted, no words getting through—only his impassioned breaths.

"You what?" Somehow in the laden seconds that passed between them, they'd grown closer. His masculine scent, a blend of earth and musk, launched a thrilling tingle through her. He reached out, tucking a chunk of hair behind her ear, his fingers gentle yet commanding. His thumb remained on her cheekbone, tracing the delicate lines of her face.

Cora held her breath. How many times had she pictured their kiss and remembered how it had radiated through her? Since that time, she'd convinced herself her memory had failed her, that she alone carried a false sense of euphoria about that moment. Yet standing here, letting her eyes wander his face, she couldn't deny the electricity between them.

Ellis's hand came to rest at the base of her neck, his fingertips softly pulsing. His intense gaze dropped to her lips, lingering there an agonizing few seconds before returning to her eyes. His throat bobbed, his jaw working. So much dwelt behind his yearning expression, yet silence engulfed them.

"*Please,* Cora." His voice faltered. "Please come with me. I need to know you are safe."

A hardened ache speared through her chest. If only she could. If only circumstances would allow her to close the distance between them and press her lips to his. To run away with him. But reality could never be so beautiful, nor so uncomplicated. Perhaps he felt affection for her in this moment, but what would happen when he woke from his dream and she was still the same soiled harlot? She doubted her spirit could survive such mutilation.

"I'll get her, and I'll help her escape when the time is right."

"No." He grasped her shoulder blade. "You won't get out alive."

"I will." She implored him, her head dropping to the side. "I always do. I've survived far more than you know."

Ellis took another gasping breath. "What can I say to convince you?"

"You can't, Ellis. I'm sorry." Stepping back, she let his hand fall away from her. Better he didn't touch her and awaken the longings within she didn't understand. "Where should I go when we leave here?"

He hesitated a moment longer before relenting with a sigh. "Come to the jail. I'll wait for you there, day and night. Just promise me you'll come."

Despite her trepidation, Cora nodded. "I'll come." If she could find a way to survive this, she would come.

Twenty

EERIE QUIET SHROUDED THE brothel, the tense stillness palpable as Cora spent the night perched atop her bed with a knife
in one hand, her eyes never leaving the closed door. Only a
whisper of wind remained from the gale that had swept over
them earlier. The rest of the house slept in unconscious bliss,
never suspecting the horror buried beneath their already tenu-
ous sense of joy.

From the lobby below, the clock chimed four o'clock—four
strident calls to announce the ungodly hour when not even
songbirds had yet awakened from their nests. Cora sat up and
adjusted her thick skirts. She had imagined at first she might
last the night and devise a plan of escape on the morrow. Yet as
the hours wore on and sleep eluded her, she'd donned her dress
and boots, ready for whatever came.

Rubbing her palm against one eye, she yawned and arched her
back. Much more of this and she would succumb to sleep whether
she wanted to or not. Pushing off the bed, she faced her door. It

was time. No good could come of waiting until morning, and a growing premonition told her waiting any longer could be lethal.

Bending low, she tucked her knife into a sleeve at her thigh and let her skirts fall back to the floor. *You can do this.* Yet even as she reminded herself, sweat seeped into the folds of her dress, her heart high in her throat.

The door groaned beneath her hands as she eased it open. The hallway, clouded with murky shadows, emanated a silent chill. Cora tiptoed past the doors of sleeping girls and across the landing, keeping on until she reached the stairway.

Her gaze cast into the shadows where Ellis had escaped mere hours ago. The urge to flee down the back stairs was almost overwhelming, but she couldn't abandon Damaris. The way forward held only death or redemption.

With every creak of the stairs as she lightly descended them, Cora grimaced. One wrong move and Madam Carey would have her head on a silver platter. When she reached the foyer below, she swiftly moved through the blue-black shadows, following the faint stream of moonlight pouring in from the windows.

The house was nothing but a darkened maze this time of night, a labyrinth fit for bumping knees and stubbing toes. Cora felt her way along the passageway toward the room Damaris slept. Only the rustle of her skirts and gentle tap of her feet across the floorboards accompanied her journey.

The common sleep room lay near the kitchen, a vast space meant for storage where Madam Carey housed the women who earned lower commissions or had fallen out of her favor. Soft sounds of slumber rose from the women's beds as Cora slipped past them. She licked her lips, intent on a single bed at the end, where Damaris's barely discernible shape lay. Her long, dark hair flowed freely across her pillow, her body curled on its side.

Ignoring the thud of her protesting heart, Cora crept to the side of Damaris's bed and leaned over her. "Damaris!" She prodded her gently. "Damaris, wake up."

The woman roused, a look of confusion knitting her brow. "What?" she asked, much too loudly.

Cora held her finger over her lips. "Quiet." She gestured for Damaris to follow, hoping she could see her in the dim light.

"What? I don't understand." Damaris squinted through the dark. "Who's there?"

Exhaling, Cora dropped to her knees on the floor and leaned close. "Damaris, you must be quiet. It's Cora. You need to leave with me right away. It isn't safe here for either of us."

Damaris's eyes popped open, white beneath the moon. She nodded swiftly, throwing back her blanket and swinging her legs over the side of the bed.

A rustling to her left froze Cora in her tracks. She glanced over at Allison's bed, occupied by a second figure curled around her. *Jorgen.* Her blood went cold. If he discovered her here, she would find no mercy.

"Quick, get back into bed," she whispered.

Damaris started. "What?"

"Pretend like you're asleep. Do it now." With a soft push, Cora propelled Damaris back and lifted the hem of her own skirt. Doing her best to make no sound, she scampered back between the rows of beds.

Allison groaned behind her, stirring in her bed. Her voice murmured, followed by Jorgen's deep timbre, as Cora broke through the door leading to the kitchen.

"Stop right there!" Jorgen's commanding voice sailed across the room, waking other girls from their sleep.

Cora broke into a run across the shadowed kitchens as feet pounded the floor after her. If she could only get to her bedroom in time, she might have a chance of escaping this. But the footsteps grew louder, gaining on her. Just before she reached the hallway, a hand snatched the collar of her dress and yanked her backward.

With the force of his pull, Cora flew back and collided with his solid body. Her bones rattled. She slid to the floor, pain lancing across her back and shoulders.

Hands like a vulture's claws clamped around her arms and flipped her onto her back. Tugging her up by a handful of her hair, Jorgen examined her face in the moonlight. Triumph captured his every sinister feature before his lips spread in a grin. "You didn't get enough of me the other night, did you? I knew you wanted more."

Cora scowled up at him. "I would rather bed a dog."

His coiled hand yanked her hair again, eliciting a wince through her teeth. "You're awfully mouthy for a girl I'm about to beat the tar out of."

Despite her determination to remain unmoved, a whimper formed on her lips. "Madam Carey will make nothing off me if you beat me. She won't allow it."

Running footsteps pattered the kitchen floor before Allison peered over his shoulder. Her face twisted on sight of Cora. "I knew it was you. You were trying to steal from me, weren't you? You have everything, and still you want more."

Cora pressed her lips together. Better Allison believe her ridiculous fantasies than know the truth.

"Come on." Jorgen hooked a hand under her arm and hauled her to standing. "I've had enough of your misbehavior. I'm taking you to Madam Carey."

The madam's quarters sat in the east wing of the sprawling house, a large set of rooms skirted by a flower garden. Cora kept her chin up as Jorgen dragged her through the ornate door toward an elaborate sitting room. Madam Carey stiffly sat on a tufted settee, garbed in a shimmering satin robe, her salt-and-pepper hair braided down her back.

Her face, normally powdered and painted to perfection, appeared sallow in the light from her rose-adorned kerosene lamp. Her shrewd eyes silently condemned Cora as Jorgen shoved her into a chair and breathlessly stood back. Madam Carey had never looked so haggard and old, her cheekbones accentuated by shadows, her deep-set eyes lined and weary.

"I dislike being dragged from my bed." Her gaze flicked from Cora to Jorgen. "I presume there is an explanation for all of this."

Jorgen slammed his hands down on the back of Cora's chair, quaking it. "I caught this one sneaking around the common sleeping room. She was up to no good."

"I see." The madam's jaw tensed. "And what type of no good was this?"

"I have yet to find out. I brought her in here before I succumbed to the urge to kill her."

Madam Carey's expression remained unimpressed, unfeeling. "I appreciate your inclinations toward violence when the need arises, but in this case, I would appreciate hearing her argument first"—she tossed him a warning glance—*"before* I hear your reasoning for being in the common sleeping room."

Jorgen stepped back, Cora's chair relieved of its weight. The intoxicating scent of Madam Carey's incense filled the room with a deceivingly calm ambiance.

Shifting atop her plush pillows, she regarded Cora with the look of a queen surveying her wayward subjects. "I'm ready for your explanation now, girl—if you have one. Out with it."

Cora gulped back the stinging rage and fear battling within her. The only plausible explanation for all of this would surely leave her as a casualty in Madam Carey's game.

"Forgive me, Madam Carey. I thought I heard noises coming from that room. I wanted to be sure everyone was unharmed."

The madam's lips twisted. "What kind of noises?"

Wiping her palms on her skirts, Cora allowed herself a fleeting glance in Jorgen's direction. He stared her down, fists at the ready, the veins in his neck popping. "It could have been pain, or I suppose it could have been—"

"Yes, I know what it could have been." Madam Carey's irritation with Jorgen seethed through her every pore.

He stomped toward her. "She's a liar. She didn't hear anything. We were only sleeping." At the madam's calm, upraised hand, he retreated.

"So you came to inspect what you thought was a problem, or perhaps gain a bit of useful information." Her fingers feathered toward Cora's disheveled skirts. "But that doesn't explain your attire. Why are you fully dressed and in boots, my dear?"

Cora's stomach constricted, her tongue suddenly dry. She never dressed like this in the brothel—not even to have breakfast. "I couldn't very well have come down in my underthings, now could I? Not with *him* on the loose."

Jorgen sneered. "A poor man's excuse for a lie. If she were really concerned, she would have come at once."

"Unfortunately, I am inclined to agree." Madam Carey set her fingers, bare of their usual rings, against her jawline. "I heard something about a theft."

Cora put on her best look of worry, hesitating a moment before relenting. "She took it from me first. I had no recourse but to take it back as she slept." Whatever *it* was.

The madam's tongue clicked with the shake of her head. "After all these years with me, you still lie to me. Whatever am I going to do with you?"

Her biting words of retribution, Cora held at bay. Lie? Yes, she'd told a white lie to save her life, but what grander sins lay at Madam Carey's feet? The ink on Cora's proof of sale had probably not even dried yet.

"I do have an idea, madam." Cora found her voice despite her insides tremoring and threatening to spill themselves across the settee. "I think I know a way to mend this."

Madam Carey's brow hooked with interest. "Go on."

Cora glanced over her shoulder at Jorgen. "I'd like to tell you alone, if you don't mind."

Jorgen huffed, but ultimately obeyed the madam's shooing fingers, his feet dragging behind him as he went.

The room felt colder, smaller with just the two of them in it. Cora looked into Madam Carey's steady gaze, determined to match her confidence. "I know I've sinned against you, madam. I feel it in my soul."

A derisive laugh bubbled on the madam's lips. "You won't get far groveling, my dear. You know how I feel about grovelers."

"I don't intend to." Cora's hands fisted in her lap. "I do wish to make amends, however. You were right. I've forgotten my place here. I never should have questioned your judgment or thought I could get on without you. You took me in when I was so young. I suppose I learned to take you for granted over the years—but I don't want to now."

The hint of softness tinged Madam Carey's features. "That's refreshing to hear. May I ask what brought about this change of heart?"

"Ellis McCraw."

"Ellis McCraw?" She laughed again, the sound ringing with malice. "What did that backward excuse for a sheriff possibly do to affect you?"

Cora's feet tucked beneath her chair. *Tread lightly.* The only path ahead was straightforward. "He came here tonight. He tried to get me to run away with him."

Lips parting, Madam Carey released the breath of someone punched in the gut. "My dear, I did not expect you to say that." Rising to her slippered feet, she paced before the settee. "How did he even get in here?"

"I don't know, but he did. He barged into my bedroom after my last client. He tried to convince me to leave you."

Madam Carey's questioning eyes ascended from the floor to Cora. "And you didn't."

"Of course I didn't." Cora set her hands on the arms of her chair. "This is my home. I cannot abandon it so easily."

Seconds passed, the tick of Madam Carey's gilded clock slowing Cora's breath.

She assessed her again, as if in judgment, before resuming her dignified stance. "I'm pleased to hear you think so."

Did her words pique the slightest modicum of guilt, or had the madam stomped out her conscience so long ago, she could no longer hear its voice? Cora guessed the latter as Madam Carey plucked a string of pearls from atop her dressing table and began running them through her fingers.

"I sensed that boy had certain feelings for you beyond his obvious display the night he came here." Her fingers closed around the necklace in her hand. "What else did he say?"

Cora sat back, pretending to think. "He said he loves me—that he's simply mad without me. He said I must be free of your poison."

The madam's eyes flashed. "Poison!"

Cora nodded. "He told me you cared nothing for me. That you tried to sell me to him as a bribe for his favor."

The madam's eyes shifted warily. "He said all that, did he?"

"I don't believe a word of it. He was desperate, pathetic." Cora toyed with the tassels dangling from a pillow. "He thought he could own me, just as you've warned me a thousand times of men like him."

Madam Carey smiled humorlessly. "Of all men, really."

"Anyway, I told him to get out, that I've been with you for six years and I trust you." Her shoulders lifted. "I could never trust someone like him, intent on acquiring a slave to wash his clothes and clean his house. To fulfill his carnal desires. To do as he says. I once thought I could live that kind of life, but I realize now I could never sacrifice the freedom I have here."

Holding her breath, she watched as Madam Carey turned and crossed to a table covered in crystal decanters. Had she said too much, laid her deception on so thickly, the world-weary woman would see straight through her? Yet as Madam Carey poured herself a glass of brandy, pride straightened her shoulders once again.

She turned Cora's way with two glasses in hand, a pitying simper on her lined lips.

"I believe you just learned a lesson I came to understand long ago." She slipped again to the settee with feminine grace, handing a glass to Cora. "It's a truth we all must learn in this profession. Without it, we're bound to have our spirits trampled by the masculine race."

Taking the offered glass of brandy in hand, Cora tried not to shake. "And what is that?"

"A woman with a husband may garner the respect of town folk. She may proudly raise her children and go about her days pretending to love the mundane dreariness of her life." She tapped her finger on her glass, rippling the amber liquid within. "But the euphoric facade fades quickly as her children age and don't need her anymore. As her husband grows fat and complains, and she comes to detest him more every day."

As if peering into a box of hidden treasures, Cora listened with rapt attention. Madam Carey never divulged this much of her tainted life philosophies.

The madam took a swig of her drink, pressing her lips together. "My mother was that way. She served my father tirelessly. She did everything for him, let him become the center of her life. And what did he do? As the years wore on and her looks faded, he found someone younger and prettier. He destroyed her."

She gazed at the far wall, as if looking into her past. "She made a man the center of her worship, and he all but killed her. Then he left her alone, without money or a leg to stand on. I made a decision that day when she lay on the floor, weeping for what was, the lost years she'd never get back." She blinked her uncommonly emotive eyes, finding Cora in the lamplight. "I promised myself I would never let my world revolve around a man. I would never depend on a man for my happiness or my financial stability. I promised myself I would stand on my own two feet, no matter what I had to do or where I needed to go."

She nodded toward Cora's untouched glass of brandy. Cora dipped her head and sipped the acidic beverage, barely feeling its warm sting as it funneled down her throat. She sat forward, enthralled with every word.

"Sex is a powerful tool," Madam Carey said, twirling her glass in her hand. "It can bring a grown man to his knees, convince him of anything. Wield that power to your advantage, and you can have whatever you wish. You possess a tool that no amount of money or education or politics can surmount. You can rule."

Cora gripped her cold glass. Somewhere inside the madam, a child had once lived—full of hope and dreams of her future. What a job her father had done to shape her into this unfeeling person sitting here now, concerned only for gaining wealth and influence through manipulation. *God, don't let me become this person.*

"Teach me."

The madam's lips curled at Cora's whispered words. She moved to the edge of the settee and touched Cora's wrist. "I would be happy to teach you, my dear, but after everything that's transpired recently, you must understand my trust in you has been challenged."

Cora's heart thumped in her throat. "What can I do to prove myself? I'll do anything you ask." And in the process, maybe she would find a way to get Damaris out of this wretched place.

A soft hand slipped over her cheek, the madam's fingertips stroking until Cora thought she might vomit. "I do believe I know just the thing. The town Halloween party is just days away." Her eyes glittered, darkening. "I have a job for you. Do it well, and you shall become my golden girl once again."

Twenty One

THE SLEEPY TOWN OF Gold Strike came alive on Halloween. Growing up in a little town tucked among the Appalachians, Ellis had seen his share of superstitions and celebrations, but nothing like this. An entire region, torn apart by politics and crime, materialized from their backwoods homes and businesses, joining together in one common spirit.

A full moon graced the occasion, its luminance shedding across the black sky as Ellis wandered beneath it down Gold Strike's main street. Every shop on either side of the thoroughfare had its doors open with candied nuts or molasses taffy at the ready. Lanterns glowed in shop windows and dangled from rafters down the boardwalk, lending the town a radiant glow.

In quiet awe, Ellis traversed the street toward a normally empty area of town near the lumbermill, now crammed with people and festivities. The smell of butter and cooking corn reached him before he spotted a woman standing before a giant kettle positioned over a fire, popping kernels and distributing them to people lined up behind her. Farther down, children leaned over barrels of water with their hands tied behind their backs, desperate to catch apples bobbing on the surface with their teeth.

Ellis sighed, taking in the spectacle with renewed vigor. He could almost believe good had overwhelmed this place, with children running to and fro, laughter echoing from tree to tree. A trio of fiddles sang jaunty notes to the sky, enticing couples to link arms and frolic to their buoyant cadence. As if life had bent low and breathed into this place, it had erupted with hope and possibilities.

"Sheriff McCraw, I see you're in good spirits tonight." Ellis looked up to find a tall figure in a cape and mask strutting toward him.

Ellis adjusted his own red paper mache mask, a staple of the festivities, he was told. "Reverend Sommers. I didn't know if I would find you here tonight." Many of the churches back home decried the secular observance of All Hallows' Eve, warning their parishioners of inviting the devil into their lives.

"I never miss it." Reverend Sommers gave him a jovial pat on the back. "I hope you enjoy your first Halloween in our town. There's nothing else like it all year long. We go all out before winter sets in and we're stuck inside until spring."

"Ah, something to look forward to." Ellis involuntarily shuddered at the mere thought.

Reverend Sommers laughed. "It isn't all bad. It gives a man time to reflect and to think." The eyes beneath his mask turned serious as he slid closer to Ellis. "How have things been fairing for you at the jail? I heard about Adrian Fox's escape."

Escape. Did anyone actually believe it when Ellis told them Red Fox had overwhelmed his men with guns? "An unfortunate incident. I hear the boy fled the county as soon as they took him, or we would have gone straight after him with more men."

The reverend eyed him sideways a few seconds, but failed to question him further. "I suppose it's heartening to know we have law in this place at all. Many towns must do without it in these parts."

A jab at his performance as sheriff? Choosing to push past it, Ellis nodded toward a pie-eating contest set up near a stand spreading the smell of caramel apples into the air. "There's a peculiar spectacle. Who is unfortunate enough to assume those seats?"

With a breathy laugh, the reverend's smile retook his face. "I loathe to say it will be me later on tonight. But first, they've enlisted Milton Placit, a senior elder at the church, and Fred Willis from the mercantile."

"You're a good sport to participate."

He shrugged. "We need a lift in spirits around here, especially after everything that has taken place this year. I'm only doing my part."

Just then, the crowd parted and Ellis spotted Edward Carter ambling through it with his daughter on his arm. "Would you excuse me, Reverend Sommers? I need to have a word with Mr. Carter."

"Of course." The reverend genially nodded. "Just don't conduct too much business tonight. This is all about having fun. Make sure to get in a dance."

His words directed Ellis's attention back to the makeshift dance floor, now swarmed with women in glittering costumes and styled hair. His heart swelled. Would Cora be among them? He couldn't allow himself to hope. Since he'd snuck into the brothel that night, he'd thought of little else beyond her safety. Yet not a word had trickled back to him, and his efforts to return to her had been thwarted by the madam's bouncer, faithfully guarding the brothel doors.

Edward Carter met him with a solid handshake. "Good to see you here, Sheriff."

"Always a pleasure." Faith's mouth curved in a pretty smile as she curtsied demurely.

"I must admit, I'm surprised to see you here." Ellis shoved both hands in his pockets. "You live in Missoula, do you not? I've seen you twice in the space of so many weeks. Are you normally this way so often?"

Mr. Carter's laugh boomed from deep beneath his waistcoat. "It is rather a drive, but it's worth it for the Halloween festivities." His long arms gestured around him. "They are the best in the region, bar none."

"My father and I never miss a year," Faith added. "He tried to skirt the obligation this year, but I would not have it, would I, Father?"

His eyes twinkled as they swept to her. "Indeed, I was a louse to suggest it. I thought business matters too important, but ultimately I arranged my schedule to attend. A daughter is always paramount." He lovingly patted her shoulder before turning his look on Ellis. "You'll understand when you have children some day."

If I have children. Though tempting, the prospect reminded him that children of his own would never truly be safe with menaces like Red Fox and Jeremiah Anderson running around. *And I'd have to commit to a woman first.*

Thrusting the notion aside, he forced a smile. "A noble ideal, indeed. I'm glad you came. I have something I wish to discuss with you."

"Please tell me it's *not* Mrs. Tillman's huckleberry pie." Mr. Carter bent close, speaking behind his hand. "The woman refuses to leave me alone until I've tried a slice and committed to taking an entire pie home. She's relentless."

Chuckling, Ellis shook his head. "I promise I'll buy one in your stead if you humor me a moment."

"Of course." Growing serious, Mr. Carter straightened. "Faith, perhaps you'd like to—"

"Don't worry, Father. I have plenty of things to do here. Take your time."

As the young woman moseyed off to inspect the carnival games, her father watched her go. "Nearly a woman and ready to see the world." His broad chest lifted and fell. "I'm not sure I'm quite so eager to watch her go."

"A father who loves his daughter never is." A picture of his own father flashed through Ellis's mind, questioning every suitor who dared step within a foot of his unmarried daughters.

"Potential husbands are already lining up down the street, I'm afraid." Mr. Carter's brow hooked. "I don't suppose you know any actual moral, law-abiding single men, do you?"

Ellis's cheeks heated. If Mr. Carter was insinuating what it felt like, he had no interest. A girl like Faith needed a younger man who would sweep her off on wild adventures and indulge her youthful inclinations, not someone almost ten years her senior and already set in his ways. "I'll have to keep an eye out."

Before Mr. Carter would divert the conversation any longer, Ellis took the reins. "I don't wish to detain you any longer than necessary. This is a night for you and your daughter to spend together, after all. I just had a small inquiry."

Mr. Carter tipped his head, though his gaze had wandered to a group of young men performing magic tricks in the open square. "Ask away."

"Forgive me for asking, but I'm new to this place." Ellis tucked his hands behind his back. "You are on the town committee, are you not?"

"I am."

"And you—have a say in fiscal matters?"

At that, Mr. Carter's eyes swung back in quiet assessment. "Do not be afraid to ask what you wish, Sheriff. I am quite influential on the right day. I'll do what I can to assist you."

Ellis blew out a breath. "I've been going over expenses for the sheriff's office. They were in shambles after the last sheriff's tenure."

"Yes, Sheriff Jones was never much good with money." Mr. Carter glanced quickly around them. "What have you found?"

"Only that the sheriff's office cannot keep running on so few funds. The debts are mounted against it already. Besides which—"

Mr. Carter's brows raised. "Go on."

"Well, as loath as I am to admit it, we need more deputies at the ready to be available for incidents like the one we encountered recently."

Lips puffing beneath his thick mustache, Mr. Carter nodded. "I heard about Adrian Fox's escape. You think it could have been prevented with more manpower?"

"The initial murder itself could have been prevented with more manpower." Ellis shook his head. "I witnessed the gun battle myself, and I could do nothing on my own to stop it. If I had more men patrolling the streets—"

"I see what you mean." Mr. Carter heaved another sigh and crossed his arms over his chest. "But you must know the budgets are stretched thin already. It would be quite a feat to convince the rest of the board to spend more money on an institution already fully funded by the county that many consider a luxury in these parts."

Ellis's mouth opened, hesitating a moment before plunging ahead. Should he even venture into his next argument? He *had* to. "What about private benefactors—men such as yourself willing to invest money into a noble cause? To invest in the security of—daughters, for example?"

A flicker of amusement laced with something deeper flashed across Mr. Carter's face. He studied Ellis a careful moment before replying. "Perhaps I've underestimated you, Sheriff McCraw. You are not one to miss the opportunity to seek an advantage."

"I am only looking out for the good of the town, sir."

"Indeed." Mr. Carter's gaze slipped back to the melee of dancers turning about the square. "In any case, my investments are few and far between. I keep my money as consolidated as possible. The opportunity for someone to seek corruption by allegiance with your position is too high. You know that, Sheriff."

The wind, carrying the scents of baked apples and cinnamon, ruffled Ellis's hair. That was precisely what happened to Sheriff Jones. Whether a conspirator or not, Mr. Carter had refused to take his bait. At least he'd moved another step toward trusting him.

"I do, Mr. Carter. I apologize. I suppose I'm too eager to see this town freed of its moral corruption."

"A valiant effort indeed, and I do hope to assist you." He clapped the sheriff's back, pointing him toward the festivities. "Try to enjoy one night, hmm? The fleeting unity of tonight only comes but once a year."

His companion melted somewhere into the crowd as Ellis watched the jovial display around him. Townspeople laughed and sang, young and old together, rich and poor. Bonfires lit the street, sparks flying against the black night. Everywhere he looked, freedom and merriment reigned. Perhaps he should take a moment to enjoy it.

A particular form amid the dancers caught his eye. Even with her face turned, Ellis recognized her. Clad in a gown of alternating peacock blue and emerald green, her sequined skirts glinted in the firelight. Her strawberry blonde hair, swept up in an elegant style, shimmered like copper as she waltzed to and fro in another man's arms.

Ellis's chest tightened, his breath coming harder. At least he knew she was safe, though watching her whirling among the other dancers, guided by another man's hands, sent his pulse pounding. Was this anger or jealousy? He didn't care. Ellis approached the group with singular focus, ignoring the curious looks of those he passed. He'd too long tried to meet with their approval and failed. Blast what they thought.

Cora's eyes widened beneath her mask as Ellis tapped on her partner's shoulder. "May I cut in?"

The man's brow quirked. "Aw, come on, Sheriff. We're not doing anything wrong. We're just dancing."

"Nevertheless, I insist I cut in." Without waiting for a reply, he swept Cora's hand into his and fastened her against him. They had already taken off to the notes of the singing violins before the man could find words to protest.

"Well, you're certainly here to make friends, aren't you?" Her plump mouth dimpled. "You could at least show some courtesy on Halloween, Sheriff. It *is* a celebration."

A disapproving sound rumbled his throat. "I could not celebrate watching you dance with somebody else."

Her fingers constricted on his shoulder. "And do I have a say in this?"

"Of course you do." Ellis led her about the swirl of dancers, keeping up a steady pace. "Do you protest my desire to dance with you?"

"I suppose not." Her mouth tilted in a smile. "You could ask next time. Buying me at auction, barging into my room, stealing me from my dance partner. It's all a bit—"

"Unconventional?"

"Cavemanish." Her sweet laughter lit the air. "You're behaving like a brute, and I'm not to be hunted for sport, Sheriff."

His hand on the small of her back pressed lightly, compelling her closer. "And what are you, Miss Blackwood?"

Her breath hitched, her eyes searching his face from beneath her sparkling mask. "I am a woman with a will of my own. I decide my own fate."

"Madam Carey seems to think you're a fine piece of bait with which to lure me."

A cloud passed over her eyes before she looked away. "Well, Madam Carey is wrong."

Ellis momentarily lifted the hand against her back to hook her chin. When her eyes came back to his, he stilled. Something dwelt beneath them, trouble she left unvoiced. What could she possibly have to hide after the conversation they'd shared in her bedroom?

The other dancers edged closer, forcing him to press her back once more and lead her along. "What is it? What are you not saying?"

She shook her head and sighed. "It's nothing. I have nothing to hide."

"What about what we said to each other the other night? You know you need to get out of there." He glanced around at those in hearing distance, all too caught up in their own affairs to listen.

"I will get out when the time is right, I promise." Yet the look in her eyes made his stomach sour.

"Cora, she hasn't convinced you that—"

"Madam Carey has done nothing. I just have some things to do first."

His arm held her tighter, his face nearing until their breath mingled. "I won't see your sense of duty allow you to get hurt. I can't."

Her eyes fell, her impassioned breath warm against his throat. "I won't, but I can't ignore it. I can't let an innocent person suffer."

Folding her into his embrace, he let his mouth rest against her hair and the delicate skin of her ear. "Please let me help you." *Don't make me watch as you walk this path of destruction toward your eventual doom.*

She pulled back, her eyes questioning, before they descended to his lips. If only he could pull her close and kiss her. If only he could show this entire town how he felt about a woman they had scorned. But it would only put her in peril.

"Not here, Ellis." She brought the hand holding hers to his chest, her fingers squeezing his. "I'll tell you everything, but you have to come with me."

Twenty Two

CORA'S HEAD BUZZED AS she led Ellis through the crowd by the hand, the once pleasant tune of the violin now an imposing drone. The laughter rankled her nerves. The singing made her queasy. What appeared in every sense a beautiful evening had become her nightmare.

The cadence of Ellis's pulse beneath her thumb throbbed across her, her heartbeat syncing with his. How beautiful it had felt to dance in the shelter of his arms, to savor his hands pressed against her, his lips a mere breath away—but she couldn't allow such thoughts to mar the job she had to do. If only she could appease both her conscience and her heart's longing.

When they reached the edge of the crowd, Cora stopped at a booth distributing wine and plopped two coins from her reticule on the table. The man behind the counter met her eyes in shrewd understanding, bending low to retrieve the bottle Madam Carey had assured her would be there.

With trembling fingers, she accepted it, along with two glasses held out to her. Somewhere among the capering mass of excited townspeople, Madam Carey must be watching, but she wouldn't let her gaze drift beyond Ellis's face.

"Come on. I know a place where we can be alone."

Rather than allow her to lead him on, he pulled back on her hand. "Should we go off on our own?" He glanced briefly around. "We've already attracted a fair bit of attention."

"We must." Her insides quivered. *This is the only way.* Reciting the words to herself yet again, she tugged on his hand and urged him to follow. No matter what came of tonight, she must do as Madam Carey ordered. Otherwise, the plan for her and Damaris would go on as constructed. She couldn't let that happen.

The girl in question stood at the edge of the crowd, watching the dancers in awestruck wonder. Did she sense what was coming? Ever since the night Cora had tried to fashion an escape, the madam had kept them apart. Damaris's eyes flashed in quiet question toward Cora as they passed, but Cora merely shook her head once. *Not yet.* Not under Madam Carey's watchful eye.

The music and gaiety faded as Cora led Ellis beyond the cluster of buildings and into the darkened forest. Here, the lanterns and bonfires offered little light, but she knew this trail like a best friend. She could have walked it in her sleep.

A short trek down a dirt path led them between towering pines to a clearing lit just enough by the moon to see. Cora led the way to a fallen tree where someone had carved out a bench for sitting.

Easing into it, she laced her fingers with Ellis's and gently tugged until he settled onto the seat next to her. The entire charade felt like an echo of the day they met—enticing glances and furtive touches, the real person beneath her shell begging to spring forth. Would he destroy her if she did?

Breaking his hold on her, she set the glasses beside her on the log and the bottle of wine on the ground. Its cool, smooth surface blazed beneath her numb fingertips, a weapon she had no business wielding.

Instead of meeting the eyes staring back at her, she pointed herself toward the vast expanse of woods behind them. A chilling wind skittered across her skin, through the wisps of hair falling from her chignon. She had begged Madam Carey to let her wear a more practical gown, but the madam had interest only in luring her prey. What care should she harbor for the bait?

As if reading her thoughts, Ellis lifted the jacket from his shoulders and draped it over her. Warmth instantly enshrouded her.

She looked up at him with a gentle smile. "Thank you."

He said nothing, only slipped a piece of her hair behind her ear, his fingertips skimming her temple. Cora held her breath as his eyes meandered over every inch of her face as if memorizing her.

"Ellis, there's so much to say, but I—" Her voice caught, choked by the tears threatening to emerge. "I don't quite know how to find the words."

"Any word you say will do." His fingertips skidded down her jawline, sparking a shiver of ecstasy through her. His thumb pulled softly on her bottom lip.

"This is dangerous." His mere touch sparked emotions she thought she'd buried long ago.

His head shook softly. "It's only dangerous if we don't mean it, and I do. I'm tired of fighting my true feelings."

Cora closed her eyes, inhaling the intoxicating blend of pine and earth. For years she'd walked such a thin line, a rope suspended above a precipice. This man could make her fall. He'd shove her to her death with a simple brush of his fingers.

"That day we met on the trail," his voice's deep timbre hummed in her ear, "the day I kissed you—did you mean it? Or was it a ruse like you have to play with the other men?"

Her eyelids fluttered open, her vision blurring with moisture. "Of course I meant it. I had no reason to trick you."

A sigh escaped him. "That's what I'd hoped you'd say, but I convinced myself if you were really speaking the truth, you would tell me a different story."

She frowned. "What do you mean?"

His fingers found hers in the dark, lacing with them and holding tight. "It's not who you are that disturbs me, it's"—he swallowed, his eyes fearful in the dim light—"it's my own insecurity. When I think of you with another man, I—I want to kill anyone who would dare touch you."

Cora covered the back of his hand in her free one, absorbing his warmth. "You know I don't have a bit of desire for any of those other men, don't you? It's only ever been a job." Her chest swelled. "A vicious and cruel one at that."

His brow knit in pensive reflection. "But you told Jeremiah Anderson what happened between us."

"I didn't, though." She saw the look of doubt passing through his eyes and lifted his hand in hers. "I told Jeremiah Anderson nothing. Madam Carey sniffed out our connection and had Jorgen beat me until I gave up what little I had. Madam Carey told Anderson, not I."

His nostrils flared. "When I get my hands on Jorgen—"

"You can't, Ellis. Not yet. Not until it's safe." Yet the pleading in his eyes nearly broke her.

"When will it ever be safe?"

Her gaze darted through the trees to the mix of voices filtering through it. She didn't have much time. "You have to trust me. I tried to get Damaris out, but I was caught. I had to make a deal with Madam Carey."

He jolted forward. "What kind of deal?"

A bargain for my very soul. She angled her head, her emotions rising like an ocean wave. "The kind that could go very badly if we're not careful."

Ellis was on his feet now, pacing, his fingers raking back his hair. "I don't like the sound of this. Madam Carey wants only to use you."

"It's true." Realizing it still tortured her sometimes. "I always thought, even in the darkest hour within her brothel walls, that she cared for me. Perhaps not in the way a mother loves a daughter, but—" The words suspended in the starlit air. Why did it still hurt so much to admit?

He stared through the darkness back at her, his eyes compassionate. "You thought she cared a little, at least."

Cora nodded, swallowing back her tears. "Once upon a time, the job she laid on my shoulders tonight might have felt like an honor. I would have considered myself privileged that she trusted me enough to carry out her plans." Her head shook sadly. "But I realize now, in that blithe state of ignorance, she never would have told me what she really planned to do."

Ellis reached her in two easy strides. "What is she planning?" His large hands covered hers. "You can tell me. Don't you trust me now?"

She let out a tearful laugh. "Ellis, of course I trust you. When you first came to the brothel, my heart shattered. I thought—" Her voice caught. His fingers tensed around hers. "I thought you'd never see me as anything but a dirty strumpet. I thought you hated me for all my innumerable sins."

"No, Cora." His whispered breath showered her skin in warmth as he drew near. "I could never think that. I was hurt because I thought you'd used me, not because I ever had room to look down on you."

Cora leaned into him, allowing her forehead to rest against his downturned one. "I know that now. I see it when I look at you. You're a good man, Ellis. You're probably the best man I've ever met."

His scruffy face rubbed against hers as his head wagged. "A good man would have stopped to listen. A good man wouldn't have been so blasted impatient or humiliated you the way I did."

"I forgave you for that long ago."

"I know, but still it haunts me." His hand lifted, cupping the side of her face. "You deserve so much more than what you've accepted from life. You deserve everything."

Cora let out a shuddering cry. "If only you could see into the depths of me."

Fingers dove beneath her chin, propelling it upward. Even in the scant crystal rays of moonlight, the contents of his heart spilled open for her to behold. "I see you, Cora Blackwood." His gaze plummeted to her lips a moment before he moved in to possess them.

Cora surrendered to his kiss, melting against his sturdy frame. Brawny arms encompassed her, his fingers diving beneath her hair. Cora's heart beat wildly, her hands clutching his clothes, her lips responding to the sensuous motion of his. She could spend an eternity wrapped in this moment, bathed in his body heat, placated by his affection—but reality lurked too close. A bush rustled somewhere beyond the trail. Madam Carey could have sent Jorgen to spy on them.

Reluctantly breaking free, she held onto his tense forearms, steadying herself. "For what comes next, you must trust me."

The warning hoot of an owl carried across the forest as Ellis searched her face. Then, with confidence, he circled his arms around her waist and anchored her to him. "I trust you with my life."

"And you with mine." Her fingertips toyed with the buttons on his chest. "This may not make much sense, but it's the only way I see out." Slipping from his grasp, she turned back to the bench they'd vacated and crouched low to gather the glasses and bottle of wine.

Without question, Ellis uncorked the bottle and began pouring the claret liquid into the glass flutes she held out to him.

"Be careful with that. Don't spill." One wrong move could be devastating.

"She wants you to get me drunk, is that it?" He set the open bottle at his feet and reached for the glass she extended his way. "She wants you to seduce me so she can catch me in the act and expose me to the town."

Acid seared Cora's throat, forcing her to swallow it back. "Either that or get you so drunk you're easy to overpower." Better he believe that than the terrifying truth.

He nodded, lifting the glass to his lips.

Cora caught him by the arm. "No, Ellis. Don't drink it."

"But we need to create the illusion, at least. If they smell no alcohol on my breath, they'll know—"

"You can't drink it." Her desperate breath slammed against her chest. "Believe me, all right? Don't drink a drop of this."

As he waited for his next move, his brows wrinkled. Could she hope to pull this off? Perhaps she should just let him run now while he still had a chance. Yet the thought of poor, innocent Damaris suffering needlessly drove her onward.

"They can't be far now." She threw a furtive look over her shoulder. "We have to do this before they see us." Her eyes found his in the dark. "When I drop this glass, you have to run, understand? Not back the way we came, but straight through the trees toward the party. They won't expect you."

She grasped his muscled arm. "Damaris is standing near the pie booth. I need you to run up as quickly as you can and get her out of here. Tell her I sent you." Her fingers pulled at his shirt sleeve. "Please, you must get her out of this town before Madam Carey can destroy her whole life."

Ellis took a step toward her. "What about you? I can't leave you."

"If they're watching me, they won't be watching *her*." At the concern on his face, she licked her lips. "Listen, I have a plan. I know how I'm going to get myself out."

His jaw tensed. "I don't like any plan that involves you risking your own life."

"I have it all worked out, I promise you." She nestled her cheek against the broad hand that found her hairline. "I know Madam Carey. I know how she operates. She will believe my story."

His throat bobbed, uncertainty brimming his eyes. "You're sure?"

"I'm sure, Ellis. I have this." She brought his hand up and kissed his knuckles. "I will come to the jail as soon as it's safe. I vow to you I will this time."

His fingers laced with hers, the desperate hold of a man who didn't want to let her go. "I'm holding you to that promise, Miss Blackwood. You had better return to me."

"I will. I promise I will."

She took another cleansing breath. With one sudden movement, she snatched the glass out of his hand and threw it on the ground, far enough that it wouldn't splatter him. She did the same with her own and kicked the bottle at their feet, sending its contents splashing into the tall grass. Ellis gave her one last meaningful look before he turned and sprinted through the trees. *Thank God.*

A blood-curdling scream ripped from her lips, false tears brewing within and spilling out her eyes. It took only seconds for several figures to emerge from the pathway they'd come down, darkening the woods with their black forms.

Jorgen ran at her first, his rounded eyes taking in the spilled wine and broken glasses. He seized Cora's sobbing frame, shaking her. "What is this? What happened?"

She choked on her tears. "He refused to drink it. He must have known."

He shook her again, harder this time. "How could he possibly have known? Did you tell him?"

"I didn't tell him a thing, I swear it." Her hands rose in defense, but it didn't stop the crack of Jorgen's hand across her face.

"You must have done something, you wench."

"I didn't, I swear." She plastered her cool hand across her face as stinging pain erupted over her cheek. "Perhaps he smelled the poison in the wine."

Jorgen bore his teeth, two glowing rows of white in the moon's rays. "Where is he going now? What is he doing?"

She gasped in another stolen breath of nocturnal air. "He said something about Sheriff Jones's old house, how he thought there was evidence there."

He stiffened. "Evidence of what?"

"I don't know. He wouldn't tell me. He tried to get more out of me, but I don't know what he's talking about."

Jorgen eyed her with suspicion a few soul-chilling seconds before he bellowed in frustration. "Get to your horses," he ordered the men who'd accompanied him. "We must ride to Jones's house before it's too late. He's alone. We'll finish him there."

Relief swamped Cora as she watched the trio of men dash back up the trail, away from the path Ellis had blazed through the woods. If only he could get to Damaris in time, her plan would work. Ellis would take Damaris to safety while Jorgen and his men fruitlessly hunted him.

Lifting her skirts, Cora shook them free of dirt and brushed off her bodice. The path was bare now, an empty stretch of dirt calling to something deep within her soul. She could almost taste the freedom lying beyond, the endless possibilities awaiting her.

Seizing her skirts in two hands, she jogged across the clearing and down the path. Her heartbeat accelerated, a warm fusion of joy and excitement lifting the dank and weary spirits plaguing her all these years. She would finally be free—to love Ellis, to let him love her in return. To experience the life of a living, breathing human being—not just the shadow of a wayward soul.

The brilliant picture of it still shone in her mind as she reached the trail's end and stumbled back to the Halloween celebration, still lively as ever. The fiddles' song must have drowned out her scream for everyone but those lurking in the bushes. Cora smiled to herself. Jorgen and his men were nowhere in sight. Ellis had disappeared too, along with Damaris. She could finally breathe easy again.

Then, as if summoned from the very depths of hell itself, Madam Carey rose into her vision, her astute eyes pinned to Cora and her purposeful gait aimed straight toward her.

Twenty Three

DAMARIS'S SMALL HAND PRESSED into Ellis's palm like that of a child's. Her eyes flashed with fearful innocence his way as they snaked their way through the crowd, still jovially milling about as if nothing sinister had transpired among them.

"Where are you taking me?" she asked between gasps for air.

"To the jail. Come on"—he tugged her hand—"we must be quick."

"Am I under arrest?" Her feet battered the ground behind him, hurrying to keep up.

"You're not under arrest, but your life is in danger." Ellis peered down the lit main street toward the jail. Too many people traversed this way. They had to go elsewhere if they didn't want to be seen. Turning to his left, he pointed them toward the back of the buildings lining the street.

"Cora said the same thing." Terror edged her voice. "Who could possibly want to hurt someone like me?"

"Plenty of people—Madam Carey the first of them."

"Madam Carey?" Breath hissed through her teeth as her arm scraped along the side of a building.

"She has plans to sell both you and Cora." As they rounded the bend to the grassy stretch of land behind the buildings, Ellis stopped short and dropped Damaris's hand. Two men emerged from the shadows, hands resting on their belts. Ellis had seen them on occasion throughout town, but had acquainted himself with neither.

"Nice of you to come this way, Sheriff," the tallest one said as he stepped firmly in Ellis's path. "We saw you running out with the girl." He eyed her with a licentious glint.

Ellis stepped protectively in front of Damaris. "Madam Carey sent you, did she?"

Exchanging startled looks, the two men shared a hearty laugh. "Do you think we'd be back here if we worked for Madam Carey?" The shorter man with a handlebar mustache flicked his chin toward the girl. "I assure you, everyone in town knows how you like them girls. Thought we'd have a share in the action."

Damaris shivered, ducking behind Ellis. His stomach turned. "Thought you would have a share? What do you think this is?"

The taller man clicked his tongue. "Ain't no need for pretense here. We know you're gettin' the goods for free. If you let us in on it, we won't tell nobody."

Freeing his pistol from its holster, Ellis held it up in the moonlight. "If you don't get out of my way, I'll kill you." Enough with these childish games.

Both men put up their hands, yet they eyed his gun dubiously. "We don't want no trouble, Sheriff," the mustached man said, "especially on a night like tonight. Anyway, the way I see it, it's two against one." Quick as a flash, his hand drew his revolver. "We all have guns here."

Heat blazed over Ellis's skin and tense muscles. He could end one of these two in an instant, but the other would surely plant a bullet in Ellis before his partner fell. Neither could he afford to attract the attention of the unknowing townspeople dancing about the square. "All right. Put your guns down and we'll have a talk. We'll work something out."

The scoundrels holstered their weapons only after Ellis did, their eyes carefully tracking his every move.

His hands splayed in front of him as if in supplication, flattened against the cold night air. "Listen here. She's just a girl. She shouldn't be treated thus."

A crude look slid between them. "A girl who goes for a handsome sum of gold at Madam Carey's. Don't try to trick us. We know who she is."

Blood pulsed up Ellis's arms, filling his fists with rage. If it took his dying breath, he would fulfill his promise to Cora. He would see this girl taken to safety.

The man opened his mouth to speak again, but Ellis lurched forward like a jungle cat with claws out. The man's eyes exploded, his hands jetting for his gun a moment too late. Ellis already had him pinned to the side of the building, his fist smashing into his face.

Movement flashed beside him, prompting his elbow to collide with the next man so eager to help his friend. A yelp and a curse flew from the attacker's mouth. He stumbled back, holding his bleeding nose in both hands.

Lifting the odorous man before him up by the shirt collar, he slammed his fist into his jaw several more times before letting him sink to the ground in a heap of bloody clothing, his gun Ellis's for the taking. Whirling back on the second attacker, Ellis aimed his gun, yet he found only a figure racing into the shadows, desperately clutching his half-fallen trousers.

"Come on." Breathless, Ellis found Damaris's hand again. "Come with me."

She let out a small, exuberant laugh as she hopped over the fallen attacker's body with eyes rounder than a harvest moon. "That was something to see. No wonder Cora is so taken with you."

Even with the crash of his pounding heart and unhampered adrenaline, Ellis couldn't stop the flutter in his chest at her words.

The jail lay only a few minutes' jog from the Halloween festivities. Ellis reached it with chest pumping, his heartbeat thundering in his ears. He paused, resting his sweating palms on his thighs. "Go on in." He pointed toward the closed door. "Through that back way. It's open." He'd made it so if the need arose for a speedy escape.

The tranquil silence of the jail broke as they stomped into it. Wainwright appeared seconds later, curiosity coloring his cheeks as he leaned into the hallway. On sight of Ellis, he breathed out. "Thank God. I was preparing myself for another onslaught of outlaws."

"Lucky for you, it's just the two of us." But his eyes had already fallen across Damaris, taking her in as a bird might ogle a fish flying through the clouds.

"I need you to do something for me, Wainwright." Ellis crossed to his office. "This is Damaris. She's in grave danger." Ducking through the door, he headed straight for the emergency pack he'd thrown together for just such an occasion. "I need you to take her north to Miller's Crossing." He thrust the pack into Wainwright's hands. "This has everything you'll need—water, food, a lantern, matches."

Wainwright's mouth hinged open, his startled gaze darting between Damaris and Ellis. "You want me to go now? If she waits until morning, she can take the train."

"She can't take the train. She has to leave before anybody notices she's gone." He stepped closer, laying a hand on Wainwright's shoulder. "This is a very delicate matter. I'm trusting you to see it carried out. Do you understand?"

A flicker of doubt moved across Wainwright's face before he puffed his cheeks and nodded shakily. "I understand. I won't let you down, Sheriff."

"Good, because I'm not sure what I'd do without you at the moment." Ellis released a breath, pivoting toward Damaris. "This is my best deputy, Mr. Arnold Wainwright. You'll be safe with him."

Wainwright stood taller at the proclamation, though at his wanting stature, he could only stretch so far. "It's an honor, miss."

Damaris's lips twitched into a quick smile, her cheeks blushing.

"Take her to the Harrington Hotel. Ask for Clarice Foster, or Caleb and Lily Broderick. Tell them I'll sort out her circumstances as soon as possible. Tell them she's a friend of Cora's."

Jotting everything down in a small notebook, Wainwright glanced up at him. "Are you sure you don't want to take her yourself if this is so important?"

"No, I can't." Feet propelling him out the office door, Ellis gazed through the window admitting light from the Halloween party. A dazzling display of fireworks now lit the night sky, shimmers of blue and silver exploding across the heavens. "I have work to do here."

Ellis barely heard the retreat of their footsteps as they hurried down the hallway and out the back. He wandered to the front of the empty building, laying his hand alongside the one window facing the street. The gaiety had only intensified, crowds swelling as the night deepened. Was Cora still among them, fighting her way out?

The hairs on his neck stood on end. She should be here by now. He pressed his forehead to the cold glass, straining to see, willing her form to magically materialize in his field of vision. Why had he agreed to this plan? Why hadn't he ensured her escape? He'd failed her yet again.

I'll come as soon as it's safe. Her soft voice rang in his ears, but it couldn't shake the uncertainty shrouding him. She could be alone, afraid, injured—and he'd never know. Not while he stood in the safety of these walls, staring out like a helpless boy.

Twisting on his heel, he marched toward the front door with determination in his step. He wouldn't wait another second. He would go after her.

Cora stood at the edge of the woods, her back rigid and arms frozen. A moment earlier, pure ecstasy had lifted her steps, giving the impression of floating on air. How masterfully a single look could yank a person down.

Madam Carey blustered toward her with the force of a strong wind. Cora briefly considered running. She doubted the aging woman could catch her if she simply took off in the other direction. But the seasoned madam was no fool. She would make a scene, find a way to ensnare Cora before she even had the chance to get halfway down the street.

Her frilly, wine-colored skirts swished as she moved expertly through the crowd. The closer she came, the more displeasure Cora could discern in her black-rimmed eyes and red-tinted lips. She stopped only inches away, surveying Cora like a displeased schoolmarm assessing her problem student.

"Well, what happened?" The wrinkles around her mouth emerged, so much deeper than they normally looked.

Cora's shoulders fell. "It didn't work. He figured out the truth."

Madam Carey's shrill voice lifted in a disbelieving laugh. "It didn't work? Please. That man worships every inch of ground you walk on."

Cora trembled, remembering his thick jacket still rested across her shoulders. *A sure sign.* "I thought he did, but he scorned me. He threw down his glass of wine before I even had a chance to ask him to drink it."

Red bursts of fireworks illuminated the sky above, rimming Madam Carey's sunken eyes in light. They narrowed ever so slightly. "Do you expect me to believe the man who's been following you around these past few months like a lovestruck boy squandered his moment alone with you? Hardly. Your deception stinks from a mile away."

The fear festering inside her hardened, catching aflame as it barreled through her. "I tried to do what you asked."

"If you had tried hard enough, the sheriff would be dead by now." Madam Carey stepped forward, her voice lowering to a malicious growl. "I don't believe you're that much of a dunce, girl. Everything you set your mind to flourishes. You *chose* not to give him that poison."

Cora's teeth gritted as she stared the woman down. "Why don't you tell me my evil plan, then—if you have it all figured out?"

"Don't be impertinent with me, girl. I've owned you ever since you stepped foot in this town." She clutched her fan in blanched fingers. "I saw the way you two looked at each other when you were dancing out there. You hide your affections about as skillfully as you do your distaste for me."

Cora lifted her chin, all desire for pretense fleeing her. "So what if I do care about him? Are you going to punish me for loving a man?"

"I'm going to punish you for *lying* to me."

Cora met her unyielding stare. "I sent Jorgen and whomever else you wrangled together on a wild goose chase. So unless you expect to fight me yourself, I would suggest you get out of my way."

A silver thread of cold ire swam through Madam Carey's gaze. Then, shoulders relaxing, she whipped open her fan and fluttered it casually. "Do you really think I trusted solely in Jorgen for something so important? Do you really think I don't have an alternate plan?" Her tongue clicked. "You should know me better than that by now." Swinging her fiery gaze to the man they'd purchased wine from earlier, Madam Carey summoned him with a nod of her head.

Bitter nausea pooled in Cora's middle as the husky man abandoned his station and tramped toward her. No. *No!* This wasn't happening. She wouldn't fall into one of Madam Carey's traps yet again. Yet with each pulse-pounding second, he covered more ground.

Cora spun around, starting off at a run through the crowd. In an instant he'd caught her, his muscled arm hooking her middle. She screamed, the sound muffled by the enormous hand he plastered over her mouth.

"Do try to cooperate, dear." Madam Carey's sinister voice swam in her head. "I would hate to cause a scene on such a joyous night."

Eyes bulging, Cora looked around for anyone who could help her, anyone who would even notice her plight. Her feet kicked wildly, landing nowhere. She tried to open her lips to bite his fingers, but his hand pressed so hard she could manage only to desperately breathe through her nose. Her voice rose again, a strangled cry that died quickly amid the laughter and rollicking music.

"Give it up, dear. No one cares what happens to you." Madam Carey touched her captor's arm. "Bring her back to the brothel, would you? The barn this time. I don't want to get blood on my nice furniture."

Then, like a sudden storm brings forth a tidal wave and recedes to stillness, the man dragged her into the darkness.

Twenty Four

ELLIS'S LEGS BURNED, HIS side raging with pain as he stumbled back to the Halloween festivities he'd left only shortly before. He glanced around, his gaze ricocheting off excited couples turning about the makeshift dance floor to the booths selling everything from roasting meats to gingerbread. Everywhere he looked, the lack of her drove his gaze onward. Where could she possibly have gone?

Pushing his way through the throng of people, Ellis ran until he reached the woods. Darkness covered him in its icy chill as he sprinted down the path they'd walked to the clearing where he'd left her. Only the toppled wine bottle and broken glasses remained of their clandestine meeting.

The heady aroma of pine sifted through him as he examined the dirt. Ellis squatted low, squinting in the pale moonlight. Her dainty shoes had left impressions across the ground, accompanied by his larger prints. But there were others—several more pairs of men's boots that had trampled through here. Pulse picking up speed, Ellis raced back down the path, his eyes frantically searching for any sign of her.

When he emerged from the woods, he spotted Reverend Sommers standing near the candy booth, watching a juggler with a smile stretched across his face. He had no time for manners. Descending on the man, he caught him by the arm. "Excuse me, Reverend. I hate to interrupt."

"Nonsense. You're not interrupting a thing." Worry shone in the reverend's masked eyes. "What is it? What can I do for you?"

Catching his breath, Ellis gripped the reverend's sleeve. "Have you seen Miss Blackwood? She was here only moments ago."

The reverend frowned. "Miss Blackwood? No. Not since the two of you were dancing together." His head angled. "Is there cause for concern?"

"I don't know yet"—Ellis's chest heaved as he glanced around the party—"but if you see her, please ensure she gets to the jailhouse safely. I need to question her."

"Of course." Reverend Sommers patted him on the back. "Miss Blackwood is a good friend and a kind woman. I'll do anything I can to help."

"Thank you, sir. I must go." Without explanation, Ellis darted between children competing in a gunny sack race and made for the edge of town. Leaving behind the smells of cooking popcorn and sugared pastries, he dashed through the night toward the darker side of Gold Strike.

The front of Madam Carey's establishment bore an ominous face, with orange light flickering in the windows against the blackened, cloudless sky beyond. Jack-o'-lanterns lined the rail of its porch, their gleaming faces smiling at him as Ellis ran up the steps.

His boots thrashed the wood of the rickety floorboards as he trampled them without care. With full force, he launched at the front door, only to find it locked. Locked on a night like this, with drunken men wandering the town, easy prey for any girl who wanted to charge double for her services? Ellis pounded the door, his fists relentless, until he spotted a slip of a girl approaching through the glass.

She greeted him with a tilted smile, a shawl hanging off one shoulder and a dress barely containing her bosoms. "Relax, sugar. No need to be in such a rush."

Her manufactured Southern lilt drove pins into his nerves. "Why is the door locked?"

"Well, don't you know?" She giggled, the sound even more grating. "We always lock the door on Halloween. It's much more fun to come through the back entrance so you can see our spooky candlelit hallways."

He huffed shortly, uninterested in finding out whatever depravities those hallways contained. "I don't have time for the back entrance."

"Well, come on in this way, then." She pursed her lips, her lewd gaze descending him. "I'll take care of you right away."

"I didn't come for *that* either. Is Cora here?"

Her eyes rolled heavenward. "Cora." She practically spat the word. "You do know she's not the only girl here worth your money?"

His teeth set. "Is Cora here?"

"She's at the Halloween celebration, of course." The girl tossed her tasseled shawl. "Madam Carey insisted she go. She is her *pet,* after all."

Ellis set both hands on the doorframe, leaning over her. "You haven't seen her come back from the party?"

"I haven't seen hide nor hair of her." Irritation flickered in her eyes. "Now, do you care for a little fun or don't you?"

Without bothering to answer, Ellis pushed off the doorframe and spun toward the street. His pulse began to hammer. If she wasn't at the party and she wasn't here, only one of two possibilities remained: she'd either escaped or been caught. He couldn't take the chance of assuming the former.

The frigid air invaded his skin as he descended the porch steps and wandered into the street. Laughter from within the brothel walls tickled his ears, the roar of the raucous celebration booming from the other direction. Crystal shards of light erupted across the sky, explosions of color fizzling out as they fell to the earth. He breathed in the smoky air, dragging a hand through his hair. Other than shouting her name at the top of his lungs and hoping foolishly that she'd hear him, he had no avenues left.

A broad figure materialized from the shadows of the brothel. Ellis's body snapped to attention, his hand reaching for his gun.

"No need to try and shoot me, Sheriff," a familiar drawl gave him pause. "You already left me in a bad way enough the last time."

Ellis's hand rested on the hilt of his pistol. "If you will remember correctly, the last time we met, you tried to kill me."

"And I've learned my lesson—believe me." Jeremiah Anderson's face passed into the distant firelight, still purple and battered from Ellis's beating. "I have no desire to hurt you."

"Then why are you sneaking up on me in the dark?" Ellis carefully surveyed him. His hands were suspended in the air, away from his gun.

"Approaching you, not sneaking up." His large hands lifted higher. "I might have some information for you."

Ellis scoffed, a puff of breath clouding the air. "Like the information I had to wrestle out of you at Jones's old place?"

"It turned out to be true, didn't it?" His brow cocked in silent challenge.

"Just because it was true doesn't mean I'm going to believe everything you tell me from now on." Ellis rested his hands on his hips. "I know the kind of man you are."

Boots treading the dirt between them, Jeremiah came to rest only feet in front of him. "I am everything you say, but I still have a spark of a conscience in there somewhere."

Ellis's brows gathered. "Like the conscience you had when Sheriff Jones paid you to murder Colton Baxter?"

His hand jetted out. "Hey, I didn't murder—"

"I know you didn't murder him, but that isn't the point." Ellis peered back at him through narrow slits for eyes. "I've read Jones's correspondences. You were planning to kill Colton Baxter, even if Wesley Pierce got to him first."

Anderson swallowed, his long, stringy hair lifting on the breeze. "I won't stand here and deny it. Jones offered me a lot of money for that kill. I ain't above killin' for the right amount of cash."

The notion turned Ellis's stomach. "Jones—or your mutual benefactor?" At the revelation on Anderson's face, Ellis nodded. "I know about him too."

Anderson spat in the dirt. "You probably know a whole lot more about him than I do."

"What does that mean?"

"It means I don't." He pulled himself up, his wide shoulders set against the starry night sky. "He sent me money for doin' jobs, but only Sheriff Jones knew who he was. I never found out."

"You're lying."

Hard gaze shooting to Ellis, Anderson sucked in a deep breath. "Why would I have reason to lie?"

"Because you want to protect whoever this benefactor is. Because he's paying you still." His arms knotted over his chest. "You have a million reasons for keeping his identity a secret, and not one for telling me the truth."

Silence enveloped them as the wind whistled through the trees.

"I have a mighty fine reason, actually." Anderson's nostrils flared. "That man don't have a shred of loyalty, whoever he is. He hasn't called on me since Jones died, and rumors are spreadin' throughout the county that he's hirin' whomever he likes—Red Fox, whatever other lawless folk he can find to do his biddin' at the cheapest price."

Ellis's muscles braced as if someone had hit him. "You truly don't know who he is."

"I haven't a clue. If I did, I'd skin him and hang him up from the nearest tree." The breath escaped him, whooshing out his whiskered mouth like a long-held secret. "I ain't got but one clue, and I plan to seize upon it."

Ellis tilted his head, stepping closer. If this was a trap, he might willingly walk into it. "And what's that?"

Anderson's wild gaze floated from Ellis to the brothel walls and back again. "He's in cahoots with Madam Carey. You probably already know that by now. I heard through my sources that she's plannin' to send her lackey to meet him in just a couple days. Supposedly they're meetin' in back of the livery."

"You're sure of this?" If true, such information could enable him to have a team of deputies ready to ensnare this mysterious benefactor.

Anderson's hands opened. "Can't be sure if nothin' is true. It's just what I've heard."

"Through a reliable source, yes?"

"Very reliable." Anderson looked again to the glowing brothel. "I don't know which day, but it can't be far off. I plan on snoopin' around until I find out for myself."

Ellis shook his head. "Chasing a vendetta will never allow you to amount to much."

"Seems a vendetta is all I got these days. Also, you may not believe it, but Cora means something to me. We was friends once upon a time. I don't want to see her hurt by all this." Anderson tipped his hat. "Sheriff." Like a quiet wind, he disappeared into the shadows as quick as he'd come.

Ellis stood amid the howling winds for several more beats, recalling his words, trying to make sense of this puzzle. Even if he could discover the man responsible for funding Sheriff Jones's nefarious deeds, it would mean nothing without Cora. He had to locate her first.

Echoing off the wind's mournful moans, a distant scream caught his attention. Ellis spun in a circle, the world a disorienting stream of colors and lights. He craned his neck, straining toward the phantom sound, but the world was quiet. Had he simply imagined it, his mind overwrought with the possibility of harm befalling Cora?

The scream rose again, louder this time, unmistakable. Pointing himself toward the source of the noise, he charged into the gathering dark. It hadn't come from the brothel—that much he knew, yet several houses and outbuildings lay beyond Madam Carey's. He would have to search all night, and by then it could be too late.

Listening for the cries again, he heard nothing but the tree limbs dancing against one another, the somber drone of a bullfrog from the creek along the mill. His gaze dropped to the dirt path, barely visible beneath the moon, and his gut twisted. There in the dirt, he made out two tracks—one of a man's, the other the smaller prints of a woman's shoes, just like the ones Cora had worn in the forest.

Hurrying along the earth, he trailed them until they disappeared into an old barn, where the tracks turned to marks of someone being dragged. Ellis's heart galloped as he raced the rest of the way to the barn. Tiny droplets of blood shimmered beneath the moon's rays.

No. No! With rage and fear pulsing through every muscle of his body, he barged inside and threw back the barn door. A hefty man stood among the aromatic hay, his back to Ellis. A soul-shaking laugh reverberated off the barn walls as he held his fist high in the air. An unseen woman whimpered beneath him, her shivering cries nearly washed out by the rushing wind. *Cora.* He knew that voice anywhere.

"This will teach you to defy the madam!" The man's fist dropped down like an anvil, colliding with flesh. Cora screeched, the sound soaking into Ellis's core.

His feet propelled him across the barn in three enormous strides, his hand shooting out like a claw. He snatched the monster's shirt collar and yanked him away. With a yelp of surprise, the man lost his footing and toppled backward, crashing to the floor. Ellis straddled him in seconds, his thighs squeezing the man's writhing torso, his fists pummeling his face until he thought his fingers might shatter.

"Please, no! Please!" But the man's screaming protests fell on deaf ears.

"Do you think I care what you want?" His teeth gritted, ire seething through his every sweating pore. "Do you think you can beat an innocent woman and get away with it?"

He slammed his fist into the man's jaw again and again, battering it until his eyes rolled up in his head and unconsciousness relieved him of his burden. Breathlessly, Ellis sat back on his heels and swiped an arm over his perspiring face. His hand stung from knuckles to wrists, his bulging muscles sore—but when his eyes fell on Cora, all awareness of his own pain ran away.

She lay on her side, holding her knees to her chest like a child in the womb. Her entire body quaked, trembling breaths still lifting off her lips, splashes of crimson dotting the hay strewn around her and smearing her perfect skin.

"Cora." His heart echoed her name. Rising up, he covered the short distance between them and hunkered down above her. She drew back at the touch of his hands. "Cora, it's only me."

"Ellis?" One eye opened enough to look at him. "Is that you?"

"It's me, honey. You're safe." He didn't quite know where the word had come from, but it felt right on his lips—to call her a term of endearment. Bending low, he gently scooped her into his arms and cradled her at his chest.

Cora relaxed her head against him, her warm blood pooling at the edge of her mouth and blotching his shirt. A quiet moan passed through her lips before she collapsed into him, sleep overcoming her. Ellis held her close and carried her into the dark night, vowing never to let her go again.

Twenty Five

THE STRIDENT CALL OF a lark jolted Cora from her sleep. She scrunched up her face, rubbing her weary eyes. Her dreams had brought visions of a dark and sinister forest, of swimming through an endless ocean with no hope of finding shore. She blinked, attempting to focus her eyes. Instead of a posh room at the brothel, another one surrounded her.

Bolting up, she searched frantically around her. A firm mattress with only a single blanket and pillow and an iron frame. Bare walls. Not a single other piece of furniture adorned the tiny bedroom. She looked to the window, where soft light barely soaked through the curtains. What she'd assumed was the honey light of morning appeared to be dusk.

Cora held her head in one hand. What had happened last night? She remembered the Halloween party, Ellis's strong hands on her back as they danced, his kiss, so powerful it still tickled the nerves in her toes. Her breath hitched.

Madam Carey had caught her after that, had her dragged away. The flash of bare white knuckles rushing toward her face set her heart to pounding. She touched her lip, wincing when the sting splintered across her face. It hadn't been a dream. Had that pathetic excuse for a man beaten her senseless, then dragged her to his cabin? The possibility drove needles up her skin.

Tossing back the blanket and easing herself over the edge of the bed, she glanced around for something, *anything* she could use as a weapon. Only an empty floor answered back. What kind of a place was this?

She turned, pausing as her frantic gaze swept the bed. A folded blanket sat on the vacant space next to her rumpled sheets with a note atop it. Cora crawled over the bed, reaching for the paper and holding it up to the dying light. *I don't have much of anything that will fit you. I'm sorry. This will have to do for now.*

Relaxing, she pressed the note to her chest. *Ellis.* Yes, Ellis had rescued her. She'd nearly forgotten. For the first time, she noticed the garments on her body—mere underthings. Ellis had apparently removed her soiled and bloody dress, for she could find it nowhere in sight.

Sighing, she reached for the blanket and draped it across her shoulders. He'd seen her in less than this before. Half the town had seen her in less than this before, yet somehow her lack of clothing suddenly felt shameful.

The scent of boiling stew reached her as Cora opened the bedroom door into a sitting area. The aroma of beef and vegetables melded together, accented by some seasoning like oregano or sage. Her gaze wandered the petite room, where nothing but a single shabby chair and a bearskin rug sat before a stone hearth bright with flames. Beyond the scant living area, a small kitchen with only a table and stove sat beneath a window.

Ellis's imposing frame filled the space as he stirred the bubbling creation in an iron pot. He glanced up, then caught her in a second, longer look. "I didn't know you were awake."

"I just woke up." Cora brushed her fingers through her long hair. He'd even thought to untie it when he put her to bed. "How long have I been asleep?"

"Just last night and today." He set his spoon aside and wiped his hands on the towel draped over his shoulder. "You seemed like you needed the rest. I didn't want to disturb you."

Her fingers slid down the smooth wood of the doorframe. "I haven't been sleeping well lately. I've had a lot of nightmares."

Eyes compassionate, he set his towel on the table and ambled toward her. "I can't imagine the dreams you must have after what you've been through." He covered her hands in his. "Perhaps you'll tell me someday."

She tried to smile, but her mouth faltered. If only she could forget them instead. "They aren't worth mentioning."

"It's over now. You know that, right?" His voice was soft, comforting. "If you want to be through with it, you never have to go back."

Cora nodded, breathing against her rush of emotion. "Thanks to you. What you did for me, I—"

His fingertips cupped her jaw. "Please don't thank me. I only did what any decent man would. And besides, I have selfish reasons too." His thumb slid down her cheek. "I happen to love you."

"Ellis." She closed her eyes, the word pressing from her stifled lungs. "You think that you love me—"

"I *do*, Cora."

Her eyelids eased open, tears budding beneath them. "A hundred men have told me they loved me, but all they loved was the idea of me. All they saw was the color of my hair and a face they found appealing. All they saw was a shapely woman who would fill their bed."

"I see so much more than that." His hand smoothed back her hair. "Don't you think I see what's inside of you? Your kindness. Your love. Your unbelievable strength." His eyes watered. "I had an inkling that day on the ridge, but I never could have guessed at the depth I would find when I looked into your heart."

Cora searched his eyes a quiet moment before casting her gaze to the shadows. Could she bear for a man to look that far inside her? Would he feel the same when he truly found out how deep the shades of darkness ran in her?

"You need something to eat. How careless of me." He dropped his hold on her and made for the kitchen. "I hope you like beef stew. There isn't much else I know how to make."

"Stew sounds lovely." She gripped the blanket tighter around her. "I can't remember the last time I had a decent meal anyway. Madam Carey has been cutting corners of late, rationing our food."

His brows dove, but he simply shook his head. "No rationing here." He ladled a generous portion of stew into a tin bowl. "Why don't you have a seat by the fire? It will warm you up."

Cora laughed as she sank into the lone chair. "Where will you sit, Sheriff McCraw?"

"I'll find a place. Don't worry about me." He beamed at her as he transferred the warm bowl into her hands. "I know this place isn't much to look at. I have plans to spruce it up, but I just haven't gotten around to it."

"The endlessly active life of a sheriff." She sat back, watching him return to the kitchen and ladle a bowl for himself. "Though nothing but a bed and a chair *does* seem rather wanting for how long you've lived here."

Ellis returned with a steaming bowl in one hand. "I hardly ever come out here. In fact, no one in town even knows I live here."

"By design, I presume."

One side of his mouth tugged up. "Precisely. You're safe here. No one knows where you are."

Cora lifted her spoon and dipped it into the stew. "You've put yourself in rather a scandalous position, have you not? The local sheriff, paragon of virtue, housing a woman of the night under his very own roof?"

His brow hooked as he settled next to her on the bearskin rug. "They already whisper about me behind my back and call me a wretch. At least I can give them something tangible to talk about."

Cora bit her lip, though she couldn't suppress the smile blooming across her mouth. Ellis's homemade stew soothed her troubled senses, warming her through. She enjoyed bite after scrumptious bite, satisfied by the flavors satiating her tongue. She finished with an unladylike smirk, noting the sparkle of joy that lit Ellis's eyes.

"You're enjoying that, I see."

Lowering the bowl to her lap, she angled her head. "Don't get cocky, Sheriff. I haven't had a decent meal in days." Her lower lip sucked between her teeth. "Though I have to admit, it *was* rather tasty."

"An old family recipe." He rose to gather her bowl with his and place them on the kitchen table.

"Can I always expect such hospitable treatment from you?"

His eyes met hers, more serious than she'd intended. "You can if you want to—stay here, that is. I certainly don't want you going anywhere else."

Knitting her hands together in her lap, she stared at the crackling fire. Its warmth shrouded her toes and crept up her body like a human embrace, but its light must have displayed every emotion on her face. How strange to find herself so frightened in a place of love and safety after the torments of hell she'd walked through.

"I made you a cup of hot cocoa, too." Ellis appeared at her side, extending a ceramic cup with wisps of vapor curling out of it. "I wanted to give it a chance to cool a bit before I gave it to you."

Cora accepted the mug by the handle, holding its warm side in her other palm. "Hot cocoa?" She inhaled the sweet, aromatic blend of chocolate and milk lifting from her cup. "I don't believe I've had this since I was a child."

"Another token of comfort from my mother." He lifted his own mug high. "To new beginnings."

She tossed him a poignant smile. "To new beginnings." Could she make a fresh start after the wayward path she'd walked? Only time would tell.

Seated cross-legged before the fire, Ellis took a long drag of his cocoa and rested his brawny arms atop his knees. Cora found her gaze crawling across his rolled-up shirt sleeves, up his neck and over the planes of his strong face, accentuated by moving firelight. He was so much more than she had comprehended on that first meeting, yet the rugged man who had swept her up without apology still awakened a longing inside her she couldn't deny.

"Tell me about your mother." Her words prompted his head to swivel her way. "Tell me what's so special about her."

A look of tender pride swept over him. "What isn't special about her? She wakes up at dawn to feed the chickens and make breakfast for an army of people. She works herself to the bone and never complains. She reads Shakespeare by firelight to ensure her children are civilized and learned in this complicated world." His mouth lifted. "She always has enough room in her heart that everyone under her roof knows how loved they really are."

She gripped the handle of her mug. "She sounds incredible. And you want to marry a woman like that." It sounded more like a statement than a question.

His eyes shifted to hers. "I want to marry a woman with a pure heart."

Eyelids batting away the warmth sprouting beneath, Cora barely managed another sip of her cocoa. *Pure of heart* was the last thing anyone could call her.

"What about yours?"

She looked back in question.

"I told you about my ma; tell me about yours."

The familiar ache of remembering tugged at her. "She's a lot like me, I suppose. Determined. Stubborn. We fought constantly."

Ellis nodded toward the hair rushing freely over her shoulders. "Did you get your color from her?"

Gathering the soft strands in one hand, she pulled them between her fingers. "Yes, but hers is much redder, not blonde like mine. They call her 'Redcap' back home."

Ellis smiled, turning his mug of cocoa around in his hands. "You came from Scotland, did you not?"

Cora's lips parted. "Now, how on earth would you know that? It took me years to cover up the accent."

"Sheriff Jones somehow knew. He had the information in a file folder in his office."

"Naturally." She readjusted the blanket draped over her lap. "Madam Carey must have told him. She drilled the Scottish out of me. She said the accent made me sound like a commoner. Killed any mystery in me."

"It's a shame she wanted to change you." His head wagged. "It's a shame she got her claws in you at all."

"Yes, well, I didn't have a lot of options when I got to this town." She swallowed back the fire in her throat. "Working at Madam Carey's far exceeded dying."

Ellis set his mug on the floor, his look of sadness slashing through her. "Would you tell me about it—how you got here? What happened to you?"

She stared into her cocoa. "It isn't a pleasant tale. I doubt you really want to hear it."

"I want to hear everything about you, Cora." The softness in his voice surrounded her. "Please let me in."

Pressing her lips together, she allowed her mind to journey back there—a place she rarely went anymore. Over the years, scars had bubbled across the wounds scratched into her heart, but the pain never left. Better to avoid it than relive the horror again and again.

"I suppose I had a happy life in Scotland. We didn't have much, but we got by. I had a family who loved me, and for a long time that felt like enough."

Seconds passed, the scent of burning cedar threading through the air. "My father was a good man, but he was poor and there were many of us—*too* many to keep on feeding and housing us all. When the collectors came, we had nothing to give them."

Her stomach clenched, the day bright and vivid in her mind's eye—when creditors had stormed the house demanding payment or her father's life. "They had a bag in one hand and a rope in the other. They said if he didn't fill their bag, they would hang him from the nearest tree by the neck." Her voice shook, her hands trembling. "They threatened to kill and rape us too. They said if my father didn't produce a payment, they would take what was theirs, one way or another."

Ellis closed his eyes, hanging his head. "How old were you?"

"Thirteen. My father begged and pleaded, but they would hear no arguments. They wanted money or death, nothing else."

Moisture brightened his eyes when they revolved back to her. "You were their payment, weren't you?"

"I was just a girl. I didn't know anything about the ways of the world. They told my father they would take me on a bond of debt, that I could work off my obligation in America and then come home." Cora inhaled through her nose, the heady aroma of burning wood flowing through her. "My father agreed, on the condition that they did not touch me—a condition they failed to uphold."

She gripped the arms of the chair. "I worked for three years for a wealthy businessman who brought me west. I did everything for him. I cooked. I cleaned. I sewed gowns for his wife. My bond of service was for ten years." Taking a sip of her cocoa, she stared into the shadows flickering over the walls.

"They settled not far from here, and for a while my life was tolerable. I had food and clothing, shelter, a bed to sleep in at night, no real concerns about my safety or how I would get by. Then sickness spread across Montana." She shook her head. "I've often wondered where my life would have gone had they not died and left me alone in a foreign country with no one I knew."

Her shoulders lifted. "I suppose I avoided seven years of service, but I took a burden upon my shoulders that no sixteen-year-old should ever have to endure."

Ellis's solemn eyes found hers. "That's when you met Madam Carey."

Cora nodded, swiping away her hot tears. "I came here looking for work, and was turned away everywhere but the Wild Rose Saloon, where I was nearly accosted. Madam Carey saw the exchange, and she came to my rescue." She looked down at her clenched hands. "I realize now I was merely a business opportunity, but at the time, it felt like I'd met my guardian angel.

"She fed me, clothed me, kept me safe, even provided emotional support in those early years." Her throat constricted with emotion. "I started looking at her as the mother I'd lost in Scotland. I didn't realize how dangerous that was at the time—to allow her to hypnotize me into doing whatever she pleased."

Ellis drew his legs against his chest and encircled them with his arms. "You did what any sixteen-year-old would have done in your position."

She met his gaze in the firelight, eyes devoid of the usual judgment she had grown accustomed to. "I could have taken my chances with a miner or a mountaineer. This place is crawling with them. I knew if I didn't marry quickly enough, I would have my virtue stolen from me. I was afraid if I married too quickly, I would be tethered to somebody horrible for the rest of my days, starving or beaten or worse."

Her eyes filled. "For years, I was like one of the new girls I see at the brothel now, full of hope for something better. I thought perhaps a man would fall in love with me, take me someplace better."

Ellis's mouth tipped. "How could they resist falling in love with you?"

Her lips curved sadly. "Like I said, I've had plenty of declarations, but no actual love. Men like the idea of possessing me, the fantasy of being the center of my world." She shook her head. "When the morning comes, they go back to reality and leave me as part of their dream world."

The patter of rain began plinking off the rooftop, forming a staccato rhythm. Cora finished the last of her cocoa and leaned back into her chair. In this quiet space, amid the scent of burning logs, her skin warmed by the fire and the sound of rain peppering the windows, she could imagine herself back in Scotland. If she closed her eyes, she could see them again—her mother and father, her brothers and cousins, all gathered together beneath a thatched roof, telling stories as it stormed outside. A yearning tugged at her heart so fiercely, she could barely manage another breath.

When her eyes opened, Ellis's face filled her view. He'd crept up silently beside the chair, still on his knees. His eyes met hers, the fire illuminating golden flecks amid the blue. His strong hand covered hers on the arm of the chair, his fingers tenderly curling.

Cora smiled, turning her hand over and lacing her fingers with his. How beautifully they knit together, as if perfect stitches in a grand embroidery. "Why didn't you come to Gold Strike seven years ago and sweep me off my feet before I had a chance to ruin my life?"

His fingers tightened around hers. "I wish I had. How I wish I could have saved you from all you've had to endure." His hand reached up to smooth her hair, his thumb softly brushing her forehead.

"The truth is, I don't deserve a man like you." Her gaze pinned to her blanket. "Dozens of respectable men have come through Gold Strike, but once they learn who I am"—she inhaled through her nose—"they look at me differently—much like you did that first night in the brothel."

"Cora, I—"

"I'm not blaming you, Ellis. It must have been a shock." Her gaze climbed his throat to his shadowed face. "You deserve a good woman—one who will walk through life as your partner, free from guilt and shame."

He came closer, his hand anchoring on her jaw, his thumb stroking her chin. "I want *you*."

The sincerity in his eyes shattered her. "It's because I'm a fantasy, Ellis. Everyone wants a fantasy before they find out what's beneath it." Endeavoring to smile, she released an involuntary sob. Soon one rolled over upon the other until her body was overcome with uncontrollable weeping. Tears rushed down her face, staining her clothes.

Arms encircled her, pulling her gently from her chair. Cora clung to Ellis's shirt as if it could keep her from slipping into the hollows of her own despair. "I'm sorry. *I'm sorry*." Sorry for trusting Madam Carey, for choosing the easier path when she faced uncertainty, for failing to wait for the man holding her now.

Ellis cradled her against his solid chest, combing his fingers through her hair and rubbing her back in soothing circles. Cora cried until she had nothing left, pouring out a lifetime of grief. As the wind whistled and the logs in the fireplace tumbled over one another, she cried until fatigue at last overtook her.

Twenty Six

ELLIS CAUGHT A WHIFF of her rosewater hair long before he opened his eyes to a shimmering strand of it laying across his face. Smiling, he plucked it off his nose and returned it to the others, a honey cascade glowing softly in the morning sunlight.

He squinted, looking around the unornamented room. A fire still lit the hearth, though the warmth from its diminutive flames barely reached him now. A half-eaten pot of stew and a kettle of hot cocoa still sat on the table where he'd left them the night before. Their used mugs littered the planks next to him. Had they really fallen asleep here and not woken the whole night through?

Cora stirred beside him, stretching and muttering something in her sleep. His arm was still curled around her, nested in the feminine curve above her hip. His hand pressed her stomach through her blanket. Everything about holding her felt so incredibly right, even with the hard floorboards pushing against his aching back.

What time must it be by now? Ellis lifted the arm draped over her middle and pushed up to peer at the flood of sunlight streaming through the window. Seven o'clock? Eight? By now, Madam Carey surely had her hounds out sniffing for her runaway girl.

His gaze dropped to her perfect silhouette, outlined in sunlight. Her flawless skin, normally pink and luminous, bore bruises along her temple and cheekbone. He had to protect her, no matter the cost. If the madam got her claws around her again, her life would be over.

Ellis watched her sleeping for several minutes, the unbothered peace enfolding her. Did nightmares still plague her as she lay within his arms, or had he given her one night's rest without the world crowding in and expecting more from her than she could possibly give? She had shed so many tears last night, each a cleansing release. Ellis had held her close, refusing to let go. He would *never* let go as long as she let him stay.

With a yawn, she rolled to her back and blinked against the intrusive sunlight. When her gaze swung into his, she smirked. "Watching me sleep, were you?"

"Best morning I've had in a long while." He let his fingertips trail the long hair flowing freely over her shoulders.

Cora wrapped the blanket higher around her exposed shoulder. "We didn't even have a pillow."

"We didn't need one, apparently." Ellis sat up, stretching his back. "Just pure, uninterrupted sleep."

She gazed down at her bare toes peeking up over the edge of the blanket. Did she regret the night they'd spent together? "Yes, well, your back won't be happy with you for it. You should have gotten up and slept in your bed."

"And left you alone on the floor?" His head wagged. "I don't think so, Miss Blackwood. That's not the kind of man I am."

Color ripened her cheeks. "I'm just beginning to understand the kind of man you are, Sheriff McCraw." Her eyelids fluttered a few times, her fingertips working the edge of the blanket. "I know I laid a lot at your feet last night. I wouldn't blame you if you cut and run after everything I told you."

Cut and run? What a fickle man she took him for. Ellis bent low until his elbows made contact with the floor. Setting his chin atop his open palm, he looked her square in the eye with devastating solemnity. "You did spark a lot of serious questions. I haven't quite worked it out yet. Do you prefer eggs or biscuits in the morning?"

Light spread across her features, starting with her green eyes and moving outward. "You're certainly one for jokes after everything that's happened between us."

Ellis got to his feet, extending his arm to her until she reluctantly slipped her hand into his and let him pull her up beside him. His gaze took her in—all of her, from her abundant ribbon of loose hair to her feminine cheekbones and proud chin. His hand cupped her head, drawing her to him. "I meant what I said last night. Nothing can change how I feel about you." Closing his eyes, he let his forehead rest against hers and breathed out everything he'd pent up inside.

With a sigh of satisfaction, she swept a hand over his bristled jaw. Ellis turned into her touch, kissing the soft skin of her palm. Such simple contact, and yet his world came alive beneath her fingertips.

"I was tied around your finger with a string the minute I met you. You know that, don't you?" He smiled against her hand.

"Well, I wasn't much better." Cora inclined her head against his shoulder, leaning her weight on him. "What are we going to do?"

He played with the silky tendrils of her hair. "I don't know, but no matter what else we do today, we start with breakfast." With a quick peck to her forehead, he seized her hand and pulled her toward the kitchen.

"It's an absolute mess in here." Cora laughed, lifting the pot from the table. "This will take ages to scrub."

"Let it be for now. It can wait." He took the pot and set it back down. "Try not to think about work. It will still be here for us." He captured both of her hands in his. "Let's try to enjoy the morning, shall we?"

Cora took a breath and nodded. "I'll try." Her gaze fell to her thin chemise and corset. "I'll have to find something to wear. I can't exactly run around in this all day."

His mouth dimpled as he allowed his gaze to skitter over her. He'd never seen her so attractive, with her hair unbound and her lithe form still achingly visible beneath the blanket draped over her shoulders. "I'll get something in town when I ride in today."

"Don't you think that's a bit risky?" At his raised brow, she drew her blanket around herself tighter. "Madam Carey has to have men out looking for you. If they find you, they'll follow you back here."

He planted two hands on her upper arms, leveling his gaze with hers. "I'll be discreet. I know how to play their games better than they do. Besides"—he turned to retrieve a loaf of bread he'd left in the cupboard—"Madam Carey may have fewer friends than she thinks."

Cora frowned. "What does that mean?"

Hunkering down, Ellis pulled a small crock of butter from a low shelf and plunked it on the table along with his bread loaf. Seizing the two plums he had on hand, he set them on the table and went for his sad collection of dishes.

"I got information last night from Jeremiah Anderson, of all places."

"Jeremiah Anderson?" Her bare feet padded the kitchen floor until she stood next to him. "What on earth could he have told you?"

"Just what he knows about whoever's behind all the corruption in this town." Ellis lifted two porcelain plates from the cupboard and set them on the bare table. "Apparently, we have a mutual enemy."

"I wouldn't believe a word he says." Plopping onto the bench beside the table, Cora set her elbows atop the wood. "He works for Madam Carey."

"Yes, but I think they're edging him out. Besides, he has another interest in the matter."

Cora set her chin on her hand. "Such as?"

"Such as you." He sat down across from her. "He cares about what happens to you. He told me so himself."

Her light laugh filled the kitchen. "Jeremiah Anderson doesn't care about a single soul but himself."

"I wouldn't be so sure about that." Ellis lifted a knife, slicing through the bread. "He cared enough to tell me about Madam Carey's schemes. Perhaps he's turning a new leaf."

"Or walking us into a trap."

Watching her from the corner of his eye, he slathered butter over the bread. Her skin had darkened, her lips pouting. "He said you two had a history." Did he want to know how deep that history ran?

Cora's eyes flashed. "We have a history, all right. He tried to kill my best friend, *and* his new wife."

"And before that?" He handed her the bread, trying to keep the curiosity out of his voice.

"Before that he was a friend, I suppose—once upon a time. He was one of the first people I met in Gold Strike, one of the only ones who didn't condemn me for my profession."

"A man like Jeremiah Anderson has no room to condemn you."

"Exactly." Cora tore off a chunk of her bread. "If you're curious if we ever had a romantic connection, the answer is no. He frequented the brothel, of course, but—"

The words she spoke were enough. "I understand." Ellis leaned on the table, enjoying a bite of bread smothered in creamy butter. "Anderson isn't the prime culprit in this town's crimes, though."

Cora paused with her hand upon one of the ripe plums. "What do you mean? He and Red Fox have always dominated the crime in this town."

"I mean there's somebody more sinister at play." He shook his head, eating another bite. "I've had my suspects, but now I don't know."

Cora listened in earnest as Ellis relayed finding the letters in Sheriff Jones's office indicating a more powerful source whom Anderson worked for. "He says he only received instructions through Sheriff Jones—that he never knew the man's identity." Ellis drummed his fingers on the table. "I'm inclined to believe him."

Cora handed him a slice of plum, her soft fingers brushing his. "Who in this place is wealthy enough to contrive such plans?"

He shrugged. "There are plenty of businessmen around town who could pull it off. None who rise above the others except—" No. As much as the idea had plagued his mind of late, he couldn't voice it without proof.

"Edward Carter."

His head came up, his eyes hunting hers. "Yes. Edward Carter. How did you know that?"

"Lucky guess, I suppose." Cora sighed, plucking a piece of fruit from her plate. "He's always given me sort of an eerie feeling—like he was watching me. He doesn't come near the brothel, though. He tells his daughter Faith that I'm a stain on everything good in this place."

Ellis's chest tightened to imagine her mistreatment under men like that. "Yes, well being a deplorable human being alone doesn't make him a candidate for orchestrating a murder, I'm afraid. So far, he hasn't done or said anything to make me suspect him, even when I offered a bit of bait."

Wind rushed over the house, quaking the walls and shutters. Cora stared out the window at the trembling tree branches, savoring a bite of plum. "Didn't Colton Baxter break into Edward Carter's house, though? Maybe that was reason enough to retaliate against him."

Ellis stared into his empty plate, savoring the plum's sweet juices. "Perhaps." It didn't feel strong enough, though—not to accuse a man.

"Who else is on your list?"

Ellis blinked, his eyes coming back into focus. "You tell me. What's the biggest business in this town? Not the region, but the town itself."

Cora bit her lip in thought. "She'd never admit to running an actual business, but of course, it's Madam Carey's. She employs more people and transacts more money than any other establishment in Gold Strike." Her mouth fell open as he nodded. "You think Madam Carey could be behind the banker's murder?"

"I do, indeed. She certainly isn't above killing. You know that."

The light diminished in Cora's eyes. "I agree, but what motive would she have?"

Ellis scratched his chin. "I haven't found that part out yet, but something is sure to reveal itself with time if she is indeed who I'm looking for. Colton Baxter was stealing a lot of money from the bank, seemingly without anybody realizing it. Someone wanted to put a stop to it."

Tiny worry lines emerged around Cora's eyes. She raked a hand through her long hair, settling it over one shoulder.

"Cora, what is it? What are you not saying?"

She shook her head. "It's nothing—just a silly thought."

"No thought is silly when life and death are on the line." He reached out, covering her hand in his. "Please tell me."

Cora met his fervent gaze. "It's just that, well—" Her brow scrunched. "Reverend Sommers talks so much in his sermons about the evils of greed, about men exactly like Colton Baxter coming in and taking up everything for themselves."

Ellis nodded slowly. "I have noticed that's a passion of his."

"But is it a passion or a clever way to hide misdeeds?" At his look of confusion, her fingers opened on the table. "I just mean to say that he has the ear of everyone. People respect him and do what he says. If his motives were to turn corrupt, he could do whatever he wanted in this town."

Ellis sat forward, mulling over her words. "But a man like Reverend Sommers surely wouldn't have the kind of money to pay for the sheriff and Jeremiah Anderson to do his bidding."

"Doesn't he?" Her brows rose. "More money comes through the church every week than anywhere else. We never see what happens to it. Think about it. Everyone trusted Colton Baxter with the bank's money. Everyone trusted the sheriff with upholding the law. Why would Reverend Sommers be any different?"

Ellis washed two hands over his face and hair, his mind a jumble of activity. It was true. Reverend Sommers could be just like all the others, donning a sanctimonious front while dealing out evil deeds behind everyone's backs. How thick a cloak of evil lay over this town?

"I'm probably wrong." Cora crossed her arms over one another on the table. "Reverend Sommers has always been kind to me. He hasn't done anything to warrant my mistrust."

But has he warranted mine? Ellis's mind raced back to their every conversation, anything the reverend had ever said to him. He had certainly lent his opinions on every event in Gold Strike, from Colton Baxter's murder to Caleb Broderick's trial and everything since. How had he not noticed a minister with an inexplicably heavy hand in the politics of this town?

"You may be on to something. He was very insistent in helping my investigation." He thumped his knuckles on the table. "But a reverend conspiring with outlaws? Working with a madam to kidnap girls? I just don't see it."

Cora collected their dishes, stacking them on top of each other. "I *know* Reverend Sommers has been to the brothel before. He's convinced girls to leave it."

Ellis's head shot up, his gaze finding her in the sunlit room. "He's actively taking girls from the brothel?"

"To help rehabilitate them." Her head wagged. "Ellis, you don't think—"

"I don't put anything past anyone anymore. Someone is working with Madam Carey to sell girls. Why not him?"

She bit her lip. "I can't believe someone as kind as him could do something like that, but I'm sure that's how most people would feel about Colton Baxter if they knew the truth."

Pushing up from the bench, Ellis walked back and forth across the tiny kitchen. "There was an attempt on Reverend Sommers's life. I have letters detailing the plan, but I reckon he could have faked those too." His fingers laced with his hair. "I don't know what to believe anymore, who to trust."

"I bet you're wishing you'd stayed in Tennessee about now." Her eyebrow cocked, though the lift of her lips said she was only kidding.

Ellis's hands dropped from his head. "Even with all of Gold Strike's faults, I'd rather be here with you than anywhere else."

She smiled sadly, the sentiment not reaching her eyes.

Ellis blew out a breath. "I have the sinking feeling that we don't have much time. Anderson said this benefactor, whoever he is, plans to meet with Jorgen in the next few days behind the livery. I can only imagine what their plans are."

"Jorgen." Cora rolled her eyes to the ceiling. "I have half a mind to meet him behind the livery myself. Give him a piece of my mind."

Ellis leaned against the table, his muscles flexing. "Don't you worry. I plan to." His brow furrowed as a new thought entered his mind. "Last night at the Halloween party—Madam Carey wanted you to poison me, didn't she?"

Cora sighed. "Yes, but I didn't want you to know. Obviously I never planned to go through with it. I didn't want to worry you beyond the burden you already carried."

"But she used you to bait me."

"She did." Cora nodded. "She knew you had feelings for me. She wanted to exploit them however she could." Her expression turned serious. "Ellis, why are you looking at me like that?"

He plastered a hand over his chest. "Because last night, only one person suggested I join the dancing, where I found you. That person was Reverend Sommers."

Twenty Seven

"THIS IS A TERRIBLE idea." Cora held tight to Ellis's torso, plastering herself against his back as Honeydew charged over the verdant landscape.

Ellis grinned, pressing the hand draped over his stomach. "It doesn't seem so bad from where I'm sitting, Miss Blackwood." He'd take a thousand rides into the circles of hell itself if it meant feeling her supple form against his.

"This was your plan all along, wasn't it?" Her laugh floated up around him, sating the forest in its beautiful sound.

The road ahead, dappled in gray-green shadows, wound between evergreens thick with aromatic branches. Sunlight barely touched them here, mere trickles of luster peeping through the trees. Honeydew's hooves pounded the fresh earth, throwing chunks behind as she thundered over the rocky soil.

Thrashing the reins across her back, Ellis urged her onward. The quicker they got to Gold Strike, the sooner they could find out the truth and put an end to this madness once and for all.

"What will we do when we get there?" Cora asked from over his shoulder. "Surely we can't just ride up to the church and question Reverend Sommers about his involvement."

Ellis veered the horse to the left, avoiding a drooping tree branch. "I'm still working that out in my mind. All I know is we have to stop this meeting before it takes place. More lives could be in danger."

Her hand gripped his shirt. "Many of those women are my friends. I'll do whatever I can to end this threat to them." Her body sagged against him. "Though I can't believe I let you dress me in this."

When first he'd held up one of his loose shirts and a pair of his old riding pants from his adolescent years, Cora had balked. No way could she be seen in such masculine attire. Yet it was either his clothes or her bloodied dress from the night before. She had acquiesced only because she couldn't stand the thought of sending him to Gold Strike alone.

"I think you look rather good in my britches." The woman could turn heads in a flour sack.

Cora jabbed at his ribs in a playful manner. "You're buying me something proper the minute this is over."

As the horse broke through the treeline and entered the clearing, Ellis tugged on her reins and slid one hand over her silky coat. "Whoa now, girl."

The town of Gold Strike had risen into view—a hive of activity compared to the tranquil forest. Beneath the mid-morning sun, the town thrived with trundling wagon wheels, the clip of horse hooves, hammering and sawing. Plumes of smoke tainted the sky above the huddle of buildings. Ellis's stomach clenched. Somewhere in that frenzy, a murderer walked free.

"Where do we even start?" Cora asked, her fingers pressing his abdomen. "We can't just sit behind the livery and wait for whomever is supposed to meet Jorgen there."

Ellis squinted against the harsh rays of sunlight. "No, but we could find Jorgen and follow him. Or find a place to hide where we can see the livery's back door." He stroked the soft skin of the hand still clinging to him. If only he didn't have to bring her into this mess.

"Madam Carey has more men under her employ than I thought. I didn't recognize the man who beat me."

"Neither did I." Exhaling, Ellis swung his leg over Honeydew's back and dismounted. "We have to keep you out of sight as much as possible. You aren't safe here."

"And what about you?" Cora accepted his outstretched hand and landed in the dust beside him with swan-like grace. "Madam Carey plotted to kill you last night. She knows she's done for if she doesn't finish the job somehow."

Ellis turned his gaze to her face. She'd knotted her hair in an elegant fashion at the crown of her head, letting wisps of red-blonde cover her injuries, but still checks of purple along her cheekbone peeked out.

"I have my pistol at the ready should anyone confront me. Do you have the one I gave you?"

Cora patted the haversack she'd slung over one shoulder. "Right here. I still don't feel comfortable using it."

"The quick lesson I gave you will be enough for now." Ellis planted two hands on her shoulders. "We can do this together. I have faith."

A breath blew out her pursed lips. "If we don't, we're as good as dead anyway. We might as well go down together."

Ellis patted her cheek and grinned. "There's my positive girl."

Leaving Honeydew tethered to a tree out of sight, the pair walked hand in hand down the path toward Gold Strike. Madam Carey had more to fear from Ellis than he from her. He possessed eyewitness testimony that the madam had conspired to poison a recognized officer of the law, and would bring said charges against her as soon as he stepped foot in his office. She likely had eyes on the jail from every angle to prevent that from happening.

The weed-speckled yard behind the livery stood vacant. Had they already gone inside?

Ellis held a finger over his lips. "I'm just going to poke my head in to check." But a quick glance inside offered nothing but an empty black room emanating the earthy scent of hay.

"Come on, let's check around the front." Ellis pulled Cora through the shadowed alley between the buildings. People traversed the dirt street and boardwalk beyond the space, each too preoccupied with their own pursuits to notice the couple waiting between the buildings. Ellis craned his neck out and peered in either direction. Nobody stood in front of the livery, and he'd surely have to expose them to explore inside.

"Ellis, look." Cora's finger speared toward a form crossing the street. "Isn't that Reverend Sommers?"

His gaze trained on the black-suited man, now hastily blazing a trail toward the church. "It most certainly is. I bet he just came from the livery."

Her fingers coiled around his arm. "We should check to see if Jorgen is inside."

"We don't have time." Seizing her arm, he pulled her out of the alley and into the street. "We have to see what he's up to. Stay close to me. Keep an eye on our surroundings. If anyone approaches, warn me, all right?"

She swallowed. "All right."

Crossing the street in the open left them vulnerable to so many possible dangers, but Ellis saw no other way. Already, the reverend had passed the shops lining the street and cut through the yard toward the church steps. He had something in his hands, but Ellis couldn't make it out from this distance. A bribe, perhaps, or a payment for his part of the conspiracy?

Ducking around a passing wagon, Ellis led them through the dusty haze and onto the opposing boardwalk. Their shoes pounded the uneven boards as they ran past aghast faces and startled citizens. *It doesn't matter now. None of it matters.* He had to put a stop to these horrific crimes before another girl went missing and her wasted life was upon his head.

When they reached the churchyard, Ellis's side smarted and his breath came in hard spurts. Reverend Sommers had disappeared through the doors only moments before, his bootprints leaving a dusty trail behind him.

"Come on." Cora tugged his hand. "I know a back way into the church. I've used it many times when I wanted to listen to the sermon without being ridiculed."

Cora led them around the side of the church to a door standing along the far wall. Easing it open, she slipped inside. Ellis cast one last furtive glance around them before stepping in after her.

Inside, a darkened corridor smelling of cedar stretched before them. To the left, Ellis spied a set of purple velvet drapes leading to the sanctuary. This couldn't be far from the office the reverend employed. The room on this side of the drapes held nothing more than a few extra pews, some stacked hymnals, and a baptismal font.

"He probably went through here," Cora whispered, pulling him through the dusky passageway toward a set of doors on the opposing end.

Their shoes barely tapped the floorboards as they traveled nearer. Stray wisps of Cora's hair brushed Ellis's neck, their sweet smell like fresh blossoms after a rainstorm. Light poured from a singular door stationed on the hallway's far end. The couple crept closer, listening for voices or movements, anything that could guide them in the right direction.

When they reached the open doorway, Cora pressed to the wall and glanced inside. Her eyes went wide. Before she could provide an explanation, a figure filled the doorway, blocking out the light.

Reverend Sommers looked from Cora to Ellis, his eyes narrowed. "Were the two of you following me?"

For the first time in his life, Ellis had no answer.

Cora froze in the back hallway of the Gold Strike church, her heart in her throat. Before them stood Reverend Sommers, his form plugging the doorway, his accusatory stare darting between her and Ellis. Her fingers inched to the side, finding Ellis's and closing around them.

The reverend glanced at their intertwined hands before huffing. "I saw the two of you running up the street after me. I didn't suppose you'd sneak in here."

Her heart pounded. Could they invent an excuse and make it believable, say they'd snuck in to secretly wed? He'd see straight through it.

Ellis lifted his chin. "Why were you in such a hurry to get here from the livery, might I ask?"

The reverend gave him an incredulous frown. "I wasn't at the livery. I was at the bakery." His brows tightened. "What would make you think I was at the livery? I don't even own a horse."

"We thought—" Cora shrugged. "We thought we saw you there."

"Either way, you were making a very swift journey this way," Ellis said. "I saw you glancing over your shoulder more than once."

"Are the two of you joshing me?" He eyed them carefully. "Are you accusing me of something?"

Ellis secured his hold on her hand. "It just appears suspicious, is all."

"What? Picking up a cake for Abeline Baxter's birthday?" At their dumbfounded expressions, Reverend Sommers stepped back from his office door and swept aside his hand to reveal a white paper box sitting atop his desk.

Cora stepped forward. "Abeline Baxter's birthday? Why would that give you reason to hurry?"

Reverend Sommers sighed. "Because the quilting society is meeting here in only twenty minutes, and they want the cake to be a surprise. Why? What else could you possibly have imagined?"

Unleashing his grip on her hand, Ellis chuckled nervously. "We thought—" He glanced at Cora, reluctance in his gaze.

She leveled her chin. "There's no reason to mince words anymore, Reverend. Are you in cahoots with Madam Carey?"

The minister's surprised breath disrupted the hallway's stillness. "Madam Carey? Now I *know* you are joking. You know how I feel about her place in this town, Cora—you better than anyone."

Ellis cleared his throat. "We've been wrong about a lot of people we trusted before. You've lured several girls from the brothel, haven't you?"

"Yes, but to free them."

"Last night at the Halloween celebration, you encouraged me to dance." Ellis's chest ballooned. "Madam Carey wanted me there. She tried to use Cora to poison me."

The reverend stared back, his mouth falling open. "I never expected—" He ran a hand over his dark hair. "I only thought you might enjoy a turn about the dance floor. That's all. I'm sorry if my motivations appeared darker, but I promise you—"

"No, Reverend. It's us who owe you an apology." Ellis's rueful gaze darted Cora's way. "We never should have laid this at your doorstep. I'm rightly embarrassed by it all."

The back doors across the sanctuary opened, and footsteps wandered in. Cora met Ellis's sorrowful eyes, swallowing back the dryness in her throat. Could they really have been so devastatingly wrong about poor Reverend Sommers that they charged across miles of forest to spy on him?

"Reverend Sommers, are you in here?" a cheerful voice resounded across the sanctuary.

The reverend tossed them a doleful look before he flattened down the rumples in his jacket and turned into the sanctuary.

"Why, Mrs. Baxter, it's so good to see your face. And Miss Carter! I didn't expect to see you."

Cora sighed, trailing behind him from the dark hallway into the wide sunlit sanctuary. After everything he'd done for her, doubting the reverend to his face felt like betrayal tantamount to murder.

"I just saw Mrs. Baxter in the street. She told me about the quilt society's meeting," Faith said, still clutching the Widow Baxter's arm. "I thought I'd help her inside the church."

"I'd like to believe I'm capable all on my own"—Mrs. Baxter beamed up at Faith, her white hair glinting—"but what a dear you are." She reached up to give Faith's cheek an appreciative pat.

On sight of Ellis and Cora, Faith gasped. "I thought I saw you from down the street, but I—" She paused, her bewildered stare descending Cora. "I decided it wasn't you. Why are you in this interesting getup? Does the church have an upcoming theatrical production I know nothing about?"

Cora tried to join in their chuckling, but her head ached even to try. "It's a long story." Self-consciously, she fluffed her hair. "Too long to get into at the present moment."

Mrs. Baxter pressed a hand to her floral dress. "Ah, to be young and adventurous. I miss the hijinks of youth."

"You can still have adventures." Faith rattled her arm. "I'd bet there are plenty of bachelors in this town just waiting to take you on one."

"Oh, you." Mrs. Baxter swiped playfully at Faith, her cheeks rosy and eyes sparkling. "Wouldn't you believe it? I'll be seventy-two this week."

"Seventy-two? My, that's impressive." Faith tucked back a curl of her long blonde hair. "You must tell me your secret. I'd like to look half as good as you when I'm your age."

Cora's mouth lifted. Leave it to Faith to flatter a poor, lonely old woman. She had a heart of innocence—one Cora hoped would last her whole life through.

Ellis cleared his throat. "Excuse me, Reverend Sommers. I think we'll be on our way. We've taken up enough of your time."

"Oh, but we just got here." Faith pouted, stepping around Mrs. Baxter to take up Cora's arm. "I'd hoped we would have a minute or two to visit"—she leaned in conspiratorially—"especially without my father here to interfere."

Cora's shoulders relaxed. She was glad of that too. "Faith?" She sidled closer, her tone quieting. "Do you remember that letter I gave you to mail? Did it ever go out?" She had yet to hear back from Caleb despite her fervent request for help.

"Of course it did." A touch of doubt flickered over Faith's unbreakable smile. "I gave it to my father to mail straight away. He promised me he would post it that day."

Her father? The words triggered a foreboding sensation. "Where is your father, anyway?" She peered toward the doors through which they'd come. "I assumed the two of you would have left this morning, what with the Halloween celebrations over with."

Faith sighed with a roll of her eyes. "I thought so too, but Father said we won't be leaving until the afternoon. He had some type of business meeting he needed to see to." She swung her reticule from her hand. "I don't know much about it. He didn't want me to attend."

"Do you know where he was conducting this meeting?" Ellis asked. "I wouldn't mind having another word with him before the two of you head home."

"I'm not exactly sure." Faith pursed her lips in thought. "He was awfully tight-lipped about it, but I did see him go into the livery."

Cora stiffened, her gaze latching with Ellis's as it swung up to her. An icy chill washed over her. *Edward Carter.* If he was the man they sought, it made perfect sense. He certainly had enough money to pull strings in town, and she'd never been able to shake her uneasiness in his presence.

Faith's perfect brows wrinkled. "What's wrong? What did I say?"

Covering the tension with a laugh, Cora touched her fingertips to her lips. "I think we're all a little surprised to hear of your important father having a business meeting in the livery. Does he have business in horses now?"

"I did find it odd." Faith played with her long silk gloves. "But my father has dealings with so many different types of people. I suppose a livery is no different than anywhere else."

Cora's pulse quickened. How long did they have before that meeting was over? Could they stop whatever plans had been set in motion? Without a word, Ellis took her arm and began steering her toward the door.

"Oh, Sheriff McCraw?" Abeline Baxter's sweet voice halted them before they'd taken three steps. They both turned to see her ambling up to Ellis's side. "I thought about what you asked me when you visited my home, and there is one thing I forgot to mention."

Reaching into her bag, she pulled out a long, slim item and placed it in the palm of her hand. "When they searched my husband's clothes, they found this in his pocket the day he died, along with his other belongings. They assumed it was his and gave it to me, but"—her head shook—"he never kept this kind in our home, and I don't think he had them at work, either."

Ellis accepted the cigar from her hand, a brown cylindrical shape with embossed gold foil banding it on one end. Even at this distance, Cora caught its familiar ashy scent.

"Oh, how funny!" Faith chimed in, a careless smile stretched across her face. "My father smokes that type of cigar."

All eyes in the room shot to her.

Ellis's fingers curled around the cigar, his other hand seizing Cora's. "We have to go *now*. We don't have a second to spare." He looked toward Reverend Sommers. "Keep them here, please. I don't want more casualties."

"Casualties?" Faith stepped forward with her hand over her heart. "I don't understand. Where are you going?"

But before Cora could provide any explanation, Ellis had yanked her down the church's aisle and out the double doors.

Twenty Eight

THE SHORT RUN FROM the Gold Strike church to the livery felt like the longest Ellis had ever endured. Every muscle in his body clenched, blood rushing in his ears, his heartbeat hammering. His feet pounded the dirt, sending clouds of dust into the air. A cold reality seeped over him as he held Cora's hand. If he failed her in this moment, it could mean the end of them both.

The front of the livery, with its proud signboard and tall posts, showed no unusual activity. Ellis shouldered past a group of ladies in homespun dresses, exchanging what sounded like dull bits of gossip, and pulled Cora straight through the midst of them.

"Well, I never," said one woman with round, rosy cheeks. "Did you see who he was with? I *told* you."

Leaving their chatter behind, Ellis dove for the livery's open front, where a broad archway led to a walkway flanked in horse stalls.

Mr. Matheson, the tall and lanky livery owner, stepped out upon their arrival. "Can I help you, Sheriff?"

Barely sparing a second glance, Ellis jogged past him. "Matheson, get everyone out of the office, and out of the street if you can." From the man's flustered expression, Ellis doubted he knew the weight of the meeting taking place under his very roof.

The livery's darkness encompassed them more with every step. Ellis halted, twisting toward Cora. "You should stay here. No good can come of what we find back there."

Her mouth collapsed into a determined line. "I'll do no such thing. I'm coming with you."

"It's far too dangerous." His hand rose to cover her cheek. "If anything should happen to you—"

"It won't." The steely surety in her eyes flattened him. "I'm not about to let you rush in there alone—not if I know I can help."

After a moment's hesitation, he finally nodded. "Very well, since I know there's no stopping you. If you're going to come, at least get your gun." He watched her pull it out with tremulous fingers. "Why don't you go around back and guard the door? They won't expect anyone back there, and it will give us an added element of surprise."

"All right." She caught his wrist before he could turn away. "Ellis." Her eyes, the only bright thing in this shadowed hovel, shimmered with meaning. "You'd better come out of this alive. I love you." She rose up on her toes, planting a kiss on his lips that he felt in his soul.

Long after she'd scampered out through the livery's front and disappeared around the side, her warmth shrouded him. Ellis unholstered his gun, gripping the cold steel as he crept past stall after stall. Several horses inhabited the space, announcing their presence in stomping hooves and soft wickers. The stench of manure mingled with heady alfalfa.

Ellis scanned the dim enclosure, holding his gun to his side, yet no sign of Edward Carter or Jorgen revealed themselves. He'd almost given up hope when a flicker of lamplight caught his eye.

He squinted, inching toward the source, as deep male voices compelled him onward.

With silent footfalls, he approached the stall at the livery's far end, near the door he'd burst through earlier. Over the partition emerged the shapes of two men sitting on hay bales with a lantern on the floor between them.

Ellis leaned closer. Jorgen had what appeared to be sepia-toned photographs in one hand, presenting them to Mr. Carter one at a time. Mr. Carter grunted his approval every so often, separating some into a stack on the bale beside him. Ellis's stomach twisted. They were photographs of women. He squeezed into the stall next to them, sidling up to the partition and pressing his ear to the cracks in the wood.

"How much do you think you could get for this one?" Jorgen's unctuous Norwegian lilt carried across the stables.

"At least five hundred," Mr. Carter answered, no emotion in his voice. "She isn't the best of what you have to offer, though. Where are the rest?"

Jorgen cleared his throat. "Madam Carey wants to retain her best girls to keep her business running strong, of course. We can't offer you the ones who are making the most money."

"And the little blonde one with the attitude? What about her?" Mr. Carter shifted, his jacket rustling. "I thought you said Madam Carey had about enough of her surly ways and wanted to get rid of her."

"Cora." Jorgen growled her name, sick with distaste. "She ran off with that other one last night. Must have gotten wind of our plans. She couldn't have gotten far. We'll find them."

A dubious sound issued from Mr. Carter's throat. "You'd best find them before they go spreading around what we're doing here." A long pause, punctuated by neighs and the swish of horse tails. "Do you think the sheriff is hiding her?"

Jorgen laughed derisively. "If he is, he's a foolish man. Madam Carey wants him dead because of her."

"Foolish or no, I believe I have him in my pocket. I think I can get him to do what we need—without his knowledge, of course. He's a moral crank."

"A scourge on our town is what he is. Madam Carey thinks he'll destroy everything good about this place if we let him."

"Then we stay ahead of his game." Mr. Carter's voice edged with steel. "He believes everything I tell him. He hasn't suspected me of a thing. We can keep up our operations under his nose and without threat to us."

"I don't know—"

"I'm telling you," Mr. Carter cut him off. "The minute he started sniffing around Baxter's murder, I threw him off the scent. He suspects nothing."

Painful barbs shot through Ellis, but he forced them back. Now was not the time to soothe his wounded pride.

"What about Cora?" Jorgen asked. "She could be a real problem for us, even if we catch her. Who knows what kind of information she'll spread."

The stables went silent again before Mr. Carter's voice rose, sharp and purposeful. "Oh, I have plans for her."

"She's too valuable to kill—"

"I'm not going to kill her. I'm going to buy her." A shuffling sound filled the livery, presumably Mr. Carter getting to his feet. "Name your price and you'll have it—but you'll have to catch her first."

Memories of the Halloween party flashed across Ellis's mind. Carter had watched Cora with outward disdain, something more animal and sinister lurking behind those eyes. Now he understood it. He'd mentioned sending his daughter off to a finishing school in the fall. What a marvelous opportunity to empty his house of unwanted witnesses.

"These two. Get them ready by tonight and I'll send my agents to collect them."

Rapid breath rushed up Ellis's throat. He could put a stop to this if he simply hid out for the time being and ambushed the brothel by night with a swarm of deputies. He relaxed against the wall of the horse's stall. Everything would fall into place.

"Not that way." Carter's voice cut through his thoughts like a blade. "We can't be seen leaving together. You go out the front, and I'll exit through the back. I'll send payment with my agents."

Ellis rose on unsteady legs as the two men collected their items and prepared to depart. In just seconds, Carter would walk through the back door and run straight into Cora. His hands trembled. He couldn't let that happen.

Gripping his weapon, he stepped boldly into the lamplight. "Take another step and you're dead."

Both men froze at the sound of Ellis's voice. Jorgen turned first, the whites of his eyes as round as silver dollars. With a calmer, almost angered expression, Edward Carter pivoted back with his hands raised. His calculating gaze pinned on the gun aimed his way before meeting Ellis's eyes.

"Sheriff. There seems to be a misunderstanding."

"There is no misunderstanding here." Ellis's pistol hand steadied. "I heard enough of your conversation to know what's going on. Indeed, what's been transpiring seemingly for years behind the backs of the good citizens in this town."

Carter's head angled, the lamplight catching the glint off his bald head. "There's no need to act rashly in this situation. We can still come to an arrangement."

"An arrangement to sell women like sheep at market?" Ellis laughed humorlessly. "You're touched if you think you can bribe me over human life."

Mr. Carter's tongue clicked. "Every man has his price. I guarantee you have it too."

"Keep your money, Carter." His teeth clenched. "After everything you've done, you're going to have your neck in a noose by the end of the week. Mark my words."

A deep, haunting laugh reverberated across the stables. "Do you really think you can frighten me with your pretended power?" His head shook once. "I've been running this town an awful long time, Sheriff. I know a thing or two about people, and I hate to tell you, but the odds are stacked against you."

Ellis's jaw worked. "People deserve a home and family, a place of safety to come home to. They'll never have it with men like you on the loose, eager to make fortunes off their suffering."

Carter's lip snarled. "When people look at me, they see an expensive suit, European cologne, a gold-trimmed carriage, a sprawling house in Missoula with fields that stretch for miles. They don't care about what has to happen to make my silver shine. They only want to watch it glow."

"I'm going to expose you for everything you are."

"Try it and see what happens." His lips puckered beneath his full mustache. "Pull the wool back from their eyes. Just see if anyone listens to you, or if they're all too mesmerized by the magician's tricks."

Fire kindled in Ellis's belly, threatening to erupt across his chest and down his arms. He could end Carter's pathetic existence with one pull of his trigger, but his father's voice still echoed in the recesses of his mind. *Remember honor and duty. Live by a code of ethics. Never surrender your moral courage.*

Ellis tightened the hand holding his pistol, his gaze darting between Carter and Jorgen. Madam Carey's lackey had his fingers suspended in the air, curling toward the gun on his hip.

"Reach for that gun and it's the last thing you'll do."

His hand popped back up at the warning, his breath quickening. He looked to Carter for direction, but the hardened businessman had singular focus. His gaze drilled into Ellis, as if he could pick him apart by sheer will.

"Now, the two of you are going to kick your guns over to me, then walk out the front of this establishment with your hands on your heads." He indicated the open passage with a flick of his head. "Anything else and I shoot. Is that understood?"

Jorgen nodded shakily, complying and stepping across the hay-strewn floor the way Ellis had come. With the eyes of a watchful eagle, Carter deposited his gun on the ground and watched Jorgen's retreating form, but made no effort to move from the stall. A horse down one side of the livery bucked and neighed, the sound overwhelming the small space.

Just as Jorgen passed by Ellis, Carter lurched forward. "Now, boy! Take his gun away!" Jorgen flashed him an uncertain look, but dove toward Ellis on Carter's command.

With an assault waging from both sides, Ellis made the split-second decision to fire his gun with his right hand and attack with his left. His elbow shot backward, connecting with bone. The livery erupted in gunsmoke. His ears rang as he whirled on Carter, slamming his fist into his jaw and knocking him backward.

Though blood drenched Jorgen's pant leg, Ellis caught him from the corner of his eye, struggling to get up. In two quick strides, he descended on him, flattening Jorgen against the packed dirt floor and bashing his fist into his nose. The coward groaned, his head rolling back, his dazed eyes slipping shut.

Carter. I have to get to Carter now before he runs out that back door and finds Cora. Ellis spun back, his stomach dropping. Carter stood at the back corner of the livery before an open door, one arm snaked around Cora's chest, the other holding the pistol Ellis had given her to her temple.

She shivered within his hold, tears sprouting in her bright eyes. "I'm sorry, Ellis. I heard gunfire and I couldn't stay outside any longer. He got my gun from me."

The gun I should never have made her carry when she hadn't a clue what to do with it. Now he could very well watch her die because of his negligence.

"Put your gun down and I won't shoot her," Carter wheezed. "I have no desire to hurt a woman."

"No, only to imprison them and make money off them." Ellis's teeth clenched. "You're the worst kind of evil, Carter—the kind that masquerades as a poor man's savior. The kind with a hand on every committee, who donates money for show, while stealing it from benevolent citizens who don't have it to spare. You're disgusting."

Smeared with blood, Carter's lip snarled. "Call me what you'd like, but I know how to get a job done. Another second of this delaying and I will kill her, I promise."

"Don't do it, Ellis." Cora's tear-filled eyes shone with determination. "He'll kill you too the minute he has a chance. Let him do it. Kill him before he can hurt anyone else."

"Shut up." Carter shook her hard, inducing a whimper from her lips. His malicious gaze slid to Ellis, his thumb cocking the pistol and his finger hooking the trigger. "I'm warning you, McCraw. You put that gun down or she's dead."

A blast of fiery ice burst in Ellis's head, trickling down through his extremities. The hand holding his pistol trembled to imagine her falling, to imagine never kissing those lips again, never hearing her laugh. A lifetime without her. No death was worth it, not even Carter's.

Arms aching, Ellis lowered his pistol, crouching low to gingerly set it on the ground.

Carter's victorious laugh rankled his nerves. "Good. Just like that. Now, kick it over to me."

Ellis complied, his nostrils ballooning. How long could evil win out before love broke through its chains? His patience was wearing thin.

Carter holstered Ellis's pistol at his side and began to back his way out of the livery with the other gun still pressed to Cora's head. "Let's make this as painless as possible, shall we?" His shoes crunched hay as he retreated. "My horse is right outside. I'll ride out with her and send her back on the condition that you don't set your posse after me."

With every step he took backward, Ellis followed. What kind of game was he playing? The minute he let Carter out of his sight, the man would pull another trick out of his sleeve, spin things around to make Ellis, the newcomer, appear to be the villain, while he walked away without consequence.

He looked to Cora, whose stubborn will masked her fear. Her hair glimmered in the sunlight as they passed through the threshold and into the back alley. At least one thing he clearly understood from eavesdropping on Carter and Jorgen's conversation—Carter didn't want Cora dead. He would keep her alive for himself as long as it suited him. But what might that mean for her?

"You stay where you are, Sheriff." Carter's voice growled in his ears. "I won't have you following us." He glanced in every direction, no doubt concerned for his pristine reputation.

Despite his warning, Ellis stepped out of the livery and into the weed-speckled alley. "You can't have her that easily, Carter. I have to know she's safe."

"She'll be safe with me. I won't hurt her unless you are foolish and try to follow."

Ellis shook his head. "I heard what you told that pathetic excuse for a man back there. You plan to buy her yourself. I want to know why."

Cora's brow wrinkled in confusion, while Carter's eyes exploded. "That is not your concern. What I choose to do with my money is my own affair."

"Except when it involves human life." Ellis's hands clenched at his sides. What type of twisted plans did he have for her? Could he dare hope to get her back if he let her go now?

"You're treading on mighty thin ice." Carter angled his arm up, pushing the gun firmly into Cora's temple. "I have a lot more men in this town under my employ than you realize, McCraw. You'll both be dead before sunset if you keep this up."

More empty threats meant to distract him. Ellis kept up his slow walk toward them. "How are you going to explain this to your daughter? What is Faith going to say when she finds out you've kidnapped her friend? How is she going to look at you?"

Carter's eyes narrowed. "Leave my daughter out of this."

"She isn't much younger than Cora." Ellis crept forward with every word. If he could distract the madman long enough, perhaps he could dive for his gun. "What would you do if someone stole Faith from her bed at night and sold her to someone like you?"

"She isn't Faith. She's nothing but a filthy strumpet." Spit formed in the corners of Carter's mouth, his teeth set on edge. "Why do you care so much about a prostitute? She means nothing!" His hand rattled with every word, and Cora squeezed her eyes shut against his voice.

"She is a person, just as you used to be." The wind whipped Ellis's hair as he took another step. "She has a soul. Every one of those girls you sold from Madam Carey's has one too. One day, you will pay for your misdeeds."

From deep in his throat, Carter let out a rumbling growl, dark and cruel as the very voice of the devil. "One day God will judge me—if there is a God at all. But here on earth, I do what I want. I take what I want, and no one has the guts to stop me."

His arm coiled around Cora tighter, lifting her to her toes. "You think I want to buy this girl because I care about what happens to her? Think again. I am going to make her pay for every time she stuck up her nose at me, every time she acted above me. This"—hatred flamed in his eyes as they raked over her—"this pathetic nothing of a girl from the Highlands."

"Just as you made Colton Baxter pay?" The statement turned on a fiery light in Carter's eyes. "I know everything about what happened that day on Miner's Trail. Let her go and I'll keep the lurid details to myself. The rest of Gold Strike will never have to know."

"Are you trying to entice me with bribery?" Carter's mouth curled up wickedly. "You're already becoming what you hate. How do I know you won't go right back on your word if I release her?"

"You don't." Ellis swallowed down the lump in his throat. "We'll both have to summon a certain amount of faith in each other."

Carter glanced at his horse, still tethered to a rail behind the livery. He shifted from foot to foot. "I have an easier way to end this that won't require me to put faith in anybody but myself. A bullet for her"—he pressed his face close to Cora's neck—"then a bullet for you. No one to say a word to anybody."

Ellis froze, his palms pushing outward and fingers splayed. "And two bodies on the ground. Think about what that will look like."

"Two bodies and no witnesses. I can invent an explanation easily enough. I've done it many times before."

Sweat leaked into Ellis's shirt, his broad shoulder muscles tightening. The fervency in Carter's eyes had raised to a fever pitch, panic setting in. He'd gambled Cora's life by insisting on more talk.

Cora squirmed within Carter's hold as his arm wound tighter around her. Her forlorn eyes pleaded with Ellis.

I can't watch her die. I can't let her. Yet Carter had his pistol flush against her head, his fingers readying to fire.

"There must be something you want. Say the word and you'll have it." Anything to release her from harm's way.

Carter's head shook swiftly. "It's too late, Sheriff. You've had your chance. It's time to end this once and for all."

A single shot blasted through the alleyway, reverberating off the clapboard buildings and sending Carter's horse into a stomping frenzy. *No.* Ellis's stomach clenched, nausea climbing his throat. The sound of a body hitting the dirt drove his dread deeper. *No.*

How had he failed her so immensely? How had he let this happen? Biting smoke stung his already watering eyes. The blast of gunpowder choked him, searing his lungs and making him sputter. But he had no other care than her, Carter, the extraordinary ache already building inside him. He would kill Carter with his bare hands for this.

"Ellis." Cora's voice found him in the fog of his own fury. A dream, no doubt. A remnant of the perfect life they could have shared together. "Ellis, are you there?"

He looked up, peering through the haze as it descended to reveal her face. He shook himself. Cora still stood—shaken, but on her feet. In the dust lay a crumpled form in a fancy suit.

"Cora." Ellis covered the distance between them at a run. His arms came around her. Crushing her against him, he kissed her hair—hair that smelled like mountain lilies in spring.

"Ellis." Her voice shook.

He kissed the side of her face. "Yes, love? What is it?"

She gasped. "Ellis, look."

He pivoted back to find Carter, though seemingly shot in the side, reaching for the gun laying beside him in the dirt. With a swift stomp, Ellis plastered his hand to the ground, eliciting a stream of curses and groans from Carter's mouth. Keeping his boot squarely on Carter's palm, he reached down for the gun discarded in the dirt.

"Got any more I need to worry about?"

Carter answered with a glare, his lips pinching beneath his abundant mustache. "You'll pay for this, McCraw. If it's the last thing I do, I'll make you pay."

"I'm not the one who shot you." At the thought, Ellis frowned, his eyes swinging up to meet Cora's. She simply shook her head. Jeremiah Anderson had mentioned waiting around for this meeting, hoping for his chance at retribution. Had he fired the single bullet now spilling blood across the ground?

Straightening, Ellis peered down the alley to a revolver still aimed their way, fresh smoke billowing from the barrel. The stark face behind it looked on with sorrow haunting her wide eyes. Faith Carter slowly lowered her gun and dropped it into the dirt.

Twenty Nine

CORA BARELY MANAGED A breath from her stifled lungs. Her head swam. She squinted through the misty rays of sunlight, sure her eyes deceived her. "Faith." She stumbled past the form sprawled across the ground, painting the dirt in crimson, toward her friend.

Faith's entire body trembled, tears burgeoning in her eyes. When Cora reached her, Faith collapsed into her arms, a quivering mess of sobs and desperate gasps for air. Cora held her to her shoulder, smoothing back her long hair.

"Faith, you—" She shook her head, disbelieving. "You saved me."

"I couldn't watch him kill you. The things he said—" She shuddered, tears racking her body anew.

"Thank you, Faith." The words whispered in Faith's ear would never suffice. She owed this girl her very life. She and Ellis both did.

Pulling back, Faith swiped her wrist over her tear-stained face. "I shot my father." Her forlorn gaze pushed past Cora to the man in question. Ellis knelt over him now, unbuttoning Carter's shirt, tending to his wounds.

Faith's hands plummeted from Cora's arms. She stepped heavily over the dusty alley, her stare fixed upon her wounded father. What emotions must be coursing through her in this moment, to watch her father suffering from a wound she'd inflicted?

Gathering her skirts, she crouched low beside Ellis. Her gaze moved from the spot where Ellis attempted to stop Carter's bleeding with his own shirt to her father's face, pale beneath the sun.

"I'm the one who taught you how to shoot," he ground out, wincing as Ellis's hands moved over his injury.

Faith nodded. "You taught me for my own protection. 'Use it for good,' you said." She swallowed, her eyes misting. "Today I did."

Carter fixed her with a pained expression. "You don't understand how the world works, baby girl. Without my sacrifices, you wouldn't have a comfortable home, fine clothes, your horses. We could be stuck in some shanty somewhere with barely enough food to survive."

Her chin trembled as she looked him straight in the eye. "But was it worth the sacrifice of your dignity, Father? Was it worth your soul?"

She sniffed, directing her attention to Ellis. "What do you need from me, Sheriff?"

Ellis blinked and appeared to shake himself. "Go get help. If we can quell the bleeding, he might still survive."

She nodded once and rose to her feet. "And after that?"

He paused, his look thoughtful. "I suppose access to your home, your father's office. I'll need proof of his every crime against this town."

Donning the regal stance of a queen, Faith dusted off her hands. "I'll do anything I can."

Within minutes, she and Cora had directed the Gold Strike deputies to the scene.

"We had reports of gunfire in the livery," Wainwright said as he trotted alongside them atop his horse. "We were just on our way out here to investigate."

"There's one shot inside the livery," Cora said between breaths. "The other is behind the livery with the sheriff."

Wainwright reined in his furious stallion. "And the shooter?"

Cora snuck a glance at Faith, then bit her lip. "Everyone involved has been disarmed. There's no threat left."

When Wainwright thundered away with a group of eager deputies behind him, Cora turned to Faith and gripped her arm. "What you did back there—" She choked on her words. "You've proven yourself to be a great woman of strength and courage today. I'm so proud to be your friend."

Faith sucked in a quivering breath and attempted a smile. "You'd do it for me if the need arose. I'm sure of it. I'm going to need a friend now more than ever."

Cora took her hand, pressing her fingers. "You have a friend in me, always."

The minutes stretched thin before Ellis led Cora through the doors of the Gold Strike sheriff's office. Her legs and back ached, her shoulders weary with a burden more emotional than physical. Cora barely stumbled through the hallway and plopped into the chair Ellis extended toward her within the confines of his personal office.

"Here's some water." He thrust a canteen into her hands. "You should drink it. I'll get you some food as soon as I can."

"What about you?" She unscrewed the canteen. "You're just as weary as I am."

A long sigh pressed from Ellis's chest. "I'll get sustenance soon enough. Don't worry about me."

Raising the canteen to her lips, she watched him stoop over the desk and gather a stack of papers, then a steel nib pen from among a collection of others. Cool water rushed over her lips as he hunted beside her for ink.

"You never stop, do you?"

The question brought his head up. "I don't have time to stop. There is always something to do."

"Always someone to rescue. Some right to be wronged." Wasn't that one of the many reasons she'd found herself drawn to him like a hopeless scrap of driftwood washing ashore at high tide?

"We have enough to bring Madam Carey in on charges of kidnapping and trafficking. I have to get a judge down here as quickly as possible—a real one this time." Hunkering down near the desk beside her, he began scratching words across the page. "I've already sent my deputies out to arrest her. She's unprotected with both Carter and her dubious bouncer laid out on the doctor's table."

Cora clutched the cold metal canteen in clenched fingers. "I'd rather not be here when they bring her in." She sat forward. "What will happen to the brothel without her running it? What about all those girls?" As vile a place as it was, Madam Carey employed many women who would go hungry otherwise.

"I don't know." Ellis continued writing, his head wagging. "I only have the capacity to deal with the problems as they come. Perhaps we'll think of something."

The landscape of Gold Strike would completely alter with Edward Carter and Madam Carey behind bars. Why did the possibility both relieve and terrify her? Cora set the canteen on Ellis's desk, keenly aware of the way her hand still trembled. The feel of Carter's hot breath on her neck, his crawling hands holding her firm, still burned into her skin until she could barely sit still.

"Ellis."

He lifted one brow, his hand flying across the page. "Hmmm?"

"Ellis, look at me." Cora pushed a hand beneath his stubbled chin, directing it her way. When he finally relented and turned his eyes toward hers, a chill skittered over her. "We defeated death today. Take a moment to celebrate, would you?"

Closing his eyes, Ellis leaned his cheek into her hand. The pen in his grip dropped to the page, leaving a trail of black ink across it. When his eyelids fluttered open, he cupped her hand over his, pressing her fingertips into the rough hair speckling his jaw. "It's easier not to think about."

Cora smoothed back the sandy hair falling across his forehead. "What do you mean?"

Ellis took the hand stroking his cheek and pressed it between his warm palms. "I thought my life was over when I heard that shot ring out. I thought you were gone." Emotion tinged his voice. "I've seen a lot of people die doing what I do, but I never once felt like that before—like the very earth was giving way beneath my feet."

Cora swallowed back the burning sensation rising in her gullet. Her body shuddered to remember that split second when nothing had stood between her and Carter's bullet but the cold steel against her skin. "I felt so helpless."

"So did I." His strong jaw worked. "I've never felt so powerless. And to know it was my fault—"

"It wasn't your fault. How could it have been?"

"I pushed him." His lips pressed together. "I was scared he was going to take you and hide you away and I'd never see you again. He never would have considered killing you otherwise."

Cora turned her hand over within his grasp and laced her fingers with his. "Such a fate would have been far worse than death. I'm glad you didn't let him take me."

His eyes descended her face slowly—tortured, as if weighted with lead. "Ultimately, I could do nothing to save you. My hands were completely tied after I angered him. You saved yourself, Cora."

Her head began to shake. "No. It was Faith."

"Faith pulled the trigger, but you set that train in motion." His free hand rose to tuck a strand of strawberry blonde hair behind her ear. "Your goodness and love is effortless. You don't even see it, but I noticed it in you that very first day on the ridge, and I've watched it flourish ever since."

Ellis lifted her hand and kissed the tender skin above her knuckles. "Faith chose you above her father because she saw you both clearly for who you truly were. You showed her your heart again and again, just as you do the girls in that brothel, just as you do the people of this town who need you."

Cora inhaled shakily. "I just try to do the right thing. It's the least I can do after—" She tucked her bottom lip between her teeth. Even with him aware of her myriad of sins, she still couldn't force herself to voice them.

"It must not seem like a lot to you because being yourself comes naturally." He squeezed her hands, launching pleasant shivers through her. "I've fallen so deeply and absolutely in love with you for who you are that my heart is no longer just mine, but yours."

Cora stared into his eyes, dumbstruck. She had never imagined such affectionate sentiments reserved for her, the lowest of sinners, the least of girls from a foreign land who'd forfeited any chance of living a respectable life. Her days at Madam Carey's lined up in her mind's eye, one after the other, each a nail driving into the coffin encasing her wayward soul.

Tears bloomed in her eyes, and she gripped his hand. Her gaze meandered over them, the way they fit together so perfectly. Her soul felt at home when he held her, but what home could a woman like her ever expect to claim?

"After the things that happened between us and what we said to each other, it's difficult to believe we've come to this place." She smiled despite her tears. "I think even the animosity we harbored against each other was love in disguise."

He beamed back at her, his eyes shimmering. "It was. It always was for me."

"And that's what breaks my heart." Her voice broke. "I've learned this lesson in life the hard way. Love isn't always enough."

"But it can be." His fingers softly toyed with the tendrils of hair falling around her face. "We can make it enough."

If only. Hadn't she discovered this truth long ago, when the hands of greed had ripped her from her family, stolen her innocence, thrown her into a life of moral ambiguity?

"I pushed you away when you came to the brothel because I was scared, but I wasn't wrong to do so." She searched his entreating eyes, trying to draw strength from the depths of devotion she saw in him. "I'm in love with you enough to see that you deserve better than me, better than a town that will ridicule you when they see us together."

The muscles in his jaw clenched. "Hang them. I don't care—"

"I know you don't." Her head cocked. "Ellis, I know you would give up everything for me, and that's why I can't let you. I'm a broken, degraded woman. I chose this path a long time ago. I never intended to fall in love."

"But you did."

"Yes, I did"—she blinked back the warmth in her eyes—"even though I tried so very hard not to. I couldn't help it." Cora let her hands slip away from him, suddenly cold as she wrapped her arms around herself and hugged her body. "Our love doesn't change who I am or what I've done. I'm already ruining you by association. Half the men in this town will look at us and remember being as intimate with me as you would be. You could never be happy." Her final words dissolved into a quiet cry, her lips shivering with the moisture of her own salty tears.

"Cora." Ellis spoke her name with such reverence, it nearly shattered her. His fingers hooked her chin, propelling it up until her gaze brushed his. "I don't care what they think they know. They will never know you as intimately as I will. They had nothing but a carnal experience. They'll never know the depth of your love, your intelligence, your spirit, your good heart. What of it if they've touched the outside of you? I want what's inside. I want your soul to come home to mine."

Warm tears blurred her vision as a laugh burst from her mouth. "You make it impossible to say goodbye, don't you?"

A sad smile lifted his lips as Ellis shifted until he knelt on the floor in front of her. "You may think you have to let me go because of the position I hold in this town, but I will not lose you over a job." He found her hands again, engulfing them in his. "If this town can't accept you because of your past or me for being with you, then I'll find another one." He shrugged. "I'll take you back home to Tennessee if I have to, but I won't let other people's opinions define us."

The word echoed over and again in her mind, an extraordinary sound. Her eyes swept his determined face, the hope radiating from his gaze. "You're sure?"

"With every fiber of my being, I'm sure." He leaned close, letting his forehead fall to hers, his warm breath sending tingles across her skin. "I was taught to see the world in black and white, with no compromise, no room to understand the person beneath someone's story." His hand descended from her head to her jawline. "I don't want to do that with you. I refuse to do that with you."

Cora's hands anchored at the sides of his neck. "I think you're the first person who has truly looked at me since I first stepped foot inside Madam Carey's."

His chuckle of joy danced along her skin. "And I'm never going to stop looking at you, Cora Blackwood."

His lips found hers, wet with falling tears, the promise of a man who'd lain everything at her feet. Cora gripped the collar of his shirt, hauling him closer, basking in the security of his nearness. His arms encircled her—solid, protective, loving. Her lips moved against his, her form secure in his arms, for the first time finding solace in the cruel world around them.

Ellis's eyes sparkled when he pulled back. "We should get out of here before it's too late. Wainwright should be bringing in Madam Carey any minute."

Cora groaned, rolling her eyes. "She has to spoil everything, doesn't she?" She set her hands against his brawny chest. "You're right, though. I don't want to see her—ever again, if I can help it."

"Then you don't have to." Ellis extended his hand to her and pulled her up before him.

With an exasperated huff, she surveyed the dirtied, wrinkled men's shirt and trousers still sheathing her weary frame. "I can't believe I'm still wearing this. Please tell me you found a suitable dress for me to wear."

Mischief swam in his gaze as it ascended her approvingly. "I don't think that will be a problem."

"Good." She squirmed in the unfamiliar clothing. "Let's find me something to wear and go back to your house. I've had enough of this place for today."

Ellis watched her dust off the ill-fitting trousers. "I can't take you back to my house."

Her head popped up, her brows cinching. "Why not?"

"It wouldn't be decent. Two unmarried people alone under one roof?" His tongue clicked with his shaking head. "I couldn't put you in that kind of compromising position, Miss Blackwood. You have a reputation to think about."

A disbelieving puff of air escaped her. "A reputation? You do know you're in Gold Strike, don't you? I certainly have a reputation, but you needn't protect it."

"Still, it wouldn't be right."

Her eyes narrowed in playful suspicion. "You were fine with having me sleep in your bed yesterday, and with you on the floor last night."

"Yes, well...that was different." The slightest twinge of a grin edged one side of his mouth. "Your life was in danger and you had nowhere else to go."

Cora's hands flew to her hips. "So you're telling me I have to find somewhere else to stay because we're not married?"

"No." His hand jetted out to grasp her arm. "I'm saying the church and the minister are only a few steps away." His fingers tensed gently on her arm. "I'm ready if you are, Miss Blackwood—to make you Mrs. McCraw, that is."

At her silence and gaping mouth, he stepped away and lowered his hand. "Of course, if you aren't ready, I will by no means coerce you. I'll simply find you respectable lodging for the night, and—"

His words cut off as Cora eliminated the distance between them and pressed her mouth to his soft, inviting lips. When she opened her eyes to look at him, her heart fluttered with surety. "Take me home tonight, Sheriff. Our life together begins today."

Thank you for reading! *The Gold Strike Chronicles* conclude in book 4, *The Wolf and the Sparrow.*

Thanks

First and foremost, thank you for your patience. I've never had to delay a pre-order date before, but I realized—amid the stress—that I needed to do so for the sake of my sanity. My original plan to release these books quickly unraveled due to unexpected events this year, and I'm deeply grateful to all of you who've continued to support me through it.

Looking ahead, I plan to give myself ample time before releasing the next book, though I'll happily move that date up if circumstances allow.

To everyone who's shared their enthusiasm and appreciation for the first two books—thank you. I hope the final two are just as rewarding. To my wonderful ARC readers, a special thank you for your time, feedback, and encouragement. I can't wait to create many more stories for you to enjoy.

Books by Laurie Sanford

The Memory Chase

The Guardians' Plot
The Moon King's Bounty
Traitor Isle
To Capture a Unicorn

The Gold Strike Chronicles

The Fox and the Nightingale
The Cat and the Crow

For exclusive scenes you can't get anywhere else, head to
www.lauriesanfordbooks.com

About the Author

Laurie Sanford is a writer of historical romance, adventure, and fantasy. Her novels take readers on vivid journeys through the past, sweeping landscapes of imaginary kingdoms, and rips in time. Every story promises excitement, sweet romance, and happy endings.

Laurie attended Pacific Union College in Napa Valley, where she earned her Bachelor's Degree. She studied to become a teacher, but wound up as a dispatcher, a job she loves and finds fulfillment doing. Laurie is happily married with three children who have given her more joy than she could have ever imagined.

When she's not at work or wrangling little ones, Laurie enjoys writing (her first love that now comes fifth in line), reading or watching anything historical, traveling (38 states and 7 countries so far), exploring nature, cooking, playing guitar, and studying genealogy. Having a family is the greatest blessing she has ever been bestowed, and everything she has she owes to Jesus Christ.

www.ingramcontent.com/pod-product-compliance
Lightning Source LLC
Chambersburg PA
CBHW020301200626
46814CB00006BA/2021